MW01244628

Omnician

The Celestial

Omnician
The Celestial
By: Foster Geofrys
Published by PetDragon Creative, 2019

Hardback ISBN: 978-1-7330988-0-9
Paperback ISBN: 978-1-7330988-1-6
E-book ISBN: 978-1-7330988-2-3
Audiobook ISBN: 978-1-7330988-3-0

2	b	1	c	b	3	5	0
8	4	c	2	f	0	a	4
4	5	5	0	5	4	2	8
1	e	f	6	7	f	a	f
7	e	a	1	0	7	0	4
4	3	8	b	3	a	1	9
8	8	4	8	9	8	9	8
5	c	f	a	3	2	a	b

This is a work of fiction

For my own

personal chaos ...

The Annals of Doctor James Marshall Marcus, Esquire

"I, James Marshall Marcus, Esquire, being of sound mind and body, do begin this log to chronicle the innermost depths of my mind and psyche. As, by the grace of god, King William's School and Yale University, I, from this day forth, am to be known as Doctor James Marshall Marcus, Esquire. These writings, by my will shall be, of and by my own hand, the record of my life's work.

Allow me to speak candidly. A sneaking suspicion lurks within my innermost mind. There must be more within this universe that we, as man, do know. There are phenomena that we, within the sciences, do believe, we know to be true, but, an innate feeling within, leads me to believe, we do not. I, as a man of science, wish not, for fear of discreditation, to make these ideals known, but will, in my lifetime, find the truth and source of this disconnect... of this missing variable. I declare, here and now, to make its' discovery, my life's mission."

- Doctor James Marshall Marcus, Esquire.
  July 16th, 1746

"Tis the season! I'm to travel home to spend this holiday season with my family.

Since this research fellowship for my Alma Mater began, I've poured over aged, even ancient historical texts in efforts to restore and decipher their meanings and find a semblance of truth and a path to follow. As a research fellow, I find it difficult at times, to declare my actions and intent to my employer as purely steward in nature. Don't misunderstand my intent. This is a quest for a better understanding of our world, not one of personal or monetary gain.

I strive to better understand the world we live in and know the truth to god's plan"

- Doctor James Marshall Marcus, Esquire
  November, 15th 1746

"I've returned from my travels and to the confines of studious ventures. Upon my return, a recently rediscovered set of texts, unearthed from deep within the cavernous archives of the university by my research assistant, Samuel Stevens Neiman and in turn, have come into my possession for restoration. These texts seem to be of Nordic origination and use a dialect, with which, I am not immediately familiar. Time must be invested to detail the structure and meaning behind this dialect, but alas, I will prevail."

- Doctor James Marshall Marcus, Esquire
  February 28th 1747

"I must provide accolades where due. Samuel has deciphered this Nordic dialect, and I have reported its' significance to the University's Historical Board of Governors. We believe it to speak of five ancient cities. The first is referred to as, heat in the frozen cold. The second, as the secrets of time among the highest of rocky thorns. The third is referenced as a city swallowed by sand and time. The fourth is described as the bridge to a city below, within and above the trees, afloat in the great sea.

For the last mentioned, we've yet to decipher the section of these scrolls. As the text concludes mention of the fourth location, the structure of the dialect begins to change and we've yet to pattern the language. In reference to this fifth city, Samuel believes the fifth location to be of great significance to the author or authors, as he states, of this document as it's mention is, strangely, in a distinct and individualistic dialect. We've provided the governors details on the first four scrolls. As the last one is indecipherable, we've yet to present its existence or details of speculations.

The first mention, as named, is of the great city of Alanis. Located somewhere in the barren, far north mountainous region of Scandinavia. One could assume that, throughout time, names become mispronounced, even forgotten throughout history. Could this be reference to the mythical Great City of Atlantis? I do not wish to entertain delusions of grandeur and as a scientist, I will observe and document, prior to making conclusion.

The second, we believe, refers to a sprawling network of caves, referred as Grand Om-Tak. The text contains numerous mentions of skilled craftsmen. If the location is where we believe it to be, in the mountainous region along the Chinese border, any venture there would most likely result in failure as the terrain is much inhospitable.

Alixandra The Hidden, as deciphered, tells of a city swallowed by sand and we believe this to reference the lost city of Ubar, located somewhere on the Southern Arabian Peninsula. As read, "as the intruders encroach the entrance to our domain, the secrets within must not pass to the unworthy. As the sands claimed her prize, an impasse was imbued and the threat swallowed whole."

The fourth tells of a city, references as Gados the Green, deep below, within and above the trees and afloat in the sea. Due to the description, terrain and other factors, we believe this could be reference to one of the many islands off the coast of southern Europe. If so, one of historical importance would stand out as a prime candidate. Kriti, Sicilia or Cyprus, perhaps as is, the location of the Paphos Forest.

This scroll, with mention of the fifth location is perhaps, the most puzzling of all. It's as if the dialect inverts when deciphered but when spoken as such, would be nonsensical at best. We plan to continue efforts to decipher this scroll.

Great interest has been shown, by the governors of the university, in expedition to one or more of these locations. I myself, plan to insist on leading the research if such an endeavor indeed, comes to fruition."

- Doctor James Marshall Marcus, Esquire
  June 22nd, 1747

"It has been declared, the university will solicit funds for an expedition in search of these relics of civilization left behind and lost to time. The university wishes us to begin in search of the lost city of Ubar. I plan to insist we begin with an alternative site as relations with the Arabic peninsula are sparse at best. Despite the distance and terrain, I believe our best chance for success lies in search of the city Alanis, in the frozen north. I believe this because for civilization to survive in such a harsh climate, they would have needed a source for fresh water as all civil expansion Is dictated by the supply of natural resources. With sparse supply of wood or oils available and the climate as such, they would be in desperate need of a heat source as well. These two components should give us the best possible chance to discover one of time's forgotten secrets.

They must listen to reason."

- Dr James Marshall Marcus, Esquire
  September 12th, 1747

"Today, begins our voyage deep into the bitter cold of the Nordics in search of a lost city… The lost city. 14 men, hand selected by Samuel and myself, set out on this journey.

A local legend states, among the peaks of the Scandinavian Mountains, lies the remnants of a once ferocious and unusually active volcano. The legend says, that inside the caldera lies the remains of a once great and advanced civilization but we've found no one to tell the tale, firsthand. Ahead, in this frozen abyss, lies our destination and our prize… the riches of knowledge."

-    Dr. James Marshall Marcus, Esquire
     January 7th, 1748

"We've searched for nearly eighteen months now and have found, virtually nothing. This land is an inhospitable one to our kind and our team. When the weather is pleasant and the ice and snow subside, the jagged rocks make traversing these terrains, treacherous. When the winter comes, travels are easier but the climate slows our progress. We've lost two men since beginning this journey. One fell to his death during a climb to reach the flatlands of the range's spine and the other, frozen to death during one of the many blizzards we've encountered.

We have found various geological formations that show promise throughout the range but have yet to find the crown jewel, the caldera.

Unfortunately, we've had no initial progress on the fifth scroll"

-    Dr. James Marshall Marcus, Esquire
     June 20th, 1749

"We're into our twenty-fifth month with little to show for our efforts. The university board continues their restlessness and impatience for results and I've begun to despise visits from the board herald.

We've lost seven more men to date, all succumbed to a respiratory sickness in the late fall. Our traveling party is now down to five and the spirits of the men, nearly broken. Samuel and I know we must persevere.

During our journey, we've encountered many locals and have bartered for information along the way, to which, one stands out as most useful. A young boy, of only nine or ten years of age, seems to provide most dependable when we are at a loss to further our progress. Much, do I feel we owe to this young boy. He knows the terrain and the trails through this place but he is reluctant to join us on our journey, as our guide. Nonetheless, he has proven to be invaluable and we've become dependent on his guidance and advice.

He will insist we parts ways at times and these times have, more frequently, been days prior to our path leading us into one of the small hunting and trapping villages that dot this barren landscape. Strangely enough, once our voyage continues back into the wilderness, our paths, like clockwork, cross again.

There's something about him I can't quite equate. He has a dull, ever-present glow within his eyes of hazel and blue and green, an even at times, of a fiery red. The glow in his eyes does, at times, swell and at others, subsides in intensity. The temperature seems slightly less brutal and the snowfall, less intense, when he's accompanying us.

I've noticed he carries, in his possession, a small metallic item, he regularly holds and caresses, when he doesn't think anyone's looking. It's seemingly of great sentimental value to him.

He calls himself Elijah."

- Dr. James Marshall Marcus, Esquire
  February 2nd, 1750

"Three more men died today. We came across a sleuth of black bears chasing a herd of elk and the animals decided my men were easier sustenance to catch. Samuel and myself are the only voyagers left and we are seriously considering returning to our home shores and to our research positions. The three black bears caught my men while sleeping. Samuel and myself, with Elijah's assistance, we're able to escape the clutches of this same fate.

We've discovered much about this land and as a result, have provided the University with enough data to publish volumes about this land and its' people's survival, against all odds.

Elijah has told us, due to the availability of daylight this far north into the mountain range, there are areas that are inaccessible and we've yet to explore some of them. He's agreed to guide us to some of these. Not sure why he's changed his mind on joining our expedition. It may be because our numbers continue to dwindle.

We've stopped in a small hunting village for rest. We resume our journey to these lands in three days."

- Dr. James Marshall Marcus, Esquire
  May 13th, 1750

"According to Elijah, we're headed north to an island near the fishing village of Tromso. It's a treacherous voyage that will take time and careful effort to traverse the terrain, but he believes it may be the place we are looking for. Honestly, I have given up hope we will ever find the caldera on this voyage we've undertaken some two and a half years ago. Elijah and Samuel share hope we will succeed.

We are to cross the mountain range and make our way to the fishing islands north of the range. There, we are to follow a path and cross a strait to our destination. He has not specified beyond this.

The glow of Elijah's eyes has been brighter of late. I estimate it's an effect of the sunlight at these extreme altitudes and climates; an effect, in my opinion, similar to the Aurora Borealis.

He's began to behave peculiarly, as well. As if he's in a rush, but hesitant in his judgements. I hold out the smallest slivers of hope for our success with this location as the Governors are content with our progress, to date and that our expenses have dwindled down to near, non-existent."

- Dr James Marshall Marcus, Esquire
  May 16th, 1750

A large section of pages is missing from the annals.
They appear to have been torn from the journal.
No discernable details are available of the page's contents or present location.

Gravity.

Gravity is the one constant amongst the cosmos. Gravity attracts and destroys and binds and orphans. Without gravity all things would cease to be. Period.

With that being said, there is still a vast void out there. An endless string of reasons and purposes. All having much and at the same time, nothing to do with one another.

This is where man has failed. Man's hubris and narcissistic nature has led him down an all too familiar path. One where no existence is without discovery and no form is without definition.

This is the hard part to explain to the human race because it's in their nature to not understand what they can't witness. What you, otherwise known as the human race, fail to grasp about this universe is that there is much more out there than you choose to recognize.

Your periodic table is the crowning achievement of your existence. It represents the furthest span of understanding your civilization has achieved in your short years.
One problem remains... you have it wrong and here comes the hard part.

Matter exists throughout the universe, not configured on a table that's categorized by atomic weight, where weight is relative.

In true existence, matter is the relative, itself. Each are influenced and exert influence by the existence of each other and other factors, more so than just of said matter, itself. Now isn't the time to explain that so let's just agree that there are things among the stars you just can't understand yet.

For one, matter isn't arranged on a table. It exists, due to its' relative nature, on a sphere referred to as, well, for the sake of furthering this thought and to maximize my dear reader's comprehension, let's call it, The Existential Sphere. The periodic table you know is just a small cluster of elements grouped within a small sector, within a much larger population representing the totality of forms of matter that exists throughout the universe. You, as a civilization, know not how it's measured, else, find it, you would have.

There are three axes that mark significant measurements across the sphere. The elements located precisely at these axis intersections are called Primes or Essences or elements of prime importance within the Universal Equation. The element you refer to as Carbon lies directly at the intersection of one of these axes. On the opposite end, or negative of said axis, is the Prime or Essence known as Divinium. These essences most closely represent and anchor those characteristics to which the axes they prime, or represent. Due to the nature of a sphere, each element is surrounded and impacted in harmony, by six other elements. This collective is referred as an elemental hexagon or Elegon. Pronounced 'El · ah · gone'.

These three axes each have a positive and negative polar essence. If one were to look upon the sphere from its' equator level and directly down one of its' dimensional axes, you would be staring directly at one of these essences along, what you would refer to as a Z axis, and in turn, at your periodic table, albeit adhered to the surface of the sphere and slightly rotated about 17 degrees, your counter clockwise.

This one you are familiar with, and has already been mentioned... Carbon. Its' negative essence is known as Divinium, again... as I've already mentioned. This axis represents, as best can be explained to, and no offense intended, your primitive thought process can relate, as the collective principle. It's a dimensional existence driven and measured by individuality and influence of matter.

From this view and again, as you would describe, the Y axis is primed, or essenced, by the positive, Eternium and the negative, Infinitium. This is where explanation gets difficult to explain as you don't yet understand the grand equation. As best I can, this axis represents the useful collectivity and destination of the associated matter, as related to other matter itself.

The third and final of the major axis, the familiar X axis, is primed by the negative essence Devium and primed positive by Honorite. This axis represents an element's contribution or purpose of matter to its' ultimate destination.

As all elements are unique, as science knows it to be, each element within our collective universe possess unique characteristics. Iron can attract and repel other elements. Hydrogen can bond with nearly every element. Carbon can serve as the foundational element in support for symbiotic life. The list of examples is without end. One must remember, however, not all elements display their properties at all times and in all circumstances.

Back to Divinium for a moment. Divinium is a dull blue metallic substance in its' solid form. Unlike matter as you know it, Divinium is not affected or manipulated by temperature or pressure, but by the elements that surround it, in the absence of its' Elegon.

When exposed to gasses such as oxygen, nitrogen and hydrogen, as found in your atmosphere, it appears as identical and indiscernible from its' surroundings. Likewise, when exposed to the liquid form of these elements, it appears as such. And in these physical forms, is dormant.

But when in solid form, it can affect the matter that surrounds it. In unique cases, Divinium in its crystalline form, known as Divinine, can be used to manipulate matter... at will. Divinine by nature, is extremely unstable and is found virtually nowhere in the universe, except for one specific place This only known hospitable environment throughout the universe is within the hydrogen bonds of DNA and RNA of an extremely rare race of beings from your planet earth. They are known as the Omnicians.

- Dr. James Marshall Marcus, Esquire
  November 11th, 1764

Another large section of pages appears to be missing from the book. They appear to have been torn from the journal.
No discernable details are available of the page's contents or present location.

"Blessings are completely unpredictable. They can and will manifest, then dissipate, just like that... or, they can bounce around throughout time while taking on a life of their own....

There is no discernible rhyme or reason for these occurrences of nature, it's only to be accepted and the consequences, dealt with...

As I can best describe it, it's by and of the matter itself, its' purpose and destination, preordained and it's will... unknown."

- Dr. James Marshall Marcus, Esquire
  September 15th, 1768

"One of the strangest phenomena on this planet Earth is the idea of the point of view.

It's justified many an atrocity, vindicated the rich among the poor but also provides justice for the wronged and is why good always triumphs over evil in the end.
Ultimately, what means do points of view actually serve in the end? Are they simply the angle at which we view an occurrence or the basis for the perpetuation of life as we all know it to be?

I've been taught, historically and from an academic perspective, through a peep hole sized view of our existence. Through a point of view that's extremely narrow minded and self-serving to man itself, and his aspirations.
I've been learning as of late, that point of view is just as it suggests. The point at which you view an occurrence. It should not be used as a basis for belief. The faith, we as man, put in good and evil serves to blind us to the real purpose we exist.
Because the universal equation willed it so...

God is an object of man created for self-service. Man cannot fathom life without purpose and drive and a final destination.

It's as if you were to put a field mouse into a room with a single block of cheese, accompanied and surrounded with many false paths. Eventually the field mouse would find that cheese. He can smell it and he will find it eventually, because it is given the purpose to do so, a task to accomplish.

Man is no different, he just has the tools to define and detail that purpose in a much more colorful and palatable form.

- Dr. James Marshall Marcus, Esquire
  February 18th, 1769

Throughout the years, I've documented and detailed my innermost thoughts. Never since have I suspected I'd utter this statement, much less agree with it.

The driving force behind man's fate is not greed or pride or sloth, but none other than love. Love will lead man to perform feats that defy logic and reason.

Love leads to attachment which, leads man to fear loss or change. It is this phenomenon that will be the downfall of mankind. He will not maintain the necessary balance through personal sacrifice required for perpetuate existence.

- Dr. James Marshall Marcus, Esquire
  March 22nd, 1772

Yesterday's eve, in assisting the Master Cleric with document storage and preservation, we've came upon an unimpressively plain writing with no discernible markings. It was sealed with a stamp of wax that had since, crumbled. Of what we know, Samuel believes it to have been written during an early period of the Omnician timeline as the dialect appears heavier in Mediterranean influence. Included was no indication of author or place of origin. We've deciphered it and prior to alerting our gracious Omnician hosts, I've documented its' entirety, here.
 And it states:

1. As all who see this must know...
2. of the impending detriment we...
3. the Omnician race of this planet Earth...
4. face...
5. Through cowardice, complacency and lament...
6. our kind left destitute to the whims...
7. of lesser men...
8. *--Line left blank*
9. He who shall know me, know me...
10. for the will of Ja the Everlast...
11. determined before the first dawns...
12. for he shall forsake us...
13. and our chiefs, betray us...
14. and the soul of the Omnician kind be lost...
15. To time and sand and the fold...
16. *--Line left blank*
17. Until the time of light of dawn...
18. Hand in hand with man and Omnician...
19. Alike, the chosen must take...
20. His destined luster and his rightful throne...
21. Among the stars, throughout time...
22. And across all boundary...
23. The end of time and space...
24. So, it shall be broken...
25. Until his ascension.

We speculate but have come to no agreement as to the meaning, significance or purpose of this writing. Prose it may, indeed, be but, beautiful and vivid, it is, nonetheless...

-   Dr. James Marshall Marcus, Esquire
    January 29th, 1773

We've come across another interesting document in our search of these archives. This one, however translates in the Alanis native dialect and is much more recent.
It reads as below

1. And in the end of times, the savior will come…
2. Uniting the clans with might and will…
3. For the spirit within shall guide his way…
4. He shall emerge from the forest of loss and sadness…
5. And when need most dire, shall he be born anew…
6. Carrying the past and the future with him…
7. Stand he will, with man and omni kind alike….
8. Adaptive, not by blood, but by will …
9. for all our kinds…

Samuel believes these two writings to be of relation, potentially speaking of an ancient prophecy of the Omnician people. I retain my doubts as to the significance of these documents, but nonetheless, he insists I document them here.

- Dr. James Marshall Marcus, Esquire
  March 3rd, 1773

Time...
Interesting subject, time.

Man has described time, historically, as finite, fleeting and fundamental to the universe. Funny thing is, man couldn't be more wrong on all counts.

What is time? Some would say it's a singular existence within the universe, but he... or she... would be miscalculated.

Time is nothing more than a particular interaction, the collective of matter interacting with other matter; simply put. The aggregation of matter, in its' whole form, interacting once with other matter.

One moment, an atom of oxygen may well be interacting in one specific way, with an atom of hydrogen, then, an atom of carbon, or a different atom of hydrogen. Collectively, and in aggregate, this is time. Nothing more.

If one is skilled in the manipulation of matter, on a molecular level, one should know where to look to find an imprint of the chronological record of such interactions. Further, if one understands how to truly measure the interaction of matter, then one would, in theory, be apt to understand and interpret how given matter will eventually interact with matter of other makeups.

I'm of the belief that this skill has, indeed, been mastered by a select few. In practice, this would, most definitely, be quite the observation.

On the other hand, it could, most definitely, be our downfall...

-       Dr. James Marshall Marcus, Esquire
        August 28th, 1775

1

Christian

He sat at his computer and typed the words: a great man once said, "go up the middle, that's where the action is.",
Scratch that.
A great man once said, "the best place to be is somewhere between the decision and the execution of that decision. In the decision, there is no wrong, there is no fault… only hope and good fortune. The execution is where you are to find the error of your ways; it's where your fault is discovered and shortcomings are illuminated with the light and heat of a thousand suns…
… it's where you find her and all her folly. It's here you find mother nature and all her wrath."

"Yeah… Yeah, I'm going with that."
As he continued typing into his laptop, ideas poured from his brain and materialized onto the screen. Line after line of Times New Roman filled the hours as he prepared what was to be the last document he would ever have to write, under duress… and for free.

He will print this document, staple it in the top left corner and place it on his professor's desk, first thing. Then, there won't be another thought given to the words that were written here. That was the plan at least. Because tomorrow, he takes his last class. Late nights, early morning classes, awkward dealings with juvenile peers and the occasional drunken exchange with the overly indulgent and aggressively affectionate coed fade away as graduation day inches closer and occupies his every thought.

It had been four years since he first started living on campus and taking classes at this small private university in Dallas, Texas. When all else failed, he always found solace looking out the window of his dorm room on a rainy day, to see the silhouette of a bustling city, that he's sure represents in the minds of many, the pinnacle of man's existence. The creation of civilization. Man's triumph over nature by way of non-nomadic habitation. Solace came not from the view, but from knowing most people out there thought we were living in the greatest of times. He knew better.

What a joke, we humans are. We think only of ourselves and we don't even bother to understand the world we're destroying.

It's 1:45 am and as he stood at the southern facing window of his dorm room for surely what would be one of the last times, he solemnly gazed upon the nighttime Dallas skyline. He could see planes making final vectors to line up for approach at Love and Addison, and sometimes DFW; when the wind was coming in from the north and the planes, westbound. Most sounds came from Central Expressway and from Greek row, both just to the east, while Highland Park slept to the North. With his

18

window open, he could hear music coming from one of the year-end fraternity parties, a couple of blocks over. Guys yelling mindless bullshit chants and guzzling cheap keg beer while young girls giggled and squawked, but from this distance, he couldn't make out specifics. They were probably talking about where they'd take daddy's jet this summer or how epic their new Madison Avenue job was going to be once the fall came.

Being there would be reprehensible in his eyes. The only thing that turned his stomach more than the idea of living in this abortion of a civilization would be contributing to the celebration of it by participating in its' primary contributing driver, Blissful Ignorance.

His life would change once he left here. He wouldn't be able to harbor massive levels of disdain for society. At least not openly and all day. He would have a job to do and rent to pay.

His phone alarm sounds at 7:35. Finals day.

After throwing on a tee shirt and jeans and grabbing a granola bar, he made the short trip down to the student center to grab a coffee before his final Exploratory Literature and Philosophy class. There was a faint smell of stale beer, cigarettes and last night's obscenities in the air, all contributing to an air of excess, fear and desperation. Bloodshot eyes and sniffling were rampant this morning.

"Must have been quite the party last night,", he thought "wonder how much the coke dealers made..."

An abhorrent thought to most southerners.
"Oh my, what a down right miserable way to view this world. You ought'a be ashamed of yourself. I pray to Jesus, that you find your way."

But he was a realist. Most college kids here did coke. Whatever... to each, their own...

After a short walk, he found himself sinking into an all too familiar but uncomfortable auditorium chair for the next two hours, two rows back from the lectern. It's here, he will take his last final of his academic career.

"Don't choose the one who is beautiful to the world...
Choose the one who makes your world beautiful."

-Harry Styles

Was this some kind of joke or part of the final?
A trick-question?
A new form of irony?

Since when did the words of THE DOUCHIEST pop singer of our time deserve to be displayed among the greats at this prestigious, institution of higher learning?

"Good morning class"

Professor Hutchison was a pale, thin man in his 60s. Tenured and thrice divorced, all he treasured in life now was the shaping of young minds ... for a couple hundred grand a year and no fear of ever getting fired, that is. Oh yeah, and Johnny Walker Blue, also.

Over the past 2 decades he had authored several upmarket-fiction works that received moderate critical acclaim and sold several hundred thousand copies each. Just enough to gain him a mild following in niche art circles and create demand for his courses at the university. Just enough for a comfortable living.

"This quote on the board... What does this mean to you?"

Hands slowly went up throughout the auditorium.

"Find inner happiness", called a female voice from behind Christian.

"Find... inner... happiness...
Ok, dig a little deeper though..."

A male voice proclaimed,
"The entirety of Harry Styles' artistic talent and depth could fit into a shot glass ..."

The audience snickered.

"I'd agree it's not deep, but profound in my opinion...", retorted the professor.

Sarcastically, Christian began, "May I offer a perspective...?"

"Fuck... Here we go...", someone uttered from behind him.

"I believe this ... sentence... represents everything that's wrong with the world we live in. Seek first and only really ever, for yourself.
On the other hand, this, being written and discussed in a senior level college class just goes to prove the reach and effectiveness of both the decision makers behind the money involved in producing this ridiculous dogshit and the mediums by which we consume it.

This vapid fuck-hole is considered by many graduating high school seniors, to be one of the profound artistic visionaries of our time.
Why?
Because he tussles his hair just so and smiles?

I'm scared for the future, sir..."

There were several laughs from the back of the room.

"Vapid fuck-hole... descriptive... and quite an amusing visual...
No, the sole purpose of this ... quote... is to remind you that your opinion,
however industrial, or marginal or radical, or thought provoking it may
be... is yours.
You've worked hard to form it ... and the voice from which it's spoken.
While you're out there sharing it with the world, and hopefully profiteering
from it, never forget that you always must be able to relate to what you
write...
Defend what you say...
And put passion behind those words.
You owe this to the reader and they can see through bullshit, shallow
works ...

Others are out there doing the same.
While you may not agree with their message or delivery, they are
expressing their artistry... bearing their soul... to the world...
No matter how boiler-plate or lifeless or thin or gentrified you believe it to
be.
While you may not approve of the message or delivery, they are
expressing their inner most thoughts ... sharing their point of view, and this
furthers our human condition...

It's of my opinion that you all have written enough this semester so with
that, we're done here...
No more papers, no more thought-provoking exercises, no final..."

Cheers and applause erupted from the back half of the auditorium.

"So, congratulations on another completed semester and to those
graduating,
get out there...
think it, live it, then write it…
fact or fiction...
Unearth the corrupt...
educate the masses...
Further the cause...

Class dismissed"

And with that, his education was over.

Several weeks ago, Christian had officially landed a contributing editor
position at a website recently out of incubation. Fastli.com is a local but
growing blog style news website. With to the point, passionate and
opiniated writing and a millennial following, the site has been growing

and adding new talent. The position will allow him the freedom to write what he's passionate about. And get paid for it.

Everything about how Christian came to be employed at Fastli, as it's referred to, was strange. Against his will and for a grade, his senior lit professor, Mr. Hutchison, made attendance to at least one on campus career fair mandatory and part of the semester grade. He did this to ensure his students at least got in front of employers once while in college. The last thing he wanted was for his students to graduate and have forgotten to find a job. What kind of shaper of young minds would he have been, if he hadn't?

With a face full of disdain, Christian put on his nicest sweater over his button down, the cleanest, least holy pair of Levi's he could find, and his black Chuck Taylors. Splashed some water into his hair, brushed it to the side with his fingers and begrudgingly, headed to the student center to find gainful employment. Or, at the least, not torpedo his GPA.

Walking through the career fair, every employer represented had recruiters present. Each were talkative, positive and full of vigor. They needed these recruits and the low cost that came with them, just as much as these soon to be, former students, needed a steady paycheck. As Christian circumnavigated the room, recruiters from various corporations handed him cards and pamphlets, which mostly followed the life cycle of, recruiter's hand, Christian's hand, floor. As he approached the Fastli.com booth, he felt an instant connection … and smelled a supremely foul odor coming from somewhere inside the booth.

The booth itself was disheveled. The Fastli.com sign was slightly off center and the right side hung lower than the left by at least 3 inches. The table in the booth had no business cards or pamphlets telling prospects how great the work and environment are at Fastli. Instead, the only things on the table were what appeared to be a half empty bottle of Jim Beam, this morning's Wall Street Journal, a soft pack of Marlboro Lights, I mean Golds and what appeared to be a passed out representative half sitting in the folding chair with his, or her head buried down into folded arms. Most job seekers just walked by in judgement. Some stopped and looked, one or two even made comments as they stopped, but none were able to get the representative to raise his head from the table.

When Christian approached, the first thing that went through his head was, "Didn't this guy know he had to recruit new employees today?"

He approached the table, tapped the rep on the elbow and said, "You OK?"

After a short pause, he uttered, "I'm no expert, but I don't think that you are going to impress ideal recruits today if you're passed out."

The rep lifted his head and Christian instantly recognized JC Ryan. He was a trim man with a full head of shaggy hair and he wore squarish, plastic frame eyeglasses. His hair was slightly amess and he was wearing a Chuck Taylor hoodie and jeans. As Christian has been a follower of fastli.com since its' early days, he had seen pictures of JC and other early employees from posts on the site and had hoped to possibly apply there when he graduated.

"You know you're the first person to check on me? Someone even said, by the looks of this guy, it must suck working there...", JC remarked.

He smiled and Christian realized JC wasn't even drunk. It's a little-known fact that JC Ryan has both an IQ of 140+ and relishes in the title of consummate prankster. This was his test to find out a person's true self without even looking at them and as it turns out, is surprisingly effective. If someone doesn't care enough about another person that appears to be suffering, how can they possibly care about their employer? He was looking for people who cared and it seems he found one. The rapid-fire conversation went like this...

"What's your name?", - JC

"Christian Jones, Mr. Ryan.", - C

"JC, please...",

"You graduating this semester?", - JC

"Yes", - C

"I'm going to say a series of words and I want you to say the first word or short phrase that comes to mind... cool?", -JC

"Sure....", - C

"Civilization", - JC
"Wasted", - C

"Corporation", - JC
"Inside", - C

"Control", - JC
"Fleeting", - C

"Creation", - JC
"...uh, ok...", - C

"Man", - JC
"Flock", - C

23

"One more… "

Christian interrupts, "Time… you got me feeling so free…", sung to the melody of the French electronic music duo, Daft Punk's November 30th, 2000 hit song of the same name.
"Seriously, One more… existence", - JC
"point of view", - C

JC had written down each of the responses. He tilted his glasses down, resting them on the end of his nose in an effort to appear like he had a purpose in doing so. He held the page close to his face, moved it away, then toward, then back again, from his face, all in a single rapid and fluid motion. He spent a brief moment reviewing the answers, then lowered the page, adjusted his glasses and looked Christian in the eye.

"Boo", he said in a forceful voice.
"Boo, back …", Christian replied with a snarky grin.

"Silly Librarian…. Looking for a job?" - JC

"Yes Sir…" - C

"Well, you just found one… Welcome to fastli.com"

Apparently, The Anne Rice quote from Queen of the Damned sealed the deal for JC.
Wait… it was the movie, not the book. I don't know… maybe the book…? I didn't read it first.

Christian asked, "just curious, but what's that smell?"

"What do you mean, smell?", JC responded with the most sarcastically straight face he could muster.
If you don't know, it's a tricky face to make. It requires hiding a shit-eating grin underneath an emotionlessly straight face. It's actually quite difficult to pull off properly.

"Oh, that smell… I find personal joy in screwing with everyone at these recruiting events. It's actually a formula of my own creation… sorry bud, patent pending…"

"By the way, what does JC stand for? I've followed the site for a while and I've never seen it mentioned anywhere…", Christian asked…

"That's a conversation for another time…
Tell you what, give me your contact info and we'll send over an offer letter and stuff before this semester is out… sound good?"

"This place is going to be awesome", Christian thought to himself.

And just like that, he had his first professional job.

After providing a writing sample, he was presented with a unique position. He would have his own subpage on the site with a firewall for subscriber-only premium content. He was offered a draw for 6 months, after which, he would be expected to be driving revenue from targeted advertisers and self-sourced premium subscribers. Once his draw was paid back in full, he'd receive a cut of the revenue from his subsite. Pretty sweet deal, he thought and he'd already thought of the perfect name.

The American Malcontent.

Fastli was everything Christian had hoped it was going to be. Fast paced, no taboo topics or ideas, creatives everywhere and he was given a long leash to explore and write. After only four months, he had The Malcontent up and running, had written upwards of two dozen posts covering a wide variety of topics, had an ever-growing viewer base while averaging about four hundred clicks at an average of 85 seconds each, per day. That meant people were reading his shit. He had already accumulated two hundred and forty-six paid subscribers, averaging new paid adds in the double digits per week. All in all, that's pretty good for someone who's student loan payments haven't even kicked in yet.

He had been hustling though. Seriously.

He hit up everyone he had an email address for, within his phone. He called every contact, family member, every college friend he had, to visit his page and share his work. Over time, his page trickled throughout the web and found its way in front of people that enjoyed his point of view and crass, sometimes crude writing style. He had written about the spoiled and narcissistic future business leaders he had gone to college with, the debt slavery epidemic, the pending student loan crash, short term thinking on wall street, you know, all the things that a normal, twenty-two-year-old concerned himself with. He went guns blazing, right up the middle and it had earned him an increasing level of national exposure and notoriety. He was starting to get requests to appear and comment from some of the more obscure news network talk shows. While Christian would usually chastise the caller, then typically, hung up the phone, he was amused that they were calling him for his thoughts now.

About 10:30am on a Tuesday, his desk phone rang.

"This's Christian", he announced into the handset.

"Oh, hey JC... what can I do for you?
.... Sure, I'll be down in a second. I'm gonna stop off at the lounge and grab a coffee first ... want one? Ok, be up in a sec..."

His stomach sank. When you're in the weeds working on a story or have a deadline to publish, you tend to get slightly pissed off when you get yanked out of the zone by getting called into your boss's office, but when you don't have a thing going on and he calls you down, your mind tends to run and you assume the worst.

Christian walked down the hall of the trendy and stylishly decorated office. He made a left into the office lounge. There were a few employees inside, having a heated debate about some niche aspect of the new Red Dead Redemption game. Christian nodded to the one who looked up as he proceeded toward the Nespresso machine. Two minutes later, a Cubano / Altissio red eye was in hand and he was closing in on JC's office door.

"Hey Patricia", he said, greeting JC's assistant as he passed by her desk and through his boss's open door. He knew he wasn't getting fired today but there is always that sneaking suspicion lurking around the corner.

"Hey boss, what's up?", He asked after sitting down in one of the empty chairs in front of JC's desk.

"We need to talk Christian...", he said with a straight face. But he had seen this face before and wasn't falling for it this time.

" Aww, shit! Are you firing me? Come on man! I'm sorry... it won't happen again. It was just an upper decker... it's not even that big of a deal... I mean... it ultimately flushed on its' own, right?"

JC couldn't hold back the smirk any longer and burst into laughter. Patricia craned her head almost completely backward to peek, in the hopes of getting a glimpse of what it was that her boss found so hilarious.

"That's a good idea! I'm going to remember that one for future use...", JC said.

"Seriously though. Your sub numbers are in for the month and I just wanted to tell you that you have officially paid back and are now covering your draw in full. You're now eligible for revenue share from your sub base. 20% is the first tier with adjustment to 25% of premium sub revenue at the 1,000 mark. Congratulations... Nice Work."

He had thought he was getting close to covering but he calculated that he needed about 650 subscribers.

With a smirk he replied, "Uh... you know ... Well, you go out there and you give 110 percent... and you wanna play good ... and you hope you play good, and I think we played pretty good tonight..."

JC just shook his head, laughing audibly while lowering his face toward his desk. The movie Bedazzled was a guilty pleasure and the reference wasn't wasted, in the least.

"Be serious for a second… You're always here, kicking ass and hustling. I think you should celebrate this achievement so I covered airfare, dinners and 5 nights at my go to spot, The Decanter Hotel in Old San Juan. Flight leaves tomorrow morning at 7:49."

"But… ", Christian was stunned. This is probably the nicest thing anyone had ever done for him.
"I don't even have a passport yet.", Were the only words he could muster.

"Dude, you don't need one…. US Territory… now go home, relax and pack a bag. You have an early flight.", JC said, as he turned his attention to one of the ever-growing pile of tasks that were accumulating on his desk. "This isn't optional, by the way… go…enjoy…"
"Thank You… seriously…", Christian said somberly.

"Don't mention it… Oh, hold on… do two things for me while you're there.", He added.
"One, tomorrow night… when you land, call ahead and get a table at Marmalade. Be sure to order the popcorn shrimp and the white bean soup. Two, check out the rainforest… totally worth it…". JC picked up his phone and began dialing a number, and just like that, he was back at full speed.

"Uh… Sure Thing! Thanks Again! OK, bye.", are the best set of words he could put together at that moment.

He took a couple of steps out of JC's office and turned to see Patricia smiling with a plain white envelope in her extended hand.
"Congratulations", she mouthed as to not make a big deal in front of the rest of the office.

"You've earned it.", she said.

Christian reached out and took the envelope from her hand, then proceeded to walk back down the hall toward his office. He was blown away. He was all but convinced that people just didn't do kindnesses like this for others anymore.

Once he left the office around 3pm, the rest of the day was pretty much a blur. From the office in uptown, He grabbed an Uber back to his apartment on Thomas and Fairmount, packed a suitcase for the trip, checked a few emails, walked down to Jake's for a chili dog and a beer, went to the nearby Whole Foods to grab a few travel incidentals he'd need, then, walked back to his apartment. There was no real need to own a car when you both lived and worked in Uptown. If you had to go somewhere farther than walking distance, you can just Uber or rent one of those motorized scooters. There are usually like three of four of those outside of his apartment building at any given time. If it's more than a 30-dollar Uber ride, is it really a place worth going?

He laid in his bed preparing himself for the next 5 days. He would, literally, have nothing he'd have to do the entire time. Since college graduation and starting at Fastli, all he thought about was The Malcontent. He had dedicated himself to getting this site up, digging deep down for perspective in his writing and focused solely on the work before him. He knew no one in Puerto Rico. Not a soul. This was a bit of a scary proposition when he spent more than a few moments thinking about it. As he laid in bed, he searched the internet for things to do in PR. As he scrolled through the search results and selected links, his eyes closed and the next thing he knew, his phone was buzzing. It was 5am. Time to make the donuts.

He jumped in the shower, brushed his teeth, threw on a white T shirt and hoodie, shorts and flip-flops and packed the rest of his toiletries. A quick pat of his pockets ensured he had his wallet, phone, keys and that white envelope Patricia handed him yesterday. He pulled out his phone and opened the Uber app. Two minutes later, a car pulled up in front of his building and he hopped in, suitcase in hand, into the back seat.

"DFW right?", the driver asked.

"Yep. Terminal A please.", He replied.

"Terminal A it is, then.", And with that, the driver pulled away from the curb.

During the ride to the airport, Christian could tell the driver had been up all night, working. He kept yawning repetitively and was trying to keep himself awake. This would probably be his last trip for the evening. He actually made pretty good money driving for Uber, overnight. He would hang around the upscale bars at 1am waiting on the drunken rush of young adults to need rides home. He had been doing this for a while and was getting pretty good at distinguishing between a bar hailing an Uber to involuntarily send patrons home and users requesting rides themselves. He's done this long enough to know when someone is standing outside a building and when the hail is coming from inside the establishment. He tries to accept the ones that are standing outside because, one, he doesn't have to wait on the passenger to exit the establishment. Two, drunks usually accidentally tip better and three, the bars and restaurant owners rarely, if ever, did.

His car radio was set to Sports Radio 96.7FM The Ticket, a local sports talk radio station and the volume was louder than expected for 5:30 in the morning. Today, The Musers were talking with KoKo the Gorilla about the Cowboys, Saints game and discussing the chances this defensive performance on Thursday Night would become history's shining example of how defense should be played in this league. As usual, George seemed put out by Koko's presence. Christian was a lifelong Cowboys Football fan, having grown up in a lower middle-class Southern Dallas suburb. He liked the station and would occasionally listen.

His boss, JC on the other hand, was a P1D1 by the station's proprietary classification system and a die-hard fan of both the Cowboys and of the sport of football in general. JC would sometimes call Christian down to his office and spend hours talking all things Jerry, "D Law and the Hot Boyz", and how Jeff Heath was done a major disservice by not being inducted from the get go, his raging man crush on LVE, "DakandZeke", as JC called them, (because they're so much better together and should never, under any circumstances, be separated), how bad the Philadelphia "Keagles", and their rot gut, battery-stuffed-snowball-throwing, fanbase sucked and basically anything else NFC East related. JC had a strange and fascinating understanding of the game of football and probably would have been an excellent head coach or referee in another life.

"The radio ok?", the driver asked.
"Sure, the Ticket's fine with me...", Christian replied.
"Koko cracks me up, man!", the driver responded.

"Why are you going to the airport? Flying somewhere?", the driver asked.

Christian immediately recognized the quote from Dumb and Dumber and that the driver was probably a regular BAD Radio listener, but it was too early in the am and he hadn't yet been properly caffeinated, so instead of replying yeah, going to Aspen, he decided to play dumb and replied, "Do, What?"

The driver didn't repeat his inquiry.

The traffic hadn't yet slowed the highways to a snarling stand still, so the drive was quick to DFW Airport. Twenty minutes later, the Corolla pulled up to the Terminal A, gates 21-35 door. Christian tossed a 5 over the driver's right shoulder and said, "sorry man, it's all I got on me."
"You know you can tip through the app... right?", the driver said.
Christian's brain doesn't properly function prior to caffeine and he just smiled and shrugged his shoulders.
"that's cool man... thank you and have a good trip.", The driver responded,
As the red tail lights of the Corolla disappeared into the humid, Texas morning, Christian turned toward the door, extended the handle on his rolling suitcase and began his journey by leaving the humid Texas morning behind and stepped into the sterile, air-conditioned confines of DFW International Airport.

2
Katie

DFW airport is a sprawling set of 8 terminals, slightly bigger than the island of Manhattan. Split down the middle by an 8-lane road, the terminals are connected by an electric tram that circles the airport every 10 minutes. Terminal A is the northeast most commercial terminal and dedicated to international or over-seas routes due to the widebody nature of the necessary aircraft. Due north is the American Airlines cargo terminal and further due North is the Private GA tarmac, where the rich and famous come and go. It was here Christian's mom took him to welcome home the flight ferrying the 2011 NBA Champion Dallas Mavericks coming back from kicking the living shit out of the LeBron heavy, Heat in 6 games. This was about the time that the Ticket got it's now infamous *Why Today Doesn't Suck* Dirk drop, "Shut It Down! Let's go Home!"

As Christian ventured into the terminal to check in and exchange his tickets for a boarding pass, he noticed the airport was virtually empty at this hour. This was fantastic! No lines and no hour wait to get body cavity searched by the TSA. Those 9/11 cock suckers really did achieve their goal if it indeed, was to make flying anywhere from within the US of A really suck. He breezed through ticketing and security to find no line at the Starbuck's. With a vente dark roast, red eye in hand, he approached the gate. It was now 7:20 and there were about 35 waiting vacationers in the seating area, on their own journey to America's own little Caribbean carve out.

The gate agent, a young man with spiky, bleached blonde hair, dressed in what resembled a pilot or flight attendant uniform, only without the cool hat, aviator sunglasses, winged insignia or jacket, came over the PA.

"We would like to welcome each and every one of you to Flight 102, this morning's nonstop service to San Juan, Puerto Rico.", he announced in a cheery voice.
"We will begin boarding shortly. As this is a relatively empty flight this morning, our captain has instructed me to tell each of you that once we board, to feel free to find your own empty row. When the captain turns off the seat belt sign, prop your feet up and relax all the way to San Juan."

There was a unified chorus of gleeful cheers in response, throughout the waiting area, following that comment.

"Mr. C Jones, can you please come to Gate 28. C Jones, Gate 28", was announced over the terminal PA system.

Christian was checking emails and the national news feeds. He raised his head from his phone, surprised, and walked the 10 feet to the gate agent's podium.

30

"Mr. Jones, we have a message in your PNR that you've been upgraded to our First-Class cabin."

"For real?", he asked, excited.

"Yes sir! If you will give me that boarding pass, I'll exchange it with this one."
The seat assignment was for 1B, front row, window! A bulkhead seat on a Boeing 767 has miles of legroom. It might as well be a suite! A couple of years ago, Christian's mom retired from American Airlines after an illustrious, 25-year career at the airline's group and meeting travel desk. He's sure she called in a favor the second he had gotten off the phone with her yesterday.

"Fuck Yeah!...
"... oh, pardon me... sorry...", he muttered, lowering his voice considerably.

"No problem, sir.", The gate agent said with a grin, "we get that response a lot."

A few minutes later.

"Welcome to Flight 102, non-stop service to San Juan Puerto Rico. We'd now like to begin the preboarding process. At this time, we invite our AAdvantage Executive Platinum, Platinum and Gold members and our first-class passengers to board through gate 28."

Christian rose to his feet. A feeling best described as pride and excitement rushed over him. There is a phenomenon that happens during the pre-boarding process on every flight, every day, within every airport in the world. When preboarding is announced, every person waiting to board any given flight, immediately looks up to see who falls into this category and begins to board the plane. It's usually with extreme envy they watch and wonder, "are they a celebrity or rich or somebody important or something?",

Christian alone, approached the gate and felt the vengeance of 68 eyeballs, glaring directly at him.

After scanning his boarding pass, he made his way down the jet bridge, toward the shining silver curvature of the jet's fuselage. He was greeted by a smiling, older brunette flight attendant.

"Good morning Mr. Jones!", she proclaimed.

"Hi, how are you?", he replied as he ducked his head to cross the threshold, into the jet's cabin. He took an immediate right, into the First-Class cabin to find his seat.

First row… easy enough.

This specific aircraft hadn't yet been through the cabin update protocols since the merger. Wide, gray leather seats, variations of deep and light blue panels and sparse accents of vivid red, adorned the cabin. The coach seats were a basic blue cloth with goldenrod patterned squares. Decorations were sparse back there and the seats, much smaller. He stored his suitcase in the overhead bin and swung into his window seat. The first-class flight attendant, a considerably more attractive and younger blonde woman with a pixie cut, approached.

"Good morning Mr. Jones. I'm Katie … I'll be up here with you for the flight this morning."

He interrupted, "Christian please… I'm not a middle-aged man on a power trip."

She laughed professionally, "Ok then… Christian.", She said with a flirty grin, "Can I get you something before we depart? Perhaps a champagne, a mimosa or a Bloody Mary?"

"Just an OJ please.", He responded.

"Once we get to cruising altitude, we will be serving breakfast and are scheduled to arrive in San Juan at approximately 12:45 am, est. It's just you and me this morning so if you need anything at all, don't hesitate to let me know…"

"Sounds good, thank you.", he said.

He couldn't tell if she was being flirty or was just really good at being professional. He thought, for a moment, she may be interested in him but the idea of him being wrong about that was overwhelming. To avoid an awkward 4-hour flight, he decided that she was just a really good flight attendant. He put in his earbuds, connected to the inflight wi-fi, opened Pandora, queued up his BlackMill station and began surfing Zero Hedge headlines.

He lost himself in the trance-like music as the rest of the occupants from Gate 28's lounge began to file into the aircraft and walked right past him. He's sure he noticed some fellow passengers still harboring ill will and even a few that shot him "go to hell" glances, but he paid no mind to them as they passed. Moments later, he felt the pressure change of the cabin door being closed, the jerk of the aircraft backing away from the gate, the beginning of the departure roll and then, a few moments later, he felt his stomach drop slightly as the aircraft's massive turbines forced the one thousand-ton marvel of man's ingenuity, into the air.

The flight was uneventful. After a left turn during power out and a shallow right bank to align with the appropriate vector at level off, the aircraft was on course to paradise. During the ascent, Christian was sure he had caught Katie staring at him a couple of times from the forward jump seats but settled on the logical conclusion that she was probably just bored.

She approached him with a breakfast of eggs benedict, hash browned potatoes, a warm croissant and a variety of butters, jams and jellies. He devoured breakfast and she cleared the remnants. He asked for another orange juice and she obliged. Afterwards, he reclined his seat fully, and enjoyed a much-needed siesta to pass the time.

In all, the aircraft flew 1,987 miles over New Orleans, the Gulf of Mexico, Cuba and Haiti, then began it's decent over the Dominican Republic. Once the jet began to descent, Christian was awoken to a soft tap on the shoulder.

"Christian, we're descending over the DR. Is there anything I can get you before we enter our final approach? A coffee perhaps?", Katie asked.

"No thank you… I'm fine.", He said.

"Great, well, would mind raising your seat back to its' original upright position for me?", she said, with that same smile. Of course, he complied, while holding down the dull gray button on the arm rest.

He glanced out the window and was astonished by the view. A sea of aqua and bright blues danced and glistened, while white capped waves crested under the midday Caribbean sun. It was spectacular. The best thing about Puerto Rico is that it was relatively inexpensive, by vacation standards. After another turn or two, the ground began to approach and suddenly, the massive Michelin tires of the 767 squealed as the plane touched down, then began to slow. A couple of turns later, the airplane came to a complete stop and a ding sounded as the fasten seat belt sign went dark. He could hear rustling in the back of the plane, so he stood up, stretched briefly, retrieved his suitcase from above his seat and began to walk to the front.

Katie had already opened the cabin door and was standing in the cockpit entryway in front of, and along with the Captain and First Officer.

"Thank you for flying American Airlines. It was our pleasure today. We hope to see you again soon!", she said. All 3 crewmembers we're smiling, and why wouldn't they be? They just got to fly 1,000 tons of awesomeness to one of the most beautiful places on the planet and got paid to do so!

"Great Job, really, all of you. Very nice landing Captain!", he proclaimed.

"Thank you, sir!", he responded.

He shot one last glance at Katie. She smiled and shot him a quick wink. He returned the smile, turned left and walked outside the hatch and onto the jet bridge. The weather was warm and he noticed how much more humid it was here, than back home. It was fitting and welcoming. This was going to be a fun week, he thought.

After exiting the jet bridge, he walked into the terminal and took a left toward the baggage claim area. He didn't have a checked bag to retrieve thanks to his mother. In all her infinite wisdom and her years working for the airlines, she had instilled this one piece of advice in her children. Always carry on. During the arrival taxi announcements, Katie had mentioned that the terminal exit and car rental kiosks were accessed through the baggage claim area.

Throughout the terminal, Latin Top 40's music was playing over the PA system. The only Latin pop song he knew was Luis Fonsi's, Despacito, Ft Daddy Yankee. He didn't really care for that kind of music in particular, but he had heard that specific song about four million times over the past year. He now had that cumbia influenced beat, stuck in his head. It could be much worse, he thought to himself.

He rounded the corner into the baggage area and spotted an older Puerto Rican man, dressed in a floral shirt, khaki slacks and a straw fedora. He was holding a small, white marker board that had the name "U. Dockor", written on it in large, black marker. He paused, then grinned, shook his head and giggled to himself. Even 2,000 miles away and in the middle of the ocean, JC's jokes don't stop.

Outside, the sun was more bright and warmer that he was used to. He put on his sunglasses, about $40 on a Facebook page he came across a while ago, then walked to the curb, where a Jeep Wrangler brandishing a magnetic placard stuck to the passenger side door that read, The Decanter, waited to chauffer him to the hotel. He tossed his suitcase into the back seat and climbed in the front seat. During the short ride, the top was down, the air, fresh and moist and Old San Juan was much more colorful than online pictures, had done justice. There were palm threes everywhere and the city was bustling and lively. He assumed it would be a little more, third world down here but he was surprised as it almost felt like he was back home. He now understood why JC liked it here so much. It felt just like Texas, minus all the giant 4x4's and 18 wheelers, but with a beach in all directions.

They arrived at the boutique hotel, as the Jeep swung into the covered valet entrance. As Christian walked into the hotel lobby, he noticed a large, bottle-necked wine decanter in the middle of a modern, rectangular sofa table set longways, with a placard neatly set next to it. The placard read, "Welcome to The Decanter in Old San Juan. Please Enjoy This Locally Sourced Refreshment.", The decanter was filled with crystal clear water with a few lemon wheel slices floating in the top. That's a nice touch, Christian thought.

Once checked in, Christian took the elevator to his 4th floor room, The French Balcony Suite, directly below the hotel's rooftop lounge and bar. His balcony was large and extended to the edge of the building, almost adjacent to the street below. From his balcony, he had a view of the streets and buildings of Old San Juan and through the buildings, he could see that memorable blue sea he witnessed from 8,000 feet above, just an hour or so earlier. When he looked up, his view was of the leading edge of the bar and lounge and he could see the heads and torsos of fellow hotel patrons leaning against its' wall, enjoying the view of the city. He decided to change clothes and venture out to explore the city a bit, prior to dinner. He made a quick call down to the concierge to get him a reservation at Marmalade for one, then headed out to explore this new and intriguing place.

Christian arranged his earbuds, hit play on Pandora then walked through the streets of Old San Juan, admiring the architectures and vibrant randomization of varying colors of block, after block. Narrow streets of brick and stone clicked and clacked as patrons navigated them. He witnessed a local political rally in the plaza, saw the ships docked at the port, walked through Fort San Juan and admired the historic navy shipyard and past the aged remains of the old cockfighting arenas. Strolling around this historic city freed his mind and made him think about this city and its' generous people. It was modern, yet cut off from the rest of the 1st world and, yet, it had a soul, it had a unique spirit, all its' own.

The sun began to set, as he set in the plaza and observed Ricardo Rossello inspire his people with his grand voice. He pointed to the sky and to the crowd and said something in Spanish, to which the crowd erupted in applause and chants of "Un Termino Mas, Un Termino Mas!".

He looked down at his watch and noticed the time. 6:55pm. He hadn't quite gotten used to the time change yet. His dinner reservation was at 7:15 so he pulled out his phone and opened Uber. He noticed a nearby driver and hailed it. Forty-five seconds later, he was in the back of a white Jetta.

"The Decanter, please", he said.

"Ah, Si Senor...", said the driver.

Five minutes later, the Jetta pulled into the overhang at the hotel and he hopped out.
Just out of habit, as Christian entered the lobby, he noticed that same lobby decanter, filled with water just this morning, was now filled with a dark liquid that appeared to be red wine. Back in his room, he changed into a button-down shirt, splashed a little water on his hair, slicked it back and in two minutes, he was back downstairs for the short walk to the restaurant.

Marmalade was a trendy, high art and fashion type of establishment. Colorful, tall back chairs surrounded small, white linoleum tabletops. No chair was identical to another around each of the 15 or so tables in the multi-leveled dining room. Beautiful young women wearing body hugging dresses and sipping artistically inspired cocktails while their sharp-dressed, debonair gentlemen, enjoying various spirits, neat, occupied the majority of the restaurant's tables. It was a packed house tonight. He approached the hostess and was shown to his table near the center of the room. He was mildly underdressed and felt slightly intimidated, sitting alone.

"Good evening sir, welcome to Marmalade, you can call me Caretaker...", announced the waiter, or Caretaker, as they're apparently called here, "...may I bring you one of our hand-crafted cocktails or perhaps, a wine list?"

"That's ok... I'll have a Macallan 25, Stoned.", Their term for those large ice balls used for finer spirits.

"Fine choice sir.", responded caretaker.

"I'm ready to order if that's cool?", Christian said.

"Absolutely, sir...", said caretaker.
"I'll have the Popcorn Shrimp to start, the tiny white bean soup and for dinner, let me try the Beef Tenderloin.", Christian replied.

He felt a little uppity ordering such things, but when in Rome...

"All fantastic choices, sir... I'll have the first two courses out shortly, followed by the main...", caretaker added.

"Thank you, Caretaker... That'll do", Christian said in a sarcastically, pompous tone while smiling at the waiter. He grinned and walked away.

Christian wasn't a big food guy. Burgers and fries were the norm for him. He did, however, enjoy the view in this place. He'd never seen so much artful expression, so many beautiful women and so much pomposity, crammed into 1,100 square feet. His normal disdain had been replaced, tonight, by an obscene admiration for the snooty.

His scotch arrived and he sipped it slowly. It burned, but not the way a call or even premium liquors burned. This was different. This burn seemed to have a life of its' own. It was warm, but not overpoweringly, so... just the right amount as to suggest, "Don't shoot me like tequila or I'll fuck you up. Relax and enjoy my full body and $125 a pour, price tag."

Christian didn't care. JC had already picked up the tab for this dinner so he was going to enjoy it and try some things he'd always wanted to try. Macallan 25 was one of those things.

The Popcorn shrimp arrived and it was a small glass dish with 3 marinated and grilled shrimp atop a bed of ancho guacamole and topped with, get this, heirloom spiced popcorn. Fucking $100 a person and they serve a dish with popcorn on it? But it was by all that was, is, and has yet to be, the definition of the word, scrumptious!

Christian now understood where JC was coming from. While seemingly pompous and douchey, the popcorn shrimp was fantastic and he felt like an asshole for his first and initial judgement of it.

Next, followed the tiny white bean soup. Served in a small espresso cup and sipped like a coffee, it was topped with black truffle oil and pancetta dust... Sign me up!

Lastly, was the tenderloin with scalloped potatoes and mushroom ragout. It was, by his own description, excellent and no other words are needed to finish this sentence.

After his dinner, caretaker approached and informed Christian that dinner was on the house as JC was a regular and friend to Chef Peter Schintler and his family.

Cheap ass. He sent me to his buddy's restaurant so he didn't have to pay. It turned out to be one of the top three meals he had ever had and any ill will he may or may not have harbored, faded away along with his hunger.

During the slow stroll back to his hotel, the dinner had left him with a feeling of warmth and wholeness within his being. This was a different experience from anything he'd ever before felt. It was like the creation itself had a soul and he had consumed it. He thought, "I wonder if this is what a vampire feels like after he drinks from the neck of a pretty, young villager?". The visual he got was that of Bella Lugosi as Dracula and it made him laugh to himself.

He took the elevator up to his suite and walked out onto the terrace. The sea breeze that blew from the east and through these evening streets, was cooler than expected and he could hear the steady beat of trendy dance tunes coming from the above, rooftop lounge. He decided to go up and have another drink or two and continue the night. After all, what the hell? He's on vacation.

Christian walked into hall and took the stairs to the rooftop. The breeze was warm and blowing just slightly. There were about thirty-five patrons scattered about among the tables, surrounding a makeshift dance floor. Against the inner wall was a long bar that ran its' entire length and was lit from the underside, with red LED lights. Built into the wall, were shelves for glasses and expensive bottles of spirits from around the world. All the players were there. Remy, Louis, Armand, Macallan among others and each, as expected, were perched on their own shelf with a singular LED spotlight illuminating them all. A familiar 80's dance mix played over the speakers from the DJ booth. Christian took a seat at the bar top near the end and ordered a Grey Goose and soda... with a squeeze and twist of lemon, of course. He sat, sipping his Grey Goose and soaked up the comfortable night air and ambiance, rarely found anywhere in North Texas.

As a dance remix of Hall and Oates, Out of Touch played, Christian felt a light, familiar tab on his left shoulder.

"Christian?", a voice asked.

"Yes...", he asked, as he turned his barstool to face his visitor. It was Katie, the super-hot flight attendant from his flight this morning. He was instantly thrust into a nervous stammer.

"Hey... Uh, it's Katie, right?", he said, trying desperately to be cool, calm and most of all, collected. "I'm kidding, I remember you. What are you doing here?", he asked.

"We stay here when we have a layover on the island.", She smiled and continued, "after we dropped you off, we went back to Miami, switched planes, and hopped on a narrow body and got back as fast as we could! That big one is going on to Heathrow tonight."

Katie was with two other young female flight attendant co-workers. One's name was Ramona, a mid-twenties Puerto Rican island native, stationed in Miami. She knew the island well and enjoyed laying over here, given she could go see her parents regularly. The other's name was Sarah, a tall African American girl with short hair, also in her mid-20's. Katie took the seat next to Christian and her friends took a seat on the other side of her, sipping cocktails and laughing about who knows, what.

"So, I figured when the flight crew was laid over, they all hung out? Are the pilots staying here too?", Christian asked.

"No, we're leaving with a different flight service crew, so they are on a shorter rollover. They leave tomorrow morning, so they can't partake this evening.", She responded, smiling.

"Uh, where are my manners. Can I get you a drink? What are you having?", he asked.

"Sure... Appleton and diet please", she said, directed toward the bartender, while taking the last sip from her current glass.

"Appleton? Is that local?", Christian asked. He was nervous but doing his best to try to stay cool.

"Jamaican actually...", she continued, "my last route sent me through Montego Bay with layovers, weekly. Got a taste for it and can't shake it.",

He tried to keep eye contact and she appeared nervous as well. He noticed she kept twisting the ends of her hair and tilting her head as they talked.

"So, where are you stationed?", he asked.

"Miami, along with Ramona and Sarah, but I live in the DFW area.", She told him.

"Oh, cool! Me too, what area?", he prompted.

"Grapevine. It's close to work and if I get called in, I can deadhead quickly… ", she answered.

"That must be convenient…", he continued, "I live, kind of, behind Hotel Zaza, off McKinney.", He paused, then said,", … I don't mean to be too direct given our professional relationship but… is there a Mister Flight Attendant back home, missing you?", He instantly felt like a creep for both saying those words, and saying them in the tone in which they came out.

He was surprised to see her smile, then blush, then look down toward her feet, then finally, raise her head back up, lean in a few inches closer, look him directly in the eye and said, without being able to fight back a smile,

"There is definitely not a mister flight attendant. I'm gone too often right now to get into a relationship…. But… I have been thinking about bidding a route that would lay me over at home, most of the time.",

Now, Christian was the one blushing and grinning ear to ear.

"Oh, I'm really sorry….", He said, "my wife is going to get super pissed if I don't get back downstairs soon.", He looked at Katie with the straightest of sarcastic face. Oscar worthy stuff, for real. As he looked her in the eye, she appeared stunned, then slightly angry, until she glanced down at his lips as he struggled to hold back his grin. A wave of relief came over her face. "You suck!", she said and she playfully smacked him on the shoulder.

They both broke into laughter.

"I'm sorry, I'm totally kidding…", he said, "I'm single as can be… I'm working all the time…"

They continued talking and drinking and laughing until she looked down at his watch, realizing it was 1:20am.

"Oh shit, it's getting late…", she said, "we're supposed to be here for a three-day layover but dispatch loves to call us on day one of PR layovers and send us on half days."

"So... I'm here... on vacation... alone... by myself... in Puerto Rico... ", he struggled, "... where I know, not a soul. Knowing that, and if you're still here tomorrow... would you maybe be interested in ... I don't know... maybe going somewhere with me.... Like, I don't know... the rainforest?", he stammered.

"Well... Mister Jones... I'm sorry, but I don't date passengers.", She said with a much better and more serious, straight face. The look on his face can only be described by using a simile involving someone punching a golden retriever puppy.

Then, nervousness rained over him kind of like when you grab a wash rag that's laid over the bath tub faucet and you accidentally pull up that lever that turns on the shower head. It was then, he noticed her fighting back a smile as well...

"That doesn't feel too good now... does it?", she smirked.

He grinned with relief and said, simply ... "Touché"

She stood up, took the last sip from her highball, put one hand on Christian's shoulder, then leaned in and gave him a hug that lingered just slightly too long. As their faces touched as she pulled away, she kissed him on the cheek and whispered, "Thank you for a lovely evening Christian... See you tomorrow...".

She took a step backward, looked him square in the eyes, shot him one last smile and turned and walked away, joining both Ramona and Sarah.

He leaned back in his chair and exhaled slowly. There's no feeling quite like the one that follows, the first time you meet someone and there's instant chemistry.

Christian put two fingers up toward his throat and signaled the bartender with that universal "close me out", hand gesture. The bartender asked which room he was in and he responded, "The French something or other...", he said. The bartender charged the bill to his room and he took out 3 crisp twenties and left them on the bar. He stood up, walked to the stairs, then shortly after, disappeared into his room on the floor below. He laid in his bed with his hands behind his head, fingers interlocked and thought of nothing but Katie's big green eyes and her smile. That smile that made the rest of the world disappear. He fell asleep that night with a smile on his face and one single thought kept going through his mind, over and over again.
I fucking Love Puerto Rico!

5:15am

The TV in his hotel room turned on unexpectedly. So, did his phone. Both activated and emitted the same sound. One long, continuous, loud beep. Those of you in the US know the sound as the beginning of an Emergency Alert System activation.

Christian heard this, as he was jarred from his slumber.

Alerta De Emergencia

A solicitud de la Administracion Nacional Oceanica y Atmosferica, se trata de una alerta del Sistema nacional de alerta de emergencia. Esto es solo una pruebra.

Si esto hubiera sido una emergencia real, este mensaje habria seguido por detalles e instrucciones. Esto es solo una pruebra.

Regresamos ahora con la programacion habitual.

Translation

Emergency Alert

At the request of the National Oceanic and Atmospheric Administration, this is a test of the national emergency alert system.
This is only a test.

If this had been an actual emergency, this message would have been followed by details and instructions. This is only a test.
We will now return you to your regularly scheduled program.

"Seriously?", he said, rather forcefully, as he sat up in the bed.

He was awake now. There's no going back to sleep after that.

Christian got out of bed, threw on a t-shirt and groggily, made his way down to the lobby for a cup of coffee and a quick breakfast. As he walked past the counter in the lobby, the front desk attendant said, "Mr. Jones, Mr. Jones... We have a something for you."

"What is it?", he enquired. The front desk lady handed him a legal sized envelope.

He took the envelope and on the front was written simply, "Christian Jones"

The letter read,

Dear Christian,

I hate to leave you this letter but at 3 am this morning, the airline called furloughed and layover employees back to the Continental United States immediately. Something about a geological event or something.

I was so looking forward to seeing you again this afternoon.

My schedule, if nothing changes, will keep me out of town for the next 3 weeks but will be back in Texas after that, for a few days.

I would really like to see you again.

Below is my email. Feel free to send me a note whenever.

Truly,

Katie

PS: I check email constantly   ;-)

He was at a loss. He figured this HAD to happen because nothing could be this good for any extended amount of time. He decided, then and there, he was going to persevere and go to that damn rainforest on the other side of the island, alone. He would take a bunch of pictures of himself, with his arm extended out into thin air as if she was there with him, all along. When he saw her again, if he saw her again, he wasn't going to waste time.

Back in his room, he finished his coffee and quickly got dressed. Back downstairs, he hailed an Uber and in minutes he was headed to the east side of the island. He noticed, what looked like heavy, rush hour traffic heading in the opposite direction, which he thought was peculiar, because it was Saturday. Nevertheless, a little traffic wouldn't stop him from this grand gesture.

3

Dorado

If you're not familiar with Puerto Rico, it's part of the Greater Antilles archipelago. A quasi-rectangular shaped island, about 80 miles across, just due East of Haiti and the Dominican Republic, on the northeastern border of the Caribbean. It is home to about three and a half million people and includes several smaller islands including Mona, Culebra and Vieques. The island's appearance is similar to Hawaii, with dense greenery but with a more mellow, mountainous terrain, minus the volcanos. Just short of half of the island's population lives below the poverty line.

San Juan is located on the north west side of the island. The El Yunque Rainforest is about 25 minutes east of San Juan, just south of Highway 3. It's just a short drive to Rio Grande, head south on 191 and you're there.

As Christian's Uber cruised down the 3, he began to see the real Puerto Rico. The Puerto Rico outside of Old San Juan. Just off the freeway, the homes were small, seemingly stacked on top of one another. Older cars with smaller engines are the norm here as gas is expensive. Most restaurants that aren't Marmalade or an American Chain transplant are open air establishments. Latin inspired music is usually playing loudly and the Medalla Light flows like wine. Again, if you don't know, Medalla Light is a local pale ale, 4.5 abv, is best consumed from the 10-ounce cans for about a dollar eighty a piece and they're fucking awesome.

Going down the 3 takes you through Carolina, then Canovanas, then into Rio Grande. As you drive into the island's interior, you rise up to 300 feet above sea level. The views from the center of the island are quite beautiful. Up the mountain a way, at Yokahu Tower, is where some of the best views of the island are taken in.

As Christian's Uber driver turned south onto 191 and began to head up the mountain, he noticed the air got a bit cooler and a lot more humid rather quickly. He asked the driver to take him to the Yokahu tower. The driver wound through the narrow roads, making his way up the mountain and through a clearing to where the tower is located. Christian got out of the car and took a look around. The tower was built in 1963, of a reddish-brown stone and resembles a castle turret. A spiral staircase takes vacationers up to the top for a three hundred sixty-degree view of the Puerto Rican rainforest.

Christian negotiated the circular staircase and after a minute of climbing, he was graced with one of the most majestic views he'd ever seen. A lush, green treetop canopy encircled in the distance by white sand beaches, resort hotels, then nothing but light blue sea as far as his eyes cared to see. He could not hear traffic or the hustle and bustle of civilization or stupid college parties. This was replaced by the sounds of water crashing over rocks, tropical birds chirping and a slight breeze causing the trees to rustle and their branches, to creak. Next to him, in the center of the observation deck, was one of those pole mounted site viewers. He reached into this pocket, pulled out a quarter and dropped it into the slot. As he heard the quarter click and clank to the bottom of the machine, he began to see light through the eye piece.

He pressed his face to the viewer and the majestic view he'd previously enjoyed, was now magnified. As he swung the viewer back and forth, he could make out individual birds along the treetop, the various waterfalls throughout the rainforest and could even see cars in the far distance, driving up and down the 3. It was breathtaking.

He backed away from the viewer to compare the unenhanced view again and he contemplated the dilemma he just stumbled into. Exceptions ignored, a man, while being buried in the big city rat race, craves, even needs this tranquil outlet for his sanity. While, on the other side of the coin, the local, who lives and works on this island, yearns to live and work and succeed in big city life.

Is it nature or nurture, that embeds us with a constant yearning for greener grass from the other side of the fence? Do we just want what we don't currently have? Once we get it, can we really be content? Is it in our inherent nature to constantly want more, despite what we've already achieved? Christian begun to feel the idea for his next article starting to form... At what point in this cycle of success...

Just then, something or someone down in the canopy of the tree line caught his eye. He glanced back over at the viewer and knew that he still had some time left on his original quarter. He had failed to notice before but around the collar, where the viewer is mounted to the pole, were markings.

These markings point in the general direction of specific sites on the island. From left to right, they read, Old San Juan, above a red arrow, Loiza/Carolina, above a blue arrow, Ensenada Comezon above a green arrow, a yellow arrow was next but the name had been scratched off, Island de Flamenco, above an orange arrow and finally, Island de Vieques above a final, white arrow.

From the research Christian had done the night before his trip, he was fairly confident the yellow arrow was pointing in the direction of the Charco Los Angelitos baths, but wasn't sure as to why the label would have been scratched off. This is, coincidentally, the general direction from which, something had caught his eye.

He immediately jumped back to the viewer and swung it in the general direction of the yellow arrow, then tilted it down. Just then, through the viewer, he observes three young tourist females take a quick look around, take off their clothes and begin to wade into the baths, about 20 feet in front of the rocky waterfall. As they splashed, frolicked nude in the tropical

44

waters, Christian noticed a figure within the tree line, watching them. He couldn't make out much detail of the figure, but it seemed to be monitoring the young ladies' movements within the pool.

Suddenly, Christian noticed a faint glow coming from the silhouette, similar to when light is shown in an animal's eyes. Then, where the initial glow began, more illuminance appeared lower, seemingly from around the silhouette, as if coming from where the figure's body would be, all the way down to the ground, where it appeared to be standing. Unexpectedly, the water began to flow heavily from the rocky waterfall, forming a larger, more rapid current and arched into a more defined waterfall. The three girls, curious as to the cause of the sudden flow of water, began to swam toward the base of, then into and underneath the newly formed waterfall, then disappeared from view. That waterfall wasn't there a second ago, Christian thought.

Immediately after, the silhouette began moving toward the waterfall as well, emerged from the tree line and Christian finally saw that the figure, was indeed a young man, whose eyes were glowing a rich blue and had markings illuminated of the same blue glow, on and around his torso and legs. He ran and dove into the pool, entering the water a few feet in front of where the waterfall was now entering the lagoon. As the man's dove into the pool, the water immediately surrounding the spot he entered the pool, illuminated a bright, light aqua color, then he quickly dissipated. The flow of water coming over the newly formed waterfall, immediately slowed and returned to normal.

Christian sat staring through the viewer for few moments, expecting the women and the young man to surface, but that never reappeared. He then backed away from the viewer, wondering what it was he had just seen.

At this point, he's not sure what came over him. It can be best described as when someone spaces out for a moment, then, in an instant, the cloud is lifted and you instantly attain a complete recurrence of conscious, realize you were in the middle of a task and continue completing it as if nothing had happened. In that instant, he sprinted down the spiral staircase and headed straight toward the baths.

As he ran through the rainforest, it was as if he knew exactly where he was going, effortlessly finding each location of the best footing along the path. Every turn, tree and rock were navigated as if he ran this path every day for years. The baths are about 2,000 feet north east of the tower and Christian navigated the jungle terrain from the tower to the shore of the baths in less than three minutes.

Out of breath and bewildered by what he had just saw, Christian knelt, hands on knees, for about a minute, staring at the pool of water. He was certain the four people had already surfaced and disappeared into the forest. As he stared into the lagoon, he replayed the events over and over again. He circled the lagoon and inspected the north side of the pool, where the figure had stood in the tree line. At this point, he began to feel as if he had seen a ghost and that it may be time better spent, to forget what he thought he had seen. He quickly dismissed these thoughts because, in all reality, he's not crazy and he knew what he had just seen. Then, across the lagoon, he spotted a scattered pile of female clothing.

He took off his shirt and sat his phone on top of it, then waded out into the warm water. He swam to the spot where he last recalled seeing the girls, prior to swimming and into where he estimated, the figure dove into the pool. As he swam to the rocks where the waterfall had previously flowed down from, he noticed that among the rocks was a small passageway about the diameter of a garbage can. Despite his building curiosity, he decided not to explore further as it was now getting late and the sun would be going down soon. The last thing he wanted was to get lost in the rainforest after dark. He decided he would come back earlier in the day tomorrow and spend the whole day exploring.

He climbed out of the water and with shirt and phone in hand, glanced around the clearing. Looking uphill, he could see the tower he had previously been atop and used this landmark to try to find his way back to the road. The path uphill was long, twisting and full of exposed tree roots. He wonders how he made it down the mountain without breaking a leg or, at the least, twisting an ankle. About 30 minutes later, he emerged from the tree line to find the main road through the rainforest. From a small clearing in the forest, he pulled out his phone and hailed an Uber to begin the long ride back to The Decanter and to Old San Juan.

As Christian waited for the Uber driver to arrive, he contemplated what he thought it was, he saw. Was it some kind of Caribbean Voodoo or witchcraft maybe? Perhaps it was light refracted from carbon dioxide leaving the rainforest? Whatever it was, Christian was puzzled.

The app said the driver was turning off of the 3 so he should arrive in about 5 minutes.

Something in the east caught Christian's attention. It sounded similar to the sonic boom a military aircraft creates when they go supersonic. Soft at first, then suddenly, as intense as if he were standing directly behind the jet engine itself. The sound and air pressure were such that he could feel the boom in his chest. It nearly knocked him down to the ground. As he turned to the east, he saw, far in the distance, what appeared to be two distinct smoke trails. At first glance, they looked like small rocket engine exhaust trails, leading from somewhere on the ground. They both rose high into the sky and were close to disappearing into the clouds above. He quickly flipped his phone over to the camera app and snapped a few pictures.

Suddenly, from about 1,500 yards behind him, another boom occurred. This time, much more intense, it came from the lagoon he had just ventured from. He looked back, then up toward to the sky and at about 200 feet, he saw a silhouette of what appeared to be a man, head toward the sky with his body streamlined. A light sky-blue iridescent glow covering the figure's torso, leaving another trail of vapor, streaking straight up into the sky, aiming too, to disappear into the clouds.

"What… the… hell… is… that…", he said, aloud.

He pointed his phone and snapped a series of pictures of the moments before the figure merged with and disappeared into the clouds above.

"Yes!", he yelled, "I got it on camera!", he continued.

He pushed his phone into the damp pocket of his shorts, just as the Uber driver pulled up and came to a stop in the middle of the narrow road.

"Hey, you call an Uber?", the driver asked.

"Yes, Old San Juan, please.", He said as he climbed into the back seat.

The radio was on in the car, quietly playing Beethoven's Piano Sonata No. 14 in C Sharp, known to the layman as The Moonlight Sonata.

"Hey man, did you hear those booms?", the driver asked, "wonder if they were bombs or something…"

"yeah man, I heard them… didn't see anything though…", Christian said.

He was bold faced lying. He knew better than to mention he had taken several pictures of this phenomenon to just anyone. He would not mention anything to anyone until he had time to look the pictures that he now had on his phone.

"Can you turn on the radio?", he asked the driver, "is there an English-speaking station on the island? I want to see if they are talking about those booms.", He proclaimed.

"Sure, un momento…", the driver said as he turned the dial on the car's radio.

Over the radio he heard.

"We're sorry to interrupt but there is a developing story coming out of Luquillo. Several residents and witnesses have reported loud booms and large smoke clouds coming from within El Yunque rainforest and from central Vieques Island. As of now, it is not believed to be an attack of any kind but residents and visitors are being asked to seek shelter. The Island of Vieques is being evacuated as we speak. We will break in with updates when more information becomes available."

"I bet it's a terrorist attack or something...", the driver commented.
"I don't know man... I just hope everyone is OK... ", Christian said.

He was lying again. He knew he saw what had made those booms but he couldn't quite wrap his head around what he had seen.

Twenty minutes later, the car pulled into The Decanter. Christian handed the driver an indiscriminate amount of money. He didn't care. He knew he had to get upstairs and call JC immediately. He knew the pictures he had in his phone could put Fastli and The Malcontent in the national spotlight. Plus, he was in revenue share now. Christian made his way into the lobby, taking extra care not to make eye contact with any of the hotel employees as he feared they would ask questions about what was going on. He ducked into the elevator bank and pressed the up button on the wall probably thirty-five times before the doors slid open and he hurried inside. Thirty seconds later, the doors opened to the fourth floor and he briskly walked down the hall, swiped his key card and entered his room.

Housekeeping had been there and his room was tidy and his bed, turned down. Christian walked in and as the door shut behind him, he leaned back against the door still reeling from what he'd just experienced. As he leaned silently against the door, he pondered what exactly it was he was about to say to JC. How do you tell someone something unbelievable? Would JC think he was crazy? Only one way to find out...

Christian walked to the lounge chair closest to the window and sat down. He pulled out his phone and clicked phone, then favorites. The top number was his mother, the second, JC. As he pressed the contact for JC, his phone began the call.

"This is JC...", he answered.

"Hey, it's me...", Christian responded.

"Christian, how's the island? Are you loving it or what?", he replied.

"It's great... thanks again.... Listen... we need to talk.", Christian said.

JC could tell by the tone in his voice that he was serious about something, so in this moment, he decided to follow suit.

"What's going on there? I just heard something about some explosion or something.", JC queried.

"I don't know what's going on JC. Before I tell you this, I need you to know that I have not been drinking today or anything else like that, ok?", Christian proclaimed.

"Jesus, what is it....?", JC continued.

"I know this sounds crazy, but I saw a man fly today. I also saw a man's eyes glow blue, then dive into a pool of water and never surface... come to think of it, both of those men were glowing... sounds weird, I know... but... ", Christian said.

The line when silent for a moment.

"I took pictures with my phone and ...", Christian continued.

"Stop talking Christian...", JC interrupted,
"Listen carefully...
you didn't see a thing, you understand and you damn sure don't have any pictures on your phone...
Now, you are going to do exactly what I say in the order that I say do it...
First, pack your shit because you're leaving right now...", he instructed.

"Next, don't worry about checking out of the hotel. Patricia will call them and take care of it. Hail an Uber. Then you're going to put your phone in your pocket and don't touch it again until you see me... don't answer it... don't search anything... don't turn it off... just leave it in your pocket, as is...

Next, you're going to take all of your bags downstairs and wait for your ride. Go to Jet Aviation FBO at the airport. Tell them your name is Douglas Freeman. They will escort you to a hanger where a plane is waiting. You will get on the plane, take the last seat back row, on your right... left side of the plane.

Then, once off the ground, flip open the left arm rest storage area, take out the phone inside and call the first name in the favorites you personally recognize.

Do you understand these instructions, exactly as I've just gave them to you...?", JC concluded.

"yes, but is all this really necessary?", he asked.

"Just do it ... all... exactly as I said, OK? We'll speak when you get back here...
Oh, and by the way... if you can help it... try not to talk to anyone ... put on your headphones or something and if someone tries to make conversation, just ignore them... seriously..."

The line went dead.

Christian was spooked. He did as he was instructed and packed all his belongings, hailed an Uber then put his phone in the front pocket of his jeans, put in his headphones and tucked the cord into the pocket of his hoodie, grabbed his bag and headed out the door and to the elevator.

As he waited for the elevator, he felt the beginnings of paranoia setting in. He could have sworn, every person he came across, was staring at him. Once in the lobby, he made a bee line, directly outside. Thirty seconds later, an uber pulled up and he jumped in the back seat, with his single bag, taking the other side of the seat.

"Jet Aviation, Luis Munoz, please.", he said to the driver.

"Si Senor...", the driver responded.

"So, how was your stay in Puerto Rico, sir?", the driver asked.
Christian was silent. He decided to close his eyes as to not accidentally make eye contact with the driver and facilitate any unintended conversation.

The driver didn't repeat the question.

The airport was less than five minutes from The Decanter. As the car pulled up to the GA terminal, Christian jumped out and headed straight inside the automatic, sliding, double glass doors.

"Welcome to Jet Aviation, sir!", said an attractive young Puerto Rican woman from behind the service desk.

"My name is Douglas Freeman", Christian said, with a serious tone.

She paused for a moment, looked down at her computer monitor, then looked back at Christian and said, "This way sir..."

She led him around the end of the counter, down a short hallway and into double doors that opened into an enormous hanger. Several business jets of varying sizes and from various decades sat inside the hanger.

The biggest one, a Gulfstream 550, sat with the cabin door down and the air stairs extended. The pilots had already started their preflight checks and were preparing to depart.

"Sir, these gentlemen will be flying you today. I hope this aircraft will suffice on such short notice.", The young woman proclaimed as she held out her left arm in presentation fashion, toward the aircraft.

The Gulfstream 550 is a $50 million-dollar aircraft with current generation avionics, the largest and most comfortable cabin in its' class and can fly halfway around the world with fuel to spare. Of course, it was sufficient but apparently, she didn't know he had never been inside one of these airplanes before... much less, wasn't accustomed to flying on something, regularly, that would make this seem, subpar.

The aircraft was a thing of beauty. An off white, gloss paint, with sky blue and graphite detail, trim and designs running the length of the fuselage. A large graphite colored symbol adorned the tail, but he didn't recognize it, at a quick glance.

He looked at the woman and nodded, then walked to the stairs of the jet. He climbed the stairs, with his bag in hand, and walked into the cabin. With his bag clutched firmly, he walked to the back of the cabin and took the seat, as instructed.

The flight attendant walked up and handed him a bottle of water but didn't say a word to Christian. When he looked up at her, she simply smiled, nodded, then turned and walked away. Christian took a deep breath and was finally able to relax. The seats on this plane put the first-class seat he'd had on the flight in, to shame. They reclined fully and swiveled so you could face in any direction, one wishes.
Moments later, the plane's massive engines fired up and it began to roll under power, out into the sun. The windows on a Gulfstream are large ovals and the view is particularly special from those specific windows. Christian decided to close the shade until he was off the ground and on the way back to Dallas.

As the aircraft made its' final taxi and lined up on the runway, the massive Rolls Royce turbines spooled up and the airplane lurched forward, faster and faster. The thrust planted Christian firmly into his chair, throughout takeoff. As the nose lifted and the airplane went skyward, Christian reached to his left, gave the armrest a firm push from the edge and the compartment opened to reveal a newspaper and an iPhone 6 sitting inside. He reached for the phone and clicked the home button. The screen came to life and the background was none other than the original fastli.com Logo. He swiped the screen and pressed the phone button. The favorites list read like a who's who of the internet.
There were contacts for Tim C, Mark Z, Jeff B among others, but the first one said simply, Patricia. That's the name he pressed and the phone called someone named Patricia.

"Hello JC's old phone…", someone answered.

Christian instantly recognized the voice as JC's assistant.

"How are you, Christian? ", she asked, "How did you like Puerto Rico?"

"It was nice… and I'm good … ", he replied, "just glad to be in the air now.",

The line went silent for a moment.

"Hold for JC", she responded.

"Christian?", JC asked the second the phone was answered.

"Yeah boss...", he responded, "... and why the war torn, middle eastern, high value target-style evac? What's going on?", he asked. He was still nervous and slightly shaking, despite flying at 625 knots over Cuba.

"I'm glad you got out of there... I don't want to talk about it now. When you land in Addison, ask Michelle at the sales and charter desk to call you a taxi... not an Uber, a taxi...

Go to my house. I'll meet you there shortly.", he instructed.

"Will you, at least, tell me why all this cloak and dagger shit...?", Christian retorted.

"All I'm going to say is you never know when, who, where and how someone is listening to your phone calls... ", JC said.

"Wait, don't you mean or... not and...?", Christian asked, puzzled.

"No, I mean and... now get some rest... we've got work to do.", JC said.

The line went dead.

Christian took one last look at the phone, shook his head in an act of sarcastic dismissal, then, put the phone back in the armrest.

Christian dimmed the cabin lights from the control panel, reclined his oversized captain's chair, turned on Pandora and closed his eyes. Shortly after, Christian fell asleep, despite the mellow roar of the twin Rolls Royce engines on either side of him.

4

Dungeon

"Mr. Freeman…", the attendant said softly, as she lightly nudged Christian on the shoulder, "We've landed in Dallas."

Christian opened his eyes and immediately raised his closed fist to cover his mouth, as a yawn came on. It was now approaching midnight on a humid Dallas night. He stood up and stretched, then made his way to the front of the aircraft, where his suitcase was stowed and waiting for him. The pilots had already deplaned and went inside the FBO to make preparations for a fueling. He made his way down the air stairs and exited the aircraft into a brightly lit hanger. The outside doors had been closed and the aircraft, powered down, now connected to hanger power. Christian looked around. There were several sports cars and a couple of smaller piston airplanes inside, as well. He spotted a set of double glass doors and made his way through them into the lobby of the Executive Terminal.

A friendly blonde woman was working the front desk. The name tag she wore said her name was Michelle.

"Hello there, sir? Welcome home.", she said.

"My name is… ", Christian started.

She interrupted, "I know who you are Mr. Freeman… or should I say, Mr. Jones."

Christian was startled. Everyone had referred to him as Douglas Freeman this whole time.

"I'm a close, personal friend of JC's… By the way, I'm to call you a taxi, aren't I?", She said.

"Yes… thank you.", He replied, with a smile.

Several moments later, a yellow minivan pulled up to the front door and Christian ventured outside and climbed in.

"Where to?", the driver said.

"Um, … 3636 University…", Christian said, still holding on to a bit of apprehensiveness.

"10-4"

A quick drive down the tollway, a turn onto mockingbird and a bit of winding through residential streets later, the cab pulled up in front of a modern, white home with a steel roof and a large, glass block wall next to a red, metal front door. He hopped out of the cab and as he closed the door behind him, he realized he hadn't paid. When he turned around and reached for his wallet to pay the driver, the cab had already begun to pull away. Christian raised his hands, unsuccessfully, to get his attention as the cab disappeared into the humid darkness. He walked to the front door and just as he reached for the doorbell, the door opened and JC welcomed Christian inside.

This was the first time he had been to JC's home. It was amazing inside. The entire house was automated and the floorplan was open and airy with exposed beams and cross members. The house was decorated in clean, white walls, accented with muted gray tile floors, floor to ceiling windows and dark gray accents.

"Nice place boss...", he said.

"Just wait...", JC replied.

"How was the flight? I assume it was to your liking Mr. Freeman...", he joked.

"Yeah, what was that all about by the way? Douglas Freeman?", He asked.

"Dude, seriously... Rendition?"

JC almost always spoke in movie quotes.

"Seriously, I said we have work to do. Follow me.", said JC as he turned and began walking into the hallway, past the foyer.

"I bought this house right after we started Fastli. I couldn't care less about the neighborhood or the school district. I bought this house because of the "extras"", he proclaimed.

He led Christian down the hall and into a home office, complete with a conference room. He pulled out his phone and clicked a button. A door closed and locked behind them.

"I need to show you this now.", he said. JC tapped something else on his phone and the bookshelf against the interior wall clicked, then a section of the bookshelf began to swing open, exposing a hidden circular staircase leading to a lower floor.

"This house was built with a lower level of sorts and the family I bought it from built a safe room in it ... It's the closest thing you'll get to a basement anywhere near Dallas.", JC said.

He led Christian down the stairs, into a dimly lit, windowless room with what looked like the inner workings of the brain of a madman, printed and hung on every square inch of the walls. There were mathematical formulas, news articles, pictures and symbols and notes of all sorts scribbled, here and there. JC walked to the center of the room, turned to face Christian, then raised his arms as if in triumph and said, "Here…. This is my life's work… my inner sanctum… where the magic happens, … so to speak."

"This looks like you're trying to track down a terrorist cell or something.", Christian said.

JC sat down in an office chair and motioned to Christian to sit as well. When he sat, JC leaned forward with his elbows on his knees and said, "OK, now… tell me what you saw…"

Christian began…

"Ok, so I was at that tower in the rainforest and something caught my eye about a few thousand feet down the mountain.
It was like light shining on a lens or something.
When I looked, there were 3 girls taking off their clothes to swim in a lagoon, in an exposed clearing.
When they got in the water, I saw a figure in the tree line. He was watching them or something…

What looked like eyes, started glowing and the water flow picked up and formed a waterfall over the rocks, where before, there was just a slow trickle of water.
The girls swam over and into the waterfall and never came back out.
Then, the guy came out of the tree line and he had tattoo looking markings all over his body, that were glowing the same color as his eyes. He dove in the water and he never came back up either.
I ran down there to check it out and all I found were the girl's clothes.
When I made it back to the road, there was a big boom a way's away and I saw two distinctive, … like, jet exhaust trails going straight up into the sky.
Then, from that lagoon I was just at, another loud cracking boom and that's where I got these pictures…"

He pulled out his phone and JC stared intently at it until Christian got to the pictures and handed his phone to JC.

The photo showed a dark-haired man, straight as an arrow, looking up at the sky, with markings on his torso and arms, glowing a light sky blue.

"Holy shit, man…", JC said, "I can't believe you got this on film! This is huge!"

"What is it?", Christian asked.

JC swung his chair around and grabbed two 8 by 10 photos off his desk, spun back around and handed them to Christian.

The first was a photo from a distance of a young, red haired woman, her eyes glowing red as fire. Her arms were extended, palms out and flames were shooting from about six inches in front of her hands, out as if, from a flame thrower, to about thirty feet in front of where she stood.

The second picture was of the sky. Dark clouds had congregated over one particular area of the sky, at an unusually low altitude and with multiple lightning discharges visible, roiling internally, then further, up into the surrounding clouds. They appeared to be approximately 150 feet off the ground and in front of the menacing clouds, hovered the silhouette of a man, suspended one hundred or so feet in the air, with bright blue glowing eyes and markings along his torso... eerily similar to what he had seen just hours earlier.

"I took these pictures in eastern Europe about a year ago. I don't know who... or what they are but if what you told me is true, I think there's at least five of them.", JC said.

"Holy shit! What are they?", Christian asked,
"Aliens ... Super heroes ... Angels ... Gods, even?"

JC took a brief pause to think for a second, how to properly articulate his thoughts, into his answer.

"First, I haven't been able to find a single, definitive piece of data, through my research. Every single rabbit hole I've gone down, lead I've followed through or research strategy I've thought of, have all resulted in jack shit...

Now, to your question...", he paused, looked off into space for a second, sighed, then returned to his thought, "... I think.... The answer is yes... they are all those things... Let me explain."

He continued, "I think the inspiration for all the stories told by man, over the ages, of gods, angels, monsters, magic, aliens, super heroes, ... hell, even sasquatch... are, or were, based on these things... these beings."

He paused briefly, then continued,

"I believe, ... man... in an effort to rationalize the unknown and the incomprehensible, created the legends we know today, after witnessing something similar to what we witnessed..."
Who sounds crazy now, huh?"

Christian pondered this for a moment, then responded,

"... ok, I can get there ... my thoughts are...

If they are what you believe them to be and…
if they have, indeed, been around that long, and …
if they are anything like us, in that, they are part of a greater civilization,
they would, most likely, have a documented history, …
they must have left a trail…
and it must be written down somewhere… right?"

"What do you think all this is?", JC replied, "I've been trying to find something, somewhere ever since I took that picture… and all roads have led me nowhere."

"Well, what's your approach been?", Christian asked.

"searches of keywords, historical events, historical figures of significance… basically anything I can think of that may have been inspired by these beings…", JC said.

"There's the problem,", Christian said, "blunt force approach won't work… usually never does…", he continued,
"if you can't find anything, it's because they probably don't want anyone to… there is always a hint. It just depends on the point of view you take."

He looked over and JC had his phone in his hand and one finger pressed to the screen.
He, then heard a mechanical sound followed by a thud. It was the lock on the steel door engaging.

"That's the work we have to do… neither one of us are leaving this room until we find something.", JC said, "You hungry? Tacos from Javier's?"

"Fuck… seriously?", Christian asked, "what about Fastli and the Malcontent?"

"This IS Fastli and the Malcontent … or it will make them what they're to become", JC replied, "Now, tell me how we find what we're looking for…."

"Ok…", Christian said, as he mentally shifted gears. He loved a good challenge and this would, indeed, be a challenge.

With a receptive and reactive demeanor, he began…
"First… where's a white board and markers?"

JC walked to the wall and grabbed handfuls of pages and ripped them down, exposing a marked-up whiteboard.
He erased the entire thing without a second's thought.

Christian continued,
"what are the three biggest legends or grandiose stories, of all time? Write this down will you…?"

JC obliged and manned the white board.

"Religious Mythology… magic… and …", JC paused, "… Philly's chance at another Super Bowl.", JC joked.

"Seriously… ", Christian continued….

"Let's start with polytheistic gods… Where and when were they…", - C

"Greece and Rome are probably the oldest, Norse next…", - JC

"Let's start with the Greeks. Stories have 3 components, the teller, the environment and the story itself.

The environment is easy, Mediterranean BC. The storytellers are a bit harder as there have been many… and like with the game telephone, stories change over time and with those who tell them. Since these were the first written down, I have to assume they are the ones that have had the most time to be changed, … to have details hidden as well…", - C

"Good point… Romans too then…", - JC

"Then let's move on to the Norse …

The Norse Gods are basically the same as the Greek ones… occurring along the same time line… maybe a little before or after… but basically the same.

The tellers are many but are clustered, throughout time, in northern Europe… in the Nordics…. The gods resided in Asgard, home of the AEsir, while man, in Midgard… the worlds were connected by the tree Yggdrasil and the gods used the Bifrost, a rainbow bridge to walk between the worlds…

wait…hold on…

If the gods are based on real beings, maybe Asgard is based on a real place too.", Christian said.

"Yeah but where…", JC responded, with little delay.

"Duh… The Nordics. These…"

JC darted across the room to pull more stuff off the walls exposing a large projection screen. A quick tap of his phone lowered a projector from behind a panel within the ceiling. The projector powered up and Christian took the wireless keyboard and pulled up a map.

"… the religion was based in this relatively restrictive area… so Asgard must be here somewhere too…
Stories spoke of Asgard being high, like on a mountain top maybe…", he suggested.

"That'd take too long to find that way… They'd have hidden from view long ago… given satellite technology has been around for so long.", JC volleyed.

"Ok… the Bifrost then… a rainbow bridge… what is a rainbow?", Christian said, changing gears.

"refracted light… wait… water…. At the right time of day, the sun's reflection off of a river can appear refracted. And when water is frozen it forms a bridge…", JC added.

"water flows downhill and tend to merge with and into larger body of water, … branches…

I bet it'd look a lot like a tree if viewed from above too…!", Christian replied.

"So, we find a mountainous region in the Scandinavian region broken up by tributaries?", JC asked, clarifyingly.

"Yep! What else do you have…?", Christian concluded.

And so, the work began.

They scoured maps of the region, old and current alike, online. The Javier's delivery guy came and dropped the order at the back door, as requested. JC unlocked the door and disappeared for a moment, up the stairs and returned with Dallas' finest.

For hours, they looked at maps, trying to find something that looked like a tree within the region with no luck. Finally, Christian had had enough.

"We're never going to find this. It's just too big of a region and nothing looks like a tree. Seriously, how many people do you think, through history, went looking for Asgard and never found a thing…", he said in frustration.

"That's it!", JC proclaimed in a moment of brilliance, "We don't have find …it… let's find the right someone who went looking for it… "

"Yeah, but…", Christian replied.

"Listen, if you went looking for something and never found a thing what would you do afterwards? To save face or recoup expenses…?", JC asked.

60

"Write a book.", Christian added.

"Right, but what if you did find something... what would you do?", JC continued.

"talk about it?", Christian quipped.

"Bullshit... you would not talk about it... especially if what you found was actively and intentionally being kept hidden... you would comply to further your own knowledge

But first... you would disappear for a time, while you were busy "finding", what you've found...", JC said, enthusiastically.

"YES!! Brilliant!!", Christian said.

He began with his alma mater historical records. He spent hours among hours looking for anything that may lead him in the right direction but the timeline didn't go back far enough. SMU is associated with the UMC, successor to the Methodist Episcopal Church. The Methodists trace back to an English journey to American, by the brothers John and Charles Wesley, to gospel to the American Indians. The brother John, on his journey to the Americas, was impressed and inspired by Germanic Moravian faith. Long story short, it failed and when he returned to England, two years later, he spent time with a Moravian named Peter Bohler. All of this occurred in the 1730's.

The first recognized existence of the formal Methodist denomination was in 1784 in Baltimore, Maryland. Any existence prior to 1784, wasn't truly contemporary Methodist, but a true predecessor, nonetheless.

Through sheer luck or divine inspiration, Christian was able to find early accounting ledgers from the online archives of the First Baltimore Methodist church. After some study, he got the hang of 1700's accounting nomenclature and had discovered, through other documents, that the Methodist Episcopal Church was active in the funding of worldly exploration projects. When digging through them, he found various entries that looked promising, indicated by ledger entries coded as "KING-EXP-JMM-Expense", that appeared to show a string of expenses related to an exploration. A half an hour later, he pushed his chair back, away from the computer.

"Hey, I think I found something.", Christian said.

JC was throwing a tennis ball against the wall. The noise made by each, timed bounce and the subsequent catch were strangely hypnotic, like a grandfather clock's motion. JC sat up in his chair, rubbed his eyes and focused his attention.

"What's up?", he asked as he inched closer to the desk.

"This accounting entry, if it says what I think it does, it is a payment, actually a series of payments to a King William's School, for an exploratory research project for someone with the initials JMM."

JC got a smile on his face. He knew something but for whatever reason, he wasn't sharing it yet.

Christian continued, "So, I tracked down an alumni roster from that time period and there's a graduate with those same initials, that went on to get an early Doctorate from Yale, then returned to a position in the historical research and documents department. His name was..."

"Doctor James Marshall Marcus, Esquire...", JC uttered, with that same smile still on his face.

"Yes, ... wait... what?", Christian asked, "you knew his name this whole fucking time...?"

JC began,
"About three months ago while researching, I was going nowhere one night. I got frustrated and started going down rabbit holes as a productive distraction.
I came upon the story in an old St. John's College student newspaper of an expedition into Scandinavia by a Doctorate of History from Yale, named James Marshall Marcus and his research assistant Samuel Neiman.

I thought, *that's weird, Neiman and Marcus?*
So, I kept digging.

Turns out the initial expedition party was 16 strong and all but James and Samuel were killed within 24 months after setting out into the Nordics. Marcus and Neiman disappeared shortly afterwards in the frozen north, while searching for some lost city.

I thought nothing of it because they disappeared... I figured they died... until you said something about how many people ever went looking for Asgard and never found a thing.

I had to let you get there on your own....

I'd bet that if he found what he was looking for, he never left.", JC said.

"So, what now?", Christian asked.

"Get some sleep... we'll figure that out later.", JC said.

JC tapped the screen of his phone and the doors to his dungeon unlocked. They both exhaustedly walked upstairs. JC told Christian that he had an extra room if he wanted to crash. Christian was spent so he took

JC up on his offer. After a quick shower, Christian laid his head down on the down feather pillow and his mind raced with the wonder of what they might uncover next. In all the excitement of the past three days, he'd almost forgotten about Katie.

5

Brandon Stone

A Lincoln Town Car hurried down one of the many, narrow New York residential streets, avoiding the traffic on the major thoroughfare. As it made its' way past row after row of turn of the century brownstones, its' passenger has become increasingly anxious to reach his destination. Brandon Stone was an opinionated and arrogant man in this late 50's and the founder and chairman of The Brownstone Corporation. StoneCorp, as regularly referred to in financial circles, was an international manufacturer and supplier of various industrial goods and chemicals and, at one time, a government logistics contractor. Mr. Stone still had a full head of hair despite it being well into the salt and pepper stage and to complete the package, he was known to possess a notoriously short temper.

"What's the ETA, Carson?", he requested from the back seat.

"Not long now, sir... eight blocks away.", His driver, Carson, responded.

Brandon sighed, then held down the button as the tinted privacy divider slowly raised.

Moments later, the town car pulled close to the curb of a midtown high rise and came to a stop. The rear door opened and Mr. Stone exited the vehicle, briefcase in hand, and walked hastily into the revolving doors as the air was quite brisk this evening. The elevator took him to the top floor where the conference room was filled to capacity and awaiting a special presentation from the company's chairman. After shaking a few hands and a quick comment or two, he took a seat at the head of the 26-seat conference table. He placed the attaché on the table in front of him, then simultaneously unlocked both locks. From the case, he removed a glove that appeared to be covered with metallic scales.

As he admired the craftsmanship of the glove, he spoke,
"My esteemed and distinguished gentlemen... and ladies... welcome.

Thanks to the ingenuity or our R&D department and several other individuals that shall remain nameless at this time, I present to you, an ultra-rare substance known as Divinium.",

In his gloved hand, he held a small, dull metallic blue stone.

"This substance... this essence is like nothing you've ever seen. The state of this material isn't impacted or manipulated with temperature ... or gravity for that matter. It affects and is affected by the elements that surround it.", he said.

With the gloved hand, he lightly tossed the small stone into the air several times and each time, it immediately disappeared, then reappeared, returning back to prior form within his gloved hand, after swiping in an upward, grabbing motion.

He continues, "when exposed to oxygen or hydrogen alone, it mimics their physical properties and turns into its' gaseous state, undetectable...

When submerged in water, it does the same and enters its' liquid state, becoming nearly indecipherable from its' surroundings.

As a matter of fact, it repeats this behavior whenever exposed to any other element...

However, in contact with its' Elegon.", he says raising his gloved hand into the air,", it can impact the matter around it...

In this form, it's relatively unpredictable and unstable... but, in its crystalline form, it can manipulate matter... at will."

The entire conference room was on the edge of their seats, listening intently, all salivating over the monetizable possibilities of this new substance he held in his hands.

"The crystalline form of this substance is known as Divinine and it's been extremely difficult so far, to synthesize. We now believe we've found a viable process to harvest this substance.

Gentlemen, with this, we could control the climate and the rains, providing the ability to farm lands currently believed to be barren and grow crops at will... and end world hunger forever.

Or we could use this material for more... substantially lucrative and more specific purposes...", he said.

"Our presentation for manufacturing and deployment plan along with preliminary financial projections will be in your inbox, shortly.

Thank You"

He leaned back in his leather executive chair to a chorus of applause.

Brandon Stone had the full support of his board on most endeavors he had ever decided StoneCorp would venture into. When he decided to take StoneCorp into volatile chemicals and government contracting, the board approved and the stock rose, quarter over quarter, like clockwork.

This time was no different. He had his hands on something special and they all knew it. You can call Mr. Stone lots of things but inept is not one of them. He knows how to turn assets and resources into cash flow and that's the primary goal at StoneCorp these days... earnings.

Brandon Stone and a few members of his senior-most leadership team exited the conference room and made the short walk to his executive suites at the other end of the floor. Most were boisterous and cheery, prematurely celebrating his successful board pitch. As the entourage rounded the corner and passed through his office door, he realized he had an unannounced guest. As each member of his party realized someone was in the room, they became quiet and observant.

"Out ... now", he said to his leadership team and they swiftly filed out of his corner office.

Flanked by two shadowed figures on either side of him, he was sitting in a chair in the darkest corner of the room. He wore a dark charcoal pinstriped suit, a gray laundered, button down shirt, polished black shoes and a heavy overcoat. His dark hair was cut short and styled in the current fashion, but he spoke with such a tone and with such purpose, that it led Brandon to believe him to be much older and much more traveled, than he appeared. Brandon didn't know his real name. He was introduced to this man at a Gala, months and months ago and had only ever known him as Mr. Black.

"Mr. Black... it's so nice to see you again. I hope you've found our city's hospitality to your liking.", Mr. Stone said.

"Dispense with the pleasantries Mr. Stone. I've delivered you what you've been promised. We've detailed everything you would ever care to know to aid you in finalizing those last aspects for the refining and handling processes.

It's up to you to use it as you see fit.

With that being said, I now need something from you.", Mr. Black said.

"Anything... it's yours... just name it.", Stone responded.

"A young man, probably appearing no more than twenty-five or twenty-six years of age, possesses something of great value to me. I wish for you and your resources to retrieve it and bring the item and the one who carries it, to me. He goes by the name of Blake Lucas...", Black continued.

"I need him and the item absolutely and completely, unharmed. Do you understand?"

"What's this item?", Stone asked.

"To you,", Black said, "it would appear as a tarnished, cheap gold bracelet... but I assure you, it... and he... will be tricky to obtain. It is of significant value to me. I must tell you... it is of the utmost importance that you deliver me this... package... in the very near future... This deal has a time limit and there, most definitely, is such thing as 'a day late and a dollar short'... At this moment, I can only tell you that there is still time on the clock, but the seconds are ticking.

Bring me these two things and I will consider your debt settled.

I will send four of my best associates to accompany your men to ensure there is no lost opportunity. Do we have a deal?", Mr. Black concluded.

"Absolutely, we do.", Brandon said, smiling, ear to ear, "...but I wasn't born yesterday... what assurances do I have that once I bring you the deliverables, you won't change the terms and call the deal null and void?"

Appearing angered and annoyed, Mr. Black responded forcefully, "You don't... But as a man of my word and as a devout follower of the principle that the only asset man has in this world is his word, I assure you our deal will be upheld... Once I possess these, the harvesting and refining processes should be more than an achievable feat for you and your resources."

Mr. Black rose from his seat and reached out his hand toward Mr. Stone. Mr. Black had never offered a handshake to Mr. Stone before so Brandon took this as a sign of absolute trust and returned the gesture, shaking his hand.

"Let's celebrate, shall we... How about a drink?", Brandon said as he turned toward his cabinet and retrieved an old bottle of single malt scotch and two highball glasses. As he turned, any semblance of Mr. Black or his associates had vanished. Brandon exhaled. There was something he always found unsettling about his interactions with Mr. Black. He poured four fingers of the single malt into one of the highball glasses and sank into the oversized leather chair behind his desk. He took a slow and longing sip of the spirit, parsed his lips in response to the burn that followed, swallowed the fiery substance and exhaled.

With the bottle of scotch and the other highball glass sitting on the opposite end of his desk, he pressed a button on his control tablet.

"T, get in here!", he said at an elevated volume, in the general direction of the tablet.

Moments later, Tamara Brown, his number two and Chief Operations Officer, entered the room. Dressed in a form fitting, knee length, strapless dress, strappy heels and a designer blazer, she was described by many in financial publishing, as one of the most powerful women in business today. Well educated and even more experienced in plan execution, she was quite an impressive individual on paper. But paper didn't do her justice. She had been at Brandon's side since the beginning.

Both grew up in broken homes and from lower middle-class families. Knowing from first-hand experience how hard it was to earn a dollar, they had little experience with the increasing complexity of turning that dollar into two. They met in college in a freshman level music appreciation class that was comprised of listening and identifying classical music compositions for two and a half hours a day, twice a week. As undergrad classmates, sharing a major and similar schedule of courses, they became close, plutonic friends almost immediately and usually chose to pair together for class projects and group work. As most of the others in their graduating class chose to party their way through college, these two were wired for success at all costs, from day one.

They made a deceptively effective team. He would figure out a plan and a list of resources required, and she would procure them and together, they would execute. In fact, the startup capital they used in founding StoneCorp came from a class project.

During a sophomore level finance class, research project, while at a local watering hole, Brandon had overheard an MBA student bragging about a predictable market anomaly he was aggressively profiteering from, on behalf of the University Endowment. He shared what he'd overheard with Tamara and together, they formulated a plan to short the long position of the University endowment. This moment in their lives became defining for years to come, and would be described by some, as genius and by others, predacious.

Trading in the futures contracts market, this MBA student named Trevor, found a position's trading pattern and its' subsequent price movement, moving predictably, like clockwork. So, he stepped into the trade. He wrote a predictive algorithm to find the trade's entry point stats and front ran the long position, usually just minutes before his level 2 data analysis predicted the expected trade would commence. For weeks, he was able to get in front of one of the big trading house's market making hedge positions and profited from their 'buy weight'. All in all, pretty smart for an MBA student running college money. But if man has one fatal flaw, it's his self-absorbed need for external gratification. Early on, he bragged to his buddies, and after several weeks and after several beers, he eventually bragged to anyone who would listen.

One specific night, Trevor was six pints deep, sitting at the bar, vaguely bragging to some coeds, one of which, he hoped to accompany home. He was telling them about his conquests in NYSE futures and they didn't seem impressed whatsoever. He did, however, have Brandon's attention who was sitting just four barstools down.

In an effort to recapture the girls' attention, Trevor pulled out his cell phone and drunkenly said, "See... See... girls... this is how easy it is to make money in the market....". He opened his trading account linked to the University endowment and clicked buy on 10,000 options contracts. With a few clicks, he executed a large options trade... after hours.

Little did he know, Brandon had his cell phone out as well, watching real time, level 2 data for the NYSE futures markets. Just then, he noticed a contract long position of 10,000 contracts post on a thinly traded muni bond derivative security. Having overheard enough details, he paid his bar tab, left the bar and went straight back to his dorm. He called Tamara and told her everything he had heard. The two devised a plan.

First, he went online and opened an account with a startup online cryptocurrency exchange and a bank account with one of the many online and offshore banks that market account anonymity on the dark web. As cryptocurrency was still in its' infancy and thought of as no more than a neat computer program, it garnered no attention and no news coverage to date. Hell, Brandon probably wouldn't have even heard of it if it weren't for Tamara showing him an article on Wired that she read about an online marketplace for everything illegal.

Next, he applied for a credit card with a $20,000 USD credit limit and was approved. He then, connected it to his crypto account and performed a cash transfer to it, purchasing a large amount of bitcoin. Next, he connected the crypto account to a newly opened trading account known for low commissions and lax compliance coverage and funded it with the crypto he had bought. Next, because any research done by a student performed on behalf of the endowment is considered school property and shared with all students in an effort to be transparent and inclusive for education benefit, he searched the share drive for a file aptly named, and sure enough after a bit of digging, found what they were looking for. Under a few folders within the university share drive, they found an excel file named 'E-Muni Timing Model – Template.xls.' The file properties showed its' author as none other than Trevor, himself.

Upon opening the file, they found his most recent work, complete with the last inputs used to predict the last position and exit points.

The model was kind of cool to Brandon. It took level 2 data and found the trailing 10, 5 and 2 day, Opens, highs, lows and close price standard deviations and the same for each of the past 24 hours, incrementally. The model showed that every Thursday, by 2:45 pm, like clockwork, someone took out large positions in the security. Sometimes, it would be 1 trade of 100,000 contracts, other times, it would be combinations of multiple trades, but the total was always 100,000 by 2:45pm. Then, equally, over the next 10 hours in after-hours trading, exactly 100,000 would be sold off, for a nice profit. Good for him for finding this, Brandon thought to himself. Bad for him, for using what he learned to try to get pussy. Rookie mistake.

Brandon changed some of the inputs to show the next trade to be predicted on Tuesday, instead of Thursday, predicting an incremental buy up, instead of one single contracts trade. He saved the file. Then, he went into the file properties and deleted the entry showing that his school User ID had updated the file. While the school server had backed up the data and had the record, the file itself, did not. It's human nature to feel invincible when you have a good thing going and Brandon and Tamara were betting on this to be the case with Trevor.

On that dreaded Tuesday, at 1:30pm, Brandon, using max margin, purchased a series of contracts. First, 25,000. Then, another lot of 15,000 just a few minutes later. Tamara was also executing her part of the plan. He had done her makeup, hair and put on her most revealing Saturday night outfit. She found Trevor outside of the dorms and began flirting. He was distracted enough by her to not check his model before the alarm went off.

Alarm
Trade Underway!!

Was the alert on his Blackberry. He excused himself and quickly opened his app. 25,000 contracts should do it, he thought. He executed. Over the next ten hours, they both sold off, riding the price back down and over the next few weeks, Tamara got closer with Trevor. It now appeared to Trevor that this trade was now happening two times per week, instead of one. He didn't care, more gains for him and the endowment, he thought. He had shared what he was doing with Tamara and she, in turn, had played dumb and convinced him that executing a massive trade would get him noticed by the big hedge funds in New York. So, he took her advice and, after getting the blessing of the business school, planned a multi-million-dollar trade on behalf of the endowment.

To his detriment, he was planning it for a Tuesday.

On that Tuesday, he executed the mother of all trades. The largest the school had ever allowed a student trader to execute. His professors and classmates watched as $22 million of endowment funds were invested on the open market. Once confirm order was clicked, the room erupted in applause and cheers.

In a dorm room on the other side of campus, Brandon saw the trade execute and he, again at full leverage, shorted the security, with one massive position. This immediately caused the market for the instrument to melt down, sinking even lower than the book said it should. This put the University endowment deep in the red on its' position. Over the next 10 hours, and like clockwork, Brandon slowly unwound his short position, eventually netting about $15 million of gains on the trade, as investors bought the after-hours dip. The trading house made money on its' hedge that next Thursday, and the endowment had an insurance policy with an alumni's firm, to make it whole as the result of failed student trades. Since then, the endowment has put forth rules preventing a student from trading more than $10,000 in value on any given trade, without professor scrutiny.

Trevor didn't fare as well. Needless to say, he was ridiculed by his peers for reaching into the cookie jar one too many times. Tamara broke up with him because she can't be seen dating a loser. Convenient, I know. Nobody knows exactly what happened to Trevor but he's probably working as an accountant or a loan officer somewhere now, agonizing, every day, over where he went wrong.

Brandon, on the other hand, was ecstatic, but he could never tell a soul what they had done. Brandon immediately moved the gains back into cryptocurrency. Eventually, after graduation, he moved them again, after a few years and significant appreciation in bitcoin's notoriety and value, into an account opened in the name of a newly created entity, affectionally named, The BrownStone Corporation. The opening balance of their first corporate account was $73 million. He and Tamara were its' first two full time employees.

"What is it, Brandon", Tamara asked.

"Where are we on the harvesting and deployment plans?", he asked.

"We have the site secured and equipment is in route now. Marketing is still working on a product launch plan.", she replied.

"FP&A are done with cost projections, but need a product rollout schedule to project impact to earnings", she added.

"Good... can you have the harvesting and preliminary product rollout deck and associated financials, along with a proxy vote poll, sent out first thing in the morning?", Brandon asked.

She looked annoyed, "Yes, but they're going to change... you know that."

"Just do it, ok... I need to get the Board vote out of the way while they're still salivating.", he added.

"I'll assume you want to exempt certain... aspects... of the harvesting process. I'll just call it work in process or proprietary or something.", she responded, then immediately began to leave the room. She didn't wait for an answer to her question. In fact, she knew his answer before she had even asked it.

First thing that next morning, an email went out to each of Brownstone's board members. It said.

Confidential
For Your Eyes Only

Thank you for your time yesterday.
Attached is the preliminary plan and projections associated with the product launch as demonstrated yesterday. Do not share or discuss the contents of this email or attachments.

For your convenience, voting functionality has been included with this email to facilitate a go/no-go board decision. Please respond as soon as possible.

Regards,

Tamara Brown
Chief Operations Officer
The BrownStone Corporation
New York, New York

This message and its' contents were sent to thirteen individual email addresses.
Within five minutes, thirteen email responses, each voting Yes, appeared in Tamara's inbox.

6
Blake

The alarm went off on Christian's phone at 5:30am. He sat up in bed and turned off the alarm on his phone. With a finger, he swiped the screen and took a look at the pictures he had taken. Using two fingers, he zoomed in on each picture and examined the glowing markings along the arms and torso of the man launching upward, into the air. The photo was a bit grainy and he had difficulty making out most of the detail. In frustration, he hit the home button and the picture disappeared. He then hit the email icon, clicked compose and began writing.

Katie,

Hi, it's Christian…
I'm sorry you missed the rainforest… it was pretty cool.
How's your trip this week?

Anyway, I'll stop babbling…
When you get back in town, I'd really like to see you again.

Below is my number
Text me If you get the chance.

Bye,

Christian

He hit send.

He climbed out of bed and walked downstairs to see JC in the kitchen, making a smoothie.

"Want something while I have the blender out?", he said.

"I'm good… just going to grab a coffee on the way out…", Christian replied.

"Speaking of which,", JC said, "I have a favor...
I told Gene and Jerry that once I got Fastli up and running and built our subscriber base, I'd do a story on the Jones art collection …"
"Oh yeah…?", Christian said, not expecting this conversation to go anywhere specific.

"Yeah… and I need you to go do the interview…

I'll make the arrangements for you to interview Gene, up in the Jones suite, regarding the art collection, before the game… Jerry will be occupied during so you can pretty much have free reign to go and look around, take some pictures and see what you can see.", JC said.

"Come on man... it's Saturday and I just slept twenty-three hours... I'm exhausted from the past three days... Can't someone else do it?", Christian complained.

"No, I need you to do it ... and you never know what else you may find out ... I heard one of the artists that did two of the installation pieces is of Icelandic-Dutch descent ...", he retorted, unwavering.

"fine...", Christian said, defeated.

The next Dallas Cowboy home game was the following day. They were to face off against the Tampa Buccaneers at noon. JC made a few calls and gave Christian the details on picking up his all access press pass and other details he'd need for his assignment.

Christian hailed an Uber and took it back to his apartment. It had been a week since he had stepped foot inside and it was in desperate need of a cleaning. That would have to wait. He had something on his mind and he needed to write it down. Christian spent the next three hours agonizing over every word he wrote. He was beginning to write a lead in piece for the San Juan Occurrence, as it was being referred to in the main stream media, to post to The Malcontent.

His email read.

***
JC,

Was thinking of posting this to the malcontent once we get more details on this thing.

Let me know what you think.

I call it, Hubris with a pinch of Narcissism

"For an eternity, man has struggled to explain that which he cannot seem to fathom. There's a word for that, which escapes the depths of man's ability to comprehend and articulate. That word is phenomenon. Throughout time, it's often been misappropriated.

It's the nature of the human condition to plant flags to serve as trophies to his intellectual conquests. Trophies are the keepsakes of our journey, which bring us back to that specific epiphany. Where we achieved the evolutionary connection of cause and effect; the link between probable cause and foundational dependence.

75

Throughout the ages, man has reached to explain that which extends past his immediate understanding. Death, individuality, the occurrence of special talent and the unseen have all been subject of lore as best he can articulate. Oftentimes, we had spanned the chasm of logical disconnection with conceptualism. Telling a story to bridge the chasm is an effective mechanism to fill the void. It's also a deadly mistake.

Nature has always been a cruel mistress. Just when you're sure you've tacked to the wind and full sail, you realize she's delivered an unforeseen and devastatingly destructive variable that you've been blind to and your approach, ineffective. You've failed and must rethink all you know to be true.

But that's your trophy, your flag, your breadcrumb. That's what you take with you and that's what reminds you that you're human.

But she lets you win. Sometimes she lets him win with frequency and to the point that he believes he's won this war of attrition. It's then that he realized he's a rat, at the end of a maze and he's found the cheese. It's also in this moment, when he claims his cheddar, that he realizes a massive metal bar has snapped shut, and Is applying a calculated level of pressure to his throat.
I did say she's cruel, didn't I?

In ancient times, these tales were of gods and angels and devils. They were to be feared and to be worshipped. If you stood against them, death and disaster were their vengeance. Bright white feathered wings and golden crowns donned the heavenly, while crimson red, reptilian scales and exposed bone are the domain of the dark, and the damned. Swords clashed among the dominion of man for the rule of all.

As evolution would have man internalize his efforts of understanding, legends were born. Tales of monsters of the night, the undead, of man's struggle with himself, his past grievances and his creation filled the minds of children and stirred their thoughts and dreams. This development would have man believe he is indeed, an equal to his world. But he is, in fact, not. Not even close.

Romanticizing was his next attempt. A veil of beauty and desire replaced fearfulness, en vogue. The unexplained was no longer feared but sought after, wanted, caressed and lusted after. But she has a mind of her own and a drive that's still beyond his grasp.

As he searched the annals of the past, he created mystical stories with prose, he imagined. That which was, that which is, and, that which has not yet come to pass. Tales of triumph and glory elevated the feat of men to that of gods. But all of them were deceived.

Once he thought beyond himself and sacrificed to the detriment of his fellow man, the age of the superhero was born. With visions of grandeur and superimposition, he explained a greater cause, a universal truth and idolized his burdens. But again, he fell short.

Then he turned his gaze to the stars. His explanation of the unknown through discovery of such was his best attempt to date. But again, the true nature he searched for, remained undiscovered. It remained secret, ... and it remained safe.

All the while, the abstract was there hiding his truth under a veil of negative existence. It hid both in plain sight and buried deep in the depths of his failure. Bathed in the whitest of light and the ugliest of atrocity.

The truest place to exist is on the precipice of discovery...

Stay tuned... this is going to be a story about that.

***

JC's reply

***

This is good...
You'll have to tweak it a little depending on what we find out though....

-JC

***

Christian laid his head down and made a failed attempt to get his body back on a regular sleep schedule. He tossed and turned but couldn't shake the visuals of what he'd seen or the images in those pictures from JC's research dungeon...also, the fact that JC had a research dungeon... and he thought about Katie. He thought about what he would say to her when he saw her again. He wondered if she was thinking about him at that exact moment. He finally fell asleep a little after 2:45am.

His alarm went off at 9:00am. He was beginning to get excited for this assignment. He'd never been inside the new stadium before and he'd only ever seen Jerry and Gene Jones on TV. As his excitement built, so did his nerves. The car service arrived around 10:30 and before he knew it, the car was rounding the last corner on Randall Mill, and the stadium in all its' grand splendor, was in full view. He was brought to the underground parking garage, generally reserved for players and other franchise personnel. A nice gentleman wearing a suit and an ear piece, stood arms folded behind him, waiting to escort Christian to the suite where he was to meet Mrs. Jones and conduct the interview. Then, he was free to spend the rest of the afternoon doing as he wished. They probably thought that since he was coming to interview Mrs. Jones about her art collection, that he would spend the rest of the time taking in the pieces. Little did they know, he had an ulterior motive

"Good morning, Mr. Jones! Welcome to AT&T Stadium...", the attendant said as Christian approached.

"Thank you... happy to be here...", he replied.

As they walked to the suite, the attendant attempted to start up conversation.

"I don't believe I've had the pleasure... how are you related to the family?", he asked.

"I'm not, it's just coincidence", Christian said, somewhat annoyed because this wasn't the first time someone had assumed his relation to the infamous Jones family.

"You must get that a lot with the last name Jones ...", the attendant suggested.

As this guy continued to talk, Christian began to pity him. He realized that the center of this man's world IS the Jones family.

What hadn't quite dawned on him yet, was that sometime soon, he, along with the rest of the world, was about to have their foundations shaken to the core, by the discovery The Malcontent was about to drop on the world. The foundations of civilized society were about to up for debate.

Rome was about to burn, again.

The two men rounded the corner and walked down a partial flight of stairs and into the Jones suite. There, Gene stood in her Sunday best, waiting for the young man from the website to interview her regarding her now, world famous art collection.

"Good morning Mrs. Jones", Christian said, "thank you so much for having me...".

"It's my pleasure, ... don't mention it ... Christian, wasn't it?", she asked.

"Yes ma'am, it is.", he responded.

"Any relation?", she quipped, with a grin, similar to Jerry's, on her face.

"None that I know of...", he said, "but I could do worse, I suppose.", he returned.

"Oh, you...", she said jokingly. And with that, they sat down, next to one another, on the back row of the suite. It was just a pleasant conversation beginning as any interview would, then her charisma and charm took over and she told stories of how she had become exposed to certain artists and their work and how she came about getting some of those same artists to create one off pieces for her, to present in the stadium.

About halfway through the interview, Jerry, Stephen, Jerry Jr. and a handful of other members of the Jones family entered the suite. Gene simply looked up at her husband, gave a loving nod and a quick smile while simultaneously, half winking at him. He returned the smile and nod to his wife as he walked past to the lower level seats of the suite. You know, the seats you see him, Stephen and Jerry Jr. sitting in, when they're shown during in-game broadcasts. Christian didn't take his eyes off Gene when the entourage walked by. He didn't want to appear as if the reason he took this interview was to find a way in and ass whip Jerry about the football team. He's not sure, but he thinks that Gene recognized his focus and professionalism and appreciated it.

 "Gene, with so many fantastic pieces throughout the stadium and within your collection, do you have a favorite?", Christian asked.

"I love them all, but today is Sunday and I can't lie... not today...", she said with a mischievous grin, "... the PhopeP piece is my favorite... I just love the way she uses color in general... it's bright and fun and pops off the canvas...

I don't know if you knew this Christian, but she grew up in downtown McKinney in one of those old landmark homes... What can I say, I'm a fan...", Gene gushed.

PhopeP, pronounced *fe*oh*pee*, as I'm sure you all know, is the one and only, world-renowned painter, artist and taxidermy aficionado, famous for the paintings, Baxter the Matador, Sassy Sailor and the phenomenally detailed, Red Haired Lady. If you'll remember, she first kicked down the door and gained art world notoriety with her hit series of paintings, The Dead Rappers. She resides in Austin Texas and is supposedly one of the nicest people you could ever meet. It's too bad you wouldn't know her if you met her because to preserve her identity, much like electronic musicians Daft Punk, she wears a helmet in the form of a cartoonish, pink, taxidermized deer head, when in public.

Christian found it endearing, honest and refreshing to see someone, to whom so many look up, actually show genuine admiration for another, themselves.

To conclude the interview Christian asked,
"Mrs. Jones, given your dedication and devotion to these pieces and your absolute love for art in general, what's next for these pieces? Of course, some of the less mobile pieces are part of the stadium now... but what about the other works? For instance, Eliasson's works... could they possibly find new homes...?",

Gene responded, "Christian, these are all really great pieces and I'd hate to have to part with any of them, but if I did have to, I suppose I'd want them to go to somewhere they can be appreciated for what they are... possibly a children's museum."

"Well, thank you for the time this morning, Mrs. Jones. We hope we're able to do your wonderful collection proud with this article...", Christian said.

"I'm sure you will, young man.", she said, "the pleasure was mine."

Christian smiled, shook Mrs. Jones's hand and stood up to exit.

"Sit down!", she exclaimed, "We're not bringing you all the way down here on a Sunday, to NOT watch some football! Now go make a plate and grab a seat."

"Yes ma'am...", is all Christian could seem to muster to say in response.

For as charismatic as Jerry came off in the media, Gene just may be a little more so, than her husband. Christian made himself a plate and enjoyed a nice lunch with one of the most storied families in all of Dallas. For all he knows, he may have even been on TV when interviewing Mrs. Jones too. Not a bad little Sunday, at all.

The Cowboys took a commanding lead early and as the game wore on, and the lead only grew. During the 3rd quarter, the game was all but won, securing the Cowboys a division title for the 2018 season. Christian decided to go take some pictures of some of the art installations, as JC suggested. In particular, the Eliasson pieces. He was now intrigued by what he may see up close. He asked Gene if it would be acceptable to do so, and she responded, in kind.

Christian walked up the stairs and out into the hall that connects all the suites at this level of the stadium. The attendant was nowhere to be found and Christian actually preferred it that way. Now, he didn't have to feel like he was being watched. As he walked down the stairs toward the main concourse area, he began to feel a bit mischievous, like he was getting away with something.

Just before reaching the bottom of the stairs, he felt a cold sensation come over him. The best way to describe it would be how everyone describes the ambient temperature change associated with a ghost sighting.

A mysterious single cold spot within a warm room.

As he descended the central staircase and neared the bottom, he looked back behind him, up the stairs, then returned his gaze back to the concourse to get a sense of where the Eliasson pieces were located. Out of nowhere appeared a thin, young man, dressed in jeans, t-shirt and hoodie, zipped up completely, with shaggy hair and pale skin. Nearly out of breath, he ran directly into Christian.

"Whoa… you ok?", Christian asked, as the two collided while, each, moving at moderate speeds.

The man didn't return the gesture and instead, grabbed Christian's hand and placed something in it. He looked at Christian and said in a serious, frantic voice, "Hold on to this … just for a minute or two… I'll be back for it shortly… ", the man said, continually trying to catch his breath, "don't tell a soul you have it."

Before Christian could show opposition, he disappeared, surprisingly quickly, around the corner and out of sight. Christian looked around for him momentarily but wherever he had gone, he had gotten there quickly. Just a few moments later, a group of three men and a red-haired woman rounded the corner and appeared from within the concourse, behind the stairwell. They seemed to have been moving fast and appeared to be looking for someone. Christian instantly closed his hand around the object and had a sneaking suspicion, this was what they were looking for. As the group approached Christian, one of the men, dressed as to suggest he may well be part of an organized crime family, looked at Christian and asked, "Hey, you… have you seen a scruffy haired guy come through here….?", The other two men were now looking his way, awaiting an answer.

 "Yeah, a guy came through here a second ago… he went that way…", Christian said, pointing in the opposite direction that he had watched the stranger, disappear.

"Thanks bro…", he said, "that guy took my wallet.", He said.

As the group disappeared around the corner, Christian noticed them picking up speed. His hand, still gripping the item tightly, ever so slightly began to open, revealing a small, dainty, old golden bracelet. It glistened its' golden hue but when the light hit it just right, It gleamed with a bluish, metallic glow. It was plain and simple, but classy and elegant. On the underside, there was an inscription written in a language Christian had never seen before. Something was special about this bracelet, he could tell, but he couldn't quite make out fully, what that was.

Christian roamed around the halls and catacombs of AT&T stadium for about 15 minutes, searching for the owner of the bracelet. He looked down every hallway and up every staircase he came across and nowhere, did he find, sign of him. He glanced at one of the many monitors throughout the concourse and noticed that the Cowboys were 12:00 minutes away from winning their first Division Title in a few years. Christian closed his eyes and gave a quick and solemn fist pump, in tribute. He also thought that he'd be best served making his way to the exit and avoid getting stuck here for the next two hours. He made his way to the nearest exit, effectively finding himself exiting the stadium to the eastern side, into the courtyard where Sky Mirror stands, alongside AT&T Parkway. He pulled out his phone to hail an Uber and the app showed a driver two minutes away.

As Christian waited for his ride, he stared at the screen of his phone watching the car slowly move toward his location. Suddenly, someone from behind him nearly knocked him to the ground. Whoever it was knocked the phone from Christian's hand and he watched as his phone fell to the ground in what seemed like slow motion. As it bounced off the concrete, a large crack along with what looked like spiderwebs manifested over the entirety of its' screen.

"Watch it, you son of a bitch!", Christian said, as he picked up his phone and turned to get a good look at the drunk who had stumbled into him. He saw that it wasn't a drunk at all. It was a man, appearing exhausted, bent over with hands on knees, barely able to hold himself up while panting heavily.

"Are… You ok?", Christian asked. The man looked up at him and his eyes were glowing. Not a bright or vivid color as he witnessed in the rainforest, days prior. His eyes were aglow in a yellowish hue, almost as an animal's do when a light is shown directly into them. His hands appeared dirty and stained. He instantly noticed him to be the guy that handed him the bracelet a few minutes ago.

"… Run…", was the only word the man could muster.

Christian quickly grabbed the man's left arm and threw it over his right shoulder, then wrapped his right arm around the man's waist and helped him toward the street. Just then, his ride pulled up to the curb. Christian opened the curbside door, ushered the man into the back seat. He closed the door, then quickly ran around and entered the back seat from the street side.

"McKinney Avenue?", the driver asked, looking at his app.

Just as Christian was about to confirm, the man raised his head just enough as not to show his eyes and said, "… Record and Munger…", he uttered. Christian looked at him just as he lowered his head back down low and away from him. Christian noticed the driver looking in his rearview mirror watching what was going on in the back seat.

"Sorry man, he had too much to drink.", Christian said, thinking quickly as to avoid further delay.

"Dude, He better not puke. If he does, you're cleaning it up…", the driver responded.

"No problem… he's good", Christian replied.

Just then, the man appeared to pass out, resting his head and most of this body weight on the driver side back door. The car pulled away from the stadium and directly toward the highway, Christian glanced over at the man sharing his ride, then noticed0 in the distance, through the car window, four figures burst from the doors of the stadium and scatter throughout the courtyard, looking frantically for someone... they were looking for the man seated next to him.

As the car rounded several corners and made its' way onto the highway, the stadium began to fade into the distance. Christian looked down at his co-passenger, still slumped over in the seat next to him. He seemed to be slipping in and out of consciousness. He nudged the man with his elbow and said,

"Hey man... you going to be ok? Do you want me to call someone for you?", but there was no response. He then noticed a wallet sitting in the middle of the back seat that appears to have fallen out of the man's jacket pocket. Inside, there was twenty-seven dollars in cash, a debit card from an online bank Christian had never before heard of, several pieces of paper with random and seemingly unassociated words written on them and an expired Texas driver's license. It read...

Blake Andrew Lucas
3201 Commerce #107b
Dallas, TX 75226

Class: C
DOB 12/24/1988
Height: 6 foot 1 inches
Sex: Male
Hair: Brown
Eyes: Green
Organ Donor: No
Restrictions: None

Christian took out his phone and was instantly reminded of the past few minutes by the absolute carnage left across its' screen. What a pain in the ass. Now, he'd have to go get a new phone or get a new screen installed... at the least. Either one would be a serious inconvenience since he now had to write up Gene's interview and continue his research from the events of the past two weeks.
Dammit, and now I've got to deal this this fucking guy? He thought to himself. Christian tried to swipe the screen of his phone but instead of a home screen as the result, shards of glass splinters became embedded into the tip of his index finger.

"Mother Fucker!", he yelled, startling the driver.

83

"What's up?", the driver asked peering into the back seat through the rearview mirror.

Without a word and from a place of full-on misery, Christian conjured an Oscar worthy smile to his face and rotated the screen of his phone to show it to the driver through the rearview mirror, while titling his head to the side to point toward the lifeless body sitting next to him.

"Sucks man…", the driver said, "you should just switch phones with him… I mean, he is passed out in YOUR ride…", he said.

Not a terrible idea, Christian thought at first, but just as quickly, dismissed it. He had an interview with Gene Jones that he needed to transcribe… not to mention the pictures he still hadn't uploaded to his secure server at work. "Dammit!", he said loudly, as he was instantly reminded that he hadn't gotten any pictures of that Nordic artist's installation pieces, as JC had asked.

Downtown Dallas began to appear as if it were rising from within the center of Interstate 30. The driver looked down at his app, then back up at the mirror and said, "Record and Munger? Is there a specific address or something?", the driver asked. Christian shrugged his head and shoulders in response.

After an exit and a couple of turns, the driver arrived at the intersection, stopped, turned to the back seat and said, "Hey man, this trip will cost extra because it's a different drop-off than what you requested… they'll upcharge your card."

"That's fine…", Christian responded. He looked over and Blake Andrew Lucas had already exited the car and was staggering onto the platform of the unmarked building across the street from the old building that used to house the West End Spaghetti Warehouse. Christian followed him. He stumbled to an old steel, roll up door and fumbled with something in his pocket. Suddenly, the door began to open and he poured into the doorway and immediately turned left to stumble down a flight of stairs, to another unmarked, metal door, which opened the moment he approached it. Christian followed about eight to ten feet behind Blake and snuck into the door, just as it was closing.

The room had no windows. It appeared to once serve as a large storage closet or perhaps, during the 1940's and prior to the advent of central air, a boiler room. The room was kept neat and the cinder block walls were painted a dark color and sparsely adorned with a few small paintings. In the corner was a simple, single bed, with a dark blanket, made up with white sheets and a white pillow case. There was a round, dark wood table with a lamp on it, against the back wall and a pair of chairs upholstered in a red cloth, surrounding it. Across the room, against the other wall was a desk and chair. Centered on the desk in front of the chair, sat an older laptop with its' screen closed. It didn't appear to have been used in quite a while. On the floor next to the desk, sat a gray bag with off white lettering that appeared to be from the large, local, high end department store.

Blake had stumbled into the room and collapsed onto the bed. His face buried into the pillow and his arms folded under him, Christian could hear him trying to speak but wasn't able to make out his words.

"I can't hear you...", Christian said.

Blake turned his head to look directly into Christian's eyes. They were glowing as before but now, his face appeared to be dirty and stained as well. Beginning beneath his collar, what looked like dark blue varicose veins were emerging and crawling up the length of his neck, beginning to approach his face.

He spoke.

"Were we followed?", Blake asked.

"No", he responded curiously.

"Good.... Did they take it from you?", was his next question.

"What, that bracelet? No, I still have it... they asked me if I'd seen where you went so, I pointed them in a different direction...", Christian replied.

Blake sprung from the bed toward Christian as a rabid animal might do. Christian was startled. Blake stopped just short of arms-length away from Christian. He reached his hand out, now covered with darkened varicose veins as well and said, "Good... Thank you for that... now, the bracelet... please..."

Christian reached into this pocket and pulled out the bracelet. He extended his hand toward Blake, where the bracelet sat lifeless in his hand. Blake reached out and gently plucked the bracelet from Christian's hand.

The moment he had it in his hand, it began to glow, the now all too familiar, strange, bright blue iridescent color. He watched for a moment, as the varicose veins along Blake's hand slowly begin to fade as if they were retreating back to a mysterious place from wince, they came. Blake slipped the bracelet onto his wrist, then retreated to the bed and curled up into the fetal position, clutching the bracelet close with both hands.

"I didn't steal it if you were wondering... It was my mother's", Blake muttered quietly, "I'm sick and it's the only thing that helps..."

"Your wallet fell out of your pocket in the car... I have that as well... Blake, isn't it...?", Christian queried. There was no reaction from Blake. He laid

85

lifeless in the bed for quite a while. Christian sat low in one of the red chairs around the wooden table. He took out his phone and stared into the cracked screen. He felt as if all the world's answers were on the other side of an unlocked door, but the doorknob was scalding hot. As he wondered what kind of situation he had accidentally wandered into the middle of, he glanced over at Blake, who continued to appear lifeless, lying on the bed.

His mind wondered several things, all at once.

Who was this guy and why were they chasing him?
What was the significance of this bracelet?
What kind of disease does this guy have and why would a bracelet help?
Most of all, what the hell is with this blue glow he'd been noticing, seemingly everywhere, lately?

From nowhere, Blake said, "Get some rest...sooner or later... they'll find this place... and when they do... We need to not be here."

Christian obliged and propped his feet up on the other chair. With his phone face down on the table, he crossed his arms and closed his eyes. In the minutes before falling asleep, as thoughts ran through his mind, he wondered how he would check in with JC. According to his busted phone, it was now approaching 6pm and JC was probably starting to get concerned with his whereabouts and especially with their recent discovery, the fact that he hadn't checked in. In his mind, he pictured the staining on Blake's face, he recalled the monstrous look of those veins and how they appeared to recede the second he touched that bracelet. He pondered the significance of what it was, exactly, of which he was now involved.

Before falling to sleep, he also thought about Katie.

7

Mr. Black

In the elevator bank of a Midtown Manhattan building, a flat panel screen on the wall shows that elevator 6 was currently at floor B4, the maintenance sub-basement, one floor below the parking garage.

Elevator 6, in this specific building on the Island of Manhattan, is part of local folk lore. It is said that deep below the office buildings and the high-rise apartments and below even the subway tunnels, this elevator is the only remaining entrance to access the remains of a city, long since forgotten, once home to a technologically advanced civilization. Many have ventured into the subway tunnels over the years, half-heartedly in search of the entrance to this lost city but none have ever gained entrance or unearthed one single artifact proving its' existence.

Legend says that sometime during the fifteen or sixteen hundred's, early in the colonization of the Americas, four deep, vertical mineshafts were dug down to bedrock, by persons and for purposes unknown, on what is now known as the Island of Manhattan. In the centuries following, a densely populated city had grown up around these shafts and the specific locations of all three have since become forgotten by those who were there to remember.

That's how the legend goes, anyway, but I assure you, they are indeed, real.

The largest and oldest is located somewhere in the midtown neighborhood of Chelsea, near what's now, The Altman Building. The second and northern most shaft was dug somewhere near what is now City College of New York. The third and southernmost shaft was dug just north of Battery Park, close to where The Whitehall now stands. Knowledge of the location of the fourth shaft has since been lost to time but in all reality, was located somewhere between the Upper East side and the East Village.

Funny thing about legends is that they are most often based on some semblance of truth. In this case, the legend is wrong. The truth is, never, was the city, lost... it was just hidden and as a matter of fact, those who built it, still live there.

The elevator continued downward for quite some time. Outside of this elevator shaft, an untouched world, still hidden from the eyes of man. The shaft, surrounded by a mixture of earth and stone, welded together with an ancient concrete, shielded eyes from the world just on the other side. It passed through a deep, dark cavern that hadn't been illuminated in centuries. It's about a mile deep but only about a thousand or so yards in either direction. There's no telling what makes its' home here now. At the bottom of the cavern, sits a single structure. Surrounding the structure is a three-dimensional maze of, cliffs, crevasses, razor thin passes and other seeming natural impediments to prevent entry from all directions. In fact, the elevator shaft is basically the only viable way in, since it enters directly, through the ceiling.

The elevator finally stopped. With a ding, the doors slid open and four individuals exited the car. A large Samoan man who goes by the name George, exited first and walked in front. He was near six foot seven inches tall. Both muscular and athletic, he was the most experienced of the four. Two other men followed. The next had short blonde hair, deep blue eyes and tanned skin. He called himself Oliver. He was built like X-games athlete, being both thin and unassumingly strong. After him, a man with long, dark haired, known simply as Angel, followed behind. While just a bit shorter than Oliver and a bit older than the others and is usually spotted wearing the most current of men's trends.

Lastly, and probably the most mysterious of all, was a woman. She had long, deep red hair. While beautiful and elegant, I can assure you she is the most temperamental and deadly of the four. She answers, simply, to the letter "I". Little is known of her past or upbringing and those who venture to ask about either, have a tendency to regret doing so.

The four walked down a dimly lit hallway which ended at an old, large, wooden set of double doors. With a squeak, they opened, revealing a large, opulent and you guessed it, dimly lit, stone walled room.

"Boss", George said loudly, as the four strolled into the cavernous, candle lit room.

"Why must you four always burst in and ruin my most tranquil of moments…", said a voice from behind a tall-backed chair. As Mendelssohn's Book 2 No.6 played softly in the background, the chair slowly began to turn. A pale man sat quietly and precisely with his legs crossed and his hands folded in his lap. He had dark hair that was cut and styled in the latest fashion and he wore a dark suit and tie. A massive painting hung on the wall behind him. It was a dark and menacingly intricate mural of thousands upon thousands of tiny figures engaged in battle, with one force led by a bearded man, dressed in white, carrying a staff adorned with lightning. The other, led by a horned beast lifting a pitchfork high into the air.

"We found him and the relic.", George said.

The man lifted his head and said with a menacing grin, "Then… where is he?"

"Well… he escaped us… but we know what he looks like now… we'll get him soon.", he responded. The other three made themselves comfortable.

"I'm aware of your constant failure…", he said, seemingly annoyed, "lest you forget, I see all. Did you see who was with him? Did you follow him and find out his destination? Did you, at the least, bring me one, single piece of information, I can use?"

George responded hesitantly, "Well… Uh… He's with a human… we think they jumped into a car that sped off just as we were coming out of…"

"Enough!", he forcefully said. It echoed through the large room as the others stood silent and motionless. "George… I assigned you, above all others, to lead this… team. Don't make me regret my decision."

"Chadwick, we did everything we could to catch him… he had help. He manifested on us without the bracelet… He couldn't have gotten far… Hell, he's probably viniated and passed out in a gutter by now…", he added, confidently.

"No more excuses George… I'll do it myself.", Chadwick said as he removed his suit jacket, neck tie and shirt, revealing a canvas of intricate tattoo-like markings in black, white and varying shades of gray. They spread over the entire exposed area of his body. He neatly hung his shirt, tie then jacket on a wooden coat hanger, then walked toward the middle of the room. He sat down in lotus position on an old Persian rug and closed his eyes. Suddenly, beginning at the neck's hollow, then, as if in sequence, the markings across his chest, shoulders, arms, back and torso began to move and change. The shapes began to twist and contort, and the colors, fade and brighten, while continuously and completely filling the entirety of their boundaries as if each were a specific and essential cog in the inner workings of an intricate and complex clock. His eyes opened and what was once brown, was now black and white, silver, gold and varying shades of gray, with similar intricate shapes moving, in sequence, across both irises.

"What time did you leave?", he said, as if he were somehow watching them, looking for the exact moment they had failed to collect their bounty.

"2:47 pm", George added.

"Which door did the four of you exit?", he asked.
"East side.", he responded.

His eyes closed again and underneath his lids, his eyes moved back and forth in rapid succession.

"He stumbled into a human from behind… knocked the phone out of his hand… Shattered… He helped him to the street… Into a blue car… to the highway… East… into downtown… West End… Munger… and Record…", he told the quartet. His eyes opened and the iris of each eye suddenly reverted back to their normal deep brown state. The markings along his body ceased all movement and returned to their sedentary, prior, motionless state. He glared up at the four from his seated position in the middle of the room.

"Go, bring him and the human to me... now", he said, now visibly exhausted. The four stared at Chadwick for a brief moment, then turned and ran to the door. They rushed into the elevator and the doors closed, taking the quartet back up to the world of man. Once the doors closed, Chadwick began to groan in pain. He slowly and with the help of a nearby ottoman, carefully rose to his feet. What he had just done took every ounce of energy he had and he knew for a fact that there were more than a few still out there that would kill him if they caught even a hint of what he'd just done. Darkened veins were beginning to form starting from his neck's hollow and down onto his chest. Physically exhausted, he found himself just able to collapse onto a nearby sofa.

He reached into his pocket and pulled out a small metallic Chinese dragon figurine, no bigger than a game piece from a board game. He held it tightly in his hands for a long time. As he lay motionless on the sofa, his mind remained consumed with the task now underway. He must acquire this relic. He knew that, in this task, there's becoming less and less room for error and the time is beginning to slip away. If he fails to attain it, events will begin to be set in motion, resulting in the onset of a long, painful and arduous journey, culminating in ascension. Once the journey begins, Chadwick knows there are many dedicated to providing assistance to the journeyer and even more that will follow the Ascended. If he has any hope whatsoever, to fulfill his destiny and lead the people into the world's next chapter, he must stop him now.

As he laid on the red velvet sofa, the darkened veins around this neck slowly subsided. He was, in fact, recovering from the effects of viniation himself, as George had mentioned in conversation earlier. Chrono-induced sickness, however, is much more violent and debilitating than other blessed beings suffer. A more complicated manifestation usually results in a deeper and longer Divine Sickness, as his mother once called it.

I suppose it's about that time to tell you about a few things so understand what's actually happening. Many of the questions you are soon to have, will indeed, be answered later...

Long ago, when corruption and sloth caused the Omnician race to lose hope in their Adaptive leadership, the race fractured, causing many Omnicians to leave the safety of Omnician cities and venture out to live in the world of man. An especially vengeful and popular Precept male named Patrik, vowed to never return to the rule of the Adaptives. He scoured the earth in search of a location suitable to remain hidden from man and from which, to wage war against the Omnician bureaucracy.

As Europeans were beginning to flee to the west, Patrik and his followers took this opportunity and left for the new world. They planned to engage with the humans and help them build their cities and infrastructure. In turn, they would profiteer from their efforts all while building themselves an empire and more importantly, a war chest.

The Array of Dawn, as they collectively refer to themselves, found a suitable location on what's now known as the Island of Manhattan. They chose this location partly because of the access to the ocean, but primarily because the ground was rich as could be, with deposits of Divinium Elegon. They settled all over the island, hiding in plain sight amongst the early settlers and erected several makeshift buildings to begin their true mission, to dig down to bedrock and gain access and proximity to the Divinium. They dug four massive shafts across the island and connected each deep underground by way of a massive cavern. It is here, that The Array build their stronghold known simply as Liège.

Little did they know, the land above them would become some of the most populated, valuable and sought-after assets to have ever been touched by man. As such, The Array began acquiring the ownership rights to as much of it as they could get their hands on. After acquiring considerable holdings and ensuring access to their domain was secured, with cooperation from a fellow legionnaire within the Omnician city of Dorado, they formed an entity to handle their financial dealings and named it The Western Teuling Corporation. Fitting, as 'Tueling' is a Dutch surname that means "Toll Taker".

Throughout the decades, The Array operated in complete isolation from the rest of the Omnician Race. Completely disconnected, The Array developed a civil culture all their own, albeit it based on the complete destruction of Adaptive Rule and enslavement of mankind to the sole needs and wants of The Array. They assisted the original European settlers of the island in the financing and building of many of the original structures that solidified the basis of the infrastructure of Manhattan as we know her today. Have you ever heard the saying, "... seems like they put this building up overnight!",
Where do you think that saying came from? It's because The Array actually DID put up some of those buildings overnight. Don't get me started on the railroads...

As the west industrialized and grew into what we now know to be the world's central financial hub of one of the world's most complex economies, The Array was there. They influenced decisions and played along to interweave themselves into the fabric of each, and every level of mankind's existence. As this new American economy became more and more complex, so did The Array. Their actions provided the basis, knowledge and template for many of the complexities that are core to our way of life as we know it, today. Offshore banking, pass through treatment of entities, financial derivatives such as interest rate and credit default swaps, even some famous federal laws were based on The Array's influence.

Throughout the years, The Teuling Corporation has undergone so many mergers, acquisitions, reverse mergers, splits and changes of hand, among others, just to keep the source of capital and ownership structure shrouded. Due to these efforts, the true name and ownership structure of the original Teuling Corporation is only truly known to a small handful of people and only documented in one specific place. It resides within a file cabinet in the office of a Senior Partner at a Midtown Manhattan Law firm. Coincidentally, this law firm resides on the top floor in one of the oldest high-rise buildings in Midtown within the neighborhood of, you guessed it.

Chelsea.

8
Dalus

My Dearest Alessandro...
Hide in The Shadows, no Longer…
Stand Boldly...
Love Ferociously...
Wander Aimlessly...
Always...
Mother

"Hey... Get up ... your phone keeps going off…", Blake said.

Christian's eyes shot open. He hadn't heard Blake speak more than a three-word sentence since he handed the bracelet back to him, hours ago. He was now up and pacing the small room, like a caged lion.

"What time is it?", Christian asked.

"3:25 am... why, got somewhere to be?", Blake retorted.

"No, just...", Christian tried to respond but Blake sat down across from him, leaned in at eye level, with his knees no further than 2 inches away from his.

"Listen... thank you for holding on to this...", Blake said motioning his head toward the bracelet he was now, wearing on his wrist, "It means a lot to me... it was my mother's...
Her name was Theresa... her and my father, Patrick, passed away a long time ago...
This bracelet is all I have left of them...
So, thank you.

Now... there are some seriously bad people chasing me and I don't want you to get any more into this, than you already are... "

Christian Interrupted,
"Question... when you plowed into me outside the stadium, your eyes were glowing like a wild animal's and you had a rash that looked like dirt ... or hair... all over your hands and neck...
Then, in the car, ... it looked like you had dark veins crawling up your neck...

You put on that bracelet and instantly, the veins started to disappear... now, just a few hours later... you're totally fine...

what's with the glowing eyes...?
And that rash ...?

but mostly, how did that disappear in just a few hours?", Christian asked, intensely.

"We don't have time for me to explain in detail ...
but I'll just say this... it's a temporary condition and the bracelet helps the "rash", ...

We need to get out of here... there's a place we can go, they won't follow... and it's close to here...

When we go, we have to go fast...

Stay close...

And don't fuck around with your phone... it'll just slow us down...", Blake told Christian.

"Alright... and don't worry about the phone...", Christian snarked, "you broke it..."

Blake stared into Christian's eyes for just a short moment longer, smiled, playfully slapped him on the side of his left knee, then stood up and walked over to the desk. He took something out of the top drawer and hastily, stuck it directly into his front pocket. Christian stood up and stretched, then pushed his phone down into his front pocket. He turned to face the desk but Blake was already standing near the door.

Blake asked, "are you familiar with the tunnels under downtown?"

"I've been down there once...", Christian said.

"We've got to get down there. The entrance to the tunnels is below that glass pyramid... It's on Griffin and Elm... about seven or eight blocks... we're going straight down Lamar to Elm, then straight inside those doors, ok?

Seriously, don't look back... and don't wait for me...
Just get into the tunnels...", Blake said, in such a tone to suggest, he wasn't playing around.

He walked back to the desk and grabbed the gray plastic bag and pulled out a dark gray hoodie.

"Here... put this on...", he said, tossing the hoodie to Christian. He caught it and took a quick look. When he lifted it to the light and looked closer at it, he noticed there were muted blue threads within the weave and among the stitches. It was the same dull blue color he noticed within the bracelet's glimmer. Peculiar, he thought for a brief moment until his mind returned to the present.

95

He obliged, pulled the hoodie over his head and put it on. It fit snugly but loosened after a few moments.

"Shall we?", Blake asked one last time.

"Let's ...", Christian answered.

Blake swung the door open and bound up the stairs. Christian followed. As they stood at the metal roll up door, Blake looked at Christian and said, "now, dead serious... don't look back and don't wait for me... straight down Lamar to Elm and straight into those doors … got it?"

"I got it", Christian said.

Following a muted clang and a repetitiously slow chugging, the door opened.

It was dark and storming outside. This didn't seem like a normal Texas Storm though. As storms in North Texas usually blow in from the West, the wind was blowing steadily from the North and without the usual ebb and flow of squalling and calming breezes. It was a steady, strong wind with a heavy downpour... and it was unusually warm for a northern December wind.

Blake yelled over the wind, "STAY UNDER THE OVERHANG... AROUND THE BUILDING TO LAMAR... THEN STRAIGHT TOWARD DOWNTOWN."

Christian nodded. Just then, Blake pulled whatever it was, from his pocket and with a closed hand, held it firmly, high up on his chest. Suddenly, a shiny, liquid metal seeped from beneath his fingers and began expanding, slowly at first, then much more rapidly, wrapping itself around his chest and torso. Once completely covering his torso, it appeared to harden into a solid metal. It looked like a Roman-era breastplate with dark gray and brown colored markings circumnavigating every inch of the surface. Christian examined it for a moment, then looked Blake in the eyes, in complete and utter amazement. Blake's eyes were glowing again, but this time, they were bright yellow with a hint of green. He seemed more-calm, more determined and somehow, more at ease, this time... and he appeared to stand just a bit taller as well, with an ever-present smile across his face.
Awe-stricken, Christian mouthed something to Blake. He laughed, subtlety, in response, as he interpreted Christian's query as, "what... the... fuck..."

What happened next became a blur for Christian the moment his adrenaline kicked in. Blake was out the door first. He took a sharp left, under the overhang, hopped a waist-high gate, then ran to the end of the building. Christian followed closely behind. The hoodie he put on had begun to now radiate a light bluish color. Blake then took another sharp left and ran the length of the building, again, with Christian close behind.

Midway down the side of the building, the overhang ended and Blake and Christian found themselves running directly into a torrential downpour. They sprinted through a parking lot, then down the alleyway behind a steakhouse. They veered right to run south, down Lamar. Christian began to have tunnel vision. Everything in his peripherals began to blur as he focused on the next 50 feet in front of him.

Suddenly, about 25 feet in front of Blake, a figure began to appear in the dark, running toward them. It was a woman with bright red hair, wearing a fire engine red breastplate with illuminated red, yellow and orange markings down her arms and neck. Christian instantly recognized her from the photo in JC's research dungeon. She took a few steps, squared her feet, then threw her hands, wrists together, out in front of her. From her hands, a ball of swirling fire materialized. Small at first, it grew larger and larger. Suddenly a gust of wind rose from behind her caused the fireball to twist and snarl. Then, as it swept up within the winds, it leapt toward Blake, burning and crackling as it approached.

Another figure appeared above the woman. Floating 10 or 15 feet off the ground as if suspended by the wind, the man had long dark hair and wore a breastplate similar to the woman's, except it was smaller, a bright, sky blue color and it was illuminated along the neckline, shoulders and waistline. He also wore greaves, and gauntlets of the same color and were glowing, similarly. With a quick glance upward, Christian instantly recognized him, as well.

As the flame approached, Blake's chest plate began glowing a muddy yellow. At about the same time, the stream of fire reached Blake and was somehow, deflected six to eight inches in front of him, as if it had impacted an invisible, rounded wall.

Suddenly, Blake began to shrink in size. Much to Christian's surprise, Blake's form changed. He was now, in full sprint, in the form of a small dog. He continued running as he passed underneath the stream of fire. The moment he crossed beneath the tunnel of flame his shape again, quickly shifted. This time, into that of a hawk and he quickly shifted direction, now, on a direct course with the dark-haired man, aloft.

Once within arms-length from the aloft assailant, he returned to his original human form and buried a closed fist that appeared now, as if covered in a rusty metal glove, into the stomach of the man, leaving a large, deep dent in the midsection of the breastplate he was wearing. The man doubled over in midair, then, fell to the ground, smashing directly through the roof of a parked car. He laid motionless as Christian ran past the now destroyed, parked car.

Blake then descended to the ground just as the fiery swirl dissipated. It was as if the wind had been instantaneously turned off, by way of a valve. His trajectory, now aimed him on a direct path toward the red-haired woman. He left his feet in mid stride and extended a knee, landing a direct hit into the chest of the woman. Her armor, previously glowing neon red, went dark but absorbed the blow, somehow, without much damage. She was sent stumbling two or three steps back, then fell to the ground, rolling multiple times backward due to the force of the impact. She rolled and her back slammed into the curb. Christian ran past her, only sneaking another quick glance.

Blake landed about 8 feet in front of Christian and immediately dropped into a ground roll. He effortlessly returned to his feet and without losing any momentum whatsoever, kept pace, running down Lamar, getting closer, with every step to downtown proper. Christian had never seen anything like that and for a moment he began to replay what he'd just seen in his mind, but instead of dwelling, he focused on the task at hand. They were 5 blocks from Elm street.

Another figure approached from the right. He had short blonde hair and wore a sea blue chest plate that was glowing bright just like the others. His arms were extended and a wall of water materialized in front him. Blake instinctively jumped into the air and grabbed a light pole with his right hand, slinging himself around it. He released it just as his trajectory lined up with where the blonde man was standing. Blake extended his left leg and planted it squarely into the chest of the man. The impact drove him off his feet and backward, knocking him, head first, and into a nearby garbage dumpster. He didn't get up.

Blake planted his foot, turned and he was back at full speed within a few steps. Christian trailed just a few feet behind. They were now at Ross. With Blake leading the way, they took a left turn and their path led them directly through a parking lot. Christian was beginning to get winded and his pace began to slow. Just then, the ground began to rumble. About thirty or forty feet ahead, the ground cracked and opened as if being torn apart by an earthquake. On the other side of the ravine stood another figure. This was a very large man. He wasn't wearing armored chest plates like the others. He had no shirt on and the majority of his torso and arms bore markings that resembled tattoos only, they were illuminated by a rich, green glow. Blake began to shift again. This time, into a large wolf. He picked up speed and began to pull away from Christian. As he watched, the wolf jumped high into the air, completely clearing the abyss, stretching across the parking lot, in stride. Christian slowed, slightly, on approaching the ravine, then veered 20 feet to the right to navigate around it.

Once on the other side of the ravine and running directly toward the figure standing at the rear of the parking lot, Blake regained his true form. Running full speed, he threw a punch directly into the man's upper chest. As the man sidestepped the punch, the ground beneath Blake began to rumble. He took two steps to the left just before the ground below him collapsed into what seemed to be an endless abyss, directly below the parking lot. Blake charged the man, driving his shoulder into his abdomen, wrapped his hands around the back of his knees, then pulled his legs out from under him, driving him into the ground and directly onto his back.

Before the two hit the ground, the wolf returned and began snarling and biting at the face and neck of his attacker. Christian ran past the two deadlocked on the ground. He ran across the street to cross the bus station platform and through another parking lot. He found himself quickly closing in on a wall with its' only opening, gated by seven feet of welded steel. He timed his approach and leapt onto the gate, halfway up. He threw his leg over the top and a second later, he was on the other side, sprinting down the sidewalk, next to the pyramid. He was now on a direct path with the doors. When he burst through, he turned straight for the escalators. He looked back at the door, waiting to see Blake enter. After a few seconds, he was half way down the escalator when he began to think that Blake had been caught. He debated going back but just as he turned to a step back up the escalator, a loud shattering followed by a shower of glass, raining down from the west face of the pyramid. It was Blake crashing through the glass. He got up, with a smile still on his face and casually joined Christian on the escalator.

"Holy shit! We're not dead… ", Christian said, still trying to catch his breath. Blake laughed. His glowing eyes began to dim and the dark markings were back on his hands and neck, but there was no sign of the veins this time. He was out of breath as well but appeared to be in sheer glee, despite the torturous nature of the last three minutes.

"Ok…", Christian said still panting, "What were those things…?"

"That's Geosis", he replied, "… they're Elementae. They're the ones following me that I warned you about."

"Wait, they're what?", Christian said.

"Elementae… of the Elemento Order. They can manifest control of the elements…", he said.

"They can what?", Christian asked, confused.

The two approached the end of the escalator, hopped off and began a brisk run into the tunnels.

"Now's not the time…", Blake said, "we're almost there."

The two ran into the depths of the tunnels, past the Which Wich corporate offices and into a section of the tunnels that have long been, under construction. At one of the darkest places in the tunnels, Christian noticed Blake glancing down at his bracelet, which was now beginning to glow a rich blue color and flicker as if it we're picking up a sonar signal. As it began to flash more rapidly, Blake stopped and walked into the adjacent construction area, then, into the center of the construction site. This pathway opened into a large hollow space, possibly a section of an underground parking garage beneath one of the high rises. Blake led the them down into the rubble where some large concrete chunks were amassed down in the bottom of the rubble. He then found a specific small passage that led even lower under the buildings.

Now, his bracelet was fully illuminated and glowing brightly, shining bright enough to fully illuminate the small spaces they were crawling through.

"Do you think they're still behind us?", Christian asked.

"Nah… they won't come down here… they can't manifest this far underground… they need their Aerus to be effective.", Blake said.

"Stop… what the fuck is an Aerus?", Christian said, confused but intrigued, "and how can you do all those things? Where did you learn to do that?"

Blake stopped his downward progress through the catacombs.

"I've never been able to do most of that before. I was sure we were going to get caught and they'd take my mom's bracelet… Something feels different today…", he continued,
"Look, I really don't know how to tell you all this, but I'll just start by saying… humans aren't the only sapienl beings that inhabitant this planet. For as long as you all have been here, so have we. This is our home too. There are nowhere near as many of us as there are of you, but we live here too.", he said.
"Who's we?", Christian asked with a tone of curiosity and fear in his voice.

"We're a sapient species almost identical to homo sapiens… But …", Blake responded.

Christian interrupted, "Your aliens, aren't you?",

"No, we're not aliens… ", Blake paused, trying to keep his train of thought, despite wanting to laugh at Christian's naivety,

"You ever heard the stories of Greek or Nordic Gods? Angels and Demons? Elves… Vampires… werewolves… zombies… super heroes…? Well, that's what we are… sort of…
All those stories man tells about things he can't explain… well, most of the time, they're based on humans, seeing us … using our blessings.

Those people that were chasing us… They are Elementae… they can control the elements. That big guy is a Gaian, the blonde guy is an Ogen, that dark haired guy is an Aerus … and Crimson, that red head, well, she's an Ignes. Together they form Geosis."

Christian interrupted again, "But you changed shapes… does that make you a werewolf or something… or a shifter? Kind of like on True Blood?"

100

"Shifter is derogatory and insulting...", Blake corrected, sternly, "My Guild is that of the Therian. I can change into other forms... usually animals. But I've never been able to do most of that stuff I just did, before... Most of the time, I'll manifest into a fly or rat or something and then, just disappear"

"Wait... what do you mean, ... manifest?", Christian asked.

"Our abilities are called blessings... and we manifest them from within...", he responded.

"But how? And what's with all the glowing stuff... and that bracelet... and this hoodie?", he asked, tugging on the shoulder of the one he was still wearing.

"Let's get where we're going first... Honestly, I don't have all the answers you're looking for...", Blake said as he turned and continued their downward journey. A couple of minutes passed and following the echoes of stones tumbling into an enclosed space, Blake led Christian down into a tunnel that flattened out and continued leading further underground, albeit at a lesser pitch. As they walked, Christian began to notice that the tunnel was just going around in a circle, slowly but surely, leading lower and lower into the ground.

"How long is this tunnel?", Christian complained.

"This tunnel leads about two hundred and fifty feet underground.", Blake replied, "It's a giant spiral walkway downward. At one time, the walls of this walkway were covered in ivy and vines and flowers that bloomed bio-luminescent blooms. I never got the chance to see it, but it was said to have been beautiful."

As they rounded the next corner, Christian felt a cool draft begin to occupy the air. The temperature continued its' slight drop, the further they walked and the passage, became even darker. As they continued lower, the light from Blake's bracelet continued to illuminate the tunnel and soon after, Christian noticed that it began to open up, both wider and taller, until it was large enough to drive an 18-wheeler through with ample space on both sides. Once the pitch of the pathway flattened, the cool air began to smell strange. A smell similar to earth and rainwater mixed with just a tiny bit of decay.

Blake stopped and stood quietly for a moment as if taking in a long-awaited moment. He reached his right hand out toward the wall. He touched his now brightly glowing bracelet to the wall and a flicker of blue sparks materialized. Suddenly, veins of glowing blue, raced out, in all directions, illuminating the darkness. The veins streaked and illuminated, first the walls, then across the massive ceiling and ultimately lighting the entirety of an enormous underground cavern.

"This… is… the Lost City of Dalus", Blake said, as if introducing his girlfriend to his parents for the first time.

Most people misuse words like gigantic or awesome or enormous, or my most despised, phenomenal. When I say enormous, I mean enormous. The cavern was probably two miles long, a half of a mile wide with the ceiling rising as high as one-hundred feet. This place was amazing. And again, I'm not misusing the word. Within the cavern were the remains of a massive city that could, by today's standards, be home to thousands of people. There were paved walkways running, like veins of gold, throughout the cavern. Christian could even hear the dull roar of fast-moving water in the distance, coming from somewhere inside the cavern.

The walkways appeared to be made of a dark material similar to tar asphalt, although most of them seem to have been destroyed some time ago. Some of the buildings appeared to have once reached all the way to the ceiling of the cavern but none still stood, that did. While some of the structures stood untouched, most appeared to have been destroyed to some extent. They were crumbling and in disrepair. This whole city was in disrepair.

For a while, the two calmly and purposefully roamed the deserted and crumbling pathways, taking in the wonder of the lost city. Blake would point out specific locations and give brief, though uncertain commentary about each. Christian observed in silence. After all, he was a guest here and this was way over his head. This place was once home to the pinnacle of understanding and temperance this planet could muster and not a single living human knew it was here. At least as far as he knew.

Blake motioned for Christian to follow. He led him into one of the crumbling buildings, then down a long hallway and down into a large, circular room. It was similar to a theatre in the round, complete with rows and rows of seating separated by three, evenly spaced aisles, effectively, dividing the space into thirds. Instead of a stage in the center, there sat a raised, large, circular stone altar. It looked like a stone table but without the chairs. In the center was a large depression dug into the stone about the size of a watermelon. Surrounding it were six smaller, evenly spaced indentions. The silhouette of a sitting dog was painted onto the face of the table, though it was covered in dust and mud and had long since began to fade.

"This was the Temple of Blessings…", Blake said as he raised his hands, palms up, slightly above his shoulders, "… This is where each of my kind are brought when we're still infants and our blessings are revealed. This is where our blessing starts."

He pulled down the front collar of his shirt and tapped his neck's hollow several times. Though it was dark in the space, Christian noticed a darkened symbol surrounded by even darker symbolic looking markings resembling but noticeably not tattoos.

"When we're babies, we're branded with a mark representing our Order. Within the brand, a flake of this special metal is embedded right here and it helps to focus and cast our blessings... and grow our summonings...", he added, pulling his collar out further to expose more of his upper chest and left shoulder revealing the continuation of the markings, resembling tree roots and clearly beginning from the brand markings at the base of his neck.

Christian was astonished. He was still amazed and continued to speculate, internally, whether he was the first human to ever witness any of this. He asked, in a melancholy and somber tone, "What happened to this place?"

"Civil War...", Blake said, "Some of us try to live in harmony with the world... and some of us just want to watch it burn. A faction of radicals attempted to overtake the Elder Council... this city paid for it... this is all that's left."

"... and who is us?", Christian said, now directing his stare and focus directly at Blake.

Blake looked around at the temple. The crumbling columns that were once ancient and grand, now resemble CNN footage of Mogadishu. A city that was once lively and bustling with activity, now sits lifeless and dormant. He looked at Christian and spoke.

"This city... was once home to my people. Elementae, Kinesis, Therian and Precept lived here in peace. We have lived just out of sight of man... for a millennium.
We are the Omnicians, the blessed and the gifted...
When nature's unforgivingly harsh, we step in...
When man unintentionally throws off the balance of life, we intervene...
When life ..."

Blake stopped speaking. His eyes began to glow again as he scanned the upper levels of the temple.
Someone was here and he could sense them... and they were coming closer. At the top level of the room, he saw a faint glow coming from one of the passages. Two vivid purple dots appeared from deep within the darkness of one of the walkways.

He whispered, "Whatever you do, no matter what you hear, don't open your eyes. Do not look at them, no matter what.", Blake instructed.
Another figure came into view, next to the first. Illuminated by a vivid green glow coming from all over its' torso and arms, it appeared smaller in stature but the glow was much more intense than Blake had ever seen on any being, before. As the creatures emerged from the shadows, Blake

103

recognized the first to be a girl probably in her late twenties, eyes glowing bright purple and a young boy, not much older that eleven but with the markings of a full-fledged Master Elder.

"Therian…", the girl spoke, as she began to descend the decrepit staircase, "what business do you have here?"
"We seek shelter from the storm… our business is our own.", Blake replied, ready to take on any challenges.
"Easy, easy…", the boy said, "we mean you no offense… we just don't see outsiders often… if ever. Who do my associate and I have the pleasure of conversing with?", he asked. Blake and Christian simultaneously took notice of the timeless elegance with which the child spoke.

"My name is Blake … Therian of Sequoia", He responded, "and who are you two?"

"I am Penelope … Precept… of the Alanis Order", the girl said.

"and I am Elijah.", The boy said.

"Elementae of Alanis?", Blake queried.

"Just Elijah…", he replied, shortly and dismissively.

Alanis, a city hidden within a mountain range in Northern Scandinavia, is one of the oldest cities in the world and where Blake's ancestors originally came from. It's also the home of, arguably, the greatest collections of worldly knowledge that's ever been accumulated. The stories told throughout the centuries of Asgard and the Bifrost were supposedly inspired by Alanis.

"You two are a long way from home, aren't you?", Blake asked.

"Yes, we are", she responded. "but after Puerto Rico, we're securing certain… sites."

"Puerto Rico? What happened in Puerto Rico?", Christian asked, his interest peaked but his head down and eyes, still closed.

"and who is your friend?", Penelope asked, having almost forgotten about Blake's companion.

"I am Christian…", he responded.

"… Chrono…", Elijah interrupted, aggressively.

"A what?", Christian replied, quickly.

"No, he's human…", Blake added.

104

"Why would you bring a human here?", she asked, exasperated by what she perceived as carelessness stupidity.

"We narrowly escaped Geosis, topside... they didn't give chase once we made it into the tunnels...", Blake said, "... he saved my life earlier... and since he showed up, my blessing ... well... it's different...."

This comment got Penelope's attention. She appeared surprised as her head quickly turned, her eyes darting toward Elijah. That statement meant something to her but she didn't pry. "What's your relic?", she asked.

"I don't have one of my own... I was forced to leave home before performing passage... When my mom died, she left me her bracelet...", Blake said, raising his right hand slightly. "Her and my dad died some time ago..."

Penelope's face began to show the emotion she had been trying to hide for the past few moments. Then, she began to recite an ancient and long-forgotten passage.

"
And in the end of times, the savior will come...
Uniting the clans with might and will...
For the spirit within shall guide his way...
He shall emerge from the forest, blind...
And when need, most dire, shall he be reborn, anew...
Carrying the past and the future with him...
Stand he will, with Man and Omni kind alike....
Adaptive, not by blood, but by will ...
for all our kinds...
"
"Don't...", Elijah said, sternly, looking at Penelope.

"But... stand with Man and Omni... need most dire... not by blood but by will...?", Penelope said quietly to Elijah.

"Coincidence... That's all... Drop it...", Elijah responded, sharply.

"What are you talking about?", Blake asked. Christian was now listening intently. To himself, he cursed his broken phone, as he would have surely been taking video of all of this, had it not been.

Penelope looked at Elijah. He knew what she was about to do, but he was hoping she thought better of it. She did not. Then, she spoke.

"We're of The Celestial Order of Alanis. The guardians of the prophecy, hand to the Chief and seekers of the next Adaptive. In all our years, we've never came across an Omni who's claimed to witness a change in their

105

blessing. If what you say is true, you're a rare one Blake... or should I call you... Alessandro."

That comment stopped Blake in his tracks. He, in all his years, has never been called by that name, except long ago, by his mother and father. How did she know his given Omnician name? The blood ran from his face and he began to feel a panic setting in. "Who's that?", he said, trying to divert the conversation anywhere but where he assumed it was about to go.

"That bracelet you wear... your relic... you said it was your mother's, right?", Penelope asked.

"yeah... so... ", he stammered, "... there are lots of bracelets in this world."

She continued, "Sure... but I don't think many of them have the inscription 'My dearest Alessandro... Stand Boldly... Love Passionately...'".

Blake interrupted, "ok... I have been called that name before... by my mother..."

"Yes, we know...", she said, "Theresa was friend to the order. 25 years ago, my father, a Master Precept, ordered her first-born son at his Trial of Blessings... To keep him safe and to keep them from killing him by transcendence, my father cast and declared the boy a Therian... but we believe him to be the first Adaptive born in eight centuries. ...",

Elijah stood quietly, shaking his head in disbelief.

"You knew my mother?", he asked.

"I didn't... but my father told me stories of her.", She said.

"Wait... so... what?", Christian asked. He was confused at this point.

"Listen...", Elijah said, "if he is who you think he is... they need to come with us... now. Geosis left with their tails between their legs... you know who they work for and it won't be long before they come looking for these two and in greater numbers... who knows what... or who they'll bring, when they return."

"He's right... if you want safety, we can offer that... Come with us. We need to leave now...", Penelope said.

Christian looked at Blake as he stood, stunned and silent. Blake quickly glanced at Christian, then back at the pair and said, "We will accompany you on your request... and thank you..."

Christian chimed in, "So, where are we going again? Atlantis?"

Again, Elijah shook his head in disapproval in response.

Penelope and Elijah moved quick. It wasn't so much of a chore for Blake to keep up but Christian hadn't kept up his cardio game lately. He would fall behind and the pack would slow the pace, allowing him to catch up. This happened a few times and Elijah got sick of it.

"Can't we just leave him here?", he asked.

"No", Penelope said, "he may have a part to play yet. Can you do something please…?"

Elijah turned around just as Christian was beginning to catch up with the others. He was winded and struggling to catch his breath. Just then, Elijah's eyes and markings along his arms, otherwise known in the Omnicient culture as Summonings, instantly illuminated a bright, vivid green. The ground beneath Christian's feet began to rumble and shake, then crack and separate underneath him. The next thing he knew, the piece of earth upon which he stood, about six feet in diameter, lifted from the ground and floated gently in the air, with Christian standing on top of it.

Amongst the green glow in Elijah's eyes, flashed sparkles of a bright sky-blue luster. Christian, and the ground he stood on, begin to move forward. He began to lose his footing, so he quickly squatted down and leaned forward. Just then, the floating piece of ground he stood upon tilted forward and began moving much faster through the air, keeping perfect pace with the others as they navigated the many walkways throughout the city ruins. As they made their way to the other end of the cavern, another entrance appeared along the back wall, as a small dark tunnel. The closer they got to the back of the cavern, the larger the tunnel appeared. There were illuminated runes surrounding the mouth of the tunnel.

When they approached the entrance, their pace began to slow, Christian noticed the illuminated markings on the back of Elijah's neck fade. At the same time, the ground he stood on instantly slowed to a stop and dissolved, falling back to the ground, as did Christian along with it. Because of his stance on the platform and the velocity at which it was moving, he fell to the ground and rolled several times. As he came to rest on the ground, he noticed Elijah looking over his shoulder with a scant but mischievous smile on his face.

Christian rose to his feet and dusted himself off. "Really?", he said, with a slight glare directed toward Elijah.

"You know what they say… When in Rome…", Elijah said with a hint of uncertainty in his voice.

"Uh... touché.", Christian begrudgingly responded, not wanting to correct, embarrass and possibly anger, a being who had just levitated him on what was probably the world's first hoverboard, over the distance of more than a mile, with minimal effort.

Penelope spoke, "We're here.". The four walked another one hundred feet into the tunnel when Christian noticed something glowing in the distance. "What's that? Is it Omnician?", He was anxious but excited to use this newly learned term for the first time. For all he knew, he was the first human to knowingly befriend and associate with Omnicians. As they walked toward the glow, Elijah responded, "Uh oh P, what is it...? A Chrono?"

Penelope looked at Elijah and got a grin on her face.
"I don't know... We better not take any chances. Let's get the jump on whoever it is... just in case...",

Then, Blake began to laugh out loud.

As the four approached the opening toward the back of the tunnel, the tunnel itself appeared to end at the source of the light. As they stepped into the space, Blake, Penelope and Elijah each began to laugh. Christian looked at each of them, then at the source of the light. It was a button panel. Next to it was an elevator door. Christian was slightly embarrassed but mostly relieved. In all his time in this world, he had never been so relieved to see the doors to an elevator.

9

Baxter Neiman

With a ding, the doors to the elevator opened at the ground floor. The first thing Christian noticed was the darkness. It wasn't night, but because this particular elevator was located in the lower levels of the parking garage of the Kay Bailey Hutchinson Convention Center. Close to the Dart Rail station, this level of the parking garage was rarely populated and made for a convenient entrance and exit to Dalus. In fact, this was the original location of Dalus' grand entrance and it still would be if it weren't destroyed, completely abandoned and stripped of Divinium, that is.

The four walked through the bowels of the garage to the DART train station and took the short ride into downtown. Staying low key was how Penelope and Elijah preferred to move as of late. At a glance, they looked like brother and sister. Sometimes, they would talk as such if they suspected someone was eavesdropping. Their next stop was Akard station, then two blocks south and two blocks east.

As the train pulled into the station and the doors slid open, the quartet found themselves wading through the crowd of preoccupied commuters.

"Where are we going, by the way?", Christian asked. Blake glanced toward Penny, as Elijah referred to her, in the hopes she would explain to Christian.

"It's a long story, but we're going to Neiman Marcus.", Penelope answered.
"Seriously... Shopping... Now?", Christian said, in a condescending and snide tone.

They walked the four city blocks, two by two. Penelope paired off with Christian as Blake and Elijah talked about various goings on, a few feet in front of them.

"Ok, long story short, Neiman Marcus was founded in 1907 by A.L. Neiman, his wife Carrie and her brother Herbert Marcus. At least that's the company's official story.

In the early 1700's, a scholar named James Marshall Marcus set out on an expedition to the Scandinavian Mountains in search of a mythical city of legend.

The mention of that name engaged Christian's attention, in full and he focused intently, on every word that followed. After the terrain, climate and conditions decimated his entire expedition party, he ended up finding our home, Alanis.", Penny said, "After living among our ancestors and learning from our elders for the majority of his years, he and his research assistant, Samuel Neiman, founded a company that has since evolved into what we all know today as Neiman Marcus. Well... what humans know, at least."

"God, you have a big mouth!", Elijah interrupted.

She rolled her eyes in dismissal and continued, "...they created this company mainly to help usher us and our goods around the planet, hidden from man's attention. They just so happened to sell expensive stuff too..."

Christian was dumbfounded by this new revelation. Not so much that Neiman Marcus was, as Penny claimed, the foundation of Omnician commerce, but that, if true, such a well-known and visible company had been able to keep this big of a secret all these years. It made him wonder what other occurrences of this magnitude and significance were hiding, in plain sight? What other secret histories existed throughout this world he knew? His mind began to race, as he wondered what other secrets, he'd unearth in following this rabbit hole that was, the Omnicians. In his mind, he'd already began to formulate the release schedule for The Malcontent.

The quartet walked down Main Street, in and out of the shadows cast along the sidewalks from the tops of the high-rises. The city that once inspired awe and hope within Christian's soul now seemed different. Not so much boring or uninspiring, just less that it what it once was. As if a magician showed the crowd an unbelievable illusion followed by thunderous applause, then, immediately after, spent the next half hour under full house lights, explaining to the crowd in painstaking detail, the pledge, the turn and the prestige.

"We're here", Elijah said as the four approached the north doors. "This is the flagship location,", Penny started, "you know, this wasn't the original location. There was a fire at the..."

"I know...", Christian interrupted, "...I did undergrad at SMU... I listened to this exact story, a minimum of three times from rich sorority girl's midterm papers in freshman level informative writing class."

"Sheesh, ... don't be so grumpy... just trying to make conversation...", she replied, seemingly, mildly insulted.

"... sorry... I didn't mean to be rude...", Christian said, apologetically.

She looked at him and smiled, then winked, hinting that she appreciated the kindness.

The four walked under the orange awnings and into the beautifully modern, downtown flagship store. Elijah's path led them directly into the interior of the first floor, near the escalators.

They passed rows and rows of opulent wares, painstakingly and masterfully floor-planned to maximize the bifurcated symbiosis of art and marketing. Furstenberg, Yurman, De La Renta, Lauren, Ford, CoCo and the many other expressors of artistic decadence were displayed for the masses to drool over and for a select few, to purchase.

Elijah strolled past row after row of the most sought-after goods man has ever created, wasting no time and showing any interest for any of them, in the least. Strangely, neither did Penny, nor Blake.

As they approached the escalators, Christian notice that Blake's bracket had a mild glow as did the large teardrop pendant on Penny's necklace. Elijah wore rings. A fiery ruby adorned a gold ring he wore on his right index finger. A cluster of small deep blue sapphires sat in a silver ring on his left thumb. An emerald was set in a graphite colored metal ring on his right middle finger. Finally, a half dozen small emerald cut blue and green topaz stones, circled the face of a white gold ring on his right ring finger. The three would later find out they were together, collectively known as, The Principles.

Each stone in each ring had a unique and dull shimmer to them, coming not from the stones, but shining through them from the metals, each's mount were constructed using.

Just then, an employee approached the quartet.

"Welcome to Neiman Marcus.", She said with a smile, "is there something I can help you find today."

"We're looking for the Divine section.", Penny responded.

The employee had a confused look on her face. "I'm sorry... We don't have a ... divine section...", she said, in confusion.

Blake interrupted, "were actually just looking for a gift for our mom. I think we know where it is..."

"Ok, if you need any assistance, please let me know...", she told them.
"P... she wasn't wearing a blue scarf. You know better...", Elijah responded.

The four continued to stroll around the escalators until they were approached by an older woman wearing a crisp gray button-down shirt, black pencil skirt, heels and a rich, blue scarf, tied around her neck and knotted, slightly off center.
"How may I help you?", The woman said with an aire of omniscience, no pun intended.

"Hello, my name is Elijah.", He said, in a childish voice.
"Hello Elijah", she responded with a smile.

"We're looking for the ... Divine section", he said.

"Ah, the divine section... very good... right this way please.", She said with a continuous and ever-knowing smile.

She led them into a small alcove around a corner, beneath the escalators and from within a recessed space at the corner of the wall, casually pulled a hanging blackout curtain closed behind them.

"Now... A relic of your choosing, please?", She said quietly, but purposefully.

"Take your pick...", Elijah said as he raised his right hand. Her eyes opened widely as she'd never seen such a sight. Most Omnicians have one relic, maybe two, on most rare of occasions, on their person. Elijah was wearing three on one hand.

"Well then...", she muttered surprisingly, as she guided his hand, palm down onto a black foam pad. A deep clicking sound was heard from within the wall. Rising from the floor, a small gap began to materialize upward, along the wall, until it reached the ceiling. Then, with a deep groan, the section of the wall opened inward, exposing a dimly lit circular staircase, leading into the bowels of the building.

The staircase led down one floor and emptied into a large basement room, lit with wall sconces and turn of the century chandeliers. Dark green paint adorned the walls. Glass cases held jewelry along the perimeter of the room, while racks held unique pieces of clothing scattered around the room. An older gentleman in a black tuxedo greeted them as they entered the room.

"Greetings young Omnicians...", he said cheerfully, "Welcome to Marcus Neiman's Divine collection. I'm Baxter Franklyn Neiman, IV. What is it I can do for you, this evening?"

He scanned the entrants and immediately recognized the ringed hand of Elijah. His eyes lit up as he spoke.

"The Wanderer, is it?", he asked, directing his question toward Elijah.

"It's been a long time since anyone addressed me by the old names... oh how I do miss them...", he warmly responded, "and how does your father do these days... if I may...?", Elijah asked. The tone, timbre and cadence of his voice had changed. He now spoke as if he were a nobleman from the 16th century. Christian was amused and began to giggle under his breath. Elijah looked back at him, unamused.
"My father passed a few years ago, though I assure you, I've been more than prepared to carry this torch, my good sir.", Baxter responded.

"We need to use the Traverse ...", he said.

The Traverse was to be the pinnacle of James Marcus and Samuel Neiman's work, while living among the Omnicians, in Alanis. Unfortunately, they were long dead before it came to fruition. In an effort to help The Omnician race move around the globe and to continue to stay hidden from the ever-growing watchful eye of the human race, James and Samuel sought to create a mode of transportation using Omnician blessings. Together, they studied for decades, with the elders and their work formed the scientific foundation that made spatial traversal mobility possible.

In his Annals, Marcus detailed an idea that Blessings sometimes manifest as if they have a life and mind of their own. Some enter this world in a flash, then leave just as quickly, while others manifest and remain as if they have a purpose all their own. It took Marcus and Neiman's understudies 75 years to figure out and complete their work.

Ultimately, to create a spatial Traverse would require a complimentary series of blessings simultaneously manifested by Precept, Elemento, Kinezea and Chrono Masters to form a bridge across time and space. It was thought that each master would need to cast each time a traversing was to occur. Once the traverse was cast for the first time though, it took on a life of its own and unbeknownst to everyone, it became self-sustaining and self-stabilized. Since inception, it's been referred to simply as, The Traverse. Its' inception resulted in a stabilized rip in time and space, creating an instant doorway between the Great Library of Alanis and three separate locations in the Western Hemisphere. The first, to the Temple of Blessings in the city of Dorado. The second was to the Chief Council's Tribunal hall in the Therian City of Sequoia. And the third and its' Celestial Anchor as they called it, and the source of its' life force, was tied to a tall stone embedded in the ground around which, the Omnician city of Dalus was built. The Celestial Stone as it was known, was a 350-foot stone pillar with a 100-foot core made entirely of Divinium. It protruded 3 feet above the surface and was anchored to bedrock at its' bottom.

When the city was still alive and thriving, the pillar was covered in ivy and vines that bloomed luminescent flowers, that helped light Dalus. It would have definitely qualified as one of the wonders of the world had man ever laid eyes on it.

Notice I used the word 'was' a lot just now. The Celestial Stone was destroyed when Dalus fell. During the civil war, warring factions thought it a most important strategic position of control. Each vowed to destroy the stone if they could not control the gate, or portal, the stone created and anchored. So, during the fall and on the brink of defeat, the Chief of the Elementae pointed his army at the column and ordered them to manifest, destroying the pillar and all watched as the entirety of its Divinium core came in contact with earth's atmosphere and evaporated into nothingness.

Little did these factions know, that the capstone still remained protruding from the surface, along with a considerable sized deposit of Divinium within. It's as if the Traverse itself ensured the entirety of the Stone was not destroyed so that it may persevere. Few knew its' location and even fewer knew it survived the fall of Dalus.

These days, measures must be taken to ensure The Celestial Stone is properly cared for and maintained so it continues to remain in secret and in safe hands. This duty was graciously accepted by the ancestors of James Marshall Marcus and Samuel Neiman, who at the turn of the century, opened what's considered, the first and original Neiman Marcus Store in the Downtown district of a city named Dallas.

Baxter appeared to struggle with this request, internally. First of all, in all his years, no one has ever asked to use The Traverse. Much less, has he met a single soul that knew what The Traverse was, or that it was located in this very room. Finally, he was baffled that it appeared to be a preteen child that possessed knowledge of what may possibly be, the history's most well-kept secret. He paused for a long moment. He put his right index finger to his lips, as if trying to prevent himself from saying the absolute wrong thing in this moment.

"Young Master...", Baxter asked with a conscious effort to show compassion and empathy toward Elijah's plight, "... I've no doubt you understand the gravity of the request you've just made, but do you fully understand the potential risks this would present, to justify its' use? You certainly know traversing will create an undeniably recognizable ripple through space and time. Any Precept worth their salt will instantly realize what it is. And god forbid, a Chrono or Adaptive, if there are any left, find this place, ..."

Elijah looked at Baxter with a smirk and said, "Baxter, allow me to enlighten you ... it was I who found James and Samuel all those years ago, in Scandinavia and it was I who brought them to Alanis and it was I who helped build this stone."

"Elijah? ... You're the wanderer?", Baxter asked dumbfounded, not realizing The Wonderer, the fabled Omnician who chose a life of exile and Elijah the Ancient, the builder of the Celestial stone, were one and the same.

"My grandfather told me stories of you when I was but a child. They were shared through every generation of our family since the early 1800's ... I was certain you would have been long dead by now... I can't believe my own eyes...." Baxter said with nostalgic sincerity.

"Hate to disappoint, but no... alive and well, I'm afraid...", Elijah said.
"But how.... you're so young ... still...", Baxter said, "you must be ...what... 300 years old?", Baxter asked.

Both Christian and Blake's heads swung around the second they heard Baxter's comment and focused intently on the conversation between the two.
"334 to be precise...", Elijah said.

"You got to be shitting me!", Christian muttered.

Following his abrupt comment, both Elijah and Baxter turned to face him and while Baxter appeared unimpressed with Christian's choice of vernacular, Elijah just grinned. He always enjoyed the general chaos that followed a well-placed curse word when lobbed, like a grenade, into the middle of prim and proper, civilized conversation.

"I know the risks and I know of those who watch. But we must get to Alanis and we do not have time for delay... if there's a faster way, we're game...otherwise, we need The Traverse.", Elijah told Baxter. He was emotionless and of absolute dedication, in this proclamation.

"Very well then... I'll prepare for your passage.", Baxter said. He then turned and walked to the middle of the room where an old, weathered Loomis Fargo travel trunk sat. At first glance, anyone who was tactful enough to get into this room, probably wouldn't have given it a second look. But the second Baxter walked over to it, Christian realized it was completely out of place, given its' surroundings.
Baxter painstakingly bent down, unbuckled the leather straps holding it closed. Then he slowly lifted the lid. Christian, Blake and Penny paid close attention as none of them had any idea what would happen next. Elijah, on the other hand, paid no mind to

116

Baxter's actions. He was scanning the room while repeatedly checking and rechecking the door that led to the stairs, the only entrance into and out of the room. He indeed, knew who could possibly be watching.

The only thing visible inside the trunk was a large limestone boulder with speckles of bluish gray metallic stone only slightly visible from beneath thin spots in its' shell. A large, clear quartz crystal was embedded in the side of the limestone boulder and through it, the blue metal was considerably more visible.

"The Celestial Stone...", Penny uttered while staring into the chest in a trancelike state, "... I've only ever heard stories about this ... Stone... who would have even guessed it was right here this whole time!"

Then Baxter did something none of them expected. He unbuckled two more straps on the front of the trunk and as he pulled it away, it opened along a seam running down the front, exposing the stone in its' entirety. It was protruding from the floor as of the entire building had been built around this specific spot.

The stone was encircled by a collar of gold and jewels around its' base. The entirety of the surface of the stone was dotted with the bluish gray spots. Suddenly, as if someone turned up a dimmer switch, the dull blue metal inside began to glow through the limestone and illuminated the room with a shower of bright blue sparkles. It was if the stone knew they were in need and it was showing willingness to participate.
"It's never done THAT before...", Baxter said surprised.

He turned to the group, "now... each of you touch your relic to the stone."
Penny removed her necklace and with an open hand, placed it against the stone. Blake touched his wrist atop and Elijah, with much less couth, carelessly placed his entire right hand on top. The impact made a sound that suggested he may have knocked a piece loose. Baxter took notice and was not impressed.

Christian looked worried.

"Uh... guys...", he said, "I don't have a relic... "
Baxter looked on, as usual, in disapproval. Elijah looked at Christian and with his head, motioned to the hoodie he was

wearing. Christian pulled his hand inside the sleeve and placed it alongside the others. The stone began to react.

The glow became brighter and the speckles of light cast from the stone, begin to dance along the walls. A moment later, the light began to focus on the ceiling and the glow condensed, merging into a singularity just above the stone, forming what looked like a bright blue plasma mass six feet tall and suspended in midair. Suddenly, the center of the portal began to darken and grow until all that was left levitating above the stone was a glowing blue ring. Through the passage Christian should see stone walls, ornate and ancient furniture and books. Thousands upon thousands of books, all housed in rows and rows of tall bookshelves, skillfully crafted from stone and wood.

"Quickly then...", Baxter said, ushering them into The Traverse. Without hesitation, Elijah stepped onto the stone and into the void. Penny followed. Blake appeared apprehensive at first, but climbed in as well. Christian glanced at Baxter. Instead of seeing the usual scowl, he was surprised to receive a nod and quick grin from him, followed by a tilt of his head suggesting, get your ass in there already. Christian climbed into the stone and peered in. Without another moment of hesitation, he climbed into the waiting void.

Then, just as sudden as it appeared, the portal vanished. The illumination lighting the walls of Marcus and Neiman's dimmed, then extinguished altogether. Alone, in the lifeless room, stood Baxter. He had waited his entire life to witness this event. Generations before him had waited, unfulfilled, just as he had until now, to be part of this exact experience. He had performed his family's duty, as his father's-father's had before him. He carefully and methodically replaced the trunk around the stone, buckled the buckles and sighed with relief.
He was still alive and breathing… For now.

10
Eden

The sun had long since, gone down. It was late, but like all dedicated Chief Executives, Brandon Stone sat behind his desk, pouring over spreadsheets of projections, performance indicators, tracking metrics, virtually any and all measures related to the performance of StoneCorp ongoing operations. This no longer demanded his attention and focus. He was perpetually consumed with his current obsession. Divinium. He obsessed day in and day out about every aspect of this pending launch. Be it financial forecasts, deployment schedules, future product rollouts or visions of grandeur such as the image of himself accepting the Nobel Peace Prize, it's safe to say, he hadn't overlooked any aspect of this project.

Just then, Tamara appeared in the doorway.

"We have a visitor...", she announced.

Behind her followed a tall, round and peculiar man. Resembling Boss Hogg from the late 1900's sitcom Dukes of Hazzard, he was dressed in expensive cowboy boots, jeans, a blazer, bolo tie and of course, a white felt cowboy hat. He spoke fast, loudly, direct and quite crass. He was a walking, talking personification of the proverb, "You can take the man out of the country, but you can never take the country out of the man...", Paul was his name but he insisted everyone call him Bubba Joe.

"Paul... how are you?", Brandon said, greeting his esteemed guest.

"Goddammit! How many times have I told you? ... Call me Bubba Joe, you' sumbitch." Brandon responded with in kind, with nervous laughter.

"My apologies Bubba Joe... how was your flight?", he asked.

"Cut the shit, Stone... when are we lightin' this firecracker? My people are ready and waiting...", Bubba responded, "you keep on tellin' us tomorrow... well guess what, tomorrow's here damnit!". He completed his tirade and sunk back down into the plush leather chair he was previously occupying.

"So... Bubba...", Tamara interjected,", you'll be glad to hear that we just received approval from our board this morning. Everything is a go on our end. The last pieces of the reactor are in route as we speak. ETA to Eden is 1100 tomorrow. Once that's in place and tested, we will begin the marketing phase. Are you sure your people are ready? Don't forget that success, in the long term, rests on you and your ability to ... produce...", she said.

119

"We're ready... and don't for one second doubt us...", Bubba responded in a more serious tone, "We've got as much riding on this as you do..."
"Doubtful...", Brandon added, snidely.

"Stone, do I have to remind you that without us, this whole thing goes down the shitter, you're out a couple hundred million dollars of StoneCorp cash and you're probably lookin' for a new job next week. So, don't give me that smartass backtalk...", Bubba said. Just as he was about continue his tirade, Tamara interrupted.

"Paul, let me start by saying, I refuse to call you Bubba Joe...

Listen, we understand you and your people's unique and serious situation... We're all stressed about this and we all, collectively, just want it to go as planned. We have a lot of money riding on this and we just want to ensure that this rollout goes perfect. Do you understand? I just said WE about six times... WE are in this together, Paul.",

When Brandon managed to infuriate someone of substantial importance, Tamara naturally went into disaster recovery mode. She has been doing that often, as of late. Tamara's plea seemed to have defused Bubba Joe for this round, as he calmed and began to shuffle his feet as if he were a child that had just been pulled from the brink of a temper tantrum by his momma.

"If that's it, I suppose I'll head back and get ready to set this bastard up and running!", Bubba said as he rose to his feet. He adjusted the waistband of his pants upward, from either side, then straightened his blazer. He gave a quick tip of his hat's brim, then turned and walked out of Brandon's office. Tamara shot a strange look toward Brandon. Best described as concerned pity with a smattering of guilt, you could tell she was harboring reservations about this plan but at this point, she still hadn't voiced it.

Paul "Bubba Joe", Bradley saw himself back down to the parking garage, where he climbed into the back seat of a black Chevrolet Suburban. It pulled off in haste, headed toward the Lincoln Tunnel, then past the Meadowlands, on its way to Teterboro. Inside the Suburban, the driver peered into the rearview mirror.
"You ok, boss?", he asked.

Paul was now holding an old Colt six shooter tightly to his chest. He no longer appeared as a tall, fat southerner. He had dark blonde hair with a significantly receded hair line. He was much shorter than just a few moments earlier and carried much less weight. Dark veins had begun to form around his neck and his eyes, had now, an ever-present dull violet glow to them. He was in the beginning stages of Divinine poisoning but he was no stranger to this. He and his people dealt with this type of thing on a near daily basis.

In the old times, the Omnician race was led from Alanis by an Adaptive Chief, the last of which, the last which was named, Acedeus. During his reign, the Omnician people had been dealt a long string of abuses laid upon them by a series of complacent and corrupt Adaptive leaders. Many rose up against him and in the end, it was decided, for the good of the people, that those who wished to leave their guilds and seek homestead elsewhere, were free to do so. Many Omnicians left the safety of the cities of Alanis, Gados and Alixandria and fled west to the new world. Paul's ancestors belonged to group of artistic and fanatical Omnicians that above all else, desired complete autonomy. It was rumored, this cult of Omnicians practiced the most-taboo form of blessing manifestation known as Indistation, or Internalizing a blessing to manipulate one's own form. This differs from Therian's blessing manifestations as the toll of the manifestation is shared equally with the Therian's Exanima, or External soul.

This cult of Omnicians fled to the far west and settled underground in a rocky region of Death Valley, they so appropriately named, Eden. The Free People of Eden as they now call themselves, used 'Indi' as a form of spiritual expression and many modified their bodies to such an extent, their blessings turned against them. If an Omni Indistates too often, the modifications can become permanent, as their blessing gets stuck in effectively, overdrive. It continues to continuously manifest, to keep the modification intact, as if it were trying to keep the Omnician itself, alive. This results in a constant depletion of Divinine from within the body and reduces the threshold to which, the body becomes viniated. In turn, has led these Omnicians to seek alternative forms of Divination, or the cleansing. One who suffers from this enhanced form of viniation, will seek to consume any and all forms of Divinium available.

Generally speaking, a viniated Omnician would seek out the Baths of Divination, pools of liquified Divinium within Omnician cities that fend off viniation in a matter of minutes. Alternatively, an Omnician can rest while in contact with their relic and over a series of hours, the symptoms of viniation will subside. Unfortunately for The Augs, as they're known, ages of severe and constant viniation and treatment has dried their baths and most discarded any relics as a protest to traditional Omnician culture. Not that a relic would be of much use in severe cases of viniation. One plentiful source of Divinium The Augs have found available is in its' dormant state within the human body. It's most effectively absorbed into the Omnician body via bodily fluids, the easiest being, by way of the consumption of human blood, directly from the vein. So, to feed this constant need, The Augs have turned Eden into an oasis of vice, catering to every want, every lust and every sin, of man.

Once the last baths of Eden dried up, its' inhabitants, becoming increasingly desperate, collectively manifested the blessing Bliss as a means to ease their own suffering. As Marcus said, blessings are unpredictable, Bliss took on a life of her own and never dissipated. Anyone who enters Eden, is overcome with an intoxicating feeling, as all cares and worries are washed away and replaced with a sense of...

well… ecstasy. The Augs use Bliss to lure humans to Eden for the epic, never ending party, booze and drugs and in turn, many have stayed within the walls of Eden, for years. Because of Bliss, they don't even realize they are being used as batteries. More accurately, as blood bags.

 "I'm having a hard time buying what they're selling", Paul said, seeming to be in considerable pain, "when something seems too easy, it's usually not that great a deal. What's to stop them from taking over?", He said. He lowered his head into his hands then leaned against the door to rest.

"I don't know the answers boss... all's I know is we need this....", the driver responded. The suburban pulled up to an unmanned gate in the south end of the New Jersey airport. The window rolled down and the driver pressed a keycard to the callbox and the gate began to open. The driver pulled the suburban onto the airfield, then into a hanger a few hundred yards away. A few minutes later an aged, midsized Hawker rolled out of the hanger and, under power, began to taxi toward the runway. With clearance, it took off and vectored toward the west coast. A few hours later, the Hawker dropped off of radar near South-central Nevada, preceded below 1,500 feet and flew the last ten or so miles to an abandoned airfield. The jet circled the airfield, then, once it was clear they had no visitors, it touched down only to abruptly taxi into one of the decrepit hangers, running the length of the dusty airfield. This particular hanger was unusually large, given the state of repair of its' surroundings. The doors slid open and the pilot maneuvered the airplane inside. The doors quickly closed behind the aircraft. Then, just a moment later, it once again appeared deserted, showing not a single sign of activity.

The inside of the hanger was not as dated and ran down as the outside would have suggested. It was modernized and brightly lit. There was also little space available inside. Every single nook and cranny were filled with cars, vans and buses of all types, four wheelers, motorcycles, many different models of dune buggies and other off-road vehicles. There were even a few other airplanes buried inside, as well.

The door to the aircraft opened and two men, one being the driver from the suburban, exited the aircraft, followed by Paul. He was heavily dependent on the stair railing to brace himself. The two men helped him down the final few steps and ushered him to a nearby golf cart. They drove toward the rear of the hanger, then turned and began down a long ramp that emptied into a long underground tunnel just below the desert's surface. This tunnel continued on for several miles until, at its' end, one finds themselves staring directly at the Gates of Eden. Once back in Eden, Paul would begin to recover but time was running short.

When VIP visitors come to Eden, they are invited to fly into this air strip and are ushered down this tunnel. The entirety of the six or so miles of tunnel is lit every twenty-five feet by candlelight. Normally, an open top shuttle car ferries guests through this tunnel. Halfway down the tunnel, patrons can begin to hear the music coming from Eden and once they're within one mile, Bliss begins to take hold and by the time the shuttle car begins to slow, the guests are well under the influence of Bliss and are ready and willing to succumb to all that awaits them in this place.

Paul was well past being comforted by Bliss. He's lived here his entire life and the effects of this perpetual blessing don't impact him and most of the elder Augs anymore.

Once the golf cart rounded the last corner, the tunnel began to widen. As they exited the tunnel, Eden came into view. Eden is nestled inside a massive cavern that's lit throughout by neon lights. Spotlights circled in figure eight patterns, creating fast moving celestial bodies that raced across the ceiling of the cavern, while crowds of guests wait in lines to enter paradise. The structure itself was built of stone and large sequoia raw timbers with white linens woven along the top, sides and draped throughout the structure. The echoes of dance music fill the cavern with an eerie, offbeat rhythm while the sounds of cheers and boisterous laughter made by hundreds of attendees spilled out and echoed throughout the cavern, from inside paradise.

The golf cart sped around to the side of the building and screeched to a halt. Both men helped Paul out of the cart and ushered him inside. They rushed him up a flight of stairs and into a balcony overseeing a sea of sweaty, dancing patrons. He sat down in a low slung, wide armed chair and a young, beautiful blonde girl sat down beside him.

She raised offered her wrist and the gold bracelets she wore clanged as they slid down her arm. Her palm faced up, toward Paul. He took her by the underside of her hand and pulled it toward his mouth. He down hard on the outside of her exposed wrist, leaving blunt puncture wounds from his four top front teeth. He didn't have pointy canines that left a nice, clean, little pair of puncture wounds, as seen in the popular vampire movies of the aughts. His teeth were just normal teeth. She began to bleed heavily and he held her wrist to his mouth as the blood began to flow. He sucked, creating an air tight seal, then swallowed, then again, and again. He began to feel that all-to-familiar tingle and the veins that had since formed a dark violet spiderweb around his neck, began to subside, then disappeared entirely. He began to feel like himself again, all to the sublime house and dance rhythm of tonight's guest DJ, simply known as Brax.

The Augs were smart. They knew that to lure humans here, they needed new, fresh entertainment, so they would invite and pay handsomely, up and coming entertainers and celebrities to perform and be seen at Eden. It was a major no-no to feed while the compensated entertainment or celebrities were on the premises. They didn't want to scare off talent, but Paul played by his own set of rules. If he wanted to do it, he just would. Then, if needed, he would just cast his way out of it. He was a powerful Precept after all. His Indi manifestation was that he could take the form of anything at will, similar to a master Therian, expect he could manifest Precept as well. and it would have an effect similar to that of a love potion, on its' recipient. In turn, they would comply with his every request.

The young blonde began to show early signs of exsanguination and she was ushered away, with her now bloody arm, wrapped with some sort of special covering that would heal her wounds in very short order. It was something Paul picked up at Marcus Neiman's quite a while ago.

As the leader of The Augs, he is expected to participate in Indi regularly, but lately, he's been hesitant to do so. It has seemed to take more and more of a toll as of late and the viniation seems harder and harder to shake. He's convinced most of the elders that he should Indi only sparingly, at least until this deal with StoneCorp comes to fruition as he needs all his focus in closing this deal. For all intents and purposed though, the deed was basically done. It was all logistics at this point. The idea was that the Augs just keep doing what they do best, attracting large crowds of human partygoers, the reactor gets up and running and they'll have plenty of Divinium to keep their baths filled. Most importantly, they'd never have to feed on human blood, ever again.

"How's the night?", Paul asked Aerik, his second in charge, while wiping the blood from his lips.

"It's good. We have new guests tonight. More than usual.", He responded.

"How many?", Paul asked.

"Forty-six", Aerik responded, "I wouldn't expect much in the way of fallout... most seem to be adapting well".

Aerik was perfection in the form of tall, dark and handsome. Six foot six, muscular, quick witted and friendly, he was an Elemento. He's an Aerus to be exact but he has taught himself to manifest Oren blessings as well. He was well on his way to earning the title of Master Elemento. If, of course The Augs actually participated in the Omnician culture and traditions. Aerik's sole Indi augmentation were long, densely feathered, white angel wings, that protruded from his shoulder blades. Each one was nearly nine feet long, when fully extended. He had learned to fly using them quite well and every so often, a lucky few guests to Eden were invited to witness Aerik fly inside the cavern. Every one of the lucky few were in awe, every time.

Aerik was special. Most of The Augs and their Indi manifestations were superficial, mostly for looks or to impress others or for self-proclaimed artistic expression, with minimal utility. He, on the other hand, treated his as an enhancement of himself. He ate properly, made sure to get plenty of rest, never let himself get overly viniated, drunk or high and most of all, to prevent getting himself into a precarious situation, he never over-manifested outside of the confines of Eden.

"Anything to speak of?", Paul asked, referring to vehicles or planes or other assets the guests arrived in, as witnessed earlier, back in the hanger. If certain, well to do guests took a special liking to the debauchery at

Eden, they were offered lifetime admittance and invited and encouraged to stay, oftentimes quite opulently. Paul would get their power of attorney and would sell whatever assets they had, in moderation of course, to fund the ongoing party. If they got out of control or wanted to leave, he'd just cast them back into obedience or, even worse, he'd just let them leave. But of course, they'd have to find their way out, then, survive the extreme conditions, while walking through Death Valley in an attempt to get home. Most who were insistent on leaving, died hours or days after while roaming aimlessly in the desert. Then, the coyotes, snakes and bugs did the rest.

"Couple of sand rails and trucks... one group arrived in a newer Gulfstream V but it's under LLC... I already looked it up ...", Aerik responded. They could muscle it from its' parent entity, but it's usually more effort than it's worth.

"Well, what do we have, then?", Paul asked sarcastically.

"Dinner... Brax is almost done... that kid went six hours without a break... let's pay him, get him on his way and get fed...", Aerik said. He wasn't a huge fan of drinking blood for sustenance but, as he eloquently says, 'if you wanna find oil, you gotta do some drilling'.

A raucous round of applause erupted below, signaling the end of the DJ's set. He was then ushered off stage, replaced by the rhythmic bumping of masterly produced rarities and moments later Brax was led up to Paul's balcony.

"Wow man... that crowd is great!", Brax said, clearly under the effects of Bliss.
"You have a good time?", Paul asked, "...that was a nice set by then way.", he continued, "Anytime you want to come back and spin, just call Aerik... you're welcome here anytime, my man!", Paul smiled at young Brax and extended his hand. Brax reciprocated with a three-point hand shake, then Paul extended a medium-sized Louis Vuitton bag, stuffed with hundreds.

"This should take care of you,", he said. Brax accepted it but didn't peer inside, as he thought it, rude. "Thank you, Paul", he said, "I'll come back real soon..."
"You want to stay a while? Maybe sample the wares?", Aerik said, hinting at facilitating efforts for getting the sixteen-year-old DJ drunk, high or laid but probably a combination of the three.
"I'll pass, but I appreciate the offer! For sure!", Brax said, "it's a school night and all", he said, jokingly with a cheesy grin.

"To each, their own", Paul said with a grin, "Aerik will get you on a plane and on your way...", then he turned his attention elsewhere.

With that, Brax disappeared back into the walkway he'd entered through. Over the next ten minutes, he hopped into a golf cart and was driven back up the tunnel. Moments later he was relaxing onboard the Hawker, headed back from whence, he came. Albeit, $243,000 richer.

Eden's debauchery runs in cycles. Sometimes the music is jumping and the crowd is wild, sometimes they play trippy music that encourages hallucinational exploration and at others, they set the mood to encourage patrons to explore each other. At dinner time, they slow down the music and boys and girls dance close. This is when The Augs peel off selected guests from the crowd for VIP access. In all honesty, it's code for, "you're dinner", but the patrons never seem to mind.

The Augs are smart about feeding as well. They know that if they're overly aggressive, despite the influence of Bliss, fear can result in guests leaving and they know that's bad for business. So, they're diligent in being calming and comforting with their prey, when feeding.
Paul's phone began to ring. He picked it up, recognizing the contact, then answered in a direct, southern voice.

"This' Bubba...", he answered. Aerik stood, snickering behind him, trying not to laugh openly and loudly.

"Well that's music to my ears buddy... we're gonna jump on that sumbitch the second it gets here .. aight then...bye.", He sat his phone down on the arm of his chair and looked at Aerik. "Reactor's here...", he said, "round up a crew and get to the strip. They're pulling up in 20"

Aerik nodded and disappeared through the balcony's only entrance. He walked the floor, taking six to eight able bodied Augs with him. They piled into golf carts and headed down the tunnel, toward the hanger. Once inside the hanger, they watched through the windows until three large box vans pulled onto the tarmac, approached the hanger doors and stopped. Each bore a large StoneCorp logo, emblazoned on the sides. Aerik's crew opened the hanger doors and the three vans entered. Aerik stood, scanning the horizon as the doors closed behind the vans. The faint pounding of dance music could still be heard from deep inside.

The Augs were on the precipice of being free. Free from the burden of having to feed on humans, free from the burden of being chained to this place, free from having to live lives of reactionary existence and most of all, free from living a taboo existence as seen by the rest of the Omnician race. They soon, would take their rightful place alongside The Array.

11
Alanis

It took a moment for Christian's eyes to adjust.
The light here seemed different as was in that basement he'd just been standing in moments ago. In every direction he seemed to look, it was as if the light only made it's way to where it needed to be.

"Weird...", he said.
"What?", Blake asked.

"The light... it's ... it's following my line of sight.", He explained as he fell to his knees, then onto one side, where he laid motionless on the cold stone floor.

"I've seen this before...", Elijah said, "Quick, we have to get him to the baths!",

Blake, Elijah and Penny picked Christian up and carried him through the medieval library. The room was a massive circular space with dense walls made of carved stone blocks and the air inside felt cool, dry and aged. The ceiling was at least fifty meters high with wooden platforms encircling the outer walls, each level about 20 meters above the last. Hundreds of bookshelves lined the circular walls. Each level had multiple ladders providing access to what had to be millions of books, texts and scrolls, where, god only knows, what was transcribed.

There were several inhabitants scattered throughout this library that took quite a startle when the group of outsiders came running through.

As they carried Christian through the library, Elijah said heavily, "The Traverse wasn't meant for humans to pass through... their bodies don't possess Divinine and don't know how to react to the shock... he could very well die! We must hurry..."

They exited the library and found themselves in a grand hallway. The ceilings were adorned with murals narrated with symbols that resembled hieroglyphics that included Norse, Latin, Greek and Sanskrit characters embedded throughout. They were painted in bright colors with painstakingly intricate detail, complete with gold and silver leafing. Golden molding ran the length of the hallways, creating a gleaming border between the stone walls and the colorful ceiling images. Every ten meters or so, fixtures hung employing burning candles and oil lamps that lit the darkest of places.

Elijah led them down the hall to the right. They ran down the hall for 200 meters until entering into another cavernous room, with roughly the same size footprint as the library. The ceiling here was much lower, only about ten or fifteen meters tall. This room was much darker than the hallway before but immensely more tranquil. Both the ceiling and the room's stone walls glistened with a luminescent glow from veins of Divinium embedded inside the walls and from the reflections from dozens of large, bright blue pools scattered across its' floor. Twenty or so stone columns, styled much like the ones that were once found at the Parthenon, sat watch between the pools and towered from the floor to the ceiling. Several mirrors were positioned along the walls in a manner to suggest they were there to reflect sunlight inside. Peculiarly though, none were being used.

They brought Christian inside, found the first unoccupied pool and laid him into it. He still lay motionless, but was now neck deep in a pool of liquid Divinium. As The blue glow danced across his skin, Blake stared on, worried for his newly found friend. Several of the pools were occupied and their inhabitants took notice of the outsiders.

The older man in the pool next to Christian asked, "What happened to him? Duel?"

Elijah acknowledged the man's query with a glance and replied, "The Traverse..."

The man's face lost all emotion. It had been eons since anyone had been known to have used The Traverse. While he wasn't even sure if that thing still worked, he knew however, that anyone claiming to have used it, is either a liar or someone extremely old and of supreme importance.

A moment later, six men rounded the corner and entered the baths. All wore suits of the familiar styled and detailed armor consisting of breastplates, bearing strange symbols, greaves and gauntlets. Each man's breastplate was slightly different from the next but all shared one trait. Each appeared to have been painstakingly crafted by a master of his craft, evident in the intricate metalwork. Each had that familiar bluish hue within the metal. The soldiers each carried a spear. The heads were made of a shiny and dark metal and all were mounted on dark ash wooden staffs.

The soldiers stood in formation creating a blockade between the pool where Christian lay and the door. One of the soldiers approached, took a defensive stance and spoke,
"State your name and your business in this place..."

Penelope turned and replied, "I'm Penelope of Alanis, this is Blake Lucas of Sequoia, our friend here has taken ill..."

The soldier became more relaxed and interrupted just as Elijah came into view, "and who is your friend?"

"His name is Christian...", she replied, purposefully brief.

"How did you get here...", he continued, still speaking in a forceful manner.
Elijah interjected, "The Traverse... we arrived moments ago ... Our friend is human and he is deathly ill..."
The soldier looked upon Elijah, in judgement at first, then noticed and recognized his ringed hands.
"The Traverse?... You're the Wanderer, aren't you...?", he asked.

Elijah nodded in acknowledgement, still focused on Christian's dire state.

"... I've heard the stories of your adventures...", he said, in awe of Elijah's presence, "... how can I help?"

"Who is the Governor these days?", Elijah asked.
"Kristus...", the soldier responded.

"Tell him Penelope is back and we need to speak to the Elder Council.", Penelope said, attempting to bring Christian back into consciousness.

"On It....", he said as he turned and led the squad of the soldiers out of the baths and down the hall, at double time.

Christian's eyes began to blink, trying to adjust to the room's light. A few moments later he regained consciousness and began to look around at his surroundings.

"Where are we? ...What happened?", he asked still quite groggy.

"You're in the Divine Baths, deep inside the confines of the Omnician city of Alanis.", Penny answered.

"What's the last thing you remember...?", Elijah asked.

"Well... we went into the basement of Neiman Marcus... that, by the way, isn't supposed to exist... then, that old guy opened that chest and a magic stone projected a glowing ring that we all went through... then nothing..."
He responded.

"The Traverse...", Elijah commented.

"Huh?", Christian said.

"It's called the Traverse.... that portal thingy you're talking about...", Elijah responded condescendingly, "... it traverses time and space..."

"Cool name... ", he said groggily. "... what happened to me...?", Christian continued.

"Humans aren't meant to bypass time and space... the Divinine within us, affords our bodies a natural resilience to the polarized elemental transgressive impact...", Elijah said.

Christian chuckled. Not because he said anything overtly funny, but because such a scientific sounding phrase came out of what appeared to be, a twelve-year old's mouth.

"You've just survived Divinium poisoning...", Elijah proclaimed, in a serious tone.
Christian sat up and then it dawned on him that he'd been submerged, fully clothed, in a pool this whole time.

"Dammit! My phone!", He yelled as he stood up. Mentally, he expected his clothes to be soaked and his phone, ruined. He was surprised to find his clothes and person were perfectly dry. He reached into his pocket and pulled out his phone. Much to his satisfaction, the large crack across his screen was gone and when he pressed the home button, the screen lit up and the battery showed full.

His screen was filled with notifications. He had 16 missed calls with voicemails, missed texts from at least six people, and a whole bunch of emails.

"I don't understand... my screen... it was cracked...", he said. The look on his face was one of absolutely bewilderment.

"How's this possible?", He said, waiting for one of them to explain.

Penny spoke, "Divinium is a powerfully strange substance... these pools heal our bodies when the sickness comes on... they have all sorts of other effects on almost anything you place inside them... they just have no effect, that we know of, on the natural state of the human body..."

A serious tone dominated Elijah's voice when he added, "Do you understand now, why we stay hidden? Why we haven't invited man openly into our cities?
Why we don't share what we know with the world of man?"

"Because we'd destroy it ... or ourselves...", Christian responded. He sat just at the edge of the pool, his knees bent, his forearms resting atop them. He hung his head down between his arms and quietly pondered this world, as he now knew it to be.
After all this time, harboring disdain and resentment for his fellow man, he never thought he'd end up here. He never thought he'd feel pity for his own kind.

"After all our breakthroughs and discoveries and triumphs, we still truly know not what we do ...", he whispered, in quiet reflection.

Just then, the group of soldiers returned through the door, now accompanied by an older gentleman leading a pack of what appeared to be bureaucrats. They were talking amongst themselves, virtually oblivious to anything happening around them.

"Penelope! It's wonderful to see you again..." The man, standing front and center said.

Kristus, the governor of Alanis was tall and thin with salt and pepper hair and overly animated facial features. Penelope had previously met this man maybe once, long before he was governor, but he was treating her like a long-lost friend, returned from the dead. She sensed that something was amiss but continued to let him lead the conversation. She was curious where this would go. Perhaps he would overplay his hand and accidentally show his cards, so to speak. Only one way to find out, right?

"My soldiers tell me you're looking to speak with the Elder Council ... I'm sorry Penelope... but the council is out of session.", He told her, "... to be honest, we haven't had need for the council as of late..."

"Well, this is quite the setback...", she responded, careful to control the specific emotions, her reactions hinted toward, as she was becoming leery of this new governor and his true intentions. "When will they return to session?", She asked.

"Unfortunately, we do not expect that they plan to meet anytime soon... I, however, would be more than happy to help you in any way I can...", he said, making every effort to appear sincere. She was assured he had ulterior motives at this point.

"Master Charles asked that I return as soon as I was able and inform him of... certain goings on... outside the confines of Alanis", she said. She chose these words carefully and paid extra care to speak with the proper cadence and tone to appear to be hiding something.

He took the bait.

"Was there something specific he wanted to know?", He asked, "maybe I can relay a message to him for you... when I see him next, that is..."

"Yes, there was...", she said, "could you deliver this message...? We went to the place you asked us to go and the thing you asked me to find was nowhere to be found... we looked for the guy as well and were not able to find him either... All-in-all ... I think we're back to square one..."

"Is that it? It's a rather cryptic message, don't you think?", He asked in a tone suggesting a blatantly obviously ploy to get her to reveal more information.

"No, he specifically instructed me to report back to him and only him... in person. I'm hoping I haven't broken his trust... plus, he's the only one who knows what it was he had us looking for... he hasn't really told me much more than that...", she responded, watching his reaction. He appeared panicked now, but seemed as if he was trying to hide it.

"If that's it, I'll do my best to relay the message...", he said, with a forced grin. He then turned and whispered something to one of his underlings. He turned and exited the baths, flanked by his gaggle of bureaucrats, followed closely by the squad of soldiers.

"Something's not right...", Elijah said.

"I know,", Penny responded, "he's way too young to be named Governor...
They're up to something... and I get a sneaking suspicion I'm not going to like what we're going to find here..."

Christian was on his feet now and the quartet left the baths and made their way back down the hall, past the library and turned into the courtyard.

The courtyard of Alanis was as mystical and breathtaking as you'd expect. Nestled on the floor, deep within the caldera of a dormant volcano, the walls are covered in thick vines blooming luminescent flowers of every imaginable color. A waterfall sprayed fresh water from its' mouth at the rim of the caldera, down through the center of the courtyard. The spray from the waterfall refracted the light as it passed through the courtyard, resulting in a perpetual mist. Rainbows were created when the bioluminescent light refracted in the mist. They seemed to be visible with every passing cloud of mist. I'd suppose only God knows how water gets pushed up the mountain, only to rain down inside of it.

Throughout the city's courtyard, stone carved walkways created six or eight levels, spiraling around the walls of the caldera, eventually leading the way up to its' rim. There were walkways across the abyss and passages branching off and disappearing into the mountain's interior. Within the mountain, exists a honeycomb of tunnels, caves and passageways, creating a city hidden inside. The lower levels of the city are populated by the majority of Alanis' citizens. The higher up the mountain you go, the more ancient, influential and powerful the families occupying the spaces become.

The majority of the community spaces are located on the lower levels with exception of the Temple of Blessings. It is located on the very top level, nestled underneath the waterfall. This is where every newly born Omnician is brought when a trial of blessings is to be performed. It's a large, egg shaped cavern consisting of auditorium seating, with a large, stone alter in its' center. The Temple of Blessings is one of the most sacred places in all of Omni culture and violence within is strictly forbidden. Omnicians will travel from far and wide to attend a Trial when a new member is born to one of the ancient families, even in the dead of winter.

Sharing the very top level of Alanis are the Governor's Chambers and the Court of Elders, where the council meets and from which, the city is managed.

One level down begins the habitation spaces, who's occupancy has been fought over for since the first of days. When the city was full, it was home to nearly twenty-five thousand Omnicians. Now, only a small fraction of that live here.

Penelope and Elijah led Blake and Christian through the courtyard, up one level and into the catacombs, leading deep into the lower levels. Along their journey through the tunnels, they passed The Great Forge where blacksmiths pounded on metals of all kinds and stone masons were hard at work milling stones for various projects. Despite Omnicient mastery of the elements and of matter itself, sometimes there's no substitute for doing things the hard way. They passed the kitchens from which the entire city is fed. Tonight, it smelled like they were having grilled meats and freshly baked bread of some sort.

Through a narrow and dark passageway, the four found themselves in a meeting room of sorts. Six prominent symbols, each made of various precious metals, polished, semi-precious stones and ash wood, hung, evenly spaced, along the walls. Seating was arranged in a circle around the center of the room. There were several smaller rooms connected to this main room, but there was little available light down here and each of the smaller rooms were pitch black inside. Penelope looked around trying to find any kind of sign or clue as to the whereabouts of her kin.

"It doesn't look like anyone has been here for a while.", Penny said.

Elijah scanned the room and found a torch laying against the wall. His eyes turned a fiery red. He grabbed the torch's handle with one hand and placed his other on the business end. He, then pulled the torch across his open hand, as if it were a matchstick. It ignited in a blaze and with an ominous roar that echoed throughout the nearby catacombs. Instantly, light filled the space and any question of what had happened here, were soon to be answered.

This space used to be a residence but because it was drafty, families decided to stop raising their children this deep, within the mountain. As a result, long ago, this whole section was abandoned. Since the exodus, no one really ventured this far down anymore. Which made it perfect for use as a meeting space for a group that wished to meet in secret.

The Order of the Celestials were devout followers of the teachings and practices of the earliest of Omnicians, originating from the first Omnicians that lived within the Paphos Forest on the Island of Cypress. Long before the Great Exodus, they were devout followers of the rule of the Adaptives and after the fall, the Prophecy of the Ascension. Long ago, the Order of the Celestials shouldered the burden of protecting the secrets of the prophecy, the search for the prophesized, and as such, considered themselves responsible for seeing the legend become reality. For centuries, they spent their lives looking for signs of the chosen one and have since, found nothing. Penelope hoped Blake's presence would change that.

There appeared to have been a struggle. The room was unusually disheveled, with any and all furniture destroyed and the space, searched thoroughly. The seating in the center of the room consisted, primarily of pillows and low-slung chairs. All of the cushions had been slashed open and most were splattered with what, even from the quickest of glances, appeared to be blood. Blake glanced around the room and noticed, protruding from one of the doorways, a bare foot.

"Guys...", Blake said, motioning Elijah to move the light toward the doorway. As Elijah walked in that direction, the torch illuminated the interior of the side room. There, piled haplessly, inside the small side room, lay the bodies of a dozen men and several women, each stabbed, multiple times, in and around the chest and neck. Most had bruising and contusions about the neck and the face. They all had one thing in common, they all were of advanced age and several were clearly the bodies of the Elders Council. Due to the low humidity and low temperature this far into the mountain, the bodies had not yet begun to decompose.

Christian looked toward Penelope and noticed the tears, streaming down her face.
This was the only family she had ever known. The Elder Council and The Order of the Celestials were both dedicated to the harmonious existence of all of Earth's inhabitants. Penelope quickly felt the rage building. Whoever did this would pay, but now was not the time. She would have her vengeance on Kristus, his minions and whoever else played a part, however small, in this atrocity that was perpetrated on this most hallowed of grounds. After all, if Omnicians do anything well, it's hold lifelong grudges.

Almost immediately, Penelope ran across the room to one of the symbols hanging on the wall. She felt around the sides until the others noticed a clicking sound coming from within the wall. Down at the bottom of the wall, a small section swung inward. It was only about 3 feet tall, but once inside, the ceiling provided ample room for the largest of man to walk, comfortably. Christian took the torch and entered the door first, followed by Blake. Before entering the door, Elijah looked at Penny and said, "I'm sorry for what happened here... the Order and Council were friends to me and I, to them... if it's my last act on this Earth, I will stand with you and avenge your lost family..."

Penny put her hand on Elijah's shoulder and smiled through the tears. She bent down and climbed into the doorway, followed by Elijah, who pushed the small stone door closed. Visible on the back side of this door was the mechanism that acted as the lock for this escape tunnel's door. A series of metal levers, springs and cogs were precisely assembled along the backside of the wall. At the top of the mechanism was the symbol of its' maker.

It was a circle with three lines, each of different length and thicknesses extending from the circle's center. Each line extended in its' own direction. The first, thickest and shortest of the three lines, was at 45 degrees, the second, being the longest and thinnest, was positioned directly at 180 degrees and the third, at 315 degrees. Over the top were letters etched into the top section of the circle. One word sat there staring back at anyone who should lay eyes upon it.

WatchMaker

Wedged, haphazardly within a randomly placed tension spring gear, sat a single, tightly-sealed, paper scroll. Penelope grabbed it just as they heard commotion coming from the other side of the wall. They could clearly hear Kristus' voice, screaming at one of his underlings. He knew they had been there but it sounded like he thought Penelope and her friends had ventured back into Alanis proper. He ordered his soldiers to search the city and bring these trespassers and traitors to his quarters the second they're found.

There's no way he knew about this passageway. It was one of the most well-kept secret of the Order, because they slowly built it, over the generations, for just an occasion like this. Following her better judgement, Penelope fought the urge to go back and confront Kristus and so, not knowing where it leads, they began down the dark pathway inside the mountain. They noticed the curvature and changes of elevation along the path, under their feet. As they continued, they noticed the texture of the path began to change as well. While initially, solid stone, it seemed to become, more and more like loose gravel.

Christian held the torch and continued to walk forward, stopping for nothing. After a short while, he started to notice detail along the walls of the tunnel. After rounding a corner, the dim highlight of the tunnel's end grew larger and larger. Just before the opening, Christian could tell it was nighttime and the moon was full and bright. There was definitely a chill in the night air.

Elijah stopped the group just before they exited the pathway.

"Listen… I know this terrain… It's quite treacherous. Stay close to me and whatever you do, do not stop… not for anyone or anything.

The moment Christian stepped out of the tunnel, a cold northern wind hit him and drove an unshakable chill, deep into his bones. North Texas can get windy, cold and rainy, but this was in another league, altogether. The winds that pound the Northern Scandinavian Mountains comes directly south from the Artic and anyone who's not acclimated to the climate, finds it nearly impossible to tolerate for any extended period of time. This was just another Tuesday evening for Elijah and Penny.

"Like I said, stay close…", Elijah said just before beginning his decent down the slope.
"Wait…", Penny said, "Where are we even going?"
Elijah shrugged his shoulders and pointed aimlessly into the horizon.
Penny pulled the scroll that she just procured, from her pocket.

She loosened the leather strap, then began to delicately unroll the very old and very fragile papyrus.

It read,

Whomever shall find this message,
Let it be known you will always find shelter, protection…
and the answers you seek …
from The Watchmaker

At the bottom of the scroll, stamped on the paper was a circular symbol. It was similar to the symbol embossed on the mechanism from which Penny took the scroll, however, the lines extending from the circle's center were positioned differently.
The others watched intently while she studied the scroll.

"What's the WatchMaker?", she asked.

Blake shrugged his shoulders. Elijah's face gave an unbiased observer the impression that he knew, yet he didn't speak up. Maybe he did know, or maybe he didn't and wanted it to seem as if he did.

Christian said, "Wait… ya'll really don't know?".

The others shrugged their shoulders and stared in anticipation for Christian to share his insight. Christian began to feel an air of pride in his newly perceived usefulness.

"Come on … WatchMaker is that really old and super expensive timepiece company in Old Town London… that boutique shop with the cases holding rows and rows of metal blocks … where you pick out your metal and then help the chronographers craft your original timepiece?

Plus… that's the font from their logo…", It turns out that he picked up more than just student loans from SMU.

"Well… London it is, I suppose…", Elijah said, as he turned and faced the valley to the south west.

"How are we going to get there?", Christian asked, not even sure where, exactly they were.

Penny spoke up with a smile on her face, "Elijah, want to try that thing?", He glanced at her with a grin and a nod.

Elijah took a couple of steps away from the opening of the tunnel. He raised his arms, palms up, then looked back at Penny. His eyes immediately illuminated with a sky-blue glow. Just then, the wind went still and the temperature became pleasantly bearable. His summonings began to illuminate, beginning at his neck's hollow, then spreading across his torso and shoulders, then down his arms, visible even underneath his clothing. He slowly brought his palms together in front of his chest, fingers up. With a quick motion, he thrust his hands outward in front of him, wrists together with his palms outward. A gust of wind followed down the mountainside and along the exact path and direction in which his arms had extended and his hands were pointing.

He then pulled his arms back toward his chest and the winds responded as could be felt in the change of air pressure, rotating his hands at the wrist, forming a cylindrical pattern. The wind then began to rotate, forming a tunnel parallel to the ground directly in front of where they stood.

It was if the four of them were staring into the eye of a tornado. Mass chaos on all sides, but peaceful and calm down its' center. The funnel was about 4 meters in diameter. The winds surrounding the funnel were becoming increasingly embedded with debris, forming a cocoon of sorts.

Elijah looked over his shoulder at Penny and said, "Your turn..."

Penelope's eyes illuminated as she walked to his side. The vivid purple glow shot down her torso and across her arms simultaneously. Elijah held out his hands, palms down, encouraging the other to grab them. Christian took his left hand, and Penelope, his right. She then, extended her hand toward Blake, her eyes locked onto his. He glanced down momentarily at her extended hand, then reached out and grabbed it. She smiled, sheepishly then returned to her task at hand. An unfamiliar series of feelings came over Blake when he took Penny's hand. She felt it, as well.

"So...", Elijah said, speaking loudly to be heard over the sounds of the whipping winds, "We take this to Copenhagen... rest there... then on to Amsterdam... rest again, then to the ferries at Calais..."

"What do you mean... take this...?", Christian asked.

Elijah's only remark was, "Hold tight, now..."

A split second later, Elijah leaned forward and the four were lifted off their feet, then sucked into the vortex. What Christian was able to see through the cocoon of debris, led him to believe that they were traveling at an extremely high rate of speed across this frozen terrain. Though obstructed by the debris, he caught glimpses of snow on the ground and scattered across the sprawling peaks and valleys.

Basically, Elijah had manifested a negative pressure wind tunnel and Penny, a cloak, to shield them from any wandering eyes outside of the vortex. While it appeared to the quartet as a long hollow tunnel, all the outside world witnessed, Omnicians included, that there was a slight, cool breeze passing by.

Several moments later, Elijah instructed the others to follow his lead. He lessened his lean into the vortex and they followed suit. Up ahead, the tunnel vortex began to collapse onto itself as the eye became smaller and smaller. Elijah leaned back and spread his feet apart slightly, similar to how a parachutist prepares for the rising ground.

Just then, the vortex dissipated and the four found themselves falling to the waiting ground, several feet below. Each landed on their feet with little effort and little in the way of ill effects, though Christian suffered a bout of vertigo for a few minutes afterwards.

They soon found themselves standing waist deep in a field of tulips. As far as the eye could see, there were blooms of every imaginable color and pattern, illuminated solely by the moon. It was breathtaking for each of them.

"Could've picked a better place to land, don't you think....", Christian said, hoping his sarcasm was obvious.

"What do you mean?", Elijah asked, puzzled, "This place is beautiful... it's one of my favorite places on earth..."

Penny shook her head in disbelief and said, "He was kidding..."

"Oh...", Elijah muttered, somewhat embarrassed.

"Seriously though,", Christian said, "Where are we anyway?"

"Just West of Copenhagen...", Elijah said, "We can catch the train from here tomorrow. Now though, I need to rest ...."

A wayward Omnician can easily find assistance for his or her specific type of needs in this part of the world. Businesses that cater to Omnicians, or are operated by such, are easily identified by the markings around the threshold of a building's entrance. Certain symbols indicate specific services that are available inside. These symbols are easily missed by someone who know not, at what they're looking. They can easily be mistaken for scratches, dirt or imperfections in the material.

The four walked the short distance to the main road, in search of one specific place. Founded in 1198, this place was by far, the oldest inn in the area. This specific place, that Elijah frequents regularly, offers rooms, a full menu, has a makeshift divine bath available for any such Omni that displays need and the means. Plus, they ask few questions. Omnicians prefer avoiding places that humans tend to frequent and this place has become somewhat of a tourist attraction over the years. They seem to always have a room available when Elijah had need, in the past.

It was still dark outside but the dawn was coming soon and Elijah wanted to be out of sight when the tourists began taking to the streets and shooting photos. They approached the darkened building through the

139

pebble covered parking lot. Above the door, several symbols could be seen but the entryway was dark, and the symbols, obscured. Elijah opened the doors and strolled inside. The interior of the inn was straight out of a medieval movie. With exposed timbers, old wooden furniture, sparse decor and a blazing hearth in the center of the gathering space. The lobby was empty with the exception of workers preparing for the breakfast service. As they approached the front desk, a familiar face spotted Elijah and greeted him instantly.

"Master Elijah... how are you?", she asked, with a friendly tone.

"Doing well...", he responded, "we are in need of accommodations for the evening."

"What is it, specifically, you would like in a room?", she asked.

"I don't know about my companions, but I'd really enjoy... a bath.", He said. She immediately knew, at what he was hinting. She slid a key over the counter. The tag on the key indicated room O2, which could be easily be confused, by non-Omnician, as zero two.

"Your room is down the stairs... my apologies sir... but there is no view from this room.", She said. Elijah didn't care for a room with a view and she knew this. He wanted access to the baths and no additional questions. With Elijah's nod of approval and appreciation, the four rounded the lobby and took the stairs down to a short hall with three rooms, O2, O3 and O4. These rooms were not shown or advertised anywhere on the website or online. These rooms were specifically for Omnician need, which may surprise you, is quite often.

Inside the room, were four beds, a desk and chair and a plain, unmarked door. The beds and pillows appeared aged, but were stuffed with goose down feathers and were, in turn, surprisingly comfortable. The door inside provided the room with private access the baths. About the size of a standard fitness center steam room, the basin was about eight inches deep and only filled with about four inches of liquid Divinium. While not up to the opulent standards of Alanis or Dorado or at a time, Dalus, it more than sufficed, in function.

Blake entered the room and immediately fell into the bed closest to the wall, Christian took the one across from him, Penny chose the bed next to Blake and Elijah, the one closest to the door. While Penny, Blake and Christian talked and relaxed, Elijah got up and walked through the unmarked door. Divine baths outside of Omnician cities don't just sit filled all of the time. As Divinium is scarce, it is usually held in an internal pump system and the baths, only filled, when necessary.

Elijah disrobed while waiting for the bath to fill. His entire body was covered in scars and wounds from living a lifetime, alone in the wilderness. His summonings were only mildly darkened. Given his age, he can endure much more than a simple negative pressure vortex but he's careful to not get himself into precarious situations. His age, in part with, and even more so, the nature of his blessings, are why he's been able to stay alive this long. Once the bath filled, he climbed in for a few minutes while his energy replenished and his summonings returned to their normal state.

Elijah exited the baths and rejoined the others. Penelope and Blake were deep in conversation. Penelope was sharing stories of her childhood and her upbringing. Elijah and Christian just listened. Upon noticing Elijah, Penelope got up and excused herself to bathe. Blake and Penny's eyes remained locked until the door to the baths closed. It was as if they were the only two in the room.

Elijah fell asleep first. He seems to be, all mission, most of the time. When it's time to sleep, he sleeps, with no fanfare and no delay. Blake and Penny continued their talk until the sun was well off the eastern horizon. Until Blake, with his head propped up on one elbow, decided he needed sleep. They said their good nights as Penny turned over and pulled the covers to her neck. She had a rather large smile on her face.

Christian laid awake. Due to the rapid succession of the past days and weeks, he was having trouble keeping the timeline of occurrences straight in his own mind. He pulled out his phone and was reminded again of the past few days. He still couldn't believe everything that had happened. More missed texts, calls and emails were now awaiting his response. He opened his text messages first. The last text from JC was a couple of hours ago and said: Call me or I'm going to send the Coast Guard out to look for you... Seriously call me back...

To JC he wrote:

Sorry for the delay in getting back with you.

I'm fine...

I'll be out of contact for a bit longer tomorrow, but boy, do I have a story to tell you...

This will put Fastli front and center...

He hit send.

Next, he opened his email and scrolled down until he found an email from Katie.

He responded:

Katie,
My most sincere of apologies for the delay in responding.
I've been out of town and my phone was broken, but I recently got it fixed.
Anyway, I hope you're doing well and that you would still like to get together when you're back in town...

I know Texas doesn't have rainforests, but I bet we could find something similarly stimulating to do together...

Feel free to text me if you'd prefer...
My number is below...

Hope to see you soon,

Christian

He hit send and with a swooshing sound, the email left his drafts folder.

As he lay in bed in a strange town in northern Europe, a place, mind you, he never in a million years, expected to be today, thoughts and visions raced through his mind of all that he'd seen, witnessed and been part of over the past few days.
This was going to make one hell of a story.

12
The Factory

There's a moment during the descent phase of every flight aboard commercial or private aviation aircraft, when power is backed down to the point, that the current level of generated thrust and lift no longer overcome gravity and drag. This moment is normally accompanied by a mild, sinking feeling within the stomachs of anyone currently, on said flight. This feeling, of course, is the result of a sudden, precipitous drop in the plane's altitude. Had certain individuals known what was about to transpire, they too, would have witnessed a similar sinking feeling deep within their souls, only due to completely unrelated circumstances.

The paired throttle levers controlling the output of the two Rolls Royce turbofan engines have sat dormant for the better part of the past two hours. A hand reached for them and pulled them back to the line marked 25% power. The ominous whirling of spooling jet engines is an all too familiar sound to frequent air travelers. It becomes white noise after a while. Any frequent flyer can pinpoint the exact moment the descent is getting underway. The mild buzz, whining and whirling calms slightly and drops a few tones.

Then, like clockwork, said flyer gets that familiar feeling within their gut. The plane begins to descend and this phase of your miraculous journey is nearly at its' end.
Most feel that way, anyway. Not Mr. Black. He despised air travel. Had he not an urgent need, he would have spent 5 days in a tour bus, being driven across the country for an unannounced visit with his new friends in Eden. Mr. Black sat in the back row with his captain's chair angled toward the window. His view was partially blocked by the massive engine mounted just aft of his seat. He gripped the arms rests of his seat firmly, as the Gulfstream 450 began its' descent into the desert. George, Oliver and Angel sipped champagne, laughed and flirted with the flight attendants aboard this most lavish aircraft. I, the fourth member of Geosis, sat in a melancholy trance across the aisle from Mr. Black and stared, longingly out the large, oval window. She always seemed to have something bothering her.

Mr. Black took notice and swiveled his chair to face the center aisle.
"I… have I ever told you the story of how I came to join The Array?", he asked.
"… not that I know of, but I'm pretty sure you're about to …", she replied, annoyed.
"After college, I went to work for my father's investment firm. He and his colleagues took pride in making first and second year associate's lives absolute hell, for weeks on end, with round the clock work days. They would ask for analytics on every minute detail of a deal and contingencies for every feasible exit, prior to taking a position … Even though I was the son of a partner, I was not spared…"

She swiveled her chair to face his and began to pay attention.

"During the dotcom boom, there were an infinite number of internet related securities traded, each with its' own market of tradable derivatives. My father or one of the other partners would get a tip about a particular stock and would point half the associates at security analytics and the other half at the exit strategy...."

"Wait...", she said, holding her hand up to suggest he slow down, "you know I don't know what half of this stuff means, right...?"

"bear with me...", he said, "it's not important... I'm just providing color for my own sanity's sake...

I had gotten quite efficient at security analytics by this point and one afternoon, myself and several analysts were watching the clock in the hopes that this Friday afternoon stayed slow and we would get a rare out at 17:00.

At 16:15, my father came out of his office and called for the attention of the floor... he said, 'I just got off the phone with a broker and he mentioned a certain stock we need to look at... InfoSpace... it's an internet yellow pages of sorts... anybody know anything about the company?

Everyone remained silent. If someone spoke up and was wrong, our workload would double...."

By this point, Angel, George and Oliver had turned their attention to Mr. Black as well. The aboard flight attendants used this as an opportunity to disappear.

"If no one knows anything about this sucker... then let's get to work... Groans followed...

So, I started digging. A guy named Naveen Jain left Microsoft to found the company...Revenue comes from banner ads ... some HTML based chat rooms on the platform... growing user base... seemingly low cost of acquisition of user... merged with another dotcom recently...

After doing some digging, I found some creative accounting entries resulting in irregularities that grossly overstated revenue... But since the market hadn't noticed it yet, it was still in play...

So, I took a straightforward strategy and recommended a buy up until about $650 a share, anticipating others jumped in when the float evaporated, with a planned exit at $1,050, we could go to the partners. I walked into my father's office and told him my recommendation...

He looked up at me and said, 'Why didn't you say anything a minute ago?'
'What do you mean?' I said.

He told me, 'There's no way you did all that research already... it's been like 5 minutes... '

I looked at my watch as confusion began to set in. I, then, turned and walked back to my desk, baffled. It had felt as if I had spent three or four hours researching the ticker, but in all reality, it had been 6 minutes. That's the first time I realized my blessing... by complete accident. Needless to say, we made considerable commissions on that trade and nearly all of the subsequent ones that followed. My father put me on some of our niche, higher net worth client accounts after that. Most of the time, when we had clients visit the office it would be buy side clients hoping to overhear a conversation about a trade or professional money manager types milking their expense account, but almost never any of the old world, old money clients.

On one random Tuesday, one of our most obscure, old money clients came into the office. My father's partner addressed the floor and demanded we be on our absolute best behavior. If I can recall, I believe he even sent one analyst home to change clothes because he didn't like the suit he was wearing.

I was doing analyses for every trade on this particular client's account by this point and had still never met anyone from the organization in person. From the moment he walked in, virtually everyone remained eyes forward, glued to their monitors. The client shook a few hands, then disappeared into my father's office with the other partners.
The entire time they were in my father's office, I felt as if a pair of eyes had been staring down upon me. There I sat, building CFP models and it was as if the world had stopped or time had slowed to a crawl and I were its' only occupant. The next thing I knew, this man was standing over me. He said to me in an embracing voice...

'My name is Chartón ... I know who... and what ... you are...',

I sat, confused, staring and pondering what he had meant.
Suddenly, the most beautifully elegant brunette woman appeared next to him and said, 'come work with us... you're wasting your talents here...'.

And just as suddenly, they both were gone. From that point forward, I felt that something was missing... something else was out there I was supposed to be doing and I had to find out what it was.

I stood up, walked into my father's office and after a long pause, I relieved myself of my position, walked back to my desk, collected my belongings and took no additional time exiting the premises.

145

I walked outside of the revolving doors of his high-rise office building in lower Manhattan. A black town car sat idling just outside the door. The rear window slowly rolled down and inside sat, the woman I had seen just moments before. She motioned for me to approach the car and I did so, the passenger side door opened.

I climbed into the seat next to her and closed the door. I looked at her and said, 'What did he mean... I know what you are?' She slowly turned toward me and spoke,
'Chadwick... You'll soon have all the answers to questions you couldn't even have thought to ask...'
We drove for a bit, then arrived at another non-descript uptown building. That was the last time I saw my father.

I was taught everything I know about what we are and where we've come from, by him... and her.

I have been alongside Chartón and The Array ever since. I have never looked back."

The plane had landed several minutes ago and was currently taxiing toward the dusty, old decrepit hanger.

Outside the airplane, the hanger doors had begun to open and Aerik stepped out into the sandy air, his wings stretched high above his head. Flanked to his right, stood Titus, Eden's head of security.
Titus was a Kinetic, actually a Titanus to be precise. At birth, he was blessed with the natural ability to increase his height and body mass, at will. Historically, Titanae Masters have achieved heights of one hundred feet and thousands of pounds but for The Augs, their blessings alone had never been enough.

Titus stands eight feet, nine inches and weighs three hundred, ninety-two pounds. He is surprisingly flexible and nimble for his size. He appears to be of Latin descent, with a dark toned skin, his hair styled in a shortly-cropped mohawk and usually wore clothing consisting mainly of camouflage, in some form. In addition to being possibly the planet's largest creature to walk on two feet, his right hand and forearm have been mummified with cobalt steel, complete with four shiny metal lugs across the knuckles of the hand and fused strategically along the forearm.

His left arm was a different story completely. His left hand was missing altogether. In its' place, what looked similar to the square connector of a socket wrench. This adapter was made of metal and had been fused directly to his left wrist. It allowed for incorporation and utilization of "attachments". He currently had a large metal half-sphere attached. On the flat face of the appendage was painted, a white smiley face.

The two stood, facing the jet as it taxied toward the hanger. Instead of pulling inside as usual, the Gulfstream came to a stop on the tarmac and its' air stairs, lowered.

George, Angel and Oliver were the first down the stairs. George instantly began to size up Titus. Oliver and Angel flanked George on both sides, standing as if ready for a fight. Chadwick walked down the stairs next, followed by I.

Aerik walked out to greet the visitors. George took a few steps toward Aerik and Titus matched his efforts.

"Easy Gentlemen...", Chadwick said, "we're all friends here..."

Noticing the feathered wings of the man approaching, he said, "Ahh... you must be Aerik...", extending his hand. Aerik returned the gesture and the two shook hands for the first time.

"Yes, and you must be Mr. Black... it's an honor to finally meet you...", Aerik said with his usual charming smile, "and who might this be?", he said, as his gaze settled on I. He took a step toward her. She looked up at him and simply said, "...it's I..."

"I... like the letter? is that short for something? Maybe... Ingrid the Peaceful or Iana, the beautiful flower?", he asked.

"Close... it's Iahu ... the exalted dove...", she responded, with a brief and awkwardly forced smile.

"Your name is Iahu? How are we just now finding this out?", Oliver commented while Angel and George look on, perplexed. They have known her for years and all she's ever told them about herself was that her name was I.
"Many times, it's not about how many times you ask a question, but the method in which you do so...", she responded, all the while her eyes remained locked on Aerik's.

"May I?", Aerik asked as he turned, stood at her side and offering the crook of his arm to her.

She slid her hand beneath and gently laid it along his forearm.
The group filed into the hanger as the doors closed behind them.

The inside of the hanger was beginning to resemble a Hoarder's episode. Piles upon piles of stuff had been accumulating within the hanger for years. If all went well, there would be no need to collect this junk anymore. That's what Paul had bet the farm on, anyway.

Chadwick quipped, "Man... you guys ever think about maybe, having a garage sale...?"

This resulted in chuckles from Angel, George, Oliver and even a brief one from the perpetually mission-focused Titus. Aerik and Iahu were in their own little world, completely consumed with one another's company, as she began to feel the effects of Bliss. Aerik's flattery and light flirting did little to aid in fending it off.

The group of seven walked toward the back of the hanger where several limousine golf carts waited to drive them down the tunnels into Eden. The entertainment for the evening was none other than the world-renowned Tiesto. His hypnotic beats and melodic rhythms could be heard as soon as the golf carts began down the decline and into the tunnels.

After a short ten-minute ride, and Bliss taking hold, the four golf carts emerged into the cavern. The sight of spotlights casting their wares across the cavern's roof, the smell of fog machines and echoing sounds of electronica, filled the catacombs. The carts pulled around to the side entrance and her esteemed guests filed inside, up the back stairwell, and into Paul's balcony. Tonight, was one of Eden's famous theme parties. Officially, it is White Lingerie under Black Light but neon wigs and body paint were making their presence felt this evening, as well.
Eden is almost always a closed door, invite only, highly exclusive type of party, but in this occasion, Paul was feeling generous. In an effort to spur up interest and attendance, he decided to invite the YouTube celebrity and influencer @shland to live stream the Tiesto set, the night's events and interview partygoers. After all, if this reactor worked as expected, they'd need the place packed, daily to extract enough Divinium to meet StoneCorp's quota and skim more than their fair share, off the top.

So, by now, we all know that the human body attracts and retains Divinium. Because humans don't possess Divinine within their DNA, it cannot be utilized within the body as it lies dormant, but it can be harvested from them. It's a painless process and completely unnoticeable to the humans being farmed.

When a human's body temperature rises, the heart begins to beat faster, beginning efforts, by the body, to circulate blood faster, to deliver more nutrients to the cells in compensation for the incrementally increased caloric burn. This results in dilation of the blood vessels as well as more and more calories are being burned, resulting in heat release or perspiration, resulting in the perpetuation of this cycle, until the source of increased caloric burn is removed from the equation.

Divinium, albeit a minute amount, is easily collected from a human being during any secretion of bodily fluids, such as perspiration, saliva, blood or various other methods. If a perspiring human gets within close proximity to Divinium Elegon, the Divinium is attracted to it, as if it had been magnetized. In a sense, it has. Since its current host has become active, the Divinium reacts to the changes in its environment and becomes agitated and receptive to influence or issuing influence on its' immediate surroundings. While it may seem like the essence is being manipulated by said surrounding matter or environment, this is a different phenomenon altogether. It's actually reacting to the stimulation of said environmental changes and not the matter, itself.

So, now that we all understand that concept, The Array's plan was simple. The Augs throw epic parties by nature. They are to continue to do so, StoneCorp is to build and deploy a network of drone camera systems, controlled by an online platform that broadcasts the feeds and provides online users the ability to "pay to party", by metered control of a specific camera drone. This serves multiple purposes. Incrementally, it drives revenue and at the same time, drives demand amongst online users to subsequently, join the party, IRL, by giving them a first-hand view of what they're missing out on.

The cameras themselves were built on platforms made of Divinium Elegon. As the user buzzes the drone above and around the dance floor or elsewhere within Eden, it's constantly collecting small amounts of Divinium on each pass. The longer and closer it hovers to the crowds, the more Divinium it can collect. Hence, the pay to party plan.

It's expected that users will focus the camera feeds on beautiful men or women, which, at Eden, tend to center within more densely populated areas of the dance floors or other private areas. Higher density equals more people. More people, equals more body heat, equals more sweat, equals more collectible Divinium on each pass.

Once the Elegon plate is filled to capacity, the "pay to party", control feed ends and goes dark to the user. The drones are programmed to immediately return to the collection reactor, where it docks in an enclosed space, and inside, the Divinium is collected, stabilized, processed, inventoried, then packaged for transport. In initial estimates, it was projected a twenty-drone system would be sufficient and optimal. Any system with a drone count of higher than twenty, may begin to have psychological impacts on Eden's crowds and on the hypothesized socio-dynamics at play, resulting in disruptions in herd clustering and inefficient collection runs.

Ever heard of the proverb, less is more or the theory of demand by exclusivity? This is the foundational principle of this system's design. Collection estimates, given Eden's potential capacity of 5,000 guests, production could exceed 250 to 300 grams of solidified Divinium, per 12-hour collection time frame. While this is not a large amount, over time, collection methods are expected to gain in efficiency and effectiveness and with an increase of new arrivals and first-time guests to Eden, ripe and previously unharvested humans should result in higher yields, per guest.

Chadwick entered the balcony first, dressed in his usual, tailored suit, impeccably perfect bow tie, pocket square and shoes. Tonight, he wore red tinted sunglasses for no other reason that he thought, it looked cool.

"Well, well, well... Paul Bradley... in the flesh...", Chadwick said, cheerfully.

"That voice... you must be the notorious ... Mr. Black... how are you my
old friend?", Paul said as he rose from his seat. Paul was in Indi tonight. He
was dressed similarly to Chadwick except his face and hair was almost
identical in appearance to none other than actor Richard Armitage as
seen in the recent, gender friendly, reboot of Ocean's 8, the near polar
opposite of his appearance in movie adaptation of The Hobbit Trilogy.
His seat was overlooking the floor, now filled to the brim, with partygoers,
all gyrating in unison, through a sea of glowing foam, fog and flashing
lights. @shlands' video crew could be spotted weaving throughout the
crowd, interviewing random and uniquely dressed partygoers and
celebrities, while capturing wide shots of Eden's perpetual hedonistic
debauchery. By the brain trust's estimates, this live stream should serve as
the online equivalent of an adrenaline shot directly into the chest cavity
of Mr. Black, Paul Bradley and Brandon Stone's master plan.

In the center of the dance floor, perched on a small platform with a
spotlight affixed on him, stood Gryffin, the Gaian Aug. Gryffin was unique
as he was the only Aug to have used Indi to merge himself with another
being. In this case, an ancient vintage of Viniated Snapdragon, taken
from one of the original Omnician cities. The moment he bonded his body
with the plant, it gained consciousness and has claimed from that
moment forth, its' name to be Emba. Every evening, Gryffin's skin
"blooms", illuminated flowers that light up whatever room he occupies. He
stood in the center of the dance floor, moving to the beats while
hundreds of guests stared at him in awe of his rare and undeniable
beauty. Gryffin loved the attention. @shland and his camera crew were
briefed prior to taking the floor, to not focus their cameras on Gryffin for
longer than a few moments at a time. Some things of Eden need to stay
exclusive to Eden, was their explanation.
"How was the flight...?", Paul continued.

"I'm not too fond of air travel, but the accommodations were as
impressive as to be expected. Needless to say, we need to speak...
preferably, somewhere a slightly more... quiet...", Chadwick replied,
motioning toward the hall from which they entered. Paul obliged and the
two left their entourages on the balcony, walked down the stairs and into
a hallway lit by dimmed LED lighting, along the floor, leading toward the
backstage area of the facility. They approached a door and Paul pressed
his thumb onto a scanner. It clicked, then buzzed and he pushed the door
open. Paul's office was a large, dark room that was unusually deep. At
the back of the room sat a dense dark stained wooden desk. Along the
walls of either side of the room were rows and rows of obscure works of
art, centered around a floor to ceiling sized canvas of a completely nude
and artistically posed, brunette woman. She looked familiar but Chadwick
couldn't immediately associate a name with a face. Behind the desk, a
high back executive leather chair sat in front of a wall of glass, looking
onto and level with, the lively dance floor. A set of matching, high back

guest chairs sat in front of his desk. Just inside and to the right of the door, lay an old and colorful Moroccan rug, on which, sat a knee height conversation table, flanked by a seating area that appeared to accommodate about six. The entire room was lit by dimmed, colored LED lighting hanging from the ceiling, each pointed at the artwork and a dimmed floor lamp sat back in the corner.

"Come in ... have a seat...", Paul said, as he collapsed into one of the couches, "can I get you something?"

"I'll have a bottle of water, if you please...", Mr. Black responded.

"Sorry man, no bottles...we're green like that...", he responded, motioning to a bowl on the table in the middle of the seating area. It was chilled from sitting atop an ice block and filled with clear spheres. Each were a consumable bubble of spring water from the Nordic region and each were marked with a frosty white stamp of one of six Nordic mythological symbols. Most in the bowl were emblazoned with The Helm of Awe, Thor's Hammer, The Valknut, The Svenfnthorn or The Vegvisir. It seemed as if someone had already picked out of all the Swasticas.

"Paul, where are you on the reactor?", Chadwick asked.
"it's up... the drones seem to work... we ran a few tests and it collected, albeit much less than Brandon initially forecasted... all in all, I think it'll work... we just need to make every party bigger and better than the last...", Paul replied, popping one the Thor's Hammer spheres into his mouth, followed by an awkwardly muffled, gushing sound.

"Good, what did your test run yield?", he asked.

"We ran five drones on manual during one of the up-tempo sets earlier... We were nowhere near capacity by the way...", Paul continued as he leaned in, closer to Mr. Black.

"Two passes with each drone, which took about 2 minutes each, and if I'm not mistaken, we collected just less than .23 grams or 22.92..."

Mr. Black interrupted, "I know the conversion to milligrams... That seems light... like half what I calculated we should be able to collect...", he said, critically.
"I know, but we're not at capacity, the ambient temperature down here cools quickly when the party isn't prime, so to speak... Plus, I'm not positive of the collection patterns the drones are programmed to fly on manual... online user control may end up getting closer to the herds..."

"Whatever...", Chadwick said, then leaned in toward Paul. The thumping sound from the dance floor could still be heard through the glass, albeit, much more faintly inside his office.

"Can you close that?", he said, pointing at the glass windows. Paul reached over and grabbed a tablet sitting on the table. With a few clicks, large, dense blackout curtains began lowering from the window's upper frame. With every approaching inch toward the stained concrete, rug covered floor, the penetrating sounds muffled more and more, until the curtains reached the ground and the room was silent.

"So...", Chadwick said, in a voice barely above a whisper, "my apologies for keeping you in the dark for this long, but I assure it was for good reason."

"What now...?", Paul replied, mildly untrusting and seemingly growing angrier and potentially belligerent, by the second.

"Calm down... it's nothing.", he assured him, "I needed you to appear mildly desperate in your dealings with Brandon Stone... I wanted him to sense weakness in you, improving the probability he'll fight hard enough to convince his board to dedicate the necessary resources to this plan and ultimately, ensure it comes to fruition. You performed, splendidly."

Paul was visibly angry at this point.

"We're not giving Divinium to the humans to sell... I've got something else in mind for them... and Brandon Stone is going push this preverbal boulder up and over the mountain for us.

He plans on revealing Divinium to the world at their annual StoneCon shareholders meeting, next month. It's there, I will be the bearer of unfortunate news, that we've decided that the price we've agreed upon, is no longer valid and acquisition of the material, he'll soon be completely dependent upon, just became price inefficient for him to acquire. If I'm right, and let's be honest, I always am... he will take the bait and immediately plot revenge on us all. If he's as successful as I suspect he'll be, he will ultimately succeed in turning the entire human race against us.

That's when we show the human race that they've actually been living amongst the gods they've so eloquently worshipped all these years... that this has always been our world, we're taking back control and they'll finally be forced to realize their true role within the universe... that they amount to nothing more than a resource... they are batteries."

Paul's anger has since subsided and was replaced with a tinge of fear, when he looked into the maddening eyes of Mr. Black. He was too far along the path now to show any objection. He said, "What about Omni Proper? They'll never go along with this..."

"They'll have no choice. When man is threatened, they lash out, irrationally... they'll defend themselves against the threat by going on the offensive. Don't forget, humans outnumber us 3 million to one. Alanis and

152

Gados and Alixandria will defend themselves and be forced to join in our cause... not because they want to but, because the enemy of my enemy and all...", Chadwick said, completely convinced his plan was flawless.

Paul had no choice but to agree. He closed his eyes, took a deep breath, then slowly leaned back onto the couch. He sighed, then opened his eyes and said,
"Dude... not cool to use me like you did, but we're with you...
Maybe the humans will kill off enough of those pretentious Alanis bastards, that we can take our home back...", he said.

"That's what I wanted to hear...", Mr. Black concluded.

StoneCorp had received production counts from today's tests, directly from the sensors throughout the collection system and reactor. The initial opinions of production were adequate. They weren't blown away or anything, but at least they had a baseline, by which to set expectations. In a conversation with Paul, Tamara knew Tiesto was to perform and @shland would be live streaming the event. Seems like a perfect time to test their socio-dynamic assumptions, on which this entire plan was built, she thought.

They picked up the live stream feed from @shland's Instagram and re-broadcasted it on every site they owned. They used a crudely coded pop up window to host the feed, making it easier to sell the story that Anonymous had hacked their network and was responsible for the interruption it caused, to their corporate and government customers. Plausible deniability, all things considered, you know?

The stream went live and the plan was put in place. @shland's face, awkward and jerky, hand-held camera feed, along with the feed of his primary camera crew was posted smack dab in the center of StoneCorp's corporate site. It did, indeed, drive eyeballs. Celebrities, athletes and other well to do rich kids floated, one after another, into Ash's live stream, praising the masterful execution of Eden's hedonistic personality.

CNBC picked up coverage and once that happened, it went viral. Ashland Hobson's Instagram follower count quadrupled in a matter of hours. This turned out to be a win-win for all parties involved. Ashland grew his subscriber base exponentially, The Augs would be almost assured of increased demand for new admittance and the ability to charge more for nearly everything, and StoneCorp, well, they made out best of all. Usually, launching a new product or service is almost always a cash drain because there is normally an extended period of financial losses after a launch, while initial research and launch costs are recouped. They just launched the product and solidified a market overnight, at the low cost of twenty minutes of a coder's hourly rate and a few dollars added to the company's electric bill.

Several hours later, Mr. Black's Gulfstream 450 picked up speed as it knifed its' way through the dry desert air. The moment the wings generated the appropriate amounts of lift, the plane's nose rose from the dusty strip and the entire aircraft lifted off of the decrepit runway. As it blasted into the sky, Mr. Black, slightly more relaxed but still not a huge fan of air travel, stared out the window and watched the air field began to shrink, then fade away into the desert sands. Another component of his plan has gone off as planned. The endgame is getting closer but there is still a very dangerous variable in play, and he expected it would soon, require his undivided attention.

Across the aisle, Iahu sat, with her captain's chair angled toward the window. She, too, seemed different as she watched the airfield fade away, hand pressed against the window, but for an entirely different reason.

13

WatchMaker

Christian wasn't able to get much sleep that night. It wasn't so much, the bed or the room or even the unfamiliar smells in the air that kept him awake, as much as it was the sense of dread for tomorrow. What new and terrible things would he witness, or worse, have done to him once this trek to London starts at sunrise.

A conversation last night led to a change in plans. No longer would they seek to reach English shores by way of ferry. For whatever reason, they decided to find alternate means. It was a half day, at best, train ride from Copenhagen to London and it wasn't as easy as getting on a train and sleeping your way on to jolly ole London. Flying would have been much easier but they didn't have anonymous access to a plane at the moment and they sure as shit weren't going to risk commercial air travel, given the heightened level of security after the San Juan incident a couple of weeks ago.

The most direct route went through Hamburg, Cologne, Brussels, then on to London by way of the Chunnel, with no less than twenty stops in between. That's twenty opportunities for someone to spot them and twenty opportunities for something to go wrong.

Elijah began to stir first, well before the sun rose. He was careful not to wake the lot when he rose from his bed and slipped out the door. At the opposite end of the hall, behind an unmarked door, was another set of stairs that lead up to the ground floor and directly outside. Elijah took those stairs. It was cold and windy but the elements never seemed to bother him much. He stood with his face into the chilly morning wind and watched as the sun turned the eastern sky from black to blue, then painted the horizon with its' fiery wares, making note of each sound and every scent carried on the breeze. He had a feeling deep inside, that this may well be the last time he enjoys the sights and sounds of home for quite some time.

Penelope was next to wake. She sat up, yawned and stretched her arms high above her head. As she looked around the room, she noticed Elijah's absence. She knew exactly where he had gone. He was always more at home in the elements. As she rose and prepared for the day ahead, Blake was awoken by the subtle sound of a belt buckle clacking across the concrete floor. He too, then began to rise.

"You guys are up early…", Christian said, in his softest early morning voice.

"Elijah is going to want to get out of here pretty quickly.", Penny responded.

"Good…", he replied, "I haven't been able to sleep anyway."

He threw the blanket covering him to the side and put his bare feet onto the cold floor. Moments later, the three were dressed and making their exit. The sun had yet to fully rise as Penny scanned the room one last time. She spotted Elijah's belongings in the corner and grabbed them. The three took the stairwell up and joined Elijah outside. There, he stood, eyes closed and shirtless, his senses one with the northern wind.

"Put this on before you freeze to death!", Penny said.

He took another couple of deep breaths and obliged her request. After a quick walk back through the lobby and a farewell to the staff, they exited through the front door and made their way to the train station. The sun still hadn't yet fully risen but Penny already wore her sunglasses. While this may look odd at six am, it was quite necessary. If they were to get into a tight spot with the locals or law enforcement during this journey, she would be the one to manifest them out of trouble. As her eyes glow vivid purple when she manifests, she didn't want risk an unintended bystander noticing and things escalating from there. Despite the glow, her blessing is ideal for dealing with conflicts involving humans and would most definitely cause the least amount of collateral damage.
Blake walked by her side all the way to the train station.

"So, why do you go by Blake?", she asked.

"My mom suggested it… plus, Alessandro starts too many conversations…", he said.

"You must really miss her…", Penny said, somberly.

"I do…", he replied, appreciative of her empathy.

The sun was well into the sky when Penny first stepped onto the train platform. Every few moments she would glance to the west in hopes of seeing a train rounding the bend. The train platform was a quick stop for the eastbound trains on their way into Copenhagen and it was just that, a platform cut in half by railroad tracks. There were no creature comforts, no vending machines and no cover from the elements. They were exposed right now and there was no way of knowing who or what knew their current location, intent or destination, as of this exact moment.

A few arduous moments later, a commuter train rounded the bend and approached the platform. With a series of creaks, hisses and squeals, the train came to a stop and the doors opened. The four boarded and found a relatively isolated and unoccupied section of the train. A few dozen sounds later, the train doors closed and it began to continue eastward, one step closer to Copenhagen' Central Station.
The cabin attendant approached Penny and Blake.

"Tickets please,", she said in a monotone, repetitive and unenthusiastic cadence.

Behind her sunglasses, an almost completely obscured but nonetheless faint purple glow began to show.

"We need to purchase through Central.", She said casually, in her best Dutch accent. Due to her manifesting, the attendant heard, "we nodig hebben on tickets via het central stations te kopen...", in classic Dutch. She didn't want to attract attention or invite additional conversation by speaking English or Norwegian.

"Hoeveel?", the attendant replied.

"Drie volwassenen, een kind...", she replied with a grin and a glance toward Elijah. He overheard her response, turned and glared at her.

The attendant pulled out a tablet and with a few clicks on the screen, replied, "vierendertig euro alsjeblieft..."

Penny pulled out a nondescript credit card from her back pocket. Omnicians are early adopters of manmade technology in general, but they took a special interest and adopted, in mass, the internet when it became more widely accessible, simply for its' provided anonymity. This particular card was issued by EasyLife Financial, one of the many generic online banks. She's completely content with the idea of never having to look a bank employee in the eye and explain the source of her funds, or worse, her spending habits.

The train rolled down the tracks with the occasional jerk and shimmy, stopping every few kilometers as it continued to pick up commuting workers and tourists on its' morning trip into Copenhagen. The cars continued to fill with unfamiliar faces and Penny became more anxious and even more observant. Once they arrived at Central Station and the mainline was underway, there would be no more stops and less chance of being spotted by a less than friendly someone.

They say ignorance is bliss, and in this case they're right. Blake and Christian weren't aware of the rather unpleasant encounter Penelope and Elijah recently had with The Array. Prior to the Celestial Order being decimated, their last act had been to send Penelope on a mission to investigate San Juan and hopefully, find the chosen one.

Being one not to turn down an adventure, Elijah volunteered to escort her on her journey as a personal favor to her father. Before departing Alanis, her father and the rest of the elders briefed her on what she may come up against. In the middle of the night, just hours before she was to begin her journey, her father and the remaining elders pulled her from her slumber and explained to her that they had learned The Array had a Chrono and that he already knew the who and what she was to be in search of. If she caught even a scent of his presence, to disappear. While there may very well be other members of the Celestial Order scattered amongst other Omnician cities, after the recent events in Alanis, she considered herself to be the last one left.

Little did The Array know however, that The Celestials had already found what they had been looking for and The Chosen One, along with two thirds of the Trivium were currently in route to starting a series of chain events that, once started, would bring about the realization of the prophecy.

Once the train arrived at the station in Valby, she could relax a bit. After that, there were few stops, with most passengers exiting the train for various downtown destinations. The train stopped at Carlsberg, then directly into Central Station. As the train pulled under the overhang and into the main terminal of Central Station, Penny let out a sigh of relief. Dealing with a Chrono was a serious matter. At least that's what she remembered as one of the major lessons from Precept school when she was a child. Supposedly, they could feel back or forward in time and if they could find your whereabouts at a specific time or place, they could be there waiting for you. The idea of just going about your day, and finding a waiting chrono somewhere along your path, always caused Penny worry. She could almost empathize with Pacirus' transcendence deeming all chrono and adaptive newborns a threat and to be destroyed on discovery. Almost.

The cars turned dark as the train pulled into the station. The four exited and disappeared into the busy station. Penny and Elijah would purchase the tickets direct to London. Blake and Christian were to get some refreshments and other sundries for the long train ride ahead. Fourteen minutes later, the loudspeaker called final boarding to London for the fifteen-hour train ride. Penny and Elijah purchased a cabin to provide a little extra cover and security. After finding their cabin and taking their seats, Christian drew the shades on the glass door leading out into the aisle, which dimmed the cabin slightly. They could now relax, kick back and actually enjoy the ride, for once. Christian smiled in disbelief as he had an amusing thought run through his head. Without a passport and having not spent one single dollar on travel, he has visited two European counties, and is about to pass through several more. He began to worry slightly, as he had absolutely no idea how he would end up getting back into the United States after all this was over.

He leaned against the stained wood window frame and attempted to get some rest, despite the lively and spirited conversation Penny, Blake and Elijah were having about what awaited them in London.

Chronos are both equally, fascinating and terrifying creatures. By definition, a Chrono is an Omnician blessed with the ability to manipulate the timeline. In practice, however, they are a much different animal. Most documented Chronos have never adequately mastered the blessing and as such, supplement their inability to manipulate the timeline, with speed. While most can impact the timeline directly around themselves, they lack the ability to project the blessing further than a few feet outward and so they couple that with precise and efficient movements, giving the illusion of greater manifestation. This lack of understanding comes from a lack of knowledge and training for Chronos, due fully to The Transcendence of Pacirus. In his transcendence, Pacirus proclaimed all Adaptives and Chronos too dangerous to be allowed to live and as such, any were to be destroyed when discovered at their Trial of Blessings. Hence, the knowledge was lost to the ages. Except it wasn't. It was documented and preserved in secret by a certain faction of Omnicians as a safeguard against corrupt and tyrannical rule. These ancient documents could teach a gifted chrono how to read and manipulate the timeline.

Basically, it teaches that time is nothing more than sequential, binary interactions of matter. That's all. One moment, an oxygen atom is touching a carbon atom. Then the next, it's not. That, in a nutshell folks, is time. Explaining the "how", is a bit more complicated, but here goes. A quantum point of view states that matter is not binary, but it exists as is and as it could or could not be, simultaneously. While this has been proven to be true, in a sense, it's inclusionary in nature. The problem is that this is an accumulative view and as a result, includes something that should, first, be dis-included. The opposite of something is not nothing, but something else. It's In the previously mentioned nothing where we find the key to the Chrono blessing. All matter impacts other matter, except when it doesn't. It's in this state of space that the interaction of matter is recorded, so to speak, and with proper training, a Chrono can follow these interactions, much like how a bloodhound follows the trail of a scent and effectively, 'see' back in time. Theoretically, depending on the method and skill level of the Chrono, he or she may be able to see interactions that have yet come to pass.

Throughout the ages, this faction waited for a worthy Chrono to emerge and for ages, one did not, until Ocedeus.

Most people have experienced déjà vu or one of the lesser known déjà vecu, déjà senti or déjà visite. The former, of course being feelings of familiarity within a specific new experience. The others, event specific, feeling specific and an inexplicable understanding of a new place, respectively. These phenomena, as defined by man, are abnormalities associated with subconscious or stored memory. The Omnicians, however know what they really are. When a chrono is following a trail throughout time, the chrono 'reads' the timeline in reverse, inherently following each atom to the next by using these interaction records as a guide. As he or she reads, the Divinine within the Chrono's cells, in a sense, feels this matter, and in turn, the Chrono witnesses what the matter has witnessed. It physically and mentally exhausts the Chrono to read for a prolonged period of time or over considerable distances.

Long story short, when you feel déjà vu or a similar feeling, even something as innocent as a shiver up your spine, know that somewhere within your body exists an atom that is part of the blockchain, if you will, that a chrono is currently reading. If he or she is mediocre at best, yes, they can see what you see, hear what you hear and, even know what you're thinking. I told you it was both fascinating and terrifying.

The train was ten hours underway at this point and nearing Cologne, Germany. The initial commotion created by the Omnicians within the cabin, had long since subsided. After a long nap and a few hours of trying to find something to do, Christian took out his phone, ignored the ever-growing list of missed calls and texts and opted instead, for the notes app. Occasionally, he would jot down ideas for articles or to do lists. He began jotting down some of the extraordinary things he had seen over the past few weeks, beginning with Geosis and The Lost City of Dalus. As he clicked away on the screen, Elijah began to notice the furious pace of his typing.

For the entirety of the trip, soft piano music had been playing over the intercom speakers throughout the train cars. Mendelssohn's Book 2 No.6 was in its' fourth bar. Before he could ask about the novel Christian seemed to be writing, he noticed Christian's facial expression change from intent focus and concentration, to one that suggested someone just dragged their fingernails down a nearby chalkboard. Immediately afterwards, he looked out the window as if he had no idea of his surroundings.

Unsure if it was the change in his facial expression or the lightning fast pace at which he typed but Elijah immediately recognized what was happening, or at the least he feared what he suspected. Before Christian could turn his head to look around inside the cabin, Elijah grabbed Christian's hoodie and tossed it toward his face. It opened in midair, then landed, completely covering Christian's head. The movement caught Penny's attention and in response, she laughed. Elijah turned and looked at Penelope, his facial expression suggesting something sinister was afoot. She immediately understood his demeanor prepared for the potential coming onslaught. Christian reached up and pulled the covering from his face to see an empty cabin. He continued to glance around for a moment. He squinted his eyes while his eyeballs darted quickly and acutely underneath. He shook his head as if he were fighting off sleep, while driving the dead man's shift on a cross country road trip. He immediately noticed Elijah and Penelope both staring at him, Penny's violet glow protruding from behind her sunglasses and along her hands and forearms.

"Whoa, that was weird... ", Christian said, "... déjà vu..."

Elijah shot Penny a quick look and returned his gaze toward Christian. "What do you mean?", he said.

"You know... déjà vu... like, when you get the feeling like you're witnessing something again, but it's actually the first time?", he replied.

"Are you still feeling like that?", Penny asked, as the violet glow in her eyes began to dissipate.

"No... I just got the chills for a second, then looked out the window and could have sworn I'd been here before... It's gone now...", he responded.

Penelope looked at Elijah, fearing the worse. Blake was oblivious to the current happenings as he had been sleeping soundly this whole time, in his seat across the cabin. It was now painfully obvious that The Array, indeed, had a Chrono and it seemed that they were either getting lucky or close with their efforts. If Elijah and Penny could fend off The Array until London and find what she thinks they will at WatchMaker, then it doesn't matter if they find them or what happens to her afterwards. She would have fulfilled her Celestial Oath and brought about the coming of the next Adaptive.

For a moment, Elijah and Penny entertained the idea of getting off the train and finding an alternate, previously undetermined mode of transport, but with less than four hours left, they ultimately decided that less delay in getting into the Chunnel was the best option. The train passed through Cologne with no additional incident and no further signs of Array surveillance. At this point, Elijah thought it best to keep Christian in the dark about what had happened. No need to bring additional factors into the equation. If the Chrono had found them, then they surely would have had a fight on their hands by now. As Brussels approached then passed, the collective spirit within the cabin lightened.

In Copenhagen, Elijah had insisted on getting Eurostar exchange tickets so that the train continued on through the Chunnel without stopping, all without the four even having to open the cabin door. Blake was awake by the time the train rounded the corner near Vieux Coquelles and began it's decent under the English Channel. Once the train entered the tunnel, they were essentially home free. Elijah smiled and let out a sigh of relief as the light coming into the cabin's windows began to dim the moment the train entered the concrete tunnel and then, disappeared completely out of sight.

Twenty-three minutes later the train emerged from under Castle Hill and roared through the English countryside. It was now a comparatively, short ride to the end of the line on the north side of Old London. Elijah was the only one of the four that had ever been to England. As the train continued its' final leg, Christian stared out the window, soaking up the sight of a strange land. He knew he wouldn't get time to site see like he did in San Juan, so he took it in nonetheless, while he knew he could.

Lush, green fields filled the landscape as they inched ever closer to London's north side. A thought entered Christians mind. How could the UK remain this way when the majority of the US is covered in concrete? His conclusion is that some remain net positive while others, net negative, on the grand scale of give versus take. This wasn't a new thought to him but it began to make him increasingly sick to his stomach, as he was reminded of the fact that he's a native to one of the greatest society of consumers and takers history has ever seen. Hell, the entire country he calls home was stolen from its native inhabitants.

The train passed through Ashford, then Gravesend, then under the River Thames. So much history sat just outside the train's windows, as Christian stared, motionless. The train passed through the Eastern outskirts of London and once the train entered Queen Elizabeth Olympic Park, Elijah began to collect his belongings. Christian thought to himself that he was probably just getting antsy.

The train continued closer to the station and as it approached Highbury Corner and then under the Famous Cock, it disappeared into the London Underground. Moments later the train slowed to a stop and completing its' 14-hour trek from Denmark. The conductor began traipsing throughout the cars, providing instruction for passengers on where to pick up luggage and where to pass through customs.

Most passengers were lined up to exit the train and continue their adventures but the shades were still drawn on the door to cabin 23. The conductor knocked once, then grabbed the knob and opened the cabin door, fully expecting to see a couple, or more, drunken passengers engaged in the throes of passion. Instead, was an empty cabin, with the exception of a single, empty bag of Skittles sitting in the center of the aft bench seat. Confused, the conductor checked his manifest again, then shrugged his shoulders and continued on to the next cabin, clearing the train.

Directly below The Famous Cock, there's a bend in the train line, just as it enters the underground system and every train must slow to avoid derailing into the turn. Many still don't know but this has been a major smuggling entry point into London for decades. Elijah instructed the others to gather their belongings and the four quietly exited to the rear of the train car, through the passthrough door, then out the service hatch to the car junction coupler. As the train slowed, the four simply stepped off the train and into the tunnel. Nearby is a certain door that will continue to remain unnamed. They knocked a specified number of times, spoke the words, "I just flew into town and man, are my arms tired.", The door was opened and allowed the four inside a pitch-black room. Seconds later, the floor began to rotate under their feet. As it did so, a torch lit pathway began to emerge from left side of this circular room. This pathway led on for two hundred meters or so until it emerges from a cream-colored building, through a nondescript door, directly onto Upper Street.

London is an intriguing city with loads of history, both documented and secret. Many know of the underground projects that have happened over the centuries, building out one of the world's most complex subterranean infrastructures. This interesting city even has an old river that

163

flows through it, above ground. Surely, London still keeps some secrets from prying eyes. One of those secrets is WatchMaker.

Off a side road, around the corner, through an unmarked door, down a flight of stairs and hidden well from plain view, is the front entrance to Watchmaker. The most exclusive and least well-known chronologist in the world has its lone shoppe and manufacturing facility somewhere near the intersection of Knightsbridge and Brompton Road. WatchMaker makes classic, old style chronographs, available from a large selection of metals and leather bands and each require the daily use of a winder box, which is included in the insanely high prices of each and every timepiece. The doors are locked, so even if you can find the entrance, you can't just go in and browse. WatchMaker is by invitation and appointment only. The store makes about seventy-five watches per year, with a lifetime warranty, first option of buyback and a starting price tag of just over £85,000. If you are an individual lucky enough to get invited for an appointment to WatchMaker, that's when the real fun starts.

The inside of the shoppe is painted a dark forest green, with dark stained hard woods throughout but is kept with immaculate care. Most patrons are chauffeured to and from the shoppe via a black Bentley Flying Spur. Most of the badging has been removed from the car with the exception of a small titanium WatchMaker logo affixed to the vehicle's grille. This car ushers esteemed guests from London Airport, where most arrive via personal private jet and are chauffeured directly into the building's basement car park. From there, each patron is brought into the shoppe where they actually assist a master chronographer in building their own time piece. I'm not talking about assembly either. The showroom of the shoppe is rumored to contain multiple glass cases with hundreds upon hundreds of spectacularly rare and sought-after blocks of varying metals, each ready to be smelted and poured into one off molds, each which are kept inside WatchMaker's vault, in the off-change an owner's watch casing or band needs to be smelted and recast.

Virtually all of these metal blocks have some of the most interesting back stories. One ingot of titanium sitting in the case was rumored to be salvaged from a satellite after it reentered our atmosphere and crashed in the Ukraine. Another, a black block was said to be collected in secret from the last retired US Air Force SR-71 Blackbird. These cases are rumored to have gold, silver, titanium and a wide assortment of precious stones from a wide range of legendary sources such as The Treasure of Lima, The Romanov Jewels, The Flor De La Mar, The Lost Dutchman's Mine, The Lake Toplitz Treasure, The Crown Jewels of Ireland, The Amber Room, Yamashita's Mine, Issyk-Kul and Lost Adam Diggings, among many other equally fascinating treasure troves.

Another and my personal favorite, in this case a recently sold, high carbon, steel slug was rumored to have been collected from the center of the world's largest recorded amber guise stone. If that's true, that humpback whale it came from must have been filtering sea water for decades or centuries to collect, then subsequently, regurgitate, that much steel. Interestingly enough, when The WatchMaker smelted this steel and poured the block, it supposedly filled the shoppe with strong perfume hints, who's bouquet can still be smelled throughout, to this day. Seriously though, who really knows the truth.

It was a relatively arduous journey to Knightsbridge from Islington, given the nightmarish London traffic. Elijah opted to hail one of the thousands of black cabs that roam the narrow streets throughout the city. Like a seasoned local, he spotted one with its' roof lamp on and silently stuck his arm out. The cab slowed to a stop and Elijah approached the driver's window, as is custom, and informed the driver they were headed to Knightsbridge and Brompton Street. With a tip of the hat, the driver obliged and the four climbed into his cab, while Elijah sat up front, as is custom for the cab's hailer to ride shotgun, so to speak.

The driver was cheerful and talkative.
"Brompton, eh?", he said, in a heavy Cagney accent, "Bit a quid burning a hole, is it?"
Elijah spoke up, "It's our mom's birthday and she loves Harrod's", Christian was more than ok with Elijah taking the lead as he didn't understand a damn thing the cabbie had just said.

The black cab masterfully weaved its' way through the narrow streets, steadily making its' way south, then west. Out the window, Christian and Blake were surprised by how many of the sites they recognized from various films and photographs. Knightsbridge runs east and west, just south of Hyde Park and Buckingham palace, and as such, the closer they got to their destination, the more and more of their surroundings, the Americans began to recognize. As the cab approached the corner, the brakes squeaked slightly as it came to a stop. Penelope again, pulled the ubiquitous card from her person and as the cabbie advised it would be twenty-eight pounds or about forty-two dollars, depending on today's exchange rates, she swiped it through the back seat, mounted card reader. Just like that, the four now stood, again, on some of the world's most sought-after real estate. They were so close now that Elijah had begun to get excited at the possibility that the true prophesized Adaptive just might be walking side by side, with him down Brompton Street.

Brompton Road veers southwest from Knightsbridge and continues on for a thousand meters or so, until it splits near Thurloe Square Garden. The four walked two by two southwest, down Brompton. The street was jam packed with as many rare and expensive cars as there were rare and expensive places to spend your money here. The people watching was just as interesting. Little did any of them know, but Elijah's rings were made long ago, by WatchMaker himself. Elijah had obtained The Principles from his mentor, long ago and hadn't put two and two together until he saw the logo, back in the tunnel in Alanis. He may have been playing it up a little for Christian's sake as well, if we're being honest.

With every step that got them closer to WatchMaker, the glow and pulse of Elijah's ring became brighter and more frequent. Little did Elijah know, though, Blake was beginning to sense its' location as well. It was a hard sensation to explain. It was as if the blood coursing through his veins or something deep within his being, became magnetized and he felt he was being pulled to its' specific location.

Elijah continued to glance down at his ring but Blake had no need. He could feel the destination deep within his soul and with every turn, it only drew more potent. Midway down the street, a small, darkened gap between buildings grabbed Blake's attention as Elijah's ring lit up so much that he covered it up to prevent it from garnering unwanted attention. The two stopped simultaneously and looked at each other, befuddled.

Blake looked to the others and said, "I think this is it...", as he turned and continued down the passthrough. The pathway was narrow and dingy that led to the alleyway behind the rows of shops. The back alley was much less appealing than the Brompton facing side of the block. Rubbish was scattered in most directions and there were no shortage of creatures calling this alleyway home. The alley captured the fumes and steam from the store's exhaust pipes. Every twenty feet or so the perpetual fog gathering in the alley way became thicker. Through the dense fog billowing out of one of the larger steam pipes, Elijah spotted the door and the four disappeared inside, behind billowing cloud of steam. The scenery just inside the door looked like something straight out of a horror movie. It was dark and damp, with the constant rattling, occasional popping and the eerie whistle of an old boiler on its' last leg.

The light from Elijah's rings was now guiding the way through this darkened, nightmarish space. The further they ventured down the walkway, the darker and more-narrow the passage became, forcing them to duck under exposed pipes and low hanging building rafters, while every few moments while plumes of steam, filled the narrow passageway. The four kept moving forward, albeit at a continuously slowing pace, but something about this felt off to Penny. As she continued to look around, small details seemed to be missing. One of the boiler pipes that was spewing steam into the air, didn't seem to have any cracks or holes from where the steam seemed to be escaping and the source of the sounds, they assumed, being made by the boiler, didn't seem to be originating from one central location, as they should. Suddenly, one of the pipes erupted, letting a large and constant cloud of steam directly in front of Christian. He was startled and his entire body recoiled to avoid being scalded. Penny stepped into his fall, catching him and whispered quietly into his ear,
"this... isn't... real..."

Christian froze, unsure of what to think and slowly turned his head toward Penny and replied, "what do you mean ... not real?"

"Shh...", she whispered, while signaling with one finger over her lips, "it's a casting..."
She reached down and grabbed the backside of his right wrist and lifted his hand toward the pipe still spewing scalding steam into the air. Sure enough, it wasn't even hot. Apparently, they were in the right place. It appeared someone had cast this to deter any and all visitors. Whether they were actively casting or not, was still unknown.

A few feet ahead, a large rafter appears to have fallen and completely blocked the path. Blake could still feel the draw that had been pulling at him but he and Elijah stopped just in front of the fallen rafter.

"What now?", Blake asked Elijah.

"Move...", Penny said, pushing the two to the side as she, then Christian following just behind, walked at a hastened pace, toward the blockage.

"Yeah... Move...", Christian said to Blake, in a snarky tone, with a smirk on his face.
Just then, Penny walked into the rafter and, to Blake and Elijah's disbelief, passed directly through it. Blake was astonished but Elijah seemed mostly embarrassed. It had been a long time since he had fallen for a Precept conjuring. Once he started to look around, he began to notice the evident tale tell signs. When a precept casts, the impact on the intended, is only as good as the castor's attention to detail. The more realistic the details, the more apt the human, or Omnician brain is to accepting what it perceives, as reality. Could be one reason they say the devil's in the details.

As Blake and Elijah passed through the blockage, the four now stood in a concrete walled hall, with sparse lighting and painted a dull gray. Several feet in front of them sat a metal door also painted the same dull gray. Penny reached out and pushed the crossbar and with a click, the door opened, revealing a circular staircase, leading downward. The stairwell looked like it belonged in a medieval castle. It was lit with candle burning sconces every fifteen feet or so and the walls were built from large, vine covered stones. As the four descended the stairwell, it became quite clear that they would soon be face to face with whatever or whoever WatchMaker was. Penny began to become anxious as she sort of assumed WatchMaker had to be a Chrono or something. Whoever they were, they had a relatively decent Precept at their disposal.

The four reached the bottom of the stairs as the stairwell emptied into a foyer about thirty feet long. At the other end was another door. A tall, glass door, complete with a tall, thick, cylindrical, golden door handle vertically mounted on its' right side. The glass was tinted dark and on the upper half of the door, about the size of a basketball, was a large, prominent, gold leafed WatchMaker logo. Elijah reached for the handle and gave the door a firm pull. The door was locked. He slowly dropped his hand from the handle, then looked around either side of the door. He was looking for a touchpad or some other type of electronic card reader, of which he found none. Penny tried pulling it and again, nothing happened. Elijah tried opening it with his ringed hand, but again, nothing happened.

Just then, Christian tapped Blake on the shoulder. When Blake looked back at him, Christian motioned downward toward his wrist where his mother's bracelet was now aglow, even brighter than Elijah's rings had been before. But this glow was something different. It wasn't the usual Divinium bluish gray color but a bright blue, almost white luminescence. Blake lifted his left hand toward the door handle. The bracelet dangled and swung on his wrist as his hand approached the golden bar. As he grabbed the handle, the bracelet lit up a bright white and a loud click could be heard from inside. Blake pushed the door and it effortlessly opened inward.

The inside of the shoppe was much like it had been rumored to be. The main shoppe floor was no larger than the front room of any typical retail shop. The walls were indeed, painted that fabled forest green, but there were also accents of varying colors and patterns of dark, polished stone throughout. A massive, extremely old and probably super expensive chandelier hung from the center of the room's ten-meter high ceiling and kept the room in lighting that resembled twilight. The unattended counter was at the back of the shoppe and each wall was covered, front to back, with five rows of display cases.

These were slightly sloped, open air cases, more like shelves and not the large floor mounted, glass cases, as rumored. Each row protruded from the wall about half a meter and were made of a dark stained hardwood that smelled of mahogany. Each section of display was about two meters long, with a ten-centimeter gap on either side, separating it from the next. On each section were mounted dozens of small, circular pedestals, each covered in a flat, black felt and were individually lit from above by bright LEDs mounted to the underside of the display case above. On each pedestal, sat a single inch and a half cube of metal. At first glance they all looked identical but after further inspection, it was clear each cube was unique and special and probably had its own backstory. The four scattered and browsed the shoppe. One particular metal that caught Christian's eye had a knotted, blue mokumegane appearance, similar to that of a katana's blade. There was, indeed, a black steel cube, though there was no placard claiming it was from an SR-71 blackbird. An entire section of five rows did contain various gold, silver and titanium blocks. Penelope even spotted a blue steel cube that was more aqua than blue and she thought to herself, that it would make exquisite jewelry.

A moment later, an old man slowly walked in from the back and spotted the guests browsing the inventory. He wore a black suit jacket and matching pants, black oxford shirt and nicely shined shoes. As he stealthily approached the counter, he spoke.

"Good morning to you all...", he said, cheerfully, "welcome... to ... WatchMaker.
It's not every day we have unannounced guests. What can I do for you?", he said.

Elijah, Blake and Christian all turned to face the old man in unison. None of them had heard him enter the room or they were just too preoccupied by all these little metal blocks to notice. Penelope approached the counter. She reached into her satchel and pulled out the scroll she took from the door mechanism during their hurried departure from Alanis. The expression on the old man's face changed immediately from one of obligated cheer to one of absolute seriousness. She placed the scroll on the countertop in a smooth but precise motion and watched as the old man's wrinkled hands slowly picked up the rolled lambskin paper with matched precision and fluidity. He turned it slightly to inspect the paper. She didn't know what it was he was expecting to see. After a moment, he lowered the scroll and looked at Penny and the others.

"I suppose you can tell me where this came from?", he uttered, not so much in mistrust of whom possessed it, but more so, as if asking to observe the group's collective response. So yeah, he probably didn't trust them, either.

"The place where we found that... we also found the slain bodies of my mentors, my friends and fellow...", she paused for a moment, "... fellow ...kin", she concluded.

"Oh, my dear... ", the old man responded, "... I too, had friends among them... I'm sorry for your loss, my dear.", he said, in an honestly sympathetic and consoling manner.
"I assume because you're here, Alanis has fallen...", he said, still examining the scroll.

"Yes, the Elders were among them ... When we entered the chamber this came from, we found nothing except the dead bodies of my family and friends... he and his men...", she gasped, "...they murdered them...", she said, trying to fight back the tears that waited just below the surface. In all reality, she hasn't had a proper time of mourning, Most Omnicians have been known to hold grudges, sometimes for centuries. One would be safe in assuming that there's a better than zero chance that Penelope will hold this grudge for much longer than that.

"There, there, young one... all will be well again, just you wait and see...", the old man said, in an attempt to console her,
"... you must not dwell in the past... but persevere ...even and especially when times seem most dark ... don't forget the words of the oath you've taken ...", he said with a labored wink and a peculiar grin.

The moment the old man grinned at Penny, it caught Christian's attention and he immediately took notice. He knows he's seen that specific... no, that exact grin somewhere before, but for the life of him, in this exact moment, he couldn't recollect where. The expression on his face said it all. It was one of an instant moment of clarity combined with an unconfident confusion. You know the one... much like when a song comes on the radio and you know the artist's name, but the moment you try to speak it, even though the name is on the tip of your tongue, you just can't seem to find it

Penny took a moment to regain her composure, then motioned for Blake, "I have someone I would like you to meet...", she said, "This is Blake. Blake, this is ... ". She just realized she hadn't caught the old man's name, "I'm sorry... I didn't get your name...", she said to the old man.

"I'm just an old watchmaker, my dear, but you may call me Cyrus.", He said, nodding in Blake's direction. Blake returned the gesture. Christian looked on, his facial expression a tale tell sign of his efforts in continuing his internal search for the answer to this current quandary.

"He has something he needs to show you...", she said to Cyrus.

Staring at Blake, she motioned with her eyes, eyebrows and every other muscle in her face, all while keeping her head completely stationary, toward the bracelet on his left hand. He glanced down at his wrist where the bracelet dangled. After a long moment's pause and in one smooth motion, he grabbed the bracelet with his right hand, slipped it off his wrist and held it out in front of Cyrus. He pulled a pair of glasses from his breast pocket, slowly put them onto his face, then pulled a boom lamp attached to the counter's underside toward him. A bright light filled the immediate vicinity as it shone onto the bracelet, that by the way, still continued to glow brightly.

His facial expression changed the moment he laid eyes on the bracelet. It was as if he had seen a ghost. He knows the exact day, time and patron for whom, it was made. He knows because he was the craftsman who instructed the one who made it.

"Aww, it's quite beautiful, isn't it?", Cyrus said, "... not extravagant or overly gaudy like many ... it's simple... timeless... elegant... much like the woman whom I helped construct it, many years ago ...", he said. That comment struck Blake like a blindside hit from a pro-bowl caliber, strong safety on a defenseless receiver. The color left his face, as the entirety of his attention, now focused on the sounds Cyrus would make with his next breath.

"And how is your mother... Alessandro.", Blake was in full disbelief now. No one knew this to be his name, except a very select few. Particularly, not some absolute stranger whom he had never previously, made acquaintance. Cyrus must know more about who I am than I do, he thought to himself.

The old man's demeanor changed almost immediately. He no longer moved slowly and methodically. He now moved with guided purpose. Kind of like he's just seen, after many years, his oldest childhood friend and there was much catching up to do. Sometime in the past few moments, Elijah had approached the counter and was now standing beside Penny.

"So, Alessandro ... tell me... how is she? Still living in Sequoia, I presume?", he asked with a smile, as would a proud parent or mentor.

"She actually passed away several years ago... ", Blake replied, somberly. Cyrus immediately lowered his head, as if saying a prayer, for a brief moment.
"I'm sorry to hear that, young man...", he said as he held the bracelet between both his partially clenched hands.

He turned his gaze and his comments, toward Elijah.

"You must be... the Wanderer...Tell me...", glancing toward his ringed hand, "how do The Principles serve you? Do they still perform as they should?"

Elijah slowly lowered his head while raising his ringed hand into the jeweler's lamp. He studied the rings he wore for an abbreviated moment. He was looking for the proper words. He knew the relics he wore were old and created in part, of Divinium, but besides that, he was clueless as to what Cyrus was referring.

He smiled, with again, that recognizable smile, "You three have much to learn... You especially, my dear", he was speaking directly to Penelope now in a serious tone.

Unannounced, he clapped his hands and the sound echoed throughout the shoppe, startling the three Omnicians. Christian didn't notice as he was rapidly typing away in what appeared to be a heated text message conversation, on his phone.

"I feel like making something!", Cyrus said, his mood changing almost immediately,
"Come young Omnicians... Let us retire to my workshop...", he said, raising his right arm, palm facing the sky, directing them toward the end of the counter and to a fold in the wall, that led deeper into the interior of the shoppe. All three began to follow his lead. Christian continued the conversation on his phone.

"And I don't believe I had the pleasure of catching your name, young man.", Cyrus said to Christian. Blake, Penny and Elijah all three turned, awaiting his response.

171

"My name is Christian, sir.... Your shoppe... I absolutely love it... I'm having difficulty putting it into words... Majestic is one... Grandiose as well... Grand just doesn't provide the adequate visual... Astonishing, too...", He babbled, having difficulty thinking of what he was trying to say before words began leaving his lips.
"Chrono...", Cyrus mumbled to himself.

"No", Penelope said, placing her hand across Cyrus' forearm, "he's a human..."
Cyrus' stare immediately turned to Penny, "Why is he with you and why did you bring him here?", He seemed deeply concerned.

Blake interrupted, "He saved my life back in the states... I owe him... also... when I ran into..."

Cyrus interrupted him, "I've heard enough!", he turned his attention to Christian, "Young man... you've done a great kindness to me, in helping these three find this place... I'm feeling generous... Pick a cube... as a token of my appreciation, I shall make you a chronograph... the finest I've ever built!"

"I couldn't possibly... OK.", He replied, excited.

"Fantastic, do you have an idea of what you'd like.", Cyrus asked.

"Actually, yes... I do... my kind sir!", he responded.

Christian didn't usually speak to anyone in this tone as it reminded him of the four years of what he then perceived as insincere pomposity. The very same thing that he despised back at SMU. But there was something different about Cyrus and he felt obligated, nay, he felt he owed absolute kindness toward Cyrus, as this grand gesture was, most definitely deserving. Plus, he was giving him free reign of any of these exotic materials in the shoppe.

"I do actually...", he began,"48 milli-meter bezel, 18 mm thickness, about 120 grams... tri split push pieces in black, rotating bezel...". Cyrus took a pad out of this jacket pocket and with slightly sarcastic parse of his lips and tightening of his eyes, began notating his ramblings.

"... calendar, timer... all on a black dial with gold and white lettering... 24/21 Oyster lug band...", he continued, "visible clockwork on the case back, decent water resistance..."

Cyrus interrupted, "Could I get you a Perrier? I can only imagine how parsed you're becoming, having to recite all of this from memory...", he said, with that unique grin and a brand of sarcasm, all his own. It was in that exact moment, Christian suddenly realized from where he knew that smile and so many other things began to make sense, like falling dominoes. He didn't change his tone or his pacing though and continued,

"Just one other thing... I prefer your brand of motion... Perpetual motion takes the fun out of it... And while you're at it, can you include a few additional band options? Maybe a leather aviator or bund or maybe your unique take on an old school G10..."

"Ok... Question... Did you go to watch college or something?", Cyrus asked.

He continued his sarcastic tone and the smirk on his face, ever growing as he figured Christian had caught on, by now.

He thought for a split second and replied with equally potent snark, "No... but I did stay at a Holiday Inn Express last night...", to which he received audible gasps from Blake, Elijah and Penny. She slowly turned to look at Cyrus, only to notice he looked to be refraining from laughing. His travel companions gasped at what they perceived to be another side they've yet to see.

"Have you a material in mind... sir? Cyrus asked.

"I do... ", Christian said. He turned and walked toward the closest display which contained the blocks of gold and silver. He reached his hand out and left it hovering over several pieces of titanium. He then, directed his gaze at Cyrus and waited for his reaction. Cyrus calmly and wisely shook his head once to each side, to which Christian reacted by slowly walking backward, his hand still extended over the middle row of the display containing rows and rows of shiny blocks. He continued walking backward, awaiting some kind of signal from Cyrus. His pace carried him away from the displays of precious metals and toward some of the more unique and rare choices, but he never broke eye contact with Cyrus.

Eventually, Cyrus motioned his approval and he was standing in front of the proper display. He motioned with his head, as to suggest he move his hand up one level. Christian followed his lead and moved his open hand, in kind. Watching this was probably like watching a dad instructing his young son on the precise location of where to position the claw of one of those prize-filled, crane games. Hopefully resulting in the claw grabbing and then, carrying over a brightly colored stuffed animal, all the way to the drop zone, to have what will certainly become the young one's new 'woobie', falls into the collection bin.

Cyrus nodded slowly, with a subtle blink, suggesting that he is in the right place. Christian turned to see his hand hovering over that block of katana steel that initially caught his eye.

"Allow me to tell you about this very special metal...", Cyrus began,

"Deep within the Himalayan Mountains, below and behind a maze of razor-sharp rocks, sits the ancient Omnician city named Om-Tak... Known for its' superior craftsmanship and artisans of metallurgy, this is the location where I was initially trained in metalwork. Om-Tak has no rival in crafting and in ingenuity, just as this specific specimen, has no equal among other metals."

Cyrus approached and plucked the metal cube from its' perch. He held it under the light in his open hand and all in the room focused their attentions, on his presentation.

"The pattern on this cube is called Mokume-Gane and it's achieved by layering individual and distinct alloys, creating what's known as a billet. The specific metals used in forging this specimen are all extremely rare and found together, virtually no other place on this planet and when combined, as they have been when creating this little guy, form what's known as an Elegon."

Elijah had heard that term before.

"This particular Elegon billet was created from twenty-one rare metals, plus steel and titanium. It provides its keeper the power to wield abilities, unimaginable to and previously unseen, by this world.", He closed his hand around the cube. He then locked eyes with Christian. He began speaking more softly and his tone became gravely serious but his resolve remained, ever sharp and direct.

"I will craft this for you and to you, I entrust, it's safe keeping."

"This specific piece of matter ... it has a part to play in the grand equation of this universe... Guard this with your life, Christian.", he concluded with a deathly serious gaze, as his glasses sat low on the bridge of his nose all contributing to his conveying the paramount nature, of this message. Christian understood. Not the purpose or usage of the material, but the importance of his stewardship of it.

"I understand", Christian said with a dedication he rarely shows, assuring Cyrus that he indeed, understand the importance of this honor and privilege.

Cyrus smiled, "Ok then... let's go make a watch...", he said, then turned and began to lead them into the workshop. Blake, Elijah and Penny instantly began to follow him.

"I have to go...", Christian uttered, with disbelief and under hints of sorrow and disappointment, as his attention lifted, again, from the screen of his phone and returned to the others inside this exclusive London shoppe.

"So be it, Young Christian... We all have our parts to play.", Cyrus said as he turned away and continued toward the back of the shoppe. Blake,

Elijah and Penelope paused and looked affectionately at Christian. Blake approached and grabbed Christian's forearm, in an ancient Sequoia sign of brotherhood, "Thank you, my brother...", he said with honest admiration. Penny approached from Blake's right and placed her hand on his shoulder. With a genuine smile, she said, "I hope to see you, soon... Safe Travels". Elijah approached from the other side and extended his hand toward Christian. With playful admiration, Christian extended his hand as to shake Elijah's, but at the last second, condescendingly, reached up and tussled Elijah's hair. Elijah smiled as Christian wrapped his arm around Elijah's shoulder and hugged him.
Christian whispered to Elijah, "I'll miss you most of all, scarecrow..."

Elijah again, looked confused. Blake laughed while Penny, again, shook her head in dumbfounded disbelief.

"My driver will take you wherever you need to go.", Cyrus told Christian.

"It's my boss... he sent his plane... again...", Christian laughed, holding up his phone displaying the text message screen. He was now visibly struggling while trying to hold back the emotion that was beginning to approach the surface. He had been with these three for the most fulfilling, life changing adventure he had ever been on, and now appears to be coming to an end.

A young man, in a suit, complete with chauffer's hat emerged from the back and motioned to Christian to follow.

"Where can I take you, sir?", he asked.

"London City Airport, I think...", he said.

Christian started toward the door where they first entered the shoppe.

"Follow me...", the young man said, motioning him the opposite way. He led Christian toward the back and into the workshop. Before disappearing into the back, Christian took one last look and gave one last wave to the Omnicians he now proudly called friends, then disappeared through the door. He was unsure if he would see them again, but remained hopeful and something deep inside, told him that they'd cross paths once more. He, now had his own part to play in whatever this was.

The WatchMaker workshop appeared strangely lifeless at first glance, except, that fires in the various hearths were burning, tools seemed to be scattered strategically and purposefully and several orders were in process at and around the various workstations. After a quick absorbing glance, Christian and the driver entered a thin elevator door, which took them directly to the roof. They exited through a metal door that exited directly onto the walkway to the rooftop helipad. Again, another first for Christian. He had never ridden in a helicopter before.

"Hey, I thought you were a driver?", he asked the young man, speaking loudly to be heard over the roar of the Bell 222's turbines and rotor.

"I can drive anything!", he replied with a smirk. The two climbed inside and moments later, Christian found himself staring out the window, taking in a rare and exclusive view of London. A short but memorable few minutes later, the helicopter descended and touched down just meters away from the terminal doors of London Executive Aviation. Christian exited, gave a quick wave to Driver and in a half-crouched jog, made his way to the terminal.

It's always humorous watching people depart a helicopter.

When a helicopter's rotor is spinning, the centrifugal force generated within the blades and, to a lesser extent, the lift created by their curvature, overpowers their weight causing them to flatten out and rise level with the point at which its' rotor head is mated to the transmission. This is well above the top of a person's head that stands six foot, two inches tall but everyone always freaks out thinking they're going to get their heads chopped off by the spinning blades and departs the immediate vicinity, in a half-squatted jog. My apologies, perhaps it's just me that finds this humorous.

Moments later, Christian was sitting comfortably in one of the now, familiar captain's chairs aboard the Gulfstream, as it taxied toward runway 60. He reached into the seatback in front of him and, miraculously, pulled out his passport, complete with an arrival stamp from London customs showing two days ago. Don't know how that works, but ok, he thought to himself. He kicked back to relax during the eight-hour flight home. Just as the nose of the plane lifted into the air, he scrolled through his phone, looking for one specific thing.
Something... anything ... from Katie.

14
The Gift

I tell you this for a reason...

The tires of an airplane have one of the hardest, most underappreciated jobs on the planet. Primarily, they are to provide for a safe, secure and soft landing for the aircraft. The other factors involved, are where the true pressures, comes into play. First, the airplane itself is most likely ridiculously expensive and even more so, fragile. With every incident, and each subsequent series of law suits, a constant and continuous increase in the costs and liability associated with major aircraft ownership and operations, follow. This cycle continues in perpetuity.

Then, there's another entirely separate set of circumstances associated with the contents themselves, being transported. Usually, the goods or passengers on these aircraft tend to be of higher value. I don't mean this derogatorily or speaking in such a sense as to suggest one life is more valuable than another. I'm simply stating that, in a logical and efficient world, the more expensive and exclusive the opportunity or object in question, the more monetary value said thing, represents or demands. One simply wouldn't logically ship a shoebox-sized steel crate full of colorless, two-plus carat diamonds, on a large, oceangoing cargo ship, just as one would not logically, ship two tons of raw plastic blanks, by way of the Concord. Neither is particularly cost effective in relation to the contents being shipped. The problem this example shows is one, that is foundational, and unfortunately, embedded deep within our society. These days, value is perceived, and in turn, applied in most cases, erroneously and to undeserving vessels.

For those of you who aren't aviation enthusiasts, due to the speed at which today's jets travel, the physical requirements for these same aircraft to efficiently travel at said speeds, and due to expectation of the travelers themselves, many hours of advanced physics have been incorporated into the design and construction of any given, current generation airplane's wing design. One of the oldest and most fundamental advancements that makes today's air travel possible, are the flap and slat mechanisms.

Even grade schoolers know that wings are fundamental to a plane's ability to fly. This is due to the lift generated by its' shape. When combined with the thrust generated by its' propulsion system, or engines, it outpaces the drag, or air resistance, created by the airplane's shape and good ole' gravity, resulting in controlled flight. As aviation designers increase the size and usable load of newer airplane designs, they tend to get larger and heavier, thus, the need for lift and thrust is greater at slower speeds. There are two ways to solve for this. One is bigger engines. Bigger engines require more fuel, therefore, more weight, therefore, a continued need for a bigger engine. The other method is to generate more lift from the airframe.

Not to teach an aerodynamics class here or anything, but a wing's lift is determined by several factors, the major one being surface area on the topside of the wing. The longer it takes air to pass over the top of the wing, the more lift the wing generates. This is what those moving sections of an airplane's wing do. As they lower, they are creating a longer surface area on top of the wing, resulting in what's referred to in the biz, as a lower stall speed, or the speed in which the forces of gravity and drag, overpower the thrust and lift being generated.

Gulfstream's don't use slats in their wing designs. Instead, the wings themselves are designed as such, that the shape of the wing does most of the lift generation, eliminating the need for slats. These specific wings are, however, enormous given the size of the airplane in general and ultimately, this exclusion results in a net weight saving. This, and several other factors, provide these aircraft with the ability to use shorter runways located at smaller airports. Addison, TX is indeed, one of these smaller airports. Typically, JC stations his plane to operate from Love Field because it's closer to Dallas proper, easier for him to get to in a time crunch, and has more optionality in the form of services and maintenance facilities, in general. But today, they were instructed to fly him directly into Addison Airport. It's one of the larger, small airports around, if that makes sense. Larger, in a sense that it has the facilities and ability to regularly host full size business jets.

Seven hours later, out the starboard window, Christian watched as the ground approached from below at an ever-growingly rapid pace. There are constant minute movements along a plane's wings throughout a flight but during takeoff and landing are when they really come to life. He noticed, out the corner of his eye, that the flaps on the trailing edge of the wing, were in process of deploying downward. He could feel their impact as the plane began to slow, descend faster, and the nose, pitch upward.

"Is this Love Field?", Christian asked the attendant, as the landmarks began to become recognizable and he didn't seem to recognize many of them.

"No sir,", she responded, "we're arriving at Addison as per our instructions."

"Do you know why?", he continued. She didn't immediately respond, so he didn't press the issue.

The plane entered the box and turned toward the west, just southeast of the airport, then again, north, to line up for landing. Moments later, the aircraft taxied to a stop just off the tarmac, into a taxiway between two rows of darkened hangers. Customs paid a quick visit and since everything was in order, Christian was allowed to exit the plane and immediately climbed into a waiting car.

Christian closed the door just as the driver put the full-size sedan into gear and pulled away, toward the gate. As the automated gate opened, Christian asked the driver, "Where are we going, anyway?"

The driver had a squared-away, high and tight look to him. Though he was seated, Christian estimated he was probably six feet, four inches and judging by his shoulders, build quite solidly. He wore that aura of recently separated military, but Christian couldn't be sure. Though it was almost eight in the evening, jet lag hadn't yet begun to fully catch up with him. The driver remained silent but Christian was pretty sure where he was being taken. A few minutes later, the car turned into the parking lot of a local Mexican restaurant chain known as Uncle Julio's. Famous for mesquite grilling virtually everything on the menu, it's a regular in the conversation for the honor of Top Mexican Food in all of Dallas. Christian expected to be dropped off at the front steps, but was surprised when the driver swung the car into a parking spot just in front of the patio. He left the car running, turned to Christian and said, "He's waiting in there for you...", as he motioned to the restaurant.

"Wait... who's ... he?", Christian asked in a skeptical tone.

"JC... your boss... my boss...", he replied in a manner that suggested he was being informative, as opposed to condescending.

"Oh, right... best not keep him waiting...", Christian replied, as he opened the door. He shuffled out into the North Texas winter and made his way up the front steps and into the lobby. He entered the restaurant and after just a few feet inside, he could see the entire dining room but there was no sign of JC anywhere.

"Mr. Jones, is it?", the hostess, a young girl of about high school age, asked.
"Yes...", he retorted.

"Right this way...", she said. She led him into the restaurant's library, a small round room, separated from the main dining floor, with one large, round table inside. There, sitting alone at the table was JC, preoccupied, as usual, with something on his phone.
"Hey boss...", Christian said, as walked into the library. The hostess closed the wooden doors behind him before she walked away. He was still wearing the hoodie that Blake gave him. JC was finishing something up, as indicated by raising one finger into the air. Christian took this moment to catch his breath, take off the hoodie and drape it on the back of an unoccupied chair. He took a seat and started devouring some of the best chips and salsa in all of Dallas. After a few more clicks, he sat his phone down on the table, interlocked his fingers on the table directly in front of him and stared intently at Christian.

"So… the last thing I knew, you were going to interview Gene Jones… That was eight fucking days ago! You better have one really good story to tell me…", he said. While, at first glance, it may seem as if he was pissed, his tone actually suggested he was worried more than angry. At the least, he was concerned.

Christian began with his visit with Gene and how the interview went. He then got into the art, the bracelet, the strange guy, his broken phone and the Uber to the underground apartment. JC listened intently and as the conversation drew out longer, he became more and more captivated by the story he was hearing. Christian remained calm and in good spirits. If we're being honest, he was a totally different person today than he was eight days ago, as he now knew the truth that very few others did. Everyday happenings just weren't as major of issues to him as they once seemed.

He continued his story, providing the details he could remember about these Omnicians, Divinine, summoning markings and the accompanying illumination and the different Omnician orders, which he was still a bit fuzzy on. Then, he started in on the events of the sprint into downtown, the tunnels and the ruins of the underground city. He then told JC about Elijah, Penelope and Blake and each of their back stories, as best he could remember. JC sat on the edge of his seat, content to just listen. He continued, with the journey back to the surface and then, the downtown Neiman Marcus. JC seemed like he wanted to ask questions several times, but restrained himself. When Christian began to tell him about the Celestial Stone, JC couldn't hold back the questions any longer.

"Wait… so you're telling me… there is a magic stone… embedded in the ground… underneath AND accessible, through a hidden room, below the downtown Nieman Marcus?", JC asked, quite skeptical.

"No… I never said it was magic…", he responded, "it's a massive piece of solid Divinium encased in what looked like limestone, capable of harnessing energy to access a rip in … time and space… I guess…".

He continued with his near-death experience and both him and his phone's subsequent, miraculous recoveries. He described Alanis and there were moments that JC closed his eyes, in what Christian interpreted, were his attempts to visualize it. He then, talked about the catacombs where they found the slaughtered remains of the Celestial Order, their escape, then the events that led them to ending up in London. JC, while skeptical, seemed to be, at the least, entertained by what he was hearing. As Christian concluded his story with the details of his visit to WatchMaker, he decidedly left out certain details about what he experienced while inside the shoppe. Namely, that they were making him a timepiece and anything that had to do with its' composition. He wasn't sure why, but he had a strange feeling when he would begin to put into words, details about Cyrus and his interactions with him. So, in that exact moment, he decided to not share much detail about the shopkeeper.

"...and they flew me to the airport on a helicopter, your plane picked me up, then, that guy brought me here.", He finished his story and JC took a couple of deep breaths. It was clear, that in this exact moment, he was formulating a plan.

He looked up at Christian and began,
"Look...first and foremost, I'm glad you're ok... You had me worried for like, five days, that something bad had happened to you."

He reached down for his phone and held it at such an angle that Christian couldn't see the screen. A few clicks later and the screen returned dark.

"I don't want you to be put in this situation again so I've gotten you some help."

Just as he finished the sentence, the door to the library opened and in stepped the driver. He immediately sat down at the table along with Christian and JC.
"Let me introduce you to your new best friend. This is Killian. He works for me, in a unique capacity and he will, now and for the foreseeable future, be your shadow. He is not to leave your side."

Killian sat, listening intently, to JC's comments, with his hands bound, one open and laid across the other's closed fist, on the table in front of him. He was all of Christian's suspected six foot four, and then some, with dark hair and dark, slate gray eyes.
"Killian is great and all, but is this really necessary?", Christian commented, seeming annoyed by his new, forcibly arranged friendship.

"Yes, it is...", JC replied shortly, "You disappeared for the better part of a week... and that's not going to happen again..."

Christian looked at Killian. The look on Killian's face suggested that he, too, was annoyed by these series of events.

"Ok, now that that's out of the way... about your story...", he took a deep breath and pushed his glasses back to the top of the bridge of his nose, "I believe you ... most of it anyway... I do have some questions, so let's talk about it more, tomorrow at the office.
Oh, and one more thing... You're moving tonight. I bought the house a few doors down from mine. Killian is going to take you to your old apartment, gather what you need for the week, then, this weekend, I'll send some movers over and you guys can pack it up and move, or store it or whatever.... Consider it a bonus...", JC said as he gathered his key fob and phone and prepared to leave.

"Wait a second! You can't just force a babysitter on me! This is total bullshit. You don't own me…", Christian complained, partly because he was super annoyed and partly because jet lag was beginning to set in.

JC, now standing, looked at Christian and said, "Just stop… you disappeared, with no warning and no subsequent contact… after I sent you on a job… a job that honestly, I should have done… that's on me… but it won't happen again. Besides, I have a feeling you and Killian will get along."

Christian, annoyed, rolled his eyes briefly as he sat back into his chair. He looked in Killian's direction. He was staring at him out of the corner of his eye. As the two made eye contact, Killian jokingly blew the softest of kisses in Christian's direction. This immediately resulted in a quick, genuine laugh accompanied by a shaking head, from Christian.

"See…", JC said with a grin, "you two are getting along already…", He clicked a button on his key fob twice and from outside, the faint sounds of a twin turbo, small bore, V8 roaring to life, followed.

"Look, I have to go… The world's assholes aren't going to uproot themselves and admit their own devious intent…"

"Wait…", Christian said, "Thank you for sending the jet. Seriously… with no passport, I had no idea how I was going to get home…"

"Don't mention it…", JC replied, another step closer to the door.

"Come on… Sit back down…", Christian said, "we haven't even eaten yet…"
"I'm good…", JC replied, "But there's a Gordo on the way… combo fajitas, diablo and especial camarones, ribs, cabrito, frog legs… the works. Enjoy… and welcome home".

Before he left, he shot one last look at Christian. It was as if JC were a relieved parent, and Christian, his teenage child, home safe after his first high school party. JC had a glimmer of a smile on his face just as Christian looked up at him. The look on Christian's face spoke a thousand words that JC didn't even need to hear. Christian knew but JC didn't react. He simply turned and left the restaurant, hopped into his car and sped away, jumping on the tollway, southbound, back toward Dallas.

Christian sat back in his chair and looked at Killian for a moment. Killian sat confidently, staring right back at him.

"Do you even speak?", Christian asked, half expecting to get no response.
"Of course, I talk, dumbass", Killian responded.

The condescending retort strangely put Christian at ease and instantly, in a better mood. A few long seconds later, a couple of servers wearing black shirts and ties under their black aprons entered the library, carried a large iron skillet, on an equally large, wooden trivet. Beans, rice, guacamole, tortillas and a large plate of fajita toppings were sat in the middle of the table. Christian's mouth began to water. For the past week, what he had really been craving this whole time was now sitting directly in front of him. A little slice of home.

"Now, are we going to let this wonderful gesture of carnivorous kindness, go to waste?", Killian asked. He had already jokingly tucked a red linen napkin into the collar of his shirt and comically, had a fork in one hand and a knife in the other. Christian again, laughed and the two commenced to putting a rather significant sized dent in the sizzling platter that lay in front of them.

Forty-five minutes later, Christian and Killian pushed themselves away from the table, filled to the proverbial, brim. They talked, mainly, about what their personal experiences have been working for JC and speculation of this house he purchased, as they were soon to be, roommates. It turns out Christian's speculation was right. Killian was recently discharged from the military. He spent the past seven years as a Sea Bee in the Navy. He had been deployed for the first 5 years in Iraq, then a year in Afghanistan and finished the last year of duty stationed in Pearl Harbor, serving as an equipment operator and underwater welder. Christian seemed in awe of living on the Hawaiian Islands, but Killian ensured it wasn't all it was cracked up to be. He said you tend to get really bored, really fast, though it wasn't as bad as working on some of the smaller islands like the Caymans or god forbid, Guam. Christian tried to pay the tab but apparently, JC had seen to it that it was settled.
Killian again drove, as he and Christian made their way down to McKinney Avenue to acquire some of Christian's belongings, prior to checking out the new digs. Christian opened the door and to his surprise, his apartment was exactly as he left it. He assumed that, given the whirlwind that was last week and that JC dropped Killian the Babysitter on him the second he cleared Customs, that someone surely would have come and rooted through his place, looking for something. If someone had, he's pretty sure he knows what they would have had been looking for, after all.
He collected some essentials from inside while Killian waited in the hall. He hadn't been there five minutes when Killian began knocking on the door, which in turn, got the attention of Christian's nosey neighbor, down the hall.

Ms. Jacobson was an older lady that lived alone. I say alone but in fact, she shared her apartment with a half dozen cats. You would know she was coming because her feline entourage would proceed her, into the hall. Apparently, she didn't work because no matter what time he would come home, she would be hanging around outside in the hall or he would often run into her on the elevator. She was pleasant but regularly asked one … or five too many questions. Killian noticed a brown cat walk out into the hallway, then another, followed by Ms. Jacobson, in her PJs.

"Who's out here making all that racket!", she asked, just as Christian was locking his front door, overnight bag in hand.

"Sorry Ms. Jacobson. We're in a hurry…", Christian replied. He had always been pleasant to her but he had a knack for exiting a conversation exactly when he felt like it.

"Aren't you going to introduce me to your friend?", she hinted while, as the older folks say, making eyes at Killian. Christian definitely found the humor in this but Killian, not so much.

"Oh yeah, Ms. Jacobson, this is my friend Killian… he only dates older women… especially ones that have cats.", Christian replied, making Killian giggle to himself. He wasn't however, going to participate as he had strict orders from JC.

"Dude, we're late.", He replied, hoping to completely avoid the situation Christian had just created. Christian walked past Ms. Jacobson and Killian followed. She couldn't take her eyes off him as she watched the two, walk directly past her without making eye contact.

"Well that was rude! Christian! I'm calling management…", she screamed, hoping to get a rise out of the two. After all, she was bored nearly all the time. They did not engage but continued down the stairs and outside into the parking lot. Killian was used to this type of behavior from his fellow soldiers during his time in the military and it made him feel at ease and strangely, at home, as if he were back in Kandahar.

The two got into the car and drove away. McKinney Avenue was busy this evening with expensive cars, six or seven-deep, stopped at every red light. It was nothing compared to the likes of Knightsbridge, though. Several minutes later, the sedan turned onto University and as Killian passed JC's house, he began to slow as he neared the end of the street.

As it turns out, JC bought the house at the end of his own street. A really nice, big brick home with large trees and a circle drive way in front. It also had a three-car garage along the side of the house, providing for a quick entry and exit, if it came down to that. The porch light was on but most of the house remained dark.

Killian pulled into the circle drive. The two approached the front door and just as they reached the top step, JC opened the door from inside.

"Welcome home boys!", he said cheerfully. Christian could tell he was taking a bit of enjoyment in all of this. On the other hand, Christian guessed that this house probably cost JC two and a half million, given its'

185

location and if, on a whim, he just felt it necessary to come out of pocket for something of this magnitude, how well IS Fastli doing? Was this that easy of a decision for him to make?

Like a realtor, JC gave them the grand tour. The house was beautiful inside. Seven bedrooms and six bathrooms were most definitely a waste on two young bachelors but apparently, it was a good investment for JC. It was $4.3 million by the way and a steal at that. This house was loaded. It had been recently updated with smart "everything" throughout, a walk-in wine cellar, a theater that sat 12, two master suites, all on 3 stories, connected by two sets of staircases, an elevator and another hidden staircase from the 2nd floor master closet, down to the laundry room, just off the garage. There were actually several of these butler's nooks throughout the home providing for quick and hidden access throughout the home. The backyard had a really nice pool and seating for dozens. It really was too bad that both of them were not going to get to spend much time here.

"So, you too can fight over who gets what room when I leave… which is now… Get some sleep because we have a lot to do tomorrow.", He was looking directly at Christian as he said it. By the look on his face, JC could tell there was something on Christian's mind, something he probably wanted to get off his chest, but he didn't pry. He would let him get there on his own.

"Oh, one more thing.", JC said motioning to the pair to follow. He led them through the foyer, past the study, the elevator and made a bee line toward the garage. He was moving faster than usual.

He opened the garage door which required a hard-right turn to enter and he waited until the other two had cleared the corner to turn on the lights. There, in the middle of the garage sat a black Nissan GT-R and next to it, a black Mercedes G Wagon.

"If you guys are going to live here, I need you to look the part…", JC said, "You two probably should ride together, so figure it that out in the morning.", he said as he made his way back inside the house. Christian was in awe of the GT-R. It was his absolute favorite car of all time, a true 200 mph sleeper. Killian felt similar feelings toward the Mercedes. Both were stunned into silence and frozen, staring at the stable of horsepower sitting in front of them, at their personal disposal.

"Adios, neighbors…", he said as he slipped back through the house and out the front door. He walked the half block back to his house with a massive grin on his face that he would have never shown the two of them. It did make him feel good to provide a life, albeit temporarily, that the two would probably never be able to provide themselves at this age. As far as he was concerned, they both deserved it. His thoughts were that you never know what the future has planned for any of us anyway, so live today.

186

Just inside the garage, mounted on the wall at eye level, hung a small valet box and within, on ornate brass hooks, were two sets of key fobs.

"Hey... uh... I totally forgot but I need to get some toothpaste...", Killian said grinning while continuing to stare at the apex of German engineering before him.

"Yeah... I think I need some stuff from the store too... I, uh... didn't see any coffee in the kitchen either...", Christian replied with the same excited, enthusiastic stare and grin. It took all of about two nanoseconds for Killian to grab the Mercedes key and the two of them to climb into the G wagon.

It took a few more moments to find and press the Home1 button that opened the garage door. The two backed out of the driveway and stopped inches from demolishing the iron automated gate. A few more moments of fumbling, found that Home2 opened it. Then, the two were out exploring. In all reality, they did need to know the neighborhood and where the closest stores were, if they were to believably, live here for any extended period of time. After twenty minutes or so of wandering around the nearby neighborhoods, the G Wagon pulled back into the garage and the door closed behind it.

"So, do you want the downstairs or upstairs master?", Christian asked his new roommate.
"I'll take the downstairs, if that's cool...", Killian responded.

Christian was hoping Killian wanted the downstairs master. He enjoys taking the stairs and prefers not to live on the ground floor. The two entered the house and Christian went upstairs to unpack. The second-floor master suite was just as well appointed as the one downstairs. Christian preferred the layout of the bathroom upstairs, anyway. The real selling point was the bed. The mattress on the king-sized bed was the most plush and soft he had ever laid upon and he was looking forward to a good night's sleep. It was now closing in on midnight, so the two decided it was time to turn in for the evening. After all, he did have to return to real life tomorrow and go back to work.

Christian performed his usual bathroom ritual then climbed into the sleep cloud anchoring the center of his new chambers. This bed was a thing of fairy tales, he thought to himself as he nearly fell asleep the moment his head touched the down feather pillow. 5 am came early the next morning. As the Caribbean themed alarm sounded, he awoke from his deep sleep, feeling extraordinarily rested. The first thing he thought to himself was, "this must be why rich people always seem to be in such a good mood..." He felt more rejuvenated this morning, than he can ever remember.

The shower in the second-floor master was glorious in its' own right. One just didn't fully understand the serenity of a rainfall shower until you bathe in one for the first time. He dressed quickly for the day and made his way downstairs to the kitchen, where he found Killian, searching for a blender to make his morning smoothie.

Christian was immediately reminded of the research marathon a few weeks ago at JC's house, now, just four doors down the street. He entered the kitchen and exchanged pleasantries with his new roommate. Honestly, Christian is basically worthless before his morning coffee, so this generally becomes every day's primary mission. The two walked out into the garage and climbed into the Mercedes at six forty-five. Coffee in hand and laptop over shoulder, Christian knew today would be a busy one. Killian backed out of the driveway, cognizant of the gate this time and aimed the German SUV toward Uptown. A short eight minutes later, the pair found themselves entering the parking garage and searching for a spot nearest the elevators. Luckily at this early hour, there was quite the selection from which to choose.

A few minutes later, Killian and Christian exited the elevator and entered the office. Christian took the familiar route to his office only to find that it had been cleared out and turned into a huddle room. The inconvenience and muted rage hadn't fully taken hold yet due to the insufficient, yet growing levels of caffeine still coursing its' way into his bloodstream.

He asked the receptionist why his office had been emptied and she informed him that in his absence, JC had made a few strategic changes to the company and in turn, the seating chart. The Malcontent team was now on the other side of the floor.

"Team?", he thought to himself and obliged when she offered to show him and Killian the way. She escorted them across the office and into a newly apportioned section where the accounting and finance people used to sit. Along the back wall a lone, large office with an entire wall of windows providing a breathtaking view of the downtown skyline, waited. As the duo approached the office's door and its' accompanying receptionist desk, he read the office occupant's name from the white lettering on the frosted glass wall. Christie Jones.

JC's jokes regularly resonate with him, even during pre-caffeination. He is usually immediately reminded of their unique exchange at that SMU recruiting fair.

His new office was wide. So much so that there was a second desk at the other end. He got the sneaking suspicion that not only are he and Killian to live together, but now he must bunk with him at work too. He thanked the receptionist for showing him in and sank into his new desk chair. This one was much more comfortable that the entry level chair in which he previously spent, hours upon hours. High back in brown leather, it had all the bells and whistles, except in his experience, these executive chairs were difficult at best, to sit in while trying to type. His preconceived notions were quickly dispelled once he realized the arms swung upward, flush with the seat back, leaving ample clearance for the chair to nestle just under the lip of the desk, allowing for his elbows a resting place. It was then, he first noticed it.

In the middle of his new desk sat a slate gray box. The box itself was covered in a paper that had a velvety, matte finish. Around the entire length of the box was wrapped, a wide ribbon, deep scarlet in color, with a pristinely tied bow perfectly centered on top. The knot was tied so the ribbon's ends pointed toward the front and back of the box. On the end of the ribbon that terminated precisely at the front edge was placed a small logo, no more than an inch and a half squared, pressed into the ribbon and presenting to the recipient, from whom, this gift hails. It was the logo of the WatchMaker.

"That took all of one day?", he thought to himself.

He carefully slid the ribbon off and cracked open the box. This moment, in retrospect, was the day his life truly changed and can most aptly be equated to when Marcellus Wallace opened the briefcase in Tarantino's masterpiece, Pulp Fiction.

Nestled inside, on a bed of jet-black velvet, sat the timepiece, as promised. It was exactly as he had requested yet somehow, so much more than he imagined. As he gazed at the work of art, he noticed that familiar bluish speckling throughout the metal. To say it was unique would be doing this masterpiece, one cardinal injustice. The billeting glistened under the fluorescent lighting like nothing this world was used to seeing.

He released the clasps on the oyster band and slid the dangling metal past his hand and onto his wrist. The moment he closed the clasps, he felt an indescribable chill throughout his body. It could very much, be described as if the watch had a soul of its own and it was choosing to become one with him. A few muffled internal clicks were heard after which, the watch's second hand began to rotate, smoothly around the matte black face. Then, the minute hand clicked into place. Surprisingly, the watch was already set to the correct time. It seemed fate or destiny knew the exact moment that he would put it on and it was set to begin its life's work at this same exact moment.

The watch was heavier than he expected but it wasn't overly burdensome. Its' fit was perfect. He made a concerted effort to move his arm more than usual to build up a charge within the movement. He sat back in his chair and absorbed his situation for a moment.

From the first second he first put it on, the watch seemed to attract lots of dust and lint. It was strange because when he would attempt to clean it off with the cloth inside the winder box, the dust and lint would just vanish, only to return a few minutes later. It was quite strange but then again, so was the guy who made it for him, the place where it was offered to him and ultimately, the manner in which he found himself taking possession of it.

After some time spent admiring it, he forgot he now had a roomie that's was sitting directly across from him, probably watching him swoon over a damn watch this whole time. The visual that popped up in his head was none other than that of Gollum caressing his precious and it made him laugh audibly.

"What's so funny?", Killian asked, peering around his laptop screen.

"I was just thinking of something.", he said dismissively. He stood up and began walking across the office toward Killian.

"Check this out... this watch was on my desk when we got here...", he said while raising his left wrist as he approached Killian's desk.

Killian pushes back from his desk, Christian thought, to stand and take a closer look. He didn't stand though. He remained seated with a worried, almost frightened look on his face.

"What's wrong?", Christian asked. At the same moment, he noticed Killian's eyes. He could have sworn they were a hazel color from what he could remember, but apparently, they had speckles of a dark crimson in them as well.

Christian then noticed his hands, as they gripped the arms of his chair. Dark crimson markings began to form along the backs. Christian took a step back. He then looked back into his eyes, which were now almost entirely filled in with the dark crimson color. His glance volleyed back and forth from Killian's eyes and hands again and he began to speak.

"You're Omnician...", he uttered, definitively, under his breath, just quietly enough that Killian heard him but couldn't quite make out what it was he had said.

"I'm what?", Killian replied with a blank stare on his face. He then noticed that Christian had been looking at his hands. He looked down at them as well. When he did, he noticed the discoloration and began to formulate a plan to talk his way out of this current predicament. The very next moment, JC entered the room.

"Good morning fellas!", He said, cheerily, as he nonchalantly strolled into the office. He noticed Christian standing, frozen in front of Killian, the watch on his wrist, then Killian's summonings. When Killian noticed the direction of JC's attention, he spun around in his chair and faced the windows, seemingly in Christian's estimation, to hide his true nature.

190

JC canvassed the situation and quickly came to the realization that his humorous approach was not going to cut it. Not this time.

"Christian... sit down... let's ... all of us... talk...", he said in a serious tone. Christian cautiously walked back to his desk and dyadically, sat in one of his guest chairs. He didn't know what to believe at this point so he decided, in this moment, to listen and only react to what JC had to say.

"Ok, first of all, I see you found the package that came for you this morning...
you told me you went to WatchMaker... you never told me he was making you a timepiece... is there anything else you didn't elaborate on last night?", He asked.

"Actually, there is...", Christian began, "but I don't actually know how or where to begin...

First of all, I didn't think it pertinent to mention the watch... I thought it felt boastful so I didn't... I'm sorry if you felt slighted by my omission...

Yesterday, I also purposefully left out some details...
Specifically, about the shoppe keeper. His name was Cyrus and yesterday, every time I began to mention details about him or my interactions with him, I got a strangle feeling in my gut, like something was telling me it wasn't a good idea to do so...
I can't explain it beyond that..."

JC interrupted, "so what was it... about this shopkeeper ...?"

"He was a ninety year old man but I could have sworn I'd met him before... at first I didn't realize it, but when he heard our story, he... changed...", Christian took a breath, gathered his words for a moment and continued, "I mean, his personality changed... it was like he was immediately 50 years younger... or his actions prior, were an act for show... I'm not sure which...

But I swear it, when he grinned... that look in his eyes and across his face... I could have sworn.... it was you.", Christian stopped, now staring at JC with the express intent of seeing his reaction, in an effort to gain some form or semblance of validation in this situation.

JC paused for a long moment. He was looking for the words to fruitfully continue this conversation.

"I had to let you get there in your own...", he responded, to which two dozen different emotions sequentially passed through Christian in the span of 10 seconds. Disbelief, denial, anger, betrayal, sadness, envy, wonder, admiration, fear and a host of others took turns leading Christian to his next comment.

"Get... where... exactly?", he asked.
Killian had turned around and was now listening to the conversation happening just across the room from him.

"You know the fishing proverb, right?
Well this is the best way I know to explain it... you can give a man a fish or you can teach him to fish.

Learn the latter and a man can eat but at the end of the day, all he really knows is how to catch fish...

he doesn't understand the why...

yes, he's hungry but there's more to it than that...

at some point it's not just about providing for himself... at some point he must teach his sons and neighbors or the whole world, what he knows of fishing and how it can sustain life...
with knowledge comes a responsibility to that knowledge...

it must be shared or... it must not be shared...

it has a destination and a purpose that must be upheld... that must be allowed to follow its purpose toward fruition...

you will never really know the right path until you've felt it... lived it... you must be mindful of the pitfalls and understand the gravity of the nature of what you've learned...

An artist can paint a picture of the rain but if he's never stood in it, felt it run down his face and dampen his clothing... he can never truly articulate that feeling... that importance... there will always be something missing from his rendering, because he doesn't really know it to be true...

I had to let you get there on your own... so you'd understand... so you'd be ready to carry this torch you've been asked to carry ...", he reached down and lifted Christian's wrist along with the watch.

"This is both a sword and a shield...

With this you'll always be protected from Omnicians that wish to do you harm...
And it will force summonings to appear, keeping Omnicians from hiding their true identity from you...

but it comes with a cost...

as long as you possess this, certain Omnicians will chase you to the ends of the earth to take it from your cold, dead corpse...

That's where Killian comes in...", Killian crossed the room to stand at JC's side.

"Yes... Killian is Omnician. A Master Kinezea to be exact. He is here at my request, to protect you from those who would wish to do you harm...

And with that on your wrist ...", he said again motioning to the watch on his wrist, "there are plenty who will try.

Killian can help with that... but you must remember... keep your distance when he has to do his thing... it won't allow an Omnician to cast in your direct vicinity... not even Killian."

He ended his statement only to see even more confusion across Christian's face.
Christian continued, "So... if he's an Omnician... are you?"

"I think it's time I tell you knew what JC stands for...

it's not Jefferson Clinton as most of the internet has been led to believe...

It's Julian ... Julian Cyrus..."

It finally clicked in Christian's mind, like dominoes, that had been stacked over the course of a millennium, finally toppling, one onto the next. All the research, that aura of smarts and understanding and that annoying, recurring comment "I had to let you get there on your own...", finally made sense. He needed to understand their plight and their responsibility... and he now did.

"So ... I don't know how to ask this but... what are you?", Christian continued, "I've met Elementae, Therians, Precepts... now I live with a Master Kinezea, whatever that is...."
Killian spoke up, "Well C, a Kinezea...", Julian interrupted with a subtle raised hand just inches from where it rested by his side and Killian dropped it.

"I... am something else, entirely...", he paused. Killian turned toward Julian with concern about what he was about to say next, but he knew he owed it to Christian, and so, he continued.

"Let me tell you a story Christian,
A long time ago, the Omnicians lived, though hidden from man, as a united people throughout the world. Omni kings were from a long line of the blessed known as the Adaptives. They have somewhat of a sixth sense about this world..."

This piqued Christian's interest and he shifted his full concentration to Julian.

"that provides them a sort of reactionary invincibility against all threats, Omnician or otherwise.

Well, the first Adaptive King was named Adom. He led his people honorably, yet ferociously. His oldest childhood friend took his side and served him, as hand. His name was Kayan and he was what is now, known as a Chrono. By definition, blessed in manipulation of the timeline."

Christian was focused on the story and he began to notice patterns emerge, patterns that had been hiding in plain sight, this whole time... throughout the annals of history.

"Adom ruled for hundreds of years, with Kayan faithfully by his side, until his death. From that point forward, other Adaptives and Chronos have emerged, but not since, has one been the caliber of Adom. So, every Adaptive born since, was considered heir to the throne but none since, had ever been forced to earn it. Each were coddled by the elders and each, became corrupted or complacent. These leaders failed the people they were charged to rule.

Sometime after, an elected Prime named Pacirus declared in his transcendence, which is a form of perpetual law only issued once during the life of a ruling Prime, all Adaptives and Chronos are to be terminated at discovery. Not since, has an Adaptive reigned prime, nor a Chrono, by his side..."

Christian spoke up, "So, wait... where's Eve?"

"What do you mean?", he asked.

"Well, Adom is clearly in relation to the Bible's Adam... and Kayan, I'd assume from the story of Cain and Abel... so how does Eve tie into all this...?", he asked. Killian glanced in Julian's direction, seemingly impressed by Christian's astute observation.

"See, K... I told you he was the right one...", Julian continued, "Actually, Eva ... was Adom's wife... she herself, a Master Elementae. Together, Adom, Kayan and Eva formed what's known to the Omnicians as The Genesis Trivium.",

"The what...?", Christian asked. Even Killian looked confused at this point.

"The Trivium is essential to Adaptive rule. To rule, one must have three things, Fearlessness, Compassion and Foresight. The Trivium provides that, as one man almost never possesses all three of these gifts in abundance. The Adaptive is fearless, the Elementae, compassionate and the Chrono, insightful. Together, A Trivium provides for stable and fair rule ...
What is leadership with no checks and balances? Tyranny, right?", he asked.
Christian agreed with a nod.

"That's what the Trivium does… and why every subsequent Adaptive has failed", he paused.

The last domino in Christian's mind finally toppled, with an enlightening thud. The last little bit, he now understood and it was now written across his face.

He spoke, "So… that was you… is you… and you're you… strangely… it makes sense now… but how does that work, exactly? It must be similar to astral-projection, right?"

Julian crossed his arms and leaned back, in a moment of immense pride. Christian continued, "… you're … a Chrono… right? … and The Wanderer is an Elementae … ", he continued to search his mind, "… then Blake's … Wait… where does Penny come into all of this?"

"Who?", Julian asked, peculiarly.

"Penny… You know… Penelope… the Precept of Alanis? Come on… you don't remember…? You just saw her yesterday… as a matter of fact she's probably…", and just like that, the realization of what was happening hit Christian all at once.

A good Chrono can perform feats never before seen by man. A gifted Chrono can read the history from the matter surrounding him, but, in theory, a truly blessed Chrono could essentially become that matter, albeit for a short period of time. It would take an insane level of understanding of historical events, an even more gargantuan level of attention to detail and even more so, an ungodly amount of subtlety to manipulate the timeline effectively without changing something that would have disastrous effects on the future interaction, destination and purpose of all associated matter. Not to mention, the effects that said matter has on any and all matter it comes into contact with subsequently, and in perpetuity. In theory, quantum computing is expected to be able to perform these intricate layers of calculation, but at best, it's still in its infancy. Watson's quantum API is really just a proof of concept at this point. How could he do this? Christian appeared to become worried by this development and Julian recognized it.

"So… Is the timeline truly linear? Are we predestined or do we truly have free will?",
Christian asked, hoping to get an answer but really expecting none in response. In a moment reminiscent of Gupta from the long since cancelled NBC sitcom Outsourced, Julian bobbled his head, seemingly both confirming and negating his question, simultaneously with that familiar, mischievous smile across his face.

"So… Have you… met her yet?", he concluded, glancing upward toward Julian, his head slightly tilted to the side.

"I know not of what you speak...", Julian responded, with a carefree smile, "But I will say... that feeling you get in your gut sometimes ... the one that urged you to withhold details about the shoppe keeper from me ... continue to trust that feeling... It'll serve you well."

Christian began to feel like the conversation was leading to another parting of ways.
He stood up and started walking toward both men standing near the door. He realized he was still wearing the watch, so he slipped it off and tossed it onto the desk. Julian and Killian gasped, watching it, intently as it floated through the air and landed haphazardly and clunkily, in its' box. Killian looked at Julian and with squinted eyes and a flat smile, as to suggest..., 'Not bad at all...'

Julian reached into his jacket pocket and pulled out a small, leather journal. He extended it and Christian's hand met his halfway, grasping the other end. Julian then placed his other hand on top of Christian's.

"Everything you need is here... I trust you'll know what to do when the time comes...", He reached out and hugged Christian in a brotherly embrace. Julian turned to Killian and hugged him as well. Tears were beginning to form in Killian's eyes as he embraced his friend for what he knew to be the last time.

With a nod and one last scan around the room, Julian Cyrus turned toward the door. There stood his assistant, Patricia. She hadn't been standing there long enough to get the full scoop but she did get the jest of what was happening. After all, she was his assistant and most of what he wanted to do, she made happen. Many who knew her said she reminded them of Donna from Suits.

"Don't forget your umbrella... you never know when it'll start raining.", She said, extending it toward him with a warm smile. It was one of those classic, English styled umbrellas, complete with golden handle and bluish gray metal Ferrule. It even had a logo stamped onto the end of the crook. An all too familiar circle design with two letters embossed below.

An W sitting just above an M.

As he walked through the office and toward the elevator doors, they heard the fading sounds of humming, then the loudly sung words of Sinatra's, The Best is Yet to Come.
Later that day, the internet and broadcast media were abuzz with the day's activities.

The headlines read,

"Reclusive Media Mogul Leaves Entire Fortune to Trusted Employee"
"New Ownership Structure Filed with SEC for Fastli.com"
"Fastli.com New Chief Editor Named"

"America's Youngest Head of Major Media Outlet. Who Is Christian Jones?"

15
StoneCon

Being a publicly traded company, The BrownStone Corporation is required by law, to perform certain actions throughout the year. First and foremost, they must file quarterly and annual financial reports with the Securities and Exchange Commission, so investors have a standardized source of truth for the profitability and goings on, of said entity. They must maintain a current cap table, or a record of all stockholders. Most companies that wish for their stock to be considered an institutional quality security, must have first and foremost, stable profitability, but also quarterly earnings calls or public conference calls where the senior executives discuss financial performance and key operating metrics with interested parties.

Most who participate tend to generally be analysts at the major investment firms that provide external coverage and opinions on the decisions being made within these companies. Finally, and most importantly, an investment worthy company will host an annual stockholder's meeting to discuss the prior year's financial performance, current year's budget, market analyses, new products and any additional pertinent information a shareholder or potential investor may want to know. This is one arena in which StoneCorp shines.

Admittedly a blatant rip-off of Comic-Con, StoneCon is their take on the annual shareholder's meeting. In name, is where the intellectual imitation ends. StoneCon is attended by hundreds of thousands each year. It is where Brandon Stone and Tamara Brown launch new products, invite esteemed guests to speak and host round tables to discuss every topic under the sun that may, in some form or fashion, impact or be impacted by the operations of StoneCorp. The first three days are like am abbreviated World's Fair. The last day is a massive StoneCorp presentation. The convention, usually held in Chicago, was this year, being held in New Orleans. Every year, the convention is filled to capacity with any and all persons who wish to bring their products or services to share with the world and anyone is invited to do so.

Stone has even made several acquisitions of innovative products and services from The Forum, as it's called, over the years. During these three days of The Forum, the company hosts junior inventor competitions with the winners taking home scholarship dollars and a lucky few, earning internship positions within StoneCorp.

Stone's attractions are always head and shoulders above all others who present and this year was to be an event to remember. Teasers of this year's presentation made the rounds throughout financial media and this year was an event not to be missed. It was rumored in the press, that this year, the pinnacle of technological innovation will be presented and shared with the world.

Every single media outlet had a delegation there. Every major YouTube blogger was there as well. At least one writer from every paper and outlet on the planet, was om attendance. Except for one. Whatever it was this year, it had better deliver, for StoneCorp's sake.

The three days preceding the StoneCorp presentation began with business as usual. Thousands of businesses, hobbyists and aspiring inventors were in attendance. If awards were given out, Best in Show would have gone to Foster and Company's, Foster Home Products exposition. With the help and guidance of Joel Gibbs at GES, they put together an entire suburban city block to showcase their suite of Neighborhood Network products. They, by way of GES, spared no expense. The demo was basically a small neighborhood, complete with mockups of an anchored retail shopping center and gas station, to demonstrate their new products.

Every structure on the Foster and Company expo was open to the public and thousands of Forum goers spent hours trapesing through the makeshift city block. The products presented included *NetGain*, a residential electricity generation solution, *Foster for Men*, a line of home goods and grooming appliances specifically designed for men, *Stork*, a home automation platform for laundry service, *Jetwash*, a new take on the ceiling fan and an endless list of proprietary home automation products and solutions. Then there was the crown jewel. Named *Fetch*, it was a home automation system so advanced and cutting edge, I wouldn't be able to describe it here and do it proper justice. It was by far, the most popular exhibit among polled Forum visitors, with crowds of hundreds surrounding the exhibit, over the three days prior to StoneCorp day.

The convention center was 1.1 million square feet of expo space. StoneCorp laid claim to the New Orleans Theatre and the La Nouvelle Ballroom and these areas were closed off to the public prior to day four. The shareholders meeting and voting was to be held in the theatre and a special presentation was to follow in the ballroom. The theatre seats 4,000 but Stone had additional seating worked in where possible, raising the capacity to 4,500. Laser LED 4K projectors were casting live broadcast feeds from the stage onto forty-five, foot screens, suspended above both ends of the stage.

StoneCorp engineers and hired hands scrambled for seventy-two straight hours to get the ballroom presentation constructed and ensure everything was perfect. If the end result was any indication, they earned every dollar and accolade they received.
The morning of the StoneCorp presentation was hectic to put it mildly. Delegations from every news outlet on the planet converged on the Ernest N. Memorial Center, all at once. When the doors opened at 8:00AM, camera crews scrambled to ensure a first-rate view within the theatre. The total population of shareholder representatives in attendance, totaled about 1,300, mostly from institutional investing

houses, along with a smattering of dedicated retail investors. The remainder of seats were assigned to, who Tamara decided, would be the most impactful of media delegations. The crowds began to file in and find their assigned seats. The forward sections were roped off for shareholders and at side stage, there were sections specifically roped off for news camera crews which were the first sections throughout the theatre, to fill.

The agenda provided, stated the schedule as follows:

8:30AM: BrownStone Corporation Introduction Video

9:00AM: Financials Review
- CFO Adam D. Young
    - 2018 Financial Performance
    - 2019 Budget Presentation

10:00AM: 2018 Strategy and Market Review
- COO Tamara Brown
    - 2018 Market Review
    - 2018 Strategy Review
    - 2019 Market Forecast
    - 2019 Initiatives Presentation

11:00AM: CEO, Brandon Stone Presentation
- State of the Corporation
- View from the Crow's nest
- 2019 Talking points

12:00 PM – 5:00 PM: Special Presentation and Demonstration, La Nouvelle Ballroom
- Lunch to be served
- Prescheduled Interview sessions
- Q&A roundtables

As the attendees began to file into the theatre, last minute finishing touches were being finalized with frantic BrownStone employees, easily identifiable by the shit brown polo shirts, with the recognizable cream BrownStone Logo on the left sleeve, mated with tan slacks. Many, if not most, of the retail investors in attendance treated this day like it was Super Bowl Sunday. They were owners in this thing with most taking great pride in the production. New money investors were easily spotted amongst the parade of stockholders. They were the ones wearing sunglasses in a dimly lit theatre, waving to the cameras. One even had the audacity to pull out the finger guns and while mere feet behind an on-air CNBC reporter, gave an audible *pew, pew, pew*.

At 8:25am, the house lights signaled the presentation was imminent and the crowds began to quiet once the house lights dimmed. A video began to play. This was rather boilerplate, showing brief interviews with BrownStone employees that, of course, had nothing but positive things to say about the company. Boring corporate team building events and other Pro-BrownStone propaganda and other meaningless, corporate cheerleader type fluff filled the screens and the first few minutes. The meat and potatoes of these presentations are the financials, performance stats and the upcoming fiscal plans. Or at least that's what it should be about.

After the video ended to a loud round of applause, Patrick Garrett, BrownStone EVP of Investor Relations took the stage and served as emcee for the remainder of the presentation. His first task was to present the CFO Adam D. Young, who took the stage and spent the next thirty minutes putting the majority of the crowd to sleep with walls of numbers, projections, forecasts and related commentary. This data is vital to the successful operation of BrownStone and fascinating to industry insiders, but most people don't want to know what's in a hot dog, they just want to put mustard, onions and cheese on top and chow down.

Mr. Garrett took the stage as Mr. Young walked off to moderate applause. Next, he announced Tamara Brown to discuss corporate operations. Backstage, as Patrick delivered a two-minute prepared introduction, Brandon and Tamara stood, stage left as Tamara took one last look at her prepared notes.

"You'll do great... ", Brandon uttered, while keeping his eyes on the crowd.
"I know... ", she said with a confident smirk. Most would have taken this as a conceited response, but Brandon knew her better than anyone. She was nervous and overcompensating and he could see right through it. Just as she began to walk onto the stage, he heard a voice from behind him say, "She really is a beautiful woman.... Isn't she?"

She garnered considerably more applause and a handful of distasteful cat calls from, probably, those same sunglass-wearing, new-money investors. She, however, is the consummate professional, always dialed in and precise in her execution. She was able to keep the crowd engaged and participative to a certain extent. She educated the crowd on how they measure success within this business and even gave out gift cards for participants who showed enthusiasm in volleying back her attempts to engage the crowd, as best she could. She left the stage with a wave and a smile, to a much, more rowdy salutation. Next, was the reason everyone had come. Brandon Stone usually managed to muster an air about him when he spoke at these presentations. Mainly attributed to his dedication to the company which he founded but it could just as easy be the celebrity he relished in.

This time was different. While Tamara was on stage presenting, he was paid another unannounced visit from one Mr. Black.

"She really is a beautiful woman... isn't she?", he said just loud enough to break Brandon's focus.

"Excuse me?", he said clearly perturbed that someone would address him just before taking the stage. Until, of course, he recognized the owner of the voice.
"Mr. Black... it's nice to see you... how, by chance, did you get back here?", he asked, clearly struggling with the dual chore of getting

prepared to speak in front of 4,500 people while having a major discussion with a seriously important player in his next groundbreaking rollout.

"Oh, you know... people make mistakes... anyway, that's not important. I just needed to talk to you for a quick second...", he said in a tone that seemed cheery on the surface but deep down, was sinister as could be.

"Would you mind too terribly if we picked this up after I go on in a few minutes... I'll happily spend all the time you require....", He pleaded, becoming more and more distracted and panicky, with every passing second.

"Sorry, it can't wait... I was talking to Paul Bradley earlier and he informed me that we have a little problem with the reactor."

The color left Brandon's face as he stared at Mr. Black. "What... What's the problem?", he struggled to get the words past his lips.

"It's not so much a problem... for us, at least... but... more so ... for you... It turns out material costs are, in all reality, going to turn out to be quadruple per gram as we initially agreed. More precisely, it's 4.2 ... There's nothing we can do about that... as they say... it is, what it is..."

Brandon felt as if he were going to vomit when he looked at the stage clock and noticed it read 4:32 as it continued to tick down, approaching zero.

"Anyway, I'm sure we can still make this arrangement work... break a leg out there...",
Mr. Black said as he playfully nudged Brandon on his shoulder. Brandon stared directly into Mr. Black's eyes and the smirk across his face began to enrage him. Something had just dawned on Brandon. There would be no logical reason or need for the cost of acquisition to go up. They had the reactor and this was nothing short of extortion.

Without warning and out of an entirely emotional reaction, Brandon balled up his fist and in short order, put his shoulder into a punch that connected directly with Mr. Black's left cheek. The blow forced Mr. Black's chin into his right shoulder and blood slowly began to trickle from a newly formed cut in the left corner of his mouth. He calmly removed a handkerchief from the inside pocket of this jacket and dabbed the corner of his mouth. Then, slowly turned his head back to face Mr. Stone. Brandon was beginning to realize the potential implications of his callous and thoughtless response and began to internalize a plan centered on salvaging the rollout, despite the events of the past six second. To his surprise, Mr. Black turned to him and said, "I guess I deserved that... but I'm pretty sure you'll end up regretting it...",

He turned to face Paul Bradley, wiped the blood from his mouth again and the two disappeared backstage.

Brandon was nursing several emotions simultaneously. Mostly rage and anger but there certainly was a bit of panic and desperation in attendance, as well. He bent down, hands on knees and gasped for air. After catching his breath and calming his heart rate slightly, he noticed the stage clock was now down into the seconds. He tried his best to quickly muster his focus and get back on track. He reached behind and grabbed a bottle of water of a nearby table, took a long swig and violently threw the empty eight ouncer, randomly into the general backstage area. Tamara had begun to leave toward stage right and Patrick was beginning his prepared introduction for Mr. Stone.

The clock said thirty seconds. He rushed through ideas on how to frame this most recent development and how to make needed changes to the speech he was about to have to give. He sorted through several scenarios and each seemed insufficient. Ten seconds.

"...Now, please give a generous round of applause, for our Chairman and Chief Executive Officer, Brandon E. Stone.", Patrick Garrett said as he extended his left hand toward stage left.

Brandon emerged from the side of the stage, straightening his jacket and even though they had no idea what had just happened, he visibly and jokingly shook off the turmoil of the last few minutes, for the crowd. He glanced to stage right and noticed Tamara, in complete shock with mouth, gaped open, after witnessing his perceived tantrum from across the stage. He gave her a nod and a quick smile. It really is too bad that she completely saw right through it, as if his thinly veiled attempt at reassurance was wet toilet paper. He took an audible breath, caught by his lavalier microphone and began.

"Thank you, Patrick...", he said, trying to stall just long enough to give himself another second or two.

"Welcome... everyone to the BrownStone Corporation Annual Shareholder's meeting.", A brief round of applause followed.

"You've already heard about our financial performance from Adam D. Young and a review of our operational metrics and strategy from Tamara Brown... I could stand up here and continue to review measures and metrics or spin up some unique take on this year's performance and sell you on why we performed better that expected or... why you should care...

But I don't want to do that... I don't want to waste my time... and honestly, I don't want to waste yours either...

I had this entire speech written and prepared so much so, that I began to struggle with the tone in which I delivered it...

That's what wrong with our world today… we spend too much time focusing on the wrong parts of … everything… to be honest… collectively…

We focus on the delivery of a message, worrying about how it's received and less so on the words themselves…

We focus on perfecting the final two percent and not the foundational, first ninety-eight…

We focus on maximizing our stock price and not the good deeds we do… or could do… as a company…

We focus on where our boat is heading and not what's left in its' wake… What are we, as a company, contributing to the world?

Don't worry… I'm not having a Jerry McGuire moment up here or anything…"

The comment spurred a round of laughter from the audience.

"Earlier this year, I spent some time soul searching and began to think about… Am I… who… I thought I'd be when I graduated college? Have I done all… really any… of what I thought I could when the sky was the limit… the slate was blank and I had no worries, no responsibilities and I was wholeheartedly convinced that I could change the world? Is who I am now, worthy of who I knew I could be?

Sadly, I believe for most of us, the answer to that question is no…" He hung his head then began to pace the stage, his outward emotion becoming more somber.

"I challenge you… ask yourselves… are YOU who you thought you could be? Are you really what you envisioned you'd become? Was your childhood dream to manage institutional investments in this cold and calculating world?

… or work a job you can't stand just so you can pay a mortgage payment in a neighborhood that provides an above average school district for your children? I think that if you're honest with yourselves… you'll admit that you aren't, either… And that's ok… We're honest… we know we can do better…"

A man in a suit entered the stage from the wings, carrying an aluminum case. Brandon Stone stared directly into the camera and now. spoke to anyone watching. "For me… for us…", he said, motioning with his hands to include the entirety of the stage, "…That… stops… today…

205

Earlier this year, our research team made significant advances on a project we've been working toward..."

The man opened the case. Stone turned toward him and removed a metal glove from inside. He slid it onto his right hand, then turned back toward the audience holding up his closed fist.

"This glove...", he said, while looking toward the nearest camera, then up, to ensure the image was being broadcasted on the screens, above the stage.

"it's made of a special material...", he continued as he turned his hand over and opened his palm, "and this... this little blue metal here... this is called... Brownstonium..."
More laughter came from the audience.

"it's quite special really... while most materials here on earth react to their surroundings like heat or pressure or chemicals... this wonderful stuff... it impacts the material around it..."

He backed up a step or two for the camera, then tossed the lug of metal into the air. As expected, and to the delight of the crowd, It completely disappeared until he motioned as if he were grabbing something out of the air and it reappeared in the glove's grasp. He did this several more times only to hear the gasps of the audience grow, each time.

"It's a neat little trick but this is just the tip of the iceberg...
This material is the centerpiece of an entirely new division we're launching within The BrownStone Corporation. We've decided to call it... Savior.

With Savior's launch, we've decided that it's time that corporations give back. It's time we led our world and our peers into the future. That's why we will be leading the charge with the first of many new product launches taking aim at the biggest, toughest, most unsolvable issues our world is plagued with... and we're starting with world hunger...

In the ballroom, we've set up a demonstration of the first of many solutions to show each and every one of you how Brownstonium will change the world...
It's called the Agridome. In essence, these agridomes can speed up the time it takes to mature crops. We can grow virtually any traditional plant, to its' full maturity, in a matter of minutes... compared to traditional farming methods... that takes months."
The crowd seemed divided. Some, began to mockingly snicker, while others roared in excitement and disbelief as camera flashes began to explode throughout.

Stone turned around and slipped the glove off and placed it back into the waiting case. As the man carried the case offstage, he crossed paths with another who rolled a flatbed dolly onto the stage. Sitting on the flatbed was a steel planter box about twelve inches high, complete with a touchscreen mounted onto the side facing the audience. When it came closer to the camera, it was clear the planter was filled with soil that had faint bluish gray speckles throughout. On the touch screen, the numbers 00:00 just sat there.

The planter was left at Stone's side.

"Here…", Stone reached into his jacket pocket and removed a small envelope. From the envelope, he pulled out a single seed that he held between his thumb and forefinger. He stepped toward the camera so it could get a closer shot.
"With this one seed…", he said as he bent down and pushed it about two inches into the speckled soil, "We can feed the world…"

He stood back up and straightened his jacket again. He stood, crossed his arms behind his back and for a long moment, nothing happened. The screens above the stage showed a close up shot of the soil that lay dormant. There were muffled rumblings beginning from the audience.

Then, a gasp was heard from the crowd and to everyone's surprise, a small green sprout poked up from within the soil. It began to grow, slowly at first, then, much more rapidly, all the while clearly visible, documented and proudly displayed on the forty-foot screens above. A few moments later, it had grown into a bushy green mass approaching the height of Brandon's waist. On the screen and under some of the foliage, small green spheres began sprouting.

Within several seconds, the newly grown plant had grown a dozen large, deep red, ripe tomatoes. Stone reached down, plucked one off of the vine, put it to his lips and took an oversized bite. The tomato tasted sweet and ripe as some of its' juice trickled down the sides of his mouth. He held it out toward the camera to show the audience the inside of the tomato. It was a deep red and virtually identical to a traditionally grown tomato because… well, in all reality, it was a tomato. He then pointed down at the touchscreen on the planter, which had been started when he pressed the seed into the soil. It read 02:42.

"We can now grow anything… as quickly or as slowly, as we like…"

"Join me in feeding the world!", He concluded, raising both arms into the air. The entirety of the audience stood in unison and roared with cheers and applause that lasted the better part of two minutes.

"Please… each of you… make your way into the ballroom and we will show you our vision for the future… and thank you so much for being here…",
The spotlight that had followed him around the stage, darkened as the house flood lights began to rise. Tamara and Adam joined Brandon on

stage and the three together, waved to the cameras and the exiting crowd as a trio of piano, violin and cello played a live version of OneRepublic's, Secrets, from the orchestral pit, below.

The theatre began to empty as every soul made a mad dash for the ballroom to see what StoneCorp had in store, next.

Once the last attendees exited the doors and the song softly began its' coda, Tamara's mood instantly soured and she stepped into putting both hands into Brandon's chest, pushing him off balance.

"What the fuck was that?", Tamara asked, referring to his backstage exchange with Mr. Black.

"We just announced... just this moment... and the literal second before we do so, you go and pull some cowboy shit like that... are you trying to blow this thing up?", she asked.

"Two minutes before I took the stage, he dropped a bomb on me... They're upping the acquisition and collection cost.... 400 plus percent. Do the math in your head... that's well past profitability limits... anything we do with this shit is cost prohibitive now...
And we're completely dependent on them for collection.

You know where the reactor is... and you know they'll never let us remove it without a fight...

What do you suggest we do?", he said, frustrated.

"Shit...", Tamara uttered, realizing the girth and gravity of the shit sandwich they were both, collectively, just served. "Tell you what... ", she said, doing what she does best and in a much less hostile tone, "Let's make some lemonade... let's get through today. Let's make the best of what we've put together here and give the agridome a chance to blow them away. Let's see this through, then, we'll regroup and come up with a plan... ok?"

Adam hadn't been included in the details of the project outside of the financial planning and capital allocation aspects of getting to this point.

"Why can't we just pass those costs on to the user?", he asked.

Forgetting he had kept his money guy mostly in the dark, as to many of this program's unsavory aspects, he said, "Because we are the user... this is a goodwill play... we were planning to eat these costs until everyone and their dog begs us for our tech, then we customize the application individually, while maintaining full design and maintenance control and ensuring absolute secrecy... at 4x cost for consumables, it doesn't make sense...", he said, still languishing over his predicament.

"Can't we just make it? I mean, we have the formula, right? It's our IP, isn't it?", Adam continued.

"No, we can't...", Tamara responded until Brandon signaled for her to shut it down.
"Let's just get this done...", she said. The three left through backstage and exited the theatre.

From a darkened corner backstage, a faint purple glow was eerily visible, like a beast emerging from absolute darkness, Paul and Chadwick stood listening to the previous conversation, in its' entirety.

"He hates me... or should I say us...", Chadwick said to Paul, with a grin. The cut on his mouth had long since stopped bleeding but the swelling and bruising was starting to form.

"Yeah... just think...", Paul added, "He knows what we are and he still swung at you... I feel pretty confident that he took the bait... but how can you ensure that he will go on the offensive?"

"He will... maybe not until after he pays that 4.2 multiple a few times, which was a nice touch by the way, but he will...", Chadwick said. The two turned and disappeared, once again, backstage.

The La Nouvelle Ballroom was a few hundred yards away and the three hurriedly walked the second-floor catacombs in an attempt to arrive prior to the opening of the doors. A few minutes later, the senior-most executives of StoneCorp arrived at the back entrance of the ballroom, just in time. Luckily, the staff hadn't yet opened the doors as the crowd was taking longer than expected to congregate to the ballroom.

They entered the ballroom and briefly marveled at what they had been able to put together.

Against the back wall, a large acrylic dome covered an octagon shaped planter bed filled with the same speckled soil. Its' footprint was just larger than a backyard trampoline. Inside, several cameras were mounted to the scaffolding securing the acrylic dome and each were pointed toward a different area of the bed. Next to the dome sat the planter used in the presentation, just moments ago. Above the dome were two large screens providing visibility for everyone in attendance.

The remainder of the space was filled with tables, each set for what was to be, a three-course lunch. Between the makeshift dining room and the dome, an open kitchen was set up with two dozen chefs preparing to serve 4,000.
As the doors opened, the crowd entered the ballroom, ready to continue this journey. After some time, the attendees entered and found their assigned seats. Waiters began bringing out bottles of Italian wine and

bottles of sparkling water, stemmed glasses, bread baskets and everything else one would expect to precede a nice dinner.

Brandon grabbed the microphone and started,
"Hey everyone... welcome to the second act of our opus...", the crowd began to quiet down, "I don't know about you, but I'm starving. One of my favorite meals ... of all time... is spaghetti and meatballs. It seems to hit the spot when I've had a long day or just want to watch TV... will you join me in some spaghetti and meatballs?"
The chefs had been busy boiling water for noodles and preparing meatballs, but something was missing.

"I like Caesar salad with my spaghetti too... anybody else?", he added, with a smile on his face. Most raised their hands or whooped in approval.

He pointed up to the screens and the camera feed from inside showed a couple of gardeners, both dressed in kind, planting some kind of seed throughout the soil. One of the gardeners held up one of the tiny seeds to the camera. Moments later, heads of Romaine lettuce could be seen sprouting from within. A few moments later, the gardeners began to pluck the heads of lettuce and one of them emerged from the dome with eight or ten heads in a basket. These were then handed to one of the chefs who began the process of making salads, sized for a table. The other chefs joined in and between eggs being cracked, the scratching of wire whisks on metal bowls and the general commotion of the attendees watching the monitors, bowls of leafy greens began to appear on the tables throughout the ballroom. The attendees, while hesitant at first, started to sample the freshly grown greens and if judged by the increasing ambient volume and conversations around the room, it would be safe to say they were enjoying it.

Then, Brandon approached the aluminum planter box and picked one of the larger tomatoes from one of its' branches.

"I did say that with that one seed, we would feed the world.... Didn't I? Let's start with the 4,000 here... shall we?", he said, then turned and tossed the tomato to one of the gardeners, that then took it inside the dome. Once back on the screen, the gardener tore the tomato in half and began to scoop out the seeds and commenced to planting them, as well. The other gardener pulled a packet of seeds out of his front pocket that he began planting himself. These turned to out to be basil plants.

In a few minutes, tomatoes and fresh basil, by the bushel were being brought out of the dome to the awaiting chefs. After some chopping, tomato pressing and an artful simmer, large bowls of spaghetti and meatballs began circulating throughout the ballroom. As the smell of tomatoes and Italian sausage filled the air, Brandon couldn't help but be proud of the presentation that they had put together. Everyone seemed blown away by their method of launch and if the atmosphere were any indication, they liked the lunch as well.

Brandon and Tamara stood off to the side of the room and listened to the conversations happening all around them. Mostly, they were about how amazing this new development was. Some spoke of potential uses for this technology while others tried to figure out how this was possible. One man, a long-time veteran of print media, approached Brandon and Tamara and congratulated them.

"Mr. Stone, my congratulations on a job well done. In all my years of covering these shareholder meetings, I've never seen anything like this... dare I say, you just might get a Nobel Peace prize out of this..."

Brandon thanked him for the kind words and played coy and humble, as usual. When he walked away, Brandon again found himself thinking back to that conversation with Mr. Black and still found himself at a complete loss as to how they were going to get out of this jam. Today, he had created a monster. The world would soon have an insatiable appetite for this and he needed to figure out a profitable way forward. One thing was for sure though, he would make Mr. Black and everyone else involved, regret the day they decided to make an enemy of StoneCorp.

16
Meteorite

After a long day of shaking hands and getting current on everything Fastli, Christian decided to spend one last, quiet night at home. He knew things would soon change and he just wanted one last taste of the simple life. He cooked himself dinner consisting of pan sautéed chicken and a packet of instant ramen. He spent the remainder of the evening getting current on his backlog of texts and emails.

He had a plan. Work emails and texts, then family and friends, then Katie. The first email in his bloated inbox was from a local law firm that represented Julian and the subject line read, Regarding the Estate of Julian Cyrus. He decided to leave that one for last. The majority of emails were congratulatory in nature and from work colleagues. He replied with boilerplate responses to most of the emails and texts saying something to the tune of 'Thank you for the kind words... Hope you're doing well...' He ignored the many emails from the alumni association of his alma mater, querying about fundraising. He even had to resort to blocking the number because the calls were relentless.
Back to the law firm email, he opened the email and it read,

Mr. Jones
We represent the estate of Julian Cyrus and we have some documents we need to go through with you.

Please accept the attached meeting invite for 9:00 am tomorrow. We will gladly accommodate and meet you at your office.

We look forward to meeting you tomorrow.

Welcome to the family,
Von Erich, Adkisson & Associates

He clicked on the accept button and a few seconds later an Outlook notification reminder popped up on his screen.

On to friends and family. Most of the texts were from aunts, uncles, 1st, 2nd and 3rd cousins, twice removed, whatever that means. Each asked some variation of, "is it you? Are you the same Christian Jones we keep hearing about on the tv?", To which, he simply replied, 'Nope... I wish!", except for his mom. He told her everything. Well, not everything, per se, but all of what she needed to know, right now. After the first text, she Immediately called and he talked to her for about an hour. She refused to let him off the phone until he promised to take some time off soon and go on a trip with her. What good is having all the money in the world if you can't live a little, or worse, if it changes you?

Two days ago, while in route home, he read and re-read Katie's email response. The words she had written were burned into his memory, at this point.
 It read,

Christian,

It's been a hectic couple of weeks. After we were pulled from San Juan, we went back to DFW and had to talk to a bunch of people from the FAA and the FBI.

Since then, I've been in a dozen different hotels in as many days. I'm taking several days off next week and am looking forward to some downtime.

I'd really enjoy meeting up for dinner or drinks or something... after the two weeks I've had, maybe two drinks ...

By the way, what was it you had in mind that was similarly stimulating?

See you soon,

Katie

;-)

He's not sure when she sent it, but there was now another message from Katie within the same email thread.

He read,

Christian,

I've cut my last trip short this morning and will be flying home on Thursday. Any chance you're free and would like to get together on Friday night?

Let me know,
Katie

Christian resisted the urge to fist pump and instead, opted to scream out a loud YES! She actually asked him out. He had never been asked out on a date by a woman before. A couple seconds later, Killian burst through his door. Christian had almost forgotten he had a roommate, slash, bodyguard one floor down. The predicament in which he was currently entangled began to rear its' ugly head again. There would be no hiding Killian from Katie. Plus, how was he supposed to explain this house and these cars and... He began to panic a little.

Killian had been watching the emotional evolution develop for a few seconds now.

213

"What's wrong, man?", Killian asked.

"Nothing... just...", he paused, "this girl I met in San Juan asked me out this Friday and with everything going on... I'm not sure how I'm going to explain any of this to her.", he said, gesturing in a suggestive manner toward Killian.

"Don't worry about that now... we'll figure that out later... wait, you did say yes, right?", he asked.

Christian realized he hadn't responded yet. He typed the following.

Katie,

I'm sorry, I just saw this message.
I'd love to... err, I'd really like to see you again on Friday but I'm not sure how my wife would react to me going on a date and all...

So, ... Friday then?

;-)

Christian

He had a smirk on his face. He was really hoping she hadn't forgotten his self-described, unique brand of humor. For anyone else, writing what he just had, in an email addressed to someone you hope to date, would be tantamount to dating seppuku. But if he were right about how he expected her to interpret and respond, she may be worth the risk.

A few minutes later his phone made that swooshing sound synonymous with a new email in the chute.

Christian,

I'm really sorry to hear about your wife's feelings and all... I mean, my husband isn't crazy about it either but I think I kind of like you...
;-)

Friday it is then...
I'll text you my address...

Bye for now,
Katie

There aren't many comparable feelings in this world like having a gut feeling about someone, taking a gamble and making such a risky comment to that someone in the hopes that the person interprets your words exactly the way you intended. Let's be clear. Neither Christian, nor

Katie were actually married. He did however, now know that she may be his perfect match. Serve, volley, point Katie.

He lowered his phone and smiled. Killian asked, so Christian gave him the play by play.
"Ballsy...", Killian responded, "that could have easily blown up in your face...but since it didn't, I guess that's a sign..."

Killian wasn't what you'd call, a total slouch with the ladies. If him being 6'5" didn't help, the fact that he's a kinetic has come in handy in the past. While he generally denies doing it, he has indeed used the classic "rolled-napkin-turns-into-a-real-red-rose", trick to impress one specific lady. Again, he'd never admit it to anyone, but I'm pretty sure he also actually uttered the phrase, "Will you accept this rose?", while longingly looking into her eyes after. I just wish I could hear Danny, Corby and Mike decimate the play by play of this move with Chris Harrison during Danny's Pig Pen, all while Mino creates mass chaos by feathering in drops of Danny giving directions.

Lost by the last sentence? Why don't you look it up on your phone?

Christian began to wonder how they'd explain Killian's presence. Killian had a decent suggestion. Tell her the truth. Well, not the whole truth of course, but the truth that was good enough for his mother. The chances of her having seen something about him and Fastli in the news were fairly high. He'd have to tell her eventually anyway, so why not be up front about it now? Christian decided that this was probably the best course of action, if he was indeed, serious about her.

Something else then came to mind. He couldn't very well pick her up in the GT-R or worse, that damn G Wagon. What kind of message does that give? He'd have to rent a car a little less conspicuous or something. He looked on his dresser and noticed JC's leather-bound journal. He hadn't even looked at it since JC handed it to him, moments before his cryptic departure. Christian walked to the dresser. He curiously opened the cover. As the binding creaked, written on the first page was a large smiley face. As Christian flipped through, his panic escalated with each subsequent turn to its' next blank page. Written on the back of the last page was a colon and capital B. Across, taped to the back cover was a silver house key with 3636 etched into it and a SD Micro memory card.

Christian detached the key, looked at it for a moment, then put it in his pocket. He then, took the memory card and inserted it into the slot on his laptop. Killian approached and sat down in the chair next to Christian, to watch along. When the memory card loaded and ran, instead of a login prompt asking for a password, a message with JC's face popped up and a short interactive video played.

"Hello Christian... and I assume Killian as well...
If you're watching this, I'm gone.

I just have one question..."

The image of JC faded out and it was replaced by a Fastli logo, slightly off center and tilted to one side. Below was a text entry box with a narrow font question written above.

It simply asked, "What's that smell?"
Christian thought for a moment, then looked at Killian, who appeared lost and clueless.
After a brief moment, Christian got that smartass smirk on his face again and into the text prompt, typed...

'patent pending'

Expecting a message saying, Incorrect Password, Try Again, he was surprised to see the screen go black. Then an image of JC's face appeared on the screen with a still image of his signature, sarcastically straight face. His voice began to speak.

The video was about two hours long, during which, both Christian and Killian shed tears, were amazed and terrified by what they heard, both feared for and received strengthened hope in humanity and dreaded the upcoming year. But by the end of the video, each understood exactly, JC's wishes, mission and what must be done by them both. Their first predicament was soon to be solved.

If you're not familiar with the Dallas area, it's easily described as follows. The Dallas Fort Worth area is basically a giant diamond covering approximately 10,000 square miles of North East Texas and seems to be constructed, almost entirely of highway concrete. Bordered to the north by Denton, south by Waxahachie, west by Fort Worth and to the east, Dallas. Just slightly north of the center mark, lies the DFW International Airport, which sits on more land than the entire island of Manhattan. Interstate highways 20 and 30 run east and west while Interstates 35 and 45 provide north/south access. I35 southbound splits in Denton, with I35 East taking you south through Dallas, while I35 West takes you south through Fort Worth. They both reconvene to the south just north of Hillsboro, TX. If one were to drive from the northern junction of I35 in Denton, south with empty roads, you would reach the southern merge in a little less than ninety minutes. If there's constant traffic like usual, that same trek can take you half a day or more, especially on I35 East.

As described in JC's message, just up 35 East, to the north of Dallas, sits a nondescript building. On the southbound service road and under a bridge with no exit ramp, is home to a small, yet special used car dealership. A massive sign is attached to the building's front corner consisting of hundreds of exposed light bulbs arranged to spell HOT RIDES, in classic marque fashion. They cater to the automobile aficionado, specializing in high end and unique cars of all kinds. It's basically a toy store for middle aged men.

In more densely populated cities, car share clubs are a normal occurrence. For an initiation fee and monthly dues, you can have immediate access to a stable of cars as opposed to owning one and shouldering all the costs that come with it. Due to the size of the metroplex, starting one in Dallas would be considered by many, a huge waste of time. Hot Rides, however, figured out how to make one work. Initially launched for serious car guys with money to spend in the aftermarket, it came out of the gate, guns blazing and turned into a phenomenon, no one expected. Using an app developed by The PetDragon Group, Hot Rides was able to make the logistics of car share work across large distances.

Each member in essence, sells their car into or buys a car from the LLC at initiation. TheClub, as it's called, in turn performs all scheduled vehicle maintenance and warrantied repairs. In addition, it provides members access to automotive aftermarket component wholesaler pricing. The idea is that a member can make his car exactly what he always imagined it could be, and the entirety of the membership gets to benefit from his or her efforts. Additionally, if a member wants a different car for a specific occasion, all he or she has to do is get on the app and reserve it. A minion from the club is dispatched and delivers it. Since the club is member owned like a homeowner's association and many of the members are young professionals, they continue to think of innovative ways to make TheClub more valuable to its' family.

TheClub doesn't tolerate violence between its' members. Any members with an issue they are unable to settle between themselves, are expected to take it to the track and settle their disputes, usually with their Gran Turismo skills, or in extreme circumstances, to take it out back and prove your worth behind a real wheel. The winner is considered right, but more importantly, holds bragging rights as the better driver. Let's be honest, that's what's really important in the dichotomy of TheClub.

The coolest part about the whole thing is when, as a member, the car you're currently in, gets called in for service or upgrading. One side of their building is gated with chain link fencing and is used by the dealership. The other side of the building has an automated garage door with access controlled by a small black sphere mounted above. When a club car pulls up, it's instantly recognized. A short drive inside and into the back is where the fun starts.

As previously mentioned, many of the members are local business owners and young professionals. The entire membership is like one big family. They all bring some sort of specialty and value to the party. Within the back of the dealership, The Garage, as it's patented, is a round the clock party. Several members own local restaurants and will regularly send food and service staff over to feed the family. Others provide their services for free or cheap, for their fellow members. Out back behind The Garage, you'll find an outdoor kitchen with meats almost always on the grill, a bottomless beer fridge and numerous kegerators, horseshoe pits, professional cornhole alleys, one serious go kart track complete with graded turns and live music on the weekends. They even have an extremely talented tattoo artist that's a member and he can be found out back, giving tap out sessions. In short, it's basically a country club for gear heads. A place for guys and girls who'd rather live life surrounded by GT-R's and leather wrapped steering wheels than golf and designer handbags, any day.

The first task at hand, get a suitable car for a date. Christian and Killian looked at each other. Once Christian grinned, they both made a mad dash for the garage. Jockeying for position, Christian slipped under Killian's extended arm while gracefully gliding down the stairs, then rounded the corner, in a mad dash for to the garage door. He quickly snatched the keys to the GT-R and clicked engine start. The twin turbo V6 roared to life just as Christian hit the button, opening the garage door. It was nearly 9 pm but good thing for them, The Garage was accessible twenty-four hours a day, for members, of which JC was one of its' founders.

When JC first founded Fastli, he just so happened to drive by and notice Hot Rides one day. He ended up stopping to take a look at their inventory. A sucker for fast cars, he struck up a conversation with the manager, Mitchell. After a few visits to check out cars, JC purchased his first vehicle from them and mentioned the idea a car club, ride share concept to Mitchell and the rest, as they say, is history.

Christian, now firmly planted in the GT-R's driver's seat, stared at Killian through the windshield, until he begrudgingly set up shop in the passenger seat. They backed out of the driveway and make their way toward the Tollway. Once on the DNT, they'll hit the toll tunnel under 635, then take the high-speed toll ramp onto I35 East northbound. That's exactly what Christian did. The high-speed part, especially. Christian got it to 120 on the tollway. The car handled perfectly as if it were glued to the pavement. After taking the cloverleaf ramp at upwards of 60 mph, the car was nimble, weaving effortlessly, around other drivers before dropping out of sight and going subterranean. The echoing roar of the two large, spooling turbos led to a lazy top speed of 135 through the tunnel. Then, it was back to normal driving speeds once off the exit ramp and onto I35 as the Farmer's Branch cops keep a keen eye for cars such as this one, to pull over, just for fun.

After exiting Sandy Lake and taking the U turn, the lights of the Nissan emerged from behind the edge of the bridge support, preceded only a split second by the sounds of a downshift into second. Christian floored the accelerator. The turbos whined loudly just as the traction control engaged and the tires grabbed, launching the GT-R forward approaching nearly 100 mph in just short of a few hundred feet. The entrance to Hot Rides was approaching quickly so he let off the gas and allowed the engine to brake and slow the car. As the car downshifted and slowed, Christian and Killian noticed an unusual number of cars parked outside the shop for 9:30 at night. When they turned into the parking lot, they could hear the bumping of dance music coming from out back and Killian began to get a smile on his face. Christian glanced over and noticed the smile.

"What's that for?", he asked, as the GT-R waited at the garage door that began opening the moment the car approached it.

"You'll see...", he snickered.

The moment the door began to open Christian urged the car through the doorway. A dimly lit passageway led to The Garage, in the back of the shop. The floor and walls were painted to appear as if you were driving through a freeway tunnel, complete with the appropriate lighting. The entrance into The Garage was just at the end of the tunnel's final bend. They pulled into The Garage to see a flurry of activity. There were several exotic cars up on lifts as well as half a dozen other cars with their hoods up, having something done to each. The sparks of welders and the faint smell of burning flax filled the air just prior to being sucked through vents installed in the ceiling. Two dozen men and women along with The Garage mechanics were hard at work, preparing their rides to head a few miles down the road, to the street races, where there's cash up for grabs.

The first to spot the black GT-R was one of the staff mechanics.

"JC", he yelled in a whooping cadence. Most of the members in the direct vicinity stopped what they were doing and turned. Several of the attendees approached the Nissan as it pulled to a stop just inside The Garage. Killian opened his door first and hopped out to greetings, slapped fives and numerous fist bumps. Christian remained behind the wheel for a few moments, preparing himself for what followed. He was never a huge fan of large crowds or of being the center of attention. I think I mentioned that before but if I hadn't, it's probably an important fact to know.

Hearing the commotion coming from The Pit, as the working floor of The Garage is affectionately known, a thin man in his mid-thirties emerged from the dealership side of the shop. Mitchell was the manager of both Hot Rides and TheClub. He noticed the car that had just arrived and he got a smile on his face. When JC showed up, something interesting usually followed. Mitchell greeted his old friend Killian in the form of a somewhat, secret handshake. They gave each other a hug and just as Mitchell turned to greet JC, Christian opened the door and stepped out of the driver's seat.

"Who's this?", Mitchell asked Killian.

"Let's go talk...", Killian responded, waving for Christian to follow. The crowd surrounding the GT-R began to quiet as stares and whispers replaced the room's rowdy prelude. This clearly wasn't JC, the infamous founding member of TheClub. The three walked into the dealership side and went into Mitchell's office. With the door closed, Killian introduced Christian and commenced to explaining what had happened, in detail. Christian, leaning against the wall near the door, thought it peculiar that Killian was disclosing so much information to this Mitchell guy.

"So, we're roommates now... I guess you can treat him as if he were JC...", Killian concluded, shifting the focus of the conversation toward Christian. Mitchell was skeptical of new people as of late, but if Killian vouched for him, he must be ok. JC actually met Killian through the family here at The Garage. Killian grew up with Mitchell and in high school, the two had gained respect and a moderate following in North Dallas as being a formidable duo at the Friday and Saturday night street races off Luna Road and Northwest Highway. They were known for bringing unique rides every weekend and most usually ended up taking the evening's crown and the spoils. After high school, Mitchell continued to tinker with cars while Killian went off to serve in the military. When he returned from service, Mitchell, JC and a few others had launched TheClub and Killian nestled right back into the fold. He used to help out around The Garage, doing various odd jobs like deliveries and assisting on member installs for extra money until, by total accident, JC discovered his blessing and immediately hired him onto the Fastli payroll.

"So... it's Christian right?", Mitchell said, extending an open hand.

Christian shook his hand, "Yeah... Mitchell, right?", he replied. Mitchell had an easygoing demeanor and after a few minutes of talking between the three, it seemed he and Christian would get along quite easily. Mitchell motioned for the two to follow. He led them through the rows of exotics, sports cars and the rest of his inventory until they reached the door along the back wall leading into TheClub. Mitchell opened the door and took a few steps inside. Christian and Killian flanked him a few steps behind, on either side.

He picked up a canned air horn used specifically to call attention throughout The Garage and pressed the button. A piercing squeal blasted through The Garage, overpowering even the DJ's PA system. The DJ shut down the tunes to the apparent dislike of a large crowd of dancing girls in front of his setup. The crowd turned their attention toward Mitchell. Someone hit the buttons on the back wall, raising the automatic rollup garage doors and another hundred members out back crowded the doors to listen to Mitchell. He spoke loudly to project.

"Fam... got some bad news... Our brother JC is gone...While he'll definitely be missed, this is Christian. He is JC's friend, confidant and sole benefactor. As far as I'm concerned, he is our brother too. Let's have a moment of silence for the fallen...", the entire population standing before them each bowed their heads, crossed their hands in front of them and the entire room went silent. As bad as it may seem, the only thing going through Christian's mind at that exact moment was "Uh, Paul in ... uh...". He didn't feel too bad about it though, because he's pretty sure JC would have thought the exact same thing.

As the members began to raise their heads, Mitchell continued, "Now, how do we welcome new brothers and sisters?"

Every person standing in the crowd, in unison, raised their right hand into the air and with each index finger slightly curved toward Christian and said, in a unified, stereotypical Californian accent, "Sa Du...", It was enough to make Christian grin, as he knew exactly where that came from. He was now fairly certain that what ran through his head several moments ago had probably entered each and every person's mind at the same time, as well.

The DJ broke the silence with the intro to the Snoop, Nate & Warren G jam, So Fly and the level of rowdiness went right back to where it had been previously. The song prompted a massive sing along, starting from the first word of the first verse. Everyone eventually went back to what they were doing, previously. Mitchell stepped down into the pit and knifed through the crowd, toward the backyard with Christian and Killian close behind. While crossing through the back wall's open garage door, Mitchell reached into the nearby beer trough and grabbed a green bottle from deep within the ice. In a quick motion, he used a ring on his left hand to pop the cap and took a refreshing swig. Christian and Killian followed suit.

Out back, there were a couple hundred members congregated, many playing cornhole or horseshoes while others held fistfuls of dollars, apparently betting on the games in process. Christian, then noticed the go kart track as the scream of open throttles whined in sequence when the competition style karts rounded the curves of the track.

Christian tapped Mitchell on the shoulder.

"Mitchell, I need a car...", he suggested.

"What's wrong with that GT-R?", he asked, honestly puzzled by the question.

"I have a date... and I need something a little less... conspicuous.", he added.

"I think I got something for you...", he said, motioning for both to follow him back inside.

The three walked back through the crowd, up the stairs and back onto the showroom floor. He walked past several sedans and stopped next to a black, late model 7 series BMW. Instead of trying to sell Christian on this one, he simply turned and waiting on his opinion.

"Too ritzy...", he said, continuing to scan the showroom floor.

"I guess these are out of the question as well?", He motioned toward a champagne Bentley Silver Spur, then a black Rolls Royce Ghost parked right next to it. Something caught Christian's eye in the back.

"What's that?", He asked, pointing toward something covered by a dusty cover, wedged into the corner.

"Aww, you don't want none of that...", Mitchell said, grinning.

The three walked to the back and Mitchell ripped the cover off, revealing a completely restored 1965 Lincoln Continental convertible in pearl white. This car was his pride, joy and hands down, favorite restoration project he had ever done. He wasn't a fan of lending it out within TheClub but since Killian had to stay by Christian's side, he came to terms with the idea of his baby being shown off around town without him.

He held the keys, extended toward Christian and Killian. Just before Killian could take them out of Mitchell's hand, he pulled them back and said, "You gotta deal the GT-R first."

"What do you mean?", Christian said.

Killian explained to Christian how TheClub car share worked. Before he could take the Lincoln, he'd first have to find someone who wanted to take the GT-R off his hands. By all accounts, this shouldn't take more than about forty seconds. Christian paused for a moment, then took a quick pace back into The Garage and headed straight into The Pit.

"Hey!", he said loudly as he got the attention of several members with their heads buried under various hoods. He held the key fob to the GT-R between his thumb and index finger out in front of him, at eye level.

"Ya'll going to the races at Luna tomorrow, right? Anybody want to take this?", he posed the question while fidgeting the key fob slightly. One of the members working on an RX-7 stood and walked toward Christian.

"I'm Carlos by the way....", he said, wiping his hands with a shop rag before extending it toward Christian, "You sure you want to part with that beast? You may not get it back for a while...", he advised. Christian shook his head in affirmation and placed the key fob in Carlos' open hand.

"I'm sure...", Christian told him, with a mischievous grin, "Take this thing and go clean up...",

Carlos nodded in approval, clicked the unlock button and joined by the rest of his crew, went straight to the GT-R to check it out.

Christian looked at his watch and sighed when he noticed he had to, again, wiped off the accumulating dust. It was fifteen until midnight. He found Killian and spent a few more minutes talking with Mitchell. A few minutes later, the Lincoln was brought up front after being sent outside for a quick wash. As Mitchell and Christian were saying their farewells, Killian made his way to the driver's side, just so Christian had no confusion as to the arrangement for this special ride. The car had been retrofitted with a modern, naturally aspirated V8 pushing almost 500 horsepower. All in all, a truly respectable number given the entirety of the power gains come from moving parts, increased efficiency of designed components and from tolerances, instead of taking the easy route of incorporating forced induction. The exhaust notes from the V8 were deep and growly. Killian took extra care as he pulled out of the parking lot and began the journey back toward University Park.

While the GT-R definitely turned heads on the highway, it was nothing like cruising at 65 in this monster. When driving a sports car, one feels almost obligated to show off its' performance when someone glances over. In this car though, there's no obligation felt whatsoever to show it off. It does fine all on its' own. Half an hour later, Christian opened the garage door from his phone, while Killian took extra care to ease the car into the empty space. The steel wheels on the garage door rattled and squealed along the tracks, until a one final thud provided evidence that it had, indeed, completely closed. Tomorrow was going to be one long day so the two, with little by way of conversation, headed their separate ways.

The morning came early and Christian was completely distracted throughout the day. He didn't have managing a major media outlet on his mind, whatsoever. All he could think about all day was what this evening had in store. He managed to make it through his meeting at 9:00am and apparently, he was now the sole owner of Fastli.com, a host of other associated web sites and business assets, an entire list of real property holdings and various other businesses, along with a considerable financial securities portfolio. As 5:00 pm came, he and Killian quietly slipped out of the office and drove back to the house to prepare. It was supposed to be a warm evening tonight. Perfect for cruising with the top down.
Christian's phone buzzed. On the screen was a text notification from an 817 number he didn't have in his contacts. His stomach dropped as his pulse rose and he noticed his palms instantly became sweaty. The four-line message said,

7:00pm sharp
925 Main
Grapevine
See you at 7!
K

223

From that moment on, Christian felt as if he had an undeniably cheesy smile glued across his face, paired with a constant feeling of having to pee. I can remember getting this same feeling as a child, in the slow-passing hours prior to the family leaving to go to Six Flags over Texas. Christian hadn't given much thought to what they would do tonight. He just wanted to see her again. It had been three long weeks since San Juan. While Killian laid back on the couch and watched TV, Christian agonized over each and every detail of the goings on for the next few hours. To make it by 7, they would have to leave at 6, 6:15 at the very latest and hope 635 wasn't a parking lot.

Christian showered, shaved, fixed his much-in-need-of-a-trim, hair as best as could be done and dressed in jeans, a nice shirt and a blazer he found in the back of his closet and Chucks. In his defense, Chucks go with everything. He came downstairs to find Killian had jokingly donned a chauffer's outfit, complete with the matching hat. Christian shook his head, appreciating the implied intent to loosen him up a bit. Killian removed the jacket and hat, tossed it on the counter and the two began the trek toward DFW Airport.

Christian insisted they leave no later than 6pm and as such he and Killian made their way north, then took the loop, west onto 635. As expected, a few minutes prior, some dip-shit had been texting and now, his new Lexus was wrapped around the backside of an 18-wheeler. The mile-long line of illuminated brake lights wrapped around the clover leaf and extended all the way to Midway Road. This extracted an involuntary string of curse words from Christian's mouth.

"Easy bud...", Killian responded, "we've got plenty of time.", Killian seemed to revel in chaos. When Christian glanced over at him, he noticed his summonings along the backside of his hand were present.

"Hey... your summoning...", Christian said pointing out one major issue that neither had thought of yet. How would Katie react if she were to catch a glimpse of Killian's illuminated summonings? Or worse, what if there were some sort of Omnician confrontation involving Killian tonight? For the remainder of the drive, they spent the time formulating a plan. Since Christian had to wear the watch, he'd do so on his right hand tonight and would consciously stay on the right side of Killian, at all times. Killian also told him that it was more effective if he were to keep the watch's accumulating dust, cleaned off as much as possible.

"One more thing...", he added reaching into his shirt pocket. He pulled out two paper tickets. "I called in a favor...", he said, handing the two tickets to Christian. They were for an intimate show at an obscure cocktail bar and venue on the east side of town called The Alchemist. Playing an impromptu show tonight was Emmaline, the quartet fronted by the wonderfully talented artist, Emmaline Campbell. The meteoric YouTube sensation gained a massive social media following after a video of her and band mate Ryan Mondak covering Al Green's classic "Let's Stay Together", with their own personal, jazzy flair layered on top, went viral.

"Dude!", Christian said, "they are awesome! How'd you get these? I didn't even know they were in town for a show.", Christian had been following Emmaline since he had accidentally found and watched one of their videos. He was excited to finally see them play live. Killian then pulled out another ticket from his pocket and held it up with a smirk, once he noticed the look of concern on Christian's face, thinking he was giving up his only two tickets for him.

The Lincoln pulled up at Building D at 6:58pm. Christian mustered his courage then hopped out and walked the 12 or so feet into the arched entrance. Just as he stepped into the shade, he saw her coming down the stairs. She was wearing one of those $5 sundresses that effortlessly made any woman look like a million bucks. She wore red lipstick and her blonde hair, just a bit longer now than he had remembered. She very well could have spent all day getting ready, but Christian was pretty sure she was one of those women that can't be improved upon much, straight out of bed. As she approached the last step, her strapped heels clacked on the cobblestone steps. She glanced down one last time, then once she found herself on solid ground, up into Christian's eyes.

"Hi You!", she said with the most intoxicating of smiles. Christian melted and was now back to his normal self, a blubbering idiot, at a loss for words.

He smiled, trying with all his might to not to come off as the quintessential, pretentious Dallas douche, while looking her up and down, only to make some 20-cent comment about her appearance. He stumbled to find the words he wanted to say.

"It's nice to see you again... you look beautiful tonight...", is what came out. She smiled then blushed mildly. All in all, not bad. He wasn't immediately hating himself for opening his mouth, so that's good. He stepped to the side and led her out near the street and into the sun. Killian had lowered the top on the Lincoln and the moment she saw that car, she let out one of those part squeal, part giggles.

"A 65' Lincoln convertible! Suicide doors! Sweet! Is this yours?", She asked Christian, checking out every nook and cranny as he opened the door for her and she climbed into the back seat. Christian had a decision to make. Either he chose to sit in the back with her and possibly come off as too aggressive or he sat in the front seat and come off as uninterested. Luckily Killian had picked up on his dilemma and with squinted eyes and a forceful nod of his head, motioned for him to get in the back seat. Christian obliged and climbed in to sit next to Katie.

"I'm sorry Katie... this is Killian, my butler", Christian said, nervously joking.

"I'm not his butler... I'm his roommate", Killian retorted, turning around to introduce himself. They shook hands over the back of the seat.

"It's nice to meet you Killian...", She said.

"Who's, car?", she asked, then immediately continued, "My grandpa had this exact car! I remember when he used to drive us around and we thought it was so cool how the doors opened backwards...", still taken, aback.

"It's a friend of ours", Killian said, nonchalantly, "he restored it by hand and he doesn't trust just anyone with his car, so I told him I'd drive you guys... I hope you don't mind...", he said sincerely.

"Not at all Killian!", She said, "So, what's the plan, gentlemen?" Christian took the tickets out of this jacket pocket and handed them to Katie, to which, she again, squeal-giggled.

"I LOVE Emmaline! How'd you know they were here?", she asked. Christian graciously explained that it was Killian who found out somehow and provided him with the tickets. With her cheerful smile, she thanked them both as the Lincoln cruised south down Main, toward the highway.

The back seat of a convertible can be a windy place to sit when on the highway, but Mitchell had thought of everything when restoring this car. He lowered the interior just a tad to both make it easier to get In and out of and with the windows rolled up, it was surprisingly calm inside, despite the noise made by the wind and the road's surface.

As the car neared downtown and the traffic thickened, Killian exited the highway and took the scenic route across Oak Lawn to Lemmon, then weaved his way down through uptown Dallas until they wound up east of 75 where Lemmon turned into North Peak.

Christian and Katie talked and laughed as Killian drove but the subject Christian feared most, never reared its' ugly head into the conversation. He was sure it would come up eventually so it never really left his mind.

As the Lincoln entered Deep Ellum proper, Katie's clutch purse began to vibrate. Her phone was ringing and she fished around inside to silence it.

"Take it if you need to... I don't mind...", he said.

She smiled, then pulled her phone out. Without even looking at the screen and all the while, staring Christian directly in eyes with a sassy, smartass look on her face, she clicked the home button to silence the call. A couple of seconds later, it began to ring again. Her expression changed slightly and she appeared a bit more concerned. On the screen she saw that it was a FaceTime call from one of her roommate coworkers named Tabitha. Tabby was a tall, attractive, flight attendant with a bit more seniority than Katie and the others. Oh yeah, she was nosey and overly-protective too. She was probably calling to see if her date sucked and to make up something if Katie needed an out. Christian wondered if they had discussed that beforehand and it left a not so good feeling with him.

"Let me take this...", she said.

Christian obliged and she lifted the phone, between her and Christian and pressed accept just as Killian pulled the car up to the unmanned valet station at The Alchemist.

"Does it suck?
Are you bored?
He's a jerk after all, isn't he?
Want me to pick you up?
I'll leave now...", her voice never stopped and Katie started to laugh.

"No, I'm fine... we're actually having fun... see". She clicked the switch camera button on her phone, now showing Christian both nervously smiling and waving. She rotated her phone to reveal her surroundings and unintentionally caught Killian in her panning shot.

"Who ... was that?", Tabby asked. Katie couldn't figure out if her tone suggested she was angered at the idea of intentionally being left out of tonight's plans or if it was more of a predator, prey kind of comment. Just then Killian turned around, threw his right elbow over the seat and faced the phone.

"My name's Killian... I don't believe I've had the pleasure...", he said mustering his coolest James Dean impression.

"No, no you haven't had the pleasure yet... It's Tabby ...", she said, returned in an unmistakably, flirty manner.

"Katie... I don't like the looks of that situation ... not one bit...", she said trying to maintain her Type A demeanor, while clearly into Killian, "I'm on my way..."

"That's not...", Katie started to suggest she not, then noticed Killian motioning for her to hand him the phone.

"Listen...", Killian said as he took the phone and stared into the screen. He had that playfully sarcastic look about him again, "I don't like the way you're trying to muscle your way into my friend's special alone time with his best girl... I have half a mind to tell you where we are so can show up and I can tell you, in person, how I really feel about it...", he said, making it clear he was continuing the flirty banter.

"Promise?", She said, her voice raising an octave or two.

"Oh god...", Katie said, a bit embarrassed, as she yanked the phone out of Killian's hand.

"Fine...", she said, shooting one last look at Killian who had a cheesy grin on his face while holding both thumbs up at jaw level. Katie laughed and proceeded to send Tabby a map pin from her current location.

Katie hung up the phone and looked at Christian, slightly embarrassed, hoping he wasn't upset at having his date hijacked. Christian did feel a certain way about her roommate shoe horning in on their date.

He felt extreme relief and Katie could read it, written across his face.

The Lincoln has several admirers standing around taking photos of the car and its inhabitants. Little did Christian know that he was rapidly rising on the list of Dallas' most sought-after bachelors and that one of these photos would grace the cover of the local newspaper tomorrow morning. Because the valet wasn't there at that exact moment, Killian backed the car into a wide spot next to the valet stand and took the keys with him. The trio went inside and were sat at a table directly in front of the stage. A waitress approached and brought some menus and took a drink order.

From the corner of the room, a deep voiced shrieked, "Kllllan!", A tall brunette with short and curly hair, ran toward him, arms extended and collided into him, giving him a long overdue hug.

It was Emmaline Campbell. Christian would come to find out later, Killian grew up, during his early years, with her in Olympus, WA and she was like a little sister to him.

Killian introduced Katie and Christian to Emma. Katie waved from across the table and just as Christian extended his right hand to shake hers, Killian intervened, stood up and got between the two, his back to Christian, saying something quietly to Emma. She took a step back, waved and said, "it was nice to meet y'all... gotta go prepare... hope y'all enjoy the show!"

She waved one last time, smiled, then turned and made her way into the makeshift back stage area.

"She's really weird about physical contact before performing...", Killian said, awkwardly.
When Katie turned to look around the room, Killian got Christian's attention and motioned to Christian's right wrist, where his watch was once again, covered in dust. Annoyed, Christian attempted to stealthily, wipe it off on his pant leg. Then it dawned on him why he was motioning toward his wrist and had prevented him from getting any closer to Emma. She too, shared Killian's plight and upbringing, though hers' differed slightly. I suppose, when it rains, it pours.

A round of drinks materialized. Then another, following some small plates of finger foods Christian had ordered for the table. He had to admit this was going much better that he feared it would.

A few moments later, a commotion near the door captured the attention of most of the patrons inside. Some belligerent lady demanded the doorman let her in, despite her not having a ticket.

"Oh god...", Katie said as she put her face into her open hands, thoroughly embarrassed. Christian started to laugh under his breath.

"I got it...", Killian said. He got up from the table and walked toward the front door. He tapped the doorman on the shoulder and handed him a ticket from his shirt pocket. The doorman allowed her entry but only after she scolded him with a stout glare.
"Well, I'm sorry sweetheart... I didn't know you'd arrived...", Killian said, as he extended his arm to guide the way, "right this way..."

Tabitha didn't realize from the phone call that he was all of 6' 5", and in person, she was forced to absorb that last little bit of information. Her personality changed substantially after that. For the rest of the night, she was more or less mesmerized by Killian, often silent and openly staring at him, as he talked. According to Katie, the silence was a nice change of pace. At one point, Katie even asked if there were any way he would consider coming to work with them just so she'd be easier to work with on those long, cross country flights.

Emmaline played for about an hour and a half in front of a crowd of no more than one hundred. It wasn't that they couldn't sell tickets because they could fill any one of the many larger venues around town. It was solely because she preferred to do these intimate setting type of shows. Those in attendance were almost assured to be those fans that prefer and deserve a show like this, the most.

Killian sat on the front left side of the table with Katie sitting just behind him. Christian sat next to Katie on the backside of the table and Tabby, directly in front of him. Shortly after the lights were dimmed, and Emmaline began to play, Christian felt Katie reach for his hand. A warm and tingly feeling he hadn't felt since middle school, overcame him as he took her hand in his. She glanced at him with her intoxicating smiled, then leaned into him, laying her head on his shoulder. This was a development that he could get used to.

Eventually, Christian mustered the nerve to put his arm around her and she scooted her chair closer. And just like that, Emmaline played their last song, said a big thank you to Dallas and waved as they left the stage to gracious rounds of applause. As most were paying tabs and exiting the venue, Killian and Tabby turned around to face the table just as Emma emerged from backstage and walked directly toward their table. Tabby took notice and like a light switch was flipped, she was instantly back to her aggressive, dominating demeanor. Emma pulled up a chair, spun it around and sat down, leaning forward against the chair's back, between Killian and Katie. "So… what'd you guys think?", she asked, as she rested her chin directly onto her interlocked fingers, resting on top of the chair's back.

Congratulations and admiration came from all around the table. Except Tabitha. Her facial expression said the thousand's, consequently millions of words her mouth need not, bother uttering. Luckily, Christian and Katie both gushed continuously about her control and mastery of her instrument, despite her young years. The most ethereal compliment, 'an old soul' was even used to which Emma was most humbled and gracious. As the four and a half chatted a while longer, the staff began to show signs of closing up shop, as the house lights slowly became brighter over the course of 15 or so minutes. Emma gave Killian one last hug and then excused herself as her and her bandmates had several hundred miles to cover before they could call it a night. Noticing the subtle queues all around him, Christian hinted that it may be time to go.
"Now what?", Killian asked, suggesting that the quartet extend the evening.

"I'm good for whatever… it's Friday…", Christian said.

"Me too…", Katie added.

"I'm actually kind of tired…", Tabby said, "I just don't want to go all the way back to Grapevine… Hey… don't you guys live around here?", she said in a poor attempt to hide her ulterior motive. Killian shook his head is a manner that suggested he was flattered but more so, surprised she'd be so blatantly obvious in expression of her intentions. Katie was again, embarrassed, but Christian's response was most classic of all. The color left his face and appeared frozen like a deer in headlights.

"Uh… yeah… it's whatever…", he muttered, more so in a nervous, almost frightened fashion, than in an arrogant one. Katie saw right through it and gave him a playful elbow in the ribs for his troubles. Christian requested the check and before he could drop his Fastli card into the check presenter and hand it off to the waiting server, two additional cards clacked down on top of his. One was Katie's the other, Tabby's. Christian looked up at the two and was pleasantly surprised that neither would succumb to the idea of letting him pay the tab for the table. Either they hadn't watched the news over the past 48 hours or they had and were trying to prove a point. Either was fine with him at this exact moment in time.

Christian glanced down at his watch. After again, wiping the dust off, he noticed it was a quarter until one. If they were to go somewhere else, they didn't have much time.

"JC's...", he said, out loud, directed at Killian. He knew for a fact, they had not one drop of alcohol in their house, but JC may have had a stocked bar down the street.

"What's that...", Tabby asked, "some other bar close by or something?"

Killian turned to her and flirtingly responded, "No dear... JC was our neighbor...", he stopped, realizing where the conversation would inevitably go.

"How about this...", Christian added, "I don't want this to sound creepy or anything, but we have a pool and a nice sitting area out back... why don't we just go back to our place and have another drink?", He wasn't sure why but he instantly felt gross posing the question. To his surprise, in stride, Tabby followed with, "What are we waiting for then?"

Katie shrugged and the four, rose to their feet, much to the liking of the Alchemist staff who were patiently waiting on them to vacate the premises. There were still a few people in the parking lot when they walked out into the humid night air. A click on the Lincoln's key fob started the engine and another began the automated lowering of the top. Katie climbed into the back and just before Christian could follow her, Tabby climbed into the back seat as well. "Sorry... Girl talk...", she told Christian with a bossy but friendly smile. He tried not to take the loss of this opportunity personally, but he really wanted to sit with Katie. He had spent the entire night trying to get the nerve up to kiss her and this would have been the perfect turn of events to give it a shot. Ultimately, the night was being extended, so he hadn't yet lost his chance. Killian drove through Deep Ellum, working his way back toward University and Hillcrest. The closer they got to the SMU campus, the more, Tabby expected that they would end up pulling up into the driveway of one of the campus frat houses. After a relentless onslaught of commentary from the back seat, Killian turned west onto University and away from the campus. Her condescending comments began to subside.

A few moments later, the car was safely in the garage and Killian took Tabby and Katie on a quick tour while Christian walked down to JC's and looked for a bottle of something. He slipped out the front door and walked down the street until he now stood at the edge of the home's circle drive. Holding the key in his hand, a rush of emotions hit him like a Mack truck.

JC was gone and had left basically, his entire life to him. He reflected for a moment and had hoped that he was somewhat coming close to living up to what JC had envisioned. He knew that somewhere, sometime, JC was probably watching. He made a pact with himself, then and there, to not squander what he had been given and to not tarnish the legacy he'd been gifted. He went into the dark house and it dawned on him that this is the first time he's stepped foot inside this home, since it'd became his. A few minutes later, he emerged back into the warm night air with an unopened bottle of vodka form a local distillery and a random but probably expensive, bottle of white wine.

He walked back through the front door of the Tutor styled home and while some lights had been turned on inside, the sliding glass door was open and faint music was quietly playing from the back yard. He stopped by the kitchen and grabbed a few highball glasses and two wine glasses, then walked out the back door. The glow from two burning tiki torches danced across the surface of the pool, while the faint scent or citronella ensured Texas' hummingbird sized mosquitos would not be in attendance this evening. Killian was slouched into on one of the sun lounger chairs while Tabitha laid across the foot of the chair, her head lying on his lap. Katie sat across from them on a low-slung patio love seat. Christian walked down the steps toward the pool. After placing the glasses on the table in front of him and pouring a couple of fingers of vodka, he took the seat next to Katie. She leaned her body into his again and he put his arm around her, his hand resting in the crook of her waist, as she cuddled even closer to him. Some people just seem to be made for each other and judging by their body language, Christian and Katie seemed to be two pieces that had that naturally perfectly fit.

This was actually the first time Christian had been in the backyard of the house but he saw no reason to share that fact in this exact moment. With Katie cuddled close to him, he took an extended sip from the glass he held in his right hand and tried with all his being to enjoy these moments with her, because he knew he may not get too many more of these in the coming year.

17

Awakening

Once Christian disappeared into the back of the shop, Cyrus' demeanor changed almost instantly. No longer did he appear as if he were struggling to keep up, while time continued to pass him by. He now appeared more driven, purposeful, precise and strangely enough, youthful.

"Ok you three... follow me...", Cyrus said, as he grabbed the Elegon billet and took a purposeful path directly into his workshop. The moment he entered, the three young Omnicians witnessed something truly unique few have ever witnessed. The moment he entered the shop, the entire place came to life. The fires in the hearths began to flare and crackle. The shop filled with the banging sounds of metals being poured and worked. Blake entered first, followed by Penny and Elijah, immediately behind. There was now no sign of Cyrus at this point. Blake looked around the shop and several times he thought he saw Cyrus at one of the specific build stations but the next moment, he seemed to have vanished. Blake continued to scour the shop looking for any sign of their host.

"Where did he go?", Penelope asked, to which both Blake and Elijah had no explanation. They just continued to watch the shop as it appeared something was being built inside but for the life of them, none could figure out how or by whom. Then suddenly, Cyrus appeared from just outside of Penelope's peripheral vision.

"So... What do you think?", Cyrus asked while holding up the freshly completed watch, he had pledged to Christian. Blake, Penny and Elijah were dumbfounded. There was no possible way he could have just created that, in the short amount of time the three had been standing there.

"But... what....", Blake started, but stumbled after getting through two words.
Cyrus turned to the Omnicians and began to explain.

 "Young ones, there's apparently much you've yet to learn...", Cyrus said, still holding up the watch for the three to admire, "... lesson one, Elegons are strange and powerful things...", He held the watch out between the three, then motioned for each of them to glance to the left at an antique mirror hanging on the wall.

They simultaneously turned their heads and all noticed each-other's eyes and summonings just beginning to glow. Blake's eyes were a light yellow and his Therian summonings were fully displayed in moving patterns of brown and dark gray.

Penelope's eyes and the symmetrical markings on the backs of her hands were ablaze in a bright violet hue. Elijah's were the strangest of all. While his eyes glowed his native banner of a deep Ogen blue, his summonings were illuminated with all the banners of an Elementae Master. The green, blue, aqua, red and yellow glowing patches seemed to swim across his skin, each time narrowly dodging a strange flat gray color. From Blake's childhood spent near Sequoia, he knew of the Gaian, Aerus, Ignes, Ogen and even the much, more-rare Electrae banners, but he had never seen, nor had he been taught what this dark matte gray banner represented. ", What's that?", Blake asked, pointing out the gray as it surfaced, then subsequently disappeared, only to reappear a moment later, somewhere else.

"Audius…", Penelope said, as Elijah captivatingly watched the colors dance along the undersides of his forearms, as if it were the last moments of twilight signaling the end of a Santorini sunset, sparkling across the Mediterranean.

"It's an extraordinarily rare blessing.", Cyrus explained, "… many throughout history referred to them as sirens or banshees…",

Penelope glanced at Blake and noticed something peculiar. Within his summonings, there were sparkling speckles of white, hidden amongst and behind the dark shades of gray and hints of brown.

"Blake…", she said, calling attention to his right shoulder. Blake had never noticed this before. About the same time Cyrus also took notice and was fumbling for an eyepiece from the shelf to his right, to take a closer look. As he did so, the expression on his face told Penelope everything she needed to know about her suspicions. Cyrus, with the watch in hand, placed it on Blake's shoulder, closed his eyes and spoke, "… of man and Omnician alike… the chosen must take… His destined luster and his rightful throne… Amongst the stars…"

Penelope and Elijah collectively, gasped. It was he.

Cyrus placed the watch and bands into the winder box he had prepared for the timepiece. As he closed the lid to the box, the room began to grow dark again as the illumination from each of the summonings faded just as quickly. He sat the box aside on a workstation and walked over to a familiar mountainous landscape painting hanging on the wall. Behind the painting was a hidden wall safe. He entered the combination and the door creaked open. Cyrus pulled out a stained and tattered cloth that looked to be hundreds of years old. Wrapped inside the cloth was a skeleton key. Although covered by decades of tarnish and dust, the metal below had a visible greenish hue to it. He held the key out in front of him and stared at it through the glasses that were, again, perched on the end of his nose.

"It has been a long time since I've used this key...", he said, as if speaking nostalgically with an old friend. In all actuality, he had never used this key. It opened one door and one door only. In the back room of the workshop, an old broom closet where he kept cleaning supplies and other odds and ends, lay dormant. In the center of the floor just next to a drain grate, sat an oddly placed keyhole. He wasn't quite sure what it did, but for ages, he'd been curious about what would happen if he put that key into that keyhole. Long ago, when he was handed the reins to WatchMaker, the last act of the departing steward involved handing him that key with the ominously vague instructions of "You'll know what to do with this when the time comes...", Something inside told Cyrus that this time, was the one for which, he'd been patiently waiting.

He motioned for Blake, Penelope and Elijah to follow into the back of the shop. As he opened the storage room door, walked in and flipped the light switch on, the thought crossed Blake's mind that maybe Cyrus wasn't playing with a full deck. Nonetheless, the three followed him into the small closet and watched while he bent down and with shaky hands, struggled to insert the key into the keyhole. Once inserted and turned, a loud series of clanks startled the four occupants, as the floor of the closet began to lower, slowly rotating in a clockwise motion, down into a dark cavern below. With a muffled, echoing thud, the old, makeshift elevator reached its' destination. The moment it stopped, Divinium veins embedded within the floor began to illuminate the cavern. Then, in sequence, the veins began to crawl up the walls and across the ceiling. This space was more or less, a cave. A trickle of water could be heard from somewhere deeper inside. The walls were covered in ancient vines and flowers that grew from the base of each.

At closer inspection, and much to the delight of all, these were not run of the mill vines but rather, Viniated Snapdragons, Divine Jasmine and Illuminated Peonies, the only three known plants on earth known by the Omnicians, to react with Divinium. Each bloom bioluminescent flowers. The moment the Omnicians stepped off of the platform, the cavern knew it had visitors. Luminescence pulsed along the veins under foot until it reached the walls, at which point, every bloom on each of the Peony and Snapdragon plants lit up in sequence. The illumination continued up the walls and through the Jasmine vines, startlingly lighting the cave with hues of blue, green and white as if the blackout curtains had been flung open on an unsuspecting Vegas bachelor party at noon.

The four stood silently in awe of this place, long hidden from the destructive hands and minds of man. No one had likely stepped foot inside this cavern in upwards of two thousand years. The vines along the wall had grown dense over the years. Being the astute precept that she is, Penelope noticed something beneath the vines and she ever so carefully, parted them, revealing an entire wall of ancient writings. She did not however, recognize these runes. Despite all their years of knowledge and experiences, Elijah nor Cyrus had seen this script prior.

"Huh...", Blake commented, beneath a chuckle. He never expected to see something so far from home that reminded him so much of his childhood.

Throughout the Sequoia forests, where Blake was raised, there still remains many old and forgotten places. One of which, an old tree's hollow where he used to play with his dog as a boy, was one of those such places. It was there, inside the petrified carcass of that long since departed Sequoia tree, from which Blake recognized these writings. He spent so much time there as a boy that he had actually created his own meanings for each and every one of the runes. The same runes that now stared back at him, here, half a world and half a lifetime away.

"What is it Blake?", Penelope asked.

"His name is Alessandro...", Cyrus interrupted, suggestively speaking, seemingly, with a specific purpose.

"Sorry... I still can't get used to that... it reminds me of my mother...", he responded, "but yes... my true name is Alessandro. My mother told me to keep it secret and I never really understood why. When I was young, I'd play outside in the woods with our dog Lucky. At dusk, she'd stand on the porch and call me home... Alie, she called me for short... Unless she had to call me more than a couple of times... then she'd cup her hands around her mouth and shout Alessandro. Sometimes, I swore that the trees were carrying her voice to me, as I'd hear that calling, plain as day...", he reminisced.

"You must take your name... your real name", Cyrus said, just short of pleading, "It's primitive, but it's necessary... Your mother would have told you that long ago, were she here... When you were a boy, she told you what you needed to know about who you were to keep you safe... you don't need to be kept safe any longer... That's not who you are anymore...", he continued, "... what else do you remember about your childhood...?"

"As far back as I can remember, we always had a dog. His name was Lucky. He wasn't any kind of special breed or anything... just a normal dog but I can remember that whenever I looked into his eyes, I always felt like he was looking back at me, wondering what I was thinking... like he was looking into my soul just as much as I was looking into his...

He would roam around the valleys and woods near our home and regularly seemed to get himself into trouble. It could be a rattlesnake or bobcat or whatever... he always seemed to escape unharmed and when he got older, nearly every time he went out, I expected his luck would run out.

One day, when I was fourteen, he was wondering in the woods and stumbled upon a mama bear and her cubs... and he started barking at her...

I heard him from the house and as usual, I followed his call ...

when I got there, the mama was reared up on her hind legs and had been roaring, protecting her cubs...

I found him and immediately dropped, hands on knees, trying to catch my breath...
He walked to my side, then sat next to me, facing the bear and cubs while, just looking up at me....

I guess most people would think Lucky was trying to gain my approval for finding the bears but I knew what it was he was trying to tell me...

It was that ... this is life...

time you have with your mother and your family... that's precious... those are the building blocks of life...

Cherish those moments... one day you'll miss them...

After a few moments, the bear backed down and ushered her cubs along while she kept an eye on me and Lucky, until she made her way over the ridge and out of sight..."

Tears were streaming down his face as he continued,
"I always noticed the Lucky didn't really seem to age...

His coat was always dark brown and had very little gray in it... even as I got into my late teens...

He got tired faster and did lose a step or two over the years but he still roamed and still managed to escape sticky situations...

One day he was out roaming near the foothills and he ran across a mountain lion... he started barking again and I heard him in the distance but this time, he met his match...

He managed to limp home, mother wrapped his wounds and laid him by the fire...

I sat there for hours, rubbing his head and scratching behind his ear in the hopes that my attention would heal his wounds but as his head laid in my lap, I felt his life leave him... I felt the moment his soul left his body, when he took one last look, up at me...

I know this sounds crazy, but I swear at the moment he passed, I felt his soul... join with mine... inside of me...

a feeling of warmth... a feeling of serenity and completeness came over me...

I felt ... well ... a new understanding of the world around me... as if I were one with nature... I could see the world through his eyes...

at first, I knew something had changed but couldn't explain it...

It's different now though...

It's as if..."

The old man interrupted,
"As if you're one with the earth and it's one with you?
As if she's guiding you, while her power courses through your veins?
As if you feel all her pain and all her sadness but also her determination and hope?"

"Yes... exactly... but it's more than that...
It's like I'm an extension of her and her of me..."

He replied,
"That's the bond you feel...
It's what makes an Adaptive... so rare and so special...
You feel our planet and our home through the bond between you and your Exanima... "

"My what?", Alessandro asked.
The old man replied, "Lucky... he was your Exanima..."

When a Therian is born, the blessing gifts them an Exanima, a spirit guide of sorts. This is a being with which you share your burden of manifestation, one to learn from, hunt with and care for.

When an Adaptive is born, their blessing is similar except the Exanima takes a different form... it's a transmitter of sorts... a link between the Divinine within and the rest of the matter around you. An Adaptive is incomplete until the moment of bond... the time when that link either folds within and shrivels, leaving an Adaptive able to defend him but disconnected to the world beyond...

Or...

That link blossoms and bonds with something or someone...
The first Adaptive, Adom, bonded with his Exanima... the Earth itself...

The next four Adaptives born were coddled and protected by the Elder Ancients. They never experienced a true life... they never knew the sadness of loss...
or the joy of accomplishment... they never truly knew love... never knew selflessness or sacrifice...
and therefore, their blessing abandoned each of them...

they were deemed unworthy by ... the essence itself... as an equal...
You are the sixth Adaptive...

Whether you want to be or not...

When your link bonded... it was not with your dog, Lucky... and his name is not Lucky...", the old man said.

"What do you mean... he?", Alessandro asked.

"your Exanima was no ordinary Therian manifestation... it was the same being Adom bonded with all those years ago... He's gone by many names throughout the ages...", the old man proclaimed, "I've known him only as Ja... Ja the Essencient.

He was drawn to you and to your link to this world. He knew what you were, even before you knew yourself and that one day, you'd bond...

so, he chose you...

to teach you and to use his Essence, when the time comes.

Essencians are unique beings for sure... they don't die... not as we know it...
They are perpetual beings, pure celestial essences of will, unburdened by time, space, matter or boundary, that pass as intent... as purpose and will... throughout the cosmos...

Their energy and consciousness pass into other planes and into other beings, freely...

they become part of their companion... separate, but enjoined together as one.

They share their knowledge, determinations, circumstances and abilities ...

Be it, for honor or for malice, for joy, hope or sadness ...

The Essencient you called Lucky is the most honorable, most pure being I've ever encountered ... he is just, fearless and he is formidable ...

He embodies, no... he is... the essence of selflessness, of bravery and of justice ...

239

One would be truly blessed, indeed to encounter him in a thousand lifetimes...

I can only describe it as otherworldly to be chosen, by him, to carry the essence and his legacy... throughout time..."

The old man turned and walked toward a cabinet on the back side of the dark room.
He grabbed a small trinket and turned slowly to walk back toward Alessandro and Penny. The short journey appeared a formidable feat for the old man.

"Hold up your hand...", he instructed. Alessandro did so, palm out with fingers spread.

"Now...", he said, turning his attention to Penny, "raise yours..."

Penny was hesitant but after a few moments, she did so as well.

"Now...", he said, motioning, in an effort to suggest the two touch palms. Penny nodded, then turned toward Alessandro.

As Penny's hand grew closer to Alie's, the summoning markings along both his and her hands and forearms immediately came to life. Like clockwork, his darkened into shades of brown and tones of gray. Her markings illuminated the familiar vivid and bright purple, but something was different this time. For both of them.

Usually, Alessandro's summonings are thick and dark, covering most of the exposed skin, but were stationary. This time it's as if the markings were crawling along the skin, changing shapes and hues. Penelope never paid much attention to the markings on her hands, but they too, appeared to be wandering around in various and random patterns, briefly forming recognizable shapes and patterns, then just as quickly, becoming an indiscernible mess of violet hues.

At the moment her hand made contact with his, bright sparks, similar to static discharge ignited from every single micron of skin where their hands touched. After a moment, the sparks subsided and, in the void, replaced by a bright white haze at all points where their hands touched, even bridging the open gaps, between their palms.

It started in his fingertips. Alessandro began to feel a crawling sensation coming from under the skin of his fingers, then his hand. Beginning at the fingertips, millimeter by millimeter, his summonings began to change. The browns and grays faded to the flattest black you can imagine, then, violently, erupted in bright and glorious white runes.

Almost immediately the effervescent glow from his summonings outshined the sparks coming from his palm. They lit the entire room as if a tiny sun burned in its' center. Then, Penny pushed her fingers between his, grasping his hand with interlocked fingers. The pace of change in his summonings increased until, moments later, the white glow was halfway up his arm and continued gaining momentum. He took a step back, doubled over and dropped to a knee as the glow began to cross his chest and race down his torso, unrelentingly grasping Penny's hand the entire time. A few seconds later, the glow dimmed from his body and the sparks between his and Penny's hands extinguished. Penny's grasp on this hand loosened just as it fell to the ground. The visible markings along his body began to pulsate between a dim and intense bright white, all the while, runes and symbols of all types formed, the dissipated within the boundaries of his summoning.

A moment later, he picked his hand up off the ground and held it to his chest. He took a deep breath, then exhaled. He felt different. Everything within his field of vision was much more, clear and crisp, in excruciating detail. He could hear the cries of the world, all at once. He could feel all of the matter surrounding him, individually and collectively, simultaneously. He felt one with his surroundings and they, with him.

He put his open hand on the ground, his summonings still pulsating and aglow the brightest of white. He pushed himself off bent knee and rose to his feet. With his eyes closed, he slowly stood, then he raised his head. The entirety of his visible body, ablaze in a heavenly white glow. His summonings danced, forming millions of tiny shapes, continuously falling apart, only to reform into millions of completely different shapes repeatedly. There was no pattern and no predictability to the markings. They seemed to hold purpose, all their own. If God were to wear armor into battle, one might describe it looking much like this.

Within his neck's hollow, the faint incarnation indicating Therian was gone. In its' place, and glowing brightly was the incarnation of the Prophesized. Six small rings arranged as the points of a hexagon, each glowing brightly in different banners. A smaller ring of solid circles, each of a different banner as well, were arranged similarly, inside the outer ring. The illumination brighter among the inner ring as it appeared to rotate slowly clockwise, while another bright glow pulsated along the outer ring, rotating a bit faster in the opposite direction. An old bedtime story told to young Omnician speaks of these rings and circles as representing the harmonious existence of each of the individual Omnician orders. Alessandro opened his eyes and a blinding light filled the room. A second later, the light dimmed and as Penny, Elijah and the Old Man gazed upon him, they finally saw that the familiar yellowish green glow of a Therian was gone from Blake's eyes. In its' place, was the legendary, lightning white glow of an Adaptive. Alessandro balled his hands into fists and he instantly felt courage, honor and determination, in liquid form, flow through his veins. He felt an instant urge to right every wrong perpetuated on this world, in that exact moment. It wasn't like he felt strongly about it and seriously hoped something would be done. He knew, right as rain, in the innermost depths of his being, that he was able, willing and compelled to act. It was as if every fiber within his being was urging him to go forth and avenge the wronged.

The old man put his hand on his forearm and said softly, "Easy Ja, my old friend... he's new and inexperienced... Allow him the moments he needs to grow accustomed to you... and you with him...", the glow across his skin pulsated in response to Cyrus' touch and words. It strangely seemed to understand him.

Into Alessandro's hand, the old man placed a small weathered scroll and the trinket that he had retrieved earlier, from the cabinet.

"Here... one day, you'll be needing this again, I'm afraid...", he whispered.

Alessandro looked at the trinket in the palm of his hand. It was a small and copper in color. Squarish in shape, with a sharp point along its' top and a small, rounded shape along its' bottom. As Alessandro held It in his palm, it dissolved into a pool of golden metal and just as quickly, began to disappear as it absorbed into his open hand. He looked at his palms and suddenly, on the left, the shape of a sword manifested. On his other, partially obscured by the scroll, a circle formed looking much like an old, Roman shield, sat plain as day. Out of the corner of his eye, he noticed movement and looked up. At that moment, the old man, with a relieved smile on his face, began to fade away as if he were dust, carried away by a gust of wind. It seemed time suspended around him until his purpose had been fulfilled. And now it seems as if, it had. As the old man faded away, the black suit jacket he wore, dropped, lifelessly to the ground.

Elijah and Penelope stared on, silently from the back of the small cavernous space. They had just witnessed what no soul ever had before. The bond between an Adaptive and an Essencian was an awesome and beautiful sight to behold. Elijah now began to feel a strong compulsion to stand at his side. Then and there, he declared he would now follow Alessandro to the ends of the Earth, if need be. Not from a feeling of obligation but from one of faith. He stepped forward, his summonings glowing brightly, and took his rightful place on his left.

Penny now, too, felt an ethereal draw toward Alessandro. Because of her upbringing in the Order, she knew the role she would now have to play, after this new dawn. Her summoning a bright violet glow, she took her place on his right side. History would remember this moment as the formation of the Celestial Trivium.

Alie looked to his left and to his right. The two by his side were now more than friends. They were part of him now, as he were now, of and to them. He would die to protect them. He glanced down into his open hand.

In Alessandro's hand, the fragile seal on the scroll broke apart and the tightly wound paper began to loosen and unravel. On the old, tattered papyrus, there was one word written, in an old and timelessly, articulate handwriting.

Gados.

Made in the USA
Lexington, KY
22 November 2019